Praise for Rac

'Johns draws readers in with her richly complex characters.'
—*Daily Telegraph* on *Just One Wish*

'Polished writing, and great dialogue drive this story forward.
The perfectly structured plot holds plenty of surprises, but
it's the beautifully crafted characters that are the glue in this
wonderful novel … Utterly delightful.' —Better Reading on
Just One Wish

'If you like your chick-lit with a dash of intelligent social commentary, *Just One Wish* is the perfect summer read … sparklingly
funny, quirky and totally of this moment' —*Herald Sun*

'Johns knows how to weave the experiences of different generations of women together, with nuance and sensitivity, understanding how competing contexts shape women's choices …
Just One Wish will make you look at the women in your own
life and wonder what stories they haven't told.' —Mamamia

'Heart-warming and compassionate … Any book lover interested
in life's emotional complexities and in the events that define and
alter us will be engrossed in *Lost Without You*.' —Better Reading

'Full of heartache and joy with a twist that keeps the pages
turning … *The Greatest Gift* will appeal to fans of Jojo Moyes
and Monica McInerney.' —*Australian Books + Publishing*

'Heartbreaking and heartwarming in equal parts, Rachael
Johns' *The Greatest Gift* takes readers on a rollercoaster ride

of emotions. My advice? Make sure you have tissues handy!'
—Lisa Ireland, author of *The Shape Of Us*

'Rachael Johns has done it again, writing a book that you want to devour in one sitting, and then turn back to the first page to savour it all over again. I loved the characters of Harper and Jasper; their stories made me laugh and cry, and ache and cheer and ultimately reflect on all the many facets of that extraordinary journey called motherhood.' —Natasha Lester, author of *A Kiss From Mr Fitzgerald*, on *The Greatest Gift*

'A beautiful story of love and loss, heartbreak and hope—this is Rachael Johns at her very finest. With achingly endearing characters and a storyline that packs a punch, *The Greatest Gift* will make your heart swell as you reach for the tissues and leave you smiling when you turn the final pages. Told with warmth, empathy and wisdom, it's a book that will appeal to everyone who has laid plans for their life and discovered that life is something that can't be controlled and that even if you think you have it all worked out, you never know what's around the corner. My favourite Rachael Johns by a country mile.' —Tess Woods, author of *Love At First Flight*

'Fans of emotional, issue driven women's fiction will welcome Johns' US women's fiction debut.' —Booklist on *The Art of Keeping Secrets*

'… a compelling and poignant story of dark secrets and turbulent relationships … I fell completely in love with the well-drawn characters of Flick, Emma and Neve. They were funny and flawed and filled with the kind of raw vulnerability that makes your heart ache for them.' —Nicola Moriarty, bestselling author of *The Fifth Letter*, on *The Art of Keeping Secrets*

'Written with compassion and real insight, *The Art Of Keeping Secrets* peeks inside the lives of three ordinary women and the surprising secrets they live with. Utterly absorbing and wonderfully written, Johns explores what secrets can do to a relationship, and pulls apart the notion that some secrets are best kept. It is that gripping novel that, once started, will not allow you to do anything else until the final secret has been revealed.' —Sally Hepworth, bestselling author of *The Secrets Of Midwives*

'A fascinating and deeply moving tale of friendship, family and of course—secrets. These characters will latch onto your heart and refuse to let it go.' —USA Today bestselling author Kelly Rimmer on *The Art of Keeping Secrets*

'Rachael Johns writes with warmth and heart, her easy, fluent style revealing an emotional intelligence and firm embrace of the things in life that matter, like female friendship.' —The Age on *Lost Without You*

About the Author

Rachael is an English teacher by trade, a mum 24/7, a supermarket owner, a chronic arachnophobe and a writer the rest of the time. She rarely sleeps and never irons. Rachael writes rural romance and women's fiction and lives in rural Western Australia with her hyperactive husband, three mostly gorgeous heroes-in-training, two fat cats, one naughty dog and a very cantankerous budgie.

At 17 Rachael began writing, enlightened by the thought that she could create whatever ending she liked and so she embarked on a Bachelor of Arts in Writing. Almost fifteen years later, after joining the Romance Writers of Australia, she finally achieved her goal of publication. Since then Rachael has finaled in a number of competitions, including the Australian Romance Readers Awards. *Jilted* (her first rural romance) won Favourite Australian Contemporary Romance in 2012 and she was voted in the Top Ten of Booktopia's Favourite Australian Author poll in 2013.

Rachael loves to hear from readers and can be contacted via her website—www.rachaeljohns.com. She is also on Facebook and Twitter.

Also by Rachael Johns:

Man Drought

The Hope Junction novels
Jilted
The Road to Hope

The Kissing Season (e-novella)
The Next Season (e-novella)

The Bunyip Bay novels
Outback Dreams
Outback Blaze
Outback Ghost

Secret Confessions Down and Dusty: Casey (e-novella)

The Patterson Girls
The Art Of Keeping Secrets

Rachael Johns

The Patterson Girls

FICTION
HQ

First Published 2015
Third Australian Paperback Edition 2020
ISBN 9781489280923

THE PATTERSON GIRLS
© 2015 by Rachael Johns
Australian Copyright 2015
New Zealand Copyright 2015

Published by
HQ Fiction
An imprint of Harlequin Enterprises (Australia) Pty Limited (ABN 47 001 180 918), a subsidiary of HarperCollins Publishers Australia Pty Limited (ABN 36 009 913 517)
Level 19, 201 Elizabeth St
SYDNEY NSW 2000
AUSTRALIA

A catalogue record for this book is available from the National Library of Australia www.librariesaustralia.nla.gov.au

Printed and bound in Australia by McPherson's Printing Group

MIX
Paper | Supporting
responsible forestry
FSC® C001695

Dear Lovely Reader

This story began a few years ago when the paddocks around the town where I live were covered in what looked to me like a beautiful purple flower.

As a converted country girl, I didn't know anything about Paterson's Curse or Salvation Jane as it is sometimes called but my farming friends told me it was actually an invasive weed. At the same time another friend of mine suggested that *Paterson's Curse* would make a great title for a book. With this pretty weed and my friend's suggestion in my head, I started dreaming of a story about a curse. It soon became a family curse and the Patterson clan was born.

Initially *The Patterson Girls* was going to be another rural romance and although it still has many of the trademarks of the much-loved rural genre, there were four sisters fighting to be heard and the story grew into a family drama with a big secret at its core instead.

I'll be honest, there were times I wanted to give up and write a straight romance, but I mostly loved writing about the relationships between the sisters—their sibling rivalry and also their special bonds. All of them are remarkable women, struggling with everyday issues and I hope that every reader will be able to identify with at least one of the girls.

And for those of you who love your romance as much as I do … never fear. As there are four sisters, there are also a number of gorgeous suitors hoping to win their hearts.

So thank you from the bottom of *my* heart for picking up *The Patterson Girls*—I'm so excited to share this story with you and can't wait to hear what you think.

Happy Reading

Rachael Johns

Dedication

To my cousins—Tom, Becky and Mikey, who were the closest I had to siblings growing up and are still some of my favourite people on the planet. Love you all!

Chapter One

'Dad.' The word slipped from Lucinda Mannolini's lips on a whisper as she emerged from gate 21 at Adelaide Airport and spotted her father. Her heart squeezed. His standard uniform of black work trousers and checked shirt seemed to hang from his lanky body. In the last six months, he appeared to have gone a little whiter on top. He still stood tall though, his glasses perched on his nose and his arms folded across his chest as he waited amidst a sea of people desperate to claim their loved ones so the holiday season could kick off. Overhead, announcements were being made about delayed flights and missing passengers, but Brian Patterson looked lost in his own little world.

Thrusting her shoulders back and pushing her chin high to give an air of confidence she didn't feel, Lucinda slipped into the stream of passengers, approaching a couple so lost in their passionate reunion that they either didn't care or hadn't noticed they were holding up the traffic. Once upon a time she and Joe had been like that whenever he returned from his two weeks on the goldfields, but lately, not so much. Pushing that thought away, she stepped around them as Dad rushed forward, his arms wide

1

open for her. Her leather handbag slapped against her back as she flung herself into them and dropped her head against his strong, broad shoulders.

'Dad,' she said again as tears welled in her eyes.

'Lucinda,' he whispered back. 'My Lucinda.' His voice held raw emotion, making her feel safe and loved and needed all at once. Still holding her, he shuffled them out of the throng of people rushing past. There wasn't room for her and him *and* the tongue-locked lovers.

'How are you, sweetheart?'

His heartfelt question almost unravelled her. He was the one who had been six months without his soulmate. Although she'd been as long without her mother, living away in Perth she'd sometimes forgotten that her mum wasn't still in their South Australian home town, making beds, cooking meals and greeting guests at the Meadow Brook Motel. Living away she could still pretend that Mum was alive, but being back home for Christmas would put an end to that illusion pretty damn quick.

'I'm good,' she lied, forcing a smile. She didn't know whether to mention Mum. 'How are you?' she asked instead.

'Fine, fine,' he waved away the question as he led her towards the baggage carousel. She guessed he wasn't speaking the whole truth either but neither pressed the other for this wasn't the place for a conversation that would quite likely end in messy, messy tears—hers not entirely related to the loss of her mother.

She wasn't sure her problem was the kind one discussed with one's father. Her sisters maybe, although she doubted any of them would understand.

Madeleine might appreciate her desire to have a child but would no doubt tell her to stop being so emotional about it. She'd say science could fix almost anything these days and suggest she book herself an appointment with a fertility clinic. All very well to say, but you had to have been trying to conceive for a year before a specialist would give you the time of day and she'd only gone off the pill eight months ago. Charlie would ask if she'd tried alternative therapy and suggest she and Joe go on a yoga holiday to get in touch with their inner fertility, or worse, visit some kind of sex therapist—as if that was the problem. And Abigail—the youngest—would get her drunk to try and take her mind off it all.

The Patterson girls were as different as the four seasons. Once upon a time, before careers and in her case a husband had scattered them, they'd been close—the way Lucinda thought sisters were supposed to be—but time and distance had drawn them apart and she missed the companionship they used to share.

'Lucinda?' Dad's voice echoed around her head and she blinked. The crowds had thinned around them.

'Sorry, Dad. What did you say?'

He frowned and then shook his head. 'Abigail's plane lands in half an hour but she'll no doubt be a while getting through customs. Charlie's next, then Madeleine. We'll probably have an hour or so to wait then before Madeleine's flight, but I thought we could grab some lunch.'

'Sounds great.' Lucinda injected chirpiness into her voice and linked her arm through her father's as she looked for her suitcase.

'Dammit.' Abigail Patterson cursed and tapped her Manolo Blahnik heel against the grubby floor of the airport as she eyed the hundreds of suitcases that were doing the rounds of the carousel while weary travellers waited ready to pounce. None of them held her violin, which she'd rashly decided to leave in London. *What a stupid mistake.*

For one, she never travelled without her instrument, and doing so would likely raise suspicion amongst her dad and older sisters.

And for two, how the hell would she get through the week ahead without being able to sneak off to her room and play some Pachelbel or Vivaldi? It would be hard enough trying not to let slip her recent failure, but the first Christmas at home without Mum was going to be plain and simple hell.

However, still raw from being kicked out of the orchestra, she had barely been able to look at her beloved violin while packing for this trip two days ago. She'd shoved it under the bed and decided that a little time apart would do them good. It would give her the chance to work out what to do with herself when she returned to London. What *did* one do with oneself when the dream you'd been working towards your whole life went up like a puff of smoke?

"Scuse me, coming through.'

A short, stocky woman with a face as red as her carrot-coloured hair barged past and launched herself at a massive purple polkadotted suitcase. Abigail glared as the woman tried to wrestle her suitcase off the carousel and then felt a spark of jealous irritation when a tall, well-built blond God of a man slipped past her to assist, lifting the case as if it were no heavier than a box of movie popcorn. He smiled at the redhead as he deposited the case on a trolley and the woman started blathering her thanks. Maybe Abigail should feign difficulty with her case and he could help *her*? She glanced around the carousel again but saw no sign of it. Anyway, it wasn't much bigger than an overnighter. If there was one thing Abigail was good at—besides playing the violin—it was packing lightly but still managing to look a million dollars.

Maybe that's what she could do … start some kind of boutique travel consultancy. She would specialise in helping women like her sister Madeleine, who always took practically her whole wardrobe on holiday, to pack smarter. Not that Madeleine ever had holidays. This trip home was a necessary exception.

'I swear my stuff is always the last,' said a dreamy voice beside her.

Thoughts of the fashion-travel-consultant business fading, Abigail turned to smile at the owner of the voice. She met his gaze and her tummy fluttered at the way he looked her up and down, obviously admiring her long legs in their tiny yellow shorts and sexy heels. Perhaps there was a God after all.

'Well, this might be your lucky day, 'cause my belongings have a habit of being last as well.' The guy smiled as her fingers inched up to her hair and she flicked her straight blonde locks over her shoulders, flirting without being fully conscious of it.

'Pity there's not a bar this side of customs,' he said. 'I'd buy you a drink.'

She swallowed, warmth flooding her at the idea of sitting down for a cocktail with this guy. He could be just the kind of tonic she needed. 'Yes, pity indeed.'

'Were you on the flight all the way from London?'

She nodded. 'You?'

'Yep.' He ran a hand through his lovely thick hair. He looked like a surfer, which would account for his lovely body. 'I always tell myself that next time I'll stop over for a night somewhere, break up the journey, but I never do.'

Why-oh-why couldn't she have been seated next to him instead of the two teenagers she'd been dumped next to? Apparently their parents had been up front in first class, drinking proper champagne and not supervising their sons, who kept pestering the flight attendant for soft drinks and talking loudly about the games they were playing while the rest of the passengers were trying to sleep.

'You do this trip often then?'

'Often enough.' He hit her with that melt-your-insides smile again. 'I work in London but the fam are still in Oz. I'd be written out of the olds' will if I didn't come home for Christmas. What about you?'

'Pretty much the same.' She wasn't about to go into the details with a stranger—that one of her 'olds' had recently passed away and she technically didn't have a job anymore.

'That's my bag.' He turned away and bent over the carousel, scooping up a large navy-blue backpack just before it went in through the little hole and did another round. The action gave Abigail a rather nice view of his taut behind and she felt her tummy do that flutter thing again. She'd been so focused on her career the last few months (make that years) that she hadn't had much time for men. There'd been that brief fling with the orchestra's assistant manager, but after discovering he was married—he hadn't mentioned it of course, but she should have done her research because everyone, she later found out, knew he was—she'd been avoiding the opposite sex. She had her violin, the true love of her life, and she didn't want anything to get in the way of her career.

Unfortunately it had turned out that she didn't need anyone else to stuff it up. She'd done a perfectly good job of that on her own. She sighed as the guy turned back towards her and hit her once again with his killer smile.

'I don't suppose you want to get a drink anyway?' he said, tilting his head to one side like an adorable puppy. 'I could wait for you to get your bag and then we could …' His voice drifted off as he nodded towards the customs line and the exit that led into the rest of the airport.

Her imagination skipped forward to what he'd want to do once they'd finished their drinks. She'd never had a one-night stand before but right now the idea of a few hours in the arms of a handsome stranger was more appealing than facing her family, who would no doubt take one look at her and know something was up.

'I'd love to, but my dad and sisters will be waiting out there.'

'Damn.' He didn't hide his disappointment and it echoed her own.

She was about to suggest they exchange numbers and maybe catch up when they were both back in London, but she spotted her case out of the corner of her eye and instinctively lunged past him. 'Sorry. That's mine.'

He didn't help her like he had the middle-aged woman and when she turned back she could already see that the moment—the opportunity—was over. He was moving on, ready to get on with his own family Christmas and forget they'd ever met. She didn't even know his name.

'Well, nice meeting you. Have a good Christmas.' He heaved his backpack a little further up his shoulder, smiled and then turned away.

'Bye.' Abigail watched a moment as he headed towards customs and joined the other passengers in the line. How different her holiday could have been if she'd been able to say yes to that drink with whatever his name was. It would be something hot and masculine like Jack or Adam, of that she was certain. One drink would have led to another, which likely would have led to some red-hot fun. How she longed for some red-hot fun.

But there was no point standing here and wishing things were different. The fact was, she wasn't home for a holiday fling. She was here to help Dad get through his first Christmas without Mum. Her chest tightened at the thought, the emotion rising up into her throat, making crying in the customs line a very real possibility. It certainly put her orchestra woes into perspective.

Nothing had ever been as bad as losing Mum.

Charlotte Patterson smiled with a mixture of relief and anticipation as she waited to exit the plane. She'd almost missed this flight, which was becoming a nasty habit and would have made her the brunt of her sisters' jokes. Again. It hadn't been her fault, though. She'd been all packed and ready to go when the little old lady in the house next door had come knocking, sobbing her heart out because she'd locked her keys inside. Of course Charlie hadn't been able to leave Mrs Gianetti until she'd called the locksmith and made sure he was on his way. As a result she'd almost been late to the airport.

It had been touch and go, but thankfully her taxi driver had been a pro at negotiating Melbourne's morning traffic and she'd arrived in the nick of time. The flight had been uneventful and now she couldn't wait to disembark and see everyone. They hadn't had a family Christmas since Madeleine had moved to America five years ago and although Mum wouldn't be there, going home to be together for this first Christmas without her felt like the right thing to do.

They'd sit around the table where she used to help them with their homework and they'd share a few wines and special memories. They'd uphold Mum's Christmas traditions—attend the local church service on Christmas Eve, maybe help Dad make breakfast for the motel guests on Christmas morning and then open their presents sitting around the tree that was decorated solely with the primitive handmade ornaments she and her sisters had made in primary school. Mum had loved them and sworn she'd never ever throw them out. Charlie swallowed the lump in her throat and blinked back the water in her eyes at the thought of going back to Meadow Brook, back to their home and the motel, without Mum there to welcome them.

The line of people started shuffling forward. For a moment Charlie froze, unable to tell her legs to move as her excitement made way for fear and dread. Fear of going home and having Christmas with a gaping hole where Mum should be. Dread that her sisters' dismissive glances would turn her into the crumbling mess she was whenever they were around. She wished they'd come to Melbourne, visit her in Brunswick where she helped manage a very busy café and ran hula-hooping classes in the evening. She might not have university letters behind her name but that didn't make what she did any less important. Her sisters might think her an airy-fairy hippy but she was happy with who she was. Most of the time, at least.

'Ahem.' A man cleared his throat behind her. 'Are you waiting for anything in particular?'

'Oh. Sorry.' Startled from her reverie, she shot forward and forced a smile back to her face. She wanted this to be a good Christmas, a cathartic experience, a chance for her family to share their grief, which would hopefully assist them in their recovery and maybe, just maybe, bring them closer together again.

Striding forward, her bag swinging over her shoulder, she appeared at the top of the ramp and glanced around the faces of people waiting in the arrivals hall.

'Over here!'

Charlie turned at the sound of a familiar voice—Abigail's—and most of the dread and fear dissipated. Her heart soared as she saw her little sister waving wildly with one hand, her other arm wrapped tightly around their father. Dear Dad, he looked weary even from this distance and Charlie swore that however bad she felt these next few days, she'd remember that he probably felt worse. Lucinda was on Dad's other side; she was also waving but not as enthusiastically as Abigail. Her golden blonde hair was pulled back into a high ponytail whereas Abigail's perfectly straight tresses hung free, almost down to her bum. Charlie's eyes once again prickled with unshed tears as she rushed towards her family and threw her arms around them.

'So good to see you.' Lucinda squeezed her arm and pressed a kiss against the side of her face.

'Hello, my darling,' Dad said, his voice a little shaky. 'Good flight?'

Abigail didn't give Charlie the chance to answer. 'I love that bag,' she gushed. 'Did you make it yourself?'

Bless Abigail, thought Charlie. Despite their differences, she always made an effort.

'No.' Charlie pulled out of the embrace and shook her head. 'I bought it at the St Kilda markets last weekend.' A brief pause to swallow the lump that was back in her throat. 'Oh my gosh, it's so good to see you all.'

They all grinned back at her and then Lucinda gestured to a trolley beside them. 'Dad and I have put my stuff in the car but we thought we could collect yours, dump them and then go get some lunch before Madeleine arrives.'

'Sounds good to me.' Charlie glanced at the trolley, frowned and then looked to Abigail. 'Where's your violin?'

She swore she saw a look of discomfort flash across Abigail's face, but if it were there she covered it over quickly with a smile and a shrug. 'I decided to take a real holiday. Besides, I know how much you guys *love* listening to me practise.'

Lucinda snorted and wrapped her arm around Abigail, drawing her close. 'We *do*, we really do love it, don't we, Charles?'

'Oh yeah ... Why else do you think I agreed to come spend a week with you lot?' Charlie retorted, secretly not believing a word Abigail said and vowing to get to the bottom of whatever was going on with her. The truth was they all loved listening to Abigail play. From the moment she'd started music lessons at all of five years old, she'd been amazing.

'Girls, girls, girls.' Dad feigned a stern tone but his chuckle gave the game away. He loved seeing his daughters together, liked it when they bantered in the way they used to do when they lived together all those years ago. And Charlie liked seeing him smile, even if it didn't quite reach his eyes.

'Sorry Dad,' they said in unison, grinning at him.

Lucinda took hold of the trolley and Abigail and Charlie linked arms with Dad as they followed the hordes towards the baggage carousel. For the first time in her life, Charlie's patchwork holdall was already doing the rounds of the carousel when they arrived. Thankful they wouldn't have to wait, she scooped it up and dumped it next to Abigail's little suitcase on the trolley.

'Dad, give me your keys.' Lucinda held out her hand. 'I'll take all this to the van while you guys go and find a table.'

Charlie couldn't hide her smirk. Although the grey shadows beneath Lucinda's eyes indicated she might not have been sleeping the best lately, she was still in top organisational form. She knew her other sisters sometimes found Lucinda's bossiness stifling and annoying but it comforted Charlie. For as long as she could remember, Lucinda had been like a second mum. Four years older than Charlie and seven years Abigail's senior, she'd often made sure her younger sisters were fed and dressed when their parents were too busy with motel guests. Madeleine was the oldest but had always had her head stuck in a book, far too busy studying to bother with tiresome little sisters. It wasn't surprising that Lucinda had chosen primary school teaching as a career and been the first (and only) one of them to get married. Charlie guessed it wouldn't be long before she and Joe had children of their own to fuss over.

'There's a table over there.'

At Abigail's words, Charlie realised she'd walked from the carousels to the café without even noticing. 'Yes, that looks fine,' she said, following Abigail and Dad to the table.

Abigail slumped into a seat and picked up the menu. 'I'm having pancakes. The food on the plane was crap. What do you want, Dad?'

'Just a coffee, love.'

'What about you, Charlie?' Abigail asked.

'Give me a chance to look at the menu,' Charlie replied, not looking at Abigail but instead to her father, who looked like he'd aged more than six months. The loss of his wife and looking after the motel by himself had obviously taken its toll and Charlie felt a stab of guilt for not being more available. Living in Melbourne, she was the closest in proximity but she may as well have been in Baltimore like Madeleine or London like Abigail for all the good it did. She reached out and took his hand across the table. 'How are you, Dad?'

He squeezed back and nodded. 'I'm as good as can be expected, but seeing you three and knowing Madeleine will be here soon helps. I've missed my girls.'

'Oh, Dad.' Abigail dropped the menu back on the table and threw her arms around him.

The three of them sat there, chairs close together, holding each other tightly, not daring to say any more for fear of shedding unsightly tears in public. That was how Lucinda found them when she returned ten minutes later.

'Have you ordered yet?' she asked.

At the sound of her voice, Abigail and Charlie pulled back from their father and looked up at their older sister.

Charlie shook her head. 'We were waiting for you.'

Lucinda smiled. 'Thanks. What do you all want? My shout.'

'Oh no, we can pay for ourselves,' Charlie protested.

'Speak for yourself.' Abigail shot Charlie a glare and then smiled sweetly at Lucinda. 'I'll have pancakes with extra ice-cream please.'

Lucinda rolled her eyes. 'What kind of lunch is that?'

'You're not my mother,' Abigail snapped.

Dad flinched as if someone had come along and slapped him on the back.

Charlie saw Lucinda swallow. 'I never said I was. Fine, have whatever you like. Dad? Charlie? What do you want?'

'Just a coffee,' Dad said.

'I'll have the sweet potato quiche, with salad.' Charlie pushed back her chair to stand. 'But I'll come with you to order.' She let out a deep breath as she and Lucinda weaved their way through the few tables to the front of the café. 'How's Joe?' she asked as they waited to place their order. 'It's a pity he couldn't come with you.'

Lucinda smiled tightly. 'Everyone has to take their turn working Christmas on the mine.'

Which didn't answer Charlie's question but she decided to let it lie. Lucinda likely didn't want to dwell on the fact she was going to spend her first Christmas without her husband since they'd been married.

'I suppose so,' she said and then glanced ahead at the specials blackboard.

Madeleine Patterson grunted as she retrieved her heavy suitcase from the carousel, yanked out the handle and then started towards customs. *Hello, Adelaide.*

If she had to choose a holiday destination, Adelaide was one of the last places on earth she'd have considered. Meadow Brook—the town she'd grown up in—was the *very* last. Despite the fact that her family owned the local motel, there was nothing holiday-like about the place. Sure, thousands of grey nomads passed through on their journey along the Eyre Highway to or from Western Australia, but why some of them stayed more than a night had always been a mystery to her.

As far as Madeleine was concerned, the most attractive thing about Meadow Brook was its name, which she'd always thought far too pretty for the dry, rugged terrain of the northern Eyre Peninsula, in which the primary industry was agriculture, followed closely by mining and supposedly (although it continued to flummox her) tourism.

No, if she'd chosen to take a holiday her destination would be a resort where she could relax on the beach or a city where she could shop till she dropped, somewhere like Paris or New York, or—if she did come back to Australia—then Sydney or Melbourne. A place where her childhood friends weren't all married with babies, making her wonder if she'd sacrificed too much in order to climb the career ladder.

She sighed. This vacation wasn't about her, it was about Dad.

It had been Lucinda's idea to get them all together for Christmas, and although Madeleine's first instinct had been to say she couldn't get away from work, the guilt and grief had gotten to her. Despite the agony of that long-haul flight and her initial reluctance to come, she now found herself impatient to get through customs and see everyone. The location wouldn't matter, it would be good just to be together at this time of the year. To celebrate Mum and help Dad through this first Christmas alone.

She sniffed and dug into her bag for a tissue, unable to imagine Meadow Brook without her mother. She blew her nose, wiped her eyes and then continued on.

The line through customs moved surprisingly fast and when she got to the front of the queue she slapped her immigration form down on the counter and answered the routine questions, hoping nothing would hold her up. After the officer waved her through, Madeleine all but ran towards the doors that would see her into the arrivals hall.

It felt better than she could possibly have imagined when she spotted the faces of her family in the crowd and even better falling into their arms. There weren't a lot of words exchanged at first but their embraces said more than enough. She wasn't usually one for too much hugging, but this felt right. This coming together, this Christmas, was always going to be difficult but it was something they all needed in order to move on.

'Finally, all my girls together again,' Dad said, as he let go of her and took a step back to survey his daughters. Madeleine smiled sadly, thinking that there was one key girl missing, but she pushed that thought aside. She didn't need to make a scene in the airport.

She didn't consider herself an emotional person but maybe she was more jet lagged than she thought, because standing here among her three sisters, next to her dad, she felt an overwhelming love for all of them.

'Right, where's the van?' she asked, tapping her suitcase. 'I'm in dire need of a shower and a drink.'

'Lead the way, Dad.' Abigail linked her arm through Madeleine's as Lucinda took the handle of her case and started to walk towards the exit.

'What on earth have you got in here?' Lucinda asked. 'How long are you planning to stay?'

Everyone laughed but Madeleine shot her a warning glare. Just because Lucinda dressed like a Perth housewife, didn't mean Madeleine couldn't take pride in her appearance. It wasn't like she could buy anything she forgot on the main street of Meadow Brook, so she'd come prepared for all occasions.

Ignoring her sister, Madeleine addressed Dad as they walked out into the bright and stiflingly hot South Australian afternoon. 'Thanks for coming to collect us. We could have hired a car.'

'Nonsense.' Dad shook his head. 'I've been counting down the days. Besides, I wouldn't want any of you driving after travelling so far.'

Charlie laughed. 'Melbourne's only an hour's flight away.'

Madeleine yawned. 'How's the motel? Lots of bookings?'

Dad shrugged as they came to the ticket payment machine. He dug his wallet out of his pocket. 'It's all right. Not as many guests as we usually have at this time of the year.' He slid the ticket into the machine and then fumbled around looking for change.

'Here, I'll get this.' Lucinda whipped her purse out of her handbag and fed a twenty dollar note into the machine, which in turn spat her out some coins. She took the returned ticket and handed it to their father.

Dad and Lucinda led the way to where the old Meadow Brook Motel people mover stood tall in the sea of vehicles around it. An ageing Toyota Tarago in faded yellow with the motel's logo and name (also faded) plastered across the sides, it looked a sorry sight. Madeleine thought it was about time Dad upgraded, but now wasn't the time to start discussing such things.

Lucinda rearranged the luggage that was already in the back and then heaved Madeleine's suitcase on top.

'Careful of Abigail's violin,' Madeleine warned.

'She didn't bring it,' Lucinda replied, closing the boot with a thunk.

'What?' Madeleine peered in through the open door at Abigail, who was settling herself on the back seat. 'Why? Are you sick or something?'

Abigail glowered. 'What's the big deal? Did you bring a host of pregnant women so you could deliver their babies while you were on holiday?'

Madeleine raised her eyebrows. It wasn't like Abigail to be so snarky. Charlie and Lucinda laughed as they climbed into the car, leaving the passenger seat beside their father for Madeleine. At least she hadn't had to remind them of her travel sickness. 'Sorry for asking,' she muttered under her breath.

No one said anything more. Seatbelts were clicked into place. Dad started the ignition and then drove out of the airport, heading west as they began the three-and-a-half journey to Meadow Brook.

Chapter Two

Charlie unpacked her few things in the room she used to share with Abigail and then sat down in the middle of the floor to meditate. This was something she did every morning and occasionally at other times of the day when she felt the need to find her inner calm. Almost four hours in the van with Dad, Madeleine, Lucinda and Abigail had definitely created one of those occasions. Her nerves, which she usually thought of as mellow, felt as tight as the strings on Abigail's absent violin.

She'd done her darn best to kickstart the conversation and then keep it going but it was like trying to make banana cake from apples. She'd never been more excited to see the 'Welcome to Meadow Brook—Home of the Sandhill Dunnart' sign in her life. The sign always made her laugh because she'd never actually seen one of the tiny, grey marsupials that were supposed to live here.

Although the mostly dry, sparse terrain beside the Eyre Highway would have been the same, the journey would have been very different if Mum had still been with them. She'd have grilled them all on their latest love interests and asked if anything exciting had happened at work recently, then filled them in on all the local gossip. Although the town's population was only five hundred, there were always plenty of stories—enough drama, good and bad, to keep a soap opera writer happy for years. Laughter would have filled the van and the miles would have flown by.

But although Charlie had thrown innocuous questions at her sisters—asking each of them in turn about their lives—they'd offered monosyllabic answers before turning back to stare out the window. Dad had been almost as bad, even seeming disinterested when she asked about the motel. She was worried about him. As well as the extra grey hairs and deeper lines around his eyes, he kept drifting off into his own little world. When they were kids he could amuse them for hours with his jokes and silly ideas but he hadn't even cracked a one-liner this afternoon. And he hadn't eaten anything in the six hours they'd been together either, not even a jelly snake from the packet Abigail had passed around. Was he thinking about Mum?

Stupid question, Charlie chastised herself. Annette had been the love of his life. Together since high school, they'd not only married and raised a family but also worked together every day of their adult lives. She thought about Mum constantly, so Dad probably felt as if part of him had died.

Her heart ached at the thought. If only there was some way to help him. They'd already lost one parent, they didn't need to lose him as well. With that thought she closed her eyes, took a deep breath and tried to clear her mind.

Half an hour later Charlie felt a lot better. She stood, tamed her long brown hair into a ponytail and listened to the sounds coming from the kitchen. The banging of cupboard doors and the clanging of pots and pans indicated that her sisters had all emerged from their rooms and were contemplating dinner. Lucinda was staying in the house with Dad and Charlie, while Abigail and Madeleine had taken vacant motel rooms. They'd all shared as children but no one was in a hurry to do so now.

Yet, the motel rooms were sparse—double beds covered with mission brown comforters to match the dull carpet, a small wooden table, two vinyl chairs, a tiny TV, a kettle and a microwave—so Madeleine and Abigail would no doubt spend most of their waking hours in the house.

Charlie left her bedroom and headed down the hallway, her silver bracelets jangling on her wrists as she passed the lounge room on her way to the kitchen. Pausing, she surveyed the room and frowned. It took a moment to realise what was wrong. It was two days before Christmas and the tree that had been in the Patterson family for as long as she could remember wasn't up yet. Had Dad forgotten about it or deliberately chosen not to put it up?

Mum had loved Christmas. Maybe it was just too painful.

'Where's Dad?' she asked as she joined her sisters in the kitchen. Aside from the fact that they were all grown up, nothing much had changed since when they'd sat in there after school eating snacks and telling Mum about their day. The cupboards were still the same old chipped wood and the benchtops a ghastly shade of orange, which was strangely comforting. Charlie could almost smell the scent of Mum's Chanel perfume wafting around them.

'Gone to check on the motel,' Madeleine replied, holding up a glass of wine. 'Do you want one of these?'

'Sure, thanks.' Charlie pulled out a chair and sat down at the table as her oldest sister poured her a glass identical to those her other sisters nursed.

'Dad asked if we wanted to have dinner in the restaurant,' Abigail said, twirling her glass between her fingers, 'but we decided we'd rather eat here. Safe from all the locals coming over to ask how we're coping.'

'Good idea.' Although secretly Charlie thought it might be less painful than sitting around the table with her broken family and trying to make small talk. She took a sip, hoping the wine might help ease the tension that was again rushing to her head. Maybe it would be a short dinner—Abigail and Madeleine had both come a long way and must be exhausted, not that you could tell. Both of them looked pretty much like they'd just stepped off a Paris catwalk. Lucinda didn't care a lot about fashion but she had the supermodel looks and body as well. Only Charlie had lucked out—boring brown hair, boring brown eyes and a body that was neither fat nor slim, tall or short.

'Only problem,' Lucinda said, peering into the fridge, 'is that there's very little here to work with. Dad must be eating most nights in the motel. I've never seen the cupboards so bare.'

Madeleine shrugged from where she was leaning against the kitchen counter. 'It's a pain in the ass cooking for one, so I don't blame him. I eat out most of the time.'

Lucinda sighed. 'I suppose so. I'll borrow some ingredients from the motel and tomorrow we'll go shopping.'

Charlie was surprised she didn't comment on Madeleine's American lingo.

'Yay.' Madeleine lifted her glass in a faux toast. 'I can hardly wait. Shopping in Meadow Brook.'

Ignoring Madeleine's sarcasm, Lucinda walked off towards the door that led from the house into the back of the motel.

'The Christmas tree isn't up yet,' Charlie told them.

Abigail frowned. 'Shouldn't it be up by now?'

'I'm not sure there are any rules,' Charlie said, suddenly wishing she hadn't said anything, 'but Mum always put it up at the beginning of December. For some reason Dad hasn't. I'm not sure if it's because he doesn't want to, hasn't had the time or can't be bothered.'

'We can't have Christmas without a tree. Where will we put the presents if we don't have a tree?' Abigail sounded outraged. She pushed back her chair and then slammed her glass on the table as she stood. 'We should put it up.' With that she flounced out of the kitchen, leaving Charlie alone with Madeleine.

They both sighed at the same time.

'It's going to be harder than I thought being here without Mum,' Madeleine said, giving Charlie a rare glimpse into what she was actually feeling. 'Everywhere I look she's there. I remember her buying these glasses for my twenty-first party.' She held up the one in her hand and looked at it like it might contain the answers to a zillion world problems. 'She said she'd give them to me when I got married.'

Charlie half-smiled, remembering that party like it was yesterday. She'd been almost fifteen and she and Mitch McDonald, her best friend, had snuck a bottle of Midori (one of Madeleine's birthday presents) and some lemonade out of the house. They'd taken it to the swings behind the motel and drunk way more than they should have. Or rather she had. Mitch, despite being a tall, lanky thing, had been able to hold his drink. He'd snuck her back inside, put her to bed and left her a glass of water on her bedside table for when she woke up. The last thing she remembered was him taking off her shoes, swinging her legs onto the mattress and stroking her hair back off her forehead. Although she hadn't been sick, she'd woken the next morning with a killer headache and had never touched the green poison since.

'I remember.' Charlie took another slow sip of her wine. 'Is there a wedding on the cards?'

Madeleine almost choked on her wine. She slapped her hand against her mouth and coughed, recovering eventually to say, 'For that I'd need a man and hospital shift work is not exactly conducive to matchmaking. Most of the men I meet are married to my patients.'

'What about a woman then?' Charlie asked.

'I'll leave them to you,' Madeleine retorted, wriggling her eyebrows.

Charlie laughed. Her sisters would never let her live down the experimental kiss she'd had with one of the barmaids from the local pub on the night of *her* twenty-first. They didn't know she'd dated a couple of women since. Truth was it wasn't usually a person's gender that attracted her. It was deeper things like their sense of humour, their values—the way they looked at, and responded to, life.

Abigail waltzed back in before either of them could say anything further on the subject of men, women or relationships. 'I found it.' She bounced on the spot, far too lively for someone who'd just flown halfway across the world. 'I've put the box in the lounge room, but I can't find the decorations. Anyone know where Mum kept them?'

Madeleine shrugged and topped up her glass. 'Dad might know.'

'Maybe we should ask him if he's okay with all this before we put the tree up,' Charlie suggested, not wanting to put a dampener on Abigail's enthusiasm (which she guessed was her way of coping) but at the same time not wanting to upset Dad. The tree had always been Mum's thing.

'I'll help you look.' Madeleine downed most of her wine and then put the glass on the table. She turned to Charlie. 'I think putting the tree up will be good for Dad. For all of us. Mum loved Christmas. We need to do this for her.'

As usual Madeleine had the last word.

Charlie rubbed her lips together as Madeleine followed Abigail back out of the room and down the hallway to the storage cupboard. Her older sister's degree might not be in psychology, but she was a doctor, so maybe she knew more about dealing with grief than the rest of them. And at least they'd relaxed a bit around each other. The wine had helped, and maybe getting into the festive spirit would assist even more.

★

Lucinda pushed open the door that led from the house into the back hallway of the motel. As the door thumped shut behind her she walked forward, detouring via the reception, bar and restaurant area on her way to the kitchen. It was just after six o'clock and so she guessed Dad would be behind the bar, chatting with guests and locals as they ordered their pre-dinner drinks. There weren't a great many dinner options in Meadow Brook: the pub served counter meals and the service station greasy fast food, so the motel had always been the go-to venue for people wanting to sit down and be served. The menu wasn't flash—home-style cooking rather than five-star cuisine—but the portions were always generous and everything came with a smile. Many of the older guests chose a drink at the motel bar over having to walk down the main street after dark to drink alongside the farmhands, road workers and backpackers that frequented the pub.

But tonight, as she stepped into reception and glanced ahead to the bar and restaurant, Lucinda frowned. The smell of sizzling steak wafted towards her but only one table was occupied and one person stood, their back to her, at the bar. Dad was nowhere to be seen.

Smoothing her hands over her outfit, she rushed over, apologising to their customer as she lifted the hatch and ducked behind the bar. 'I'm so sorry, can I get you a drink?' She looked into the man's eyes as she came to stand in front of him and gasped with recognition. 'Mitch!'

'Hello stranger.' The boy who had been Charlie's best friend all through school grinned back at her, his face tanned but his eyes as bright and mischievous as ever. He leaned over the bar and pulled her into a hug. 'Heard you girls were back for Christmas. How are you?'

Lucinda smiled as she withdrew from his embrace to take a better look at him. She'd seen him briefly at Mum's funeral but there'd been so many people to talk to and barely time to say 'hi' to any of them. 'We're okay. They say the big occasions are the hardest—first Christmas, birthday, anniversaries—but at least we're all together, here for Dad.'

He nodded, his smile fading. 'Yes. It'll be good for him to have you around.'

'Speaking of families, how's yours?'

'Dad's hanging in there.' Mitch stared down at the bar, clearly uncomfortable talking about his father. Charlie, or maybe Dad, had mentioned that Rick McDonald had recently gone into full-time care. 'Macca's great, though. Did you hear that he and Kate have just had their fourth?'

'Really? That's great?' Lucinda forced a smile, trying to sound enthusiastic, but then quickly changed the subject. 'So what are you doing here? *Can* I get you a drink?'

'Yes, I'll have a Coopers Pale Ale, please.'

Lucinda spun around and scoured the glass fridge behind her. She was thankful he hadn't asked her to pull a pint as she wasn't sure she remembered how. There was little call for bar tending in the classroom. 'Um, I'm not sure we have one.'

'Never mind, I'll have a Carlton Draught instead.'

'Great.' She opened the fridge, pulled out the bottle, cracked the lid and then handed it to him. 'Are you meeting someone for dinner?'

He took a sip and then shook his head. 'Nah. Just came to see your old man. Been popping by every now and then, since … Well, you know.'

Lucinda swallowed. Yep, she knew. 'That's lovely of you.' Mitch had always been a sweetie. If he hadn't been four years younger than her and a walking extension of her sister, maybe she'd have been interested in him as more than a brother figure. He might have been a little weedy and a little nerdy in a class clown sort of way back then, but he'd filled out in all the right places and grown into one very good looking guy.

'Brian was always good to me, and after Annette died, knowing you girls weren't around. Well, I ...' He shrugged.

'Thanks so much.' She reached over the bar and squeezed his hand. 'In your opinion, how's he coping with ... with everything?'

Mitch took another long drag of his beer, sighed and then glanced back into the reception as if checking Dad wasn't in hearing distance. 'I'll be honest with you, I'm a little worried.' He gestured to the fridge behind her. 'I don't think he's keeping up with orders and Mrs Sampson'—one of the motel's long-time employees—'confided in me that some bills aren't being paid and he doesn't always bother to answer the phone. Reservations are down, and you can see for yourself that things aren't as busy as they used to be. Maybe I'm speaking out of turn, but this place used to be crowded on a Friday night.'

At that moment, the chef, Rob, came through from the restaurant and put a pizza box on the bar in front of Mitch. 'Enjoy,' he said and then tipped his head to Lucinda. 'Hi Lucinda, welcome back.'

'Thanks.' She smiled at Rob but was glad when he turned away again. He'd only been an employee for about a year and she didn't know him well enough to grill him, but she wanted to talk more to Mitch.

He opened the box and gestured to the Hawaiian pizza inside. 'Want a slice?'

She shook her head. 'Do you know where Dad is now?'

'In the office I think.' Mitch took a bite of his pizza.

Lucinda hoped he was wrong about her dad not coping, but he wasn't the type to exaggerate.

'Charlie back too?' Mitch asked, jolting her out of her thoughts.

She smiled inwardly at his fake-nonchalant tone. She'd always suspected he had a sweet spot for her sister and it looked like he still did. 'Sure is. Why don't you head on inside and say hi? I'm sure she'd love to see you.'

His cheeks flushed and he slammed down the lid on the pizza. 'Nah, maybe later. Give you all a chance to catch up. I guess now you're here I don't need to check on Brian anyway. You have a good night.' Then, leaving half his beer un-drunk, he picked up the box and all but fled from the motel.

Lucinda planted her elbows on the bar, cupping her head in her hands. If Mitch was right about Dad, that was just another worry to add to her list. She looked up again and glanced at the grey-haired couple in the restaurant. They seemed happy enough; at least Rob was looking after them. Then she looked at her watch. Should she try and give Joe a call, tell him she'd arrived safely and bid him goodnight? Or should she confront Dad to see if Mitch's worries carried any weight? Of course he'd be different now—he'd lost his wife. He was allowed to be sad, allowed to be a little more quiet than usual. They all needed time to heal. But what if it was something more serious?

Argh! She wanted to scream or cry or throw something. Why did everything have to be so damn hard?

'Hello love. I've been so excited about seeing you.'

Startled from her thoughts, Lucinda straightened and then turned to look at the motel's housekeeper, who'd just entered the bar area. A widow with two adult sons who now lived in Adelaide, Mrs Sampson had been a good friend of Mum's as well as an employee for about twenty years. Lucinda opened her arms and rushed over to give the older woman a hug. Mrs Sampson was a good cook and had a physique to match, so Lucinda's hands didn't meet around her back like they did whenever she'd hugged her mother, but the embrace was almost as comforting. She felt her eyes tearing up, but forced the waterworks down and pulled back to get a proper look at the woman whose warm, caring nature and bubbly personality had made her like a second mother to them.

The two of them held hands, looking each other over a moment. Where Mum had been a trim, lithe woman and almost six foot, there was more of Mrs Sampson to love. She still wore her greying hair in a thick plait and had often joked about being happy to grow old gracefully.

'How are you?' Lucinda asked, finally letting go of the older woman's hands.

'Feeling annoyed at myself. That's what I am. I popped home a few hours ago to feed the blasted cat, sat down on the couch for a quick cup of tea and then woke up fifteen minutes ago and realised I'd lost most of the afternoon.'

Lucinda smiled. 'You must have needed the rest.'

'What I needed,' tsked Mrs Sampson, 'was to be here when my girls arrived home and to have had dinner and your favourite desserts on the table. I suppose you're all going to eat in the restaurant instead? Rob is a fabulous cook but I thought you might prefer to be in the house tonight, this being your first night back without ...'

Her voice drifted off but Lucinda guessed what she'd been going to say. People didn't quite know how to bring her mother into the conversation without things getting awkward. Everyone was censoring themselves for fear of upsetting someone else.

'Oh no, we wouldn't expect you to do that. I find cooking therapeutic, so I'm going to whip something up.' Lucinda gestured towards the motel kitchen. 'I came to steal some ingredients from Rob.'

'Well, I'll help you anyway. Can't wait to see the others.' Mrs Sampson started towards the kitchen, but Lucinda reached out to put her hand on her arm.

'Can I ask you a question?'

'Sure. Ask away.' Mrs Sampson smiled warmly.

'It's … Dad.' Lucinda glanced towards the office and lowered her voice. 'I'm worried about him. Mitch said he might not be coping so well. That things are falling by the wayside around here.'

'Well, I won't lie. These past six months have been hard on all of us. Annette was the lifeblood of the motel and we're all struggling to work out how to continue without her, but of course, Brian the most. Don't you worry, I'm looking after him.'

'But you look tired too. When was your last day off?' Something told her Mrs Sampson was putting in more hours than someone of her age should be. And if Mitch was right about Dad struggling with bills, was she even getting paid overtime?

'I'm fine. I like keeping busy.'

Avoiding the question usually meant one thing. 'Are you going to see your boys over Christmas?'

'Not this year, love. They have their own families now, and your father needs me here.'

At that moment, Dad appeared from the office.

'I'm just going to borrow some veggies from Rob for a pasta,' Lucinda told him, not wanting him to guess they were discussing him. 'That okay?'

'Of course, love, whatever you need.' Then he smiled at Mrs Sampson. 'Hello there. Will you be joining us for dinner?'

'I shouldn't stay. I'm just going to say hello to the girls and then I'll be off.'

'Don't be silly, we'd love to have you,' Lucinda said. Maybe the older woman's presence would help ease the awkwardness when they all sat down at the table for the first time without their mother.

'Okay then, if you insist.' Mrs Sampson chuckled, clearly pleased to be invited.

'Dad, when will you be able to join us?' Lucinda asked.

'I won't be long. We're not busy tonight so Rob can handle things and then close up.'

Lucinda couldn't help but frown. 'Don't we usually have more guests at this time of year?' Lots of locals used the motel to put up extra family in town for the festive period—at least they always had in the past.

'Sometimes.' He looked past her to the big bar fridge and changed the subject. 'Shall I bring a bottle of wine?'

'Maybe a couple,' she said. 'The way Madeleine and Abigail were drinking, they've probably polished one off already.'

He chuckled and Lucinda kissed him on the cheek and then she and Mrs Sampson went through to the kitchen to beg Rob for some ingredients.

Madeleine, Charlie and Abigail were in their parents' bedroom staring into the walk-in robe. They hadn't been together in their parents' room for years and the last time they were even in the house was for Mum's funeral, so going into this very personal space felt like an invasion of privacy. But they'd turned the storage cupboard upside down and still hadn't uncovered the decorations so they'd headed in here to look in their mum's other hiding spot. It had been a big joke in their teens that Mum still thought she had a place they didn't know about to hide Christmas presents. Worst kept secret ever.

'Should her clothes still be here?' Abigail asked.

Her shaky question tore Madeleine from her memories. It wasn't only the wardrobe; the whole room looked as if Mum still slept here every night. Her pink fluffy slippers were on the floor beside the bed and a book lay splayed open to the page she must have been reading the night before she died—a rural romance with a hot bloke and a windmill on the cover. Madeleine's heart spasmed at the sight.

'It hasn't been that long. Only six months.' Charlie moved to put her arm around Abigail, her eyes still focused on Mum's side of the robe.

Madeleine also felt transfixed, staring at the outfits, many of which she recalled Mum wearing during their Skype conversations. It didn't feel that long ago. She rubbed her arms, which suddenly felt shivery despite the early evening South Australian heat.

'Yes,' Abigail mused, 'but wouldn't it depress him seeing her stuff everywhere he looked? It can't be healthy. What do you reckon, Madeleine?'

She shrugged, wishing she had a definitive answer. 'Grieving is an individual process. Having her clothes here probably makes him feel like she's still close. He may not be able to bear the thought of sorting through them just yet.'

'I guess.' Abigail sniffed. 'I can't believe she's gone. I just wish—'

'I know,' Madeleine and Charlie said at the same time.

Madeleine tried to swallow the lump in her throat. She'd felt the same way when she'd received the horrid phone call telling her that Mum had been stung by a bee at the Meadow Brook school fête, had an allergic reaction, gone into anaphylactic shock and died before anyone could call an ambulance. At fifty-eight years, Annette Patterson had been too young to die, far too full of life, and her oldest daughter hadn't been prepared. No one had even known Mum was allergic to bees, and anyway, what was a school without an EpiPen floating around in this day and age? Didn't these kinds of nightmares happen to *other* people? They were the stuff of page ten newspaper articles, stories she read about and brushed aside just as quickly. But to happen to them? The thought of never being able to ask Mum's advice again or simply hear her voice made Madeleine feel like she was underwater and running out of breath. She shook her head as memories of that awful day flashed back—she'd taken the call at work, on the ward, and had gone immediately into shock.

Thankfully Hugo had looked after her, ushering her into his office where he'd conjured a stiff drink from Lord knows where and then taken it upon himself to book her a flight home.

If it wasn't for him and Celia she didn't know how she'd have gotten through that day, nor the six months that had followed. Before she realised it, tears were streaming down her face.

'Oh Madeleine.' Abigail wrapped her arms around her and laid her head on her shoulder. Within seconds Madeleine felt her sister's own tears sopping through her shirt. She patted Abigail's back and tried to blink away her emotion—she was the oldest, supposed to be the strongest, she hadn't even cried at the funeral— but when Charlie joined them, wrapping her arms around the both of them, she lost any chance she had of winning the battle. *Tomorrow.* Tomorrow, after a good night's sleep and a therapeutic morning run, she'd be strong for everyone.

The three of them sank to the floor in a sobbing mess and that was where Lucinda found them a few minutes later.

Lucinda paused in the doorway to her parents' bedroom and stared at her sisters, wrapped in each other like some kind of messy knot. She couldn't remember the last time she'd seen Madeleine cry—maybe it was in primary school—and she almost felt like an intruder. Part of her wanted to rush over and drop to the floor beside them, to cling to her sisters and take the comfort she very much needed, but there was the worry that if she started crying, she'd never be able to stop. And not just because she was missing her mum. The other option was playing the bad guy, telling them to get their act together before Dad found them like this. But suddenly she didn't want to burden them with her worries about their father. She'd grill Mrs Sampson a little more first, watch him like a hawk herself and then come up with a game plan.

Choosing to retreat, she escaped quietly and headed back into the kitchen where she found Mrs Sampson slicing up the vegetables with a sharp knife. Her hackles rose, but she caught herself before saying anything. The woman was only trying to help. She grabbed another chopping board, knife and started on the carrots before Mrs Sampson could get to them. Between them, the capsicum, broccoli and cauliflower were all diced to an inch of themselves before they heard the other girls arguing in the lounge room.

'At it already, I hear.' Mrs Sampson chuckled. 'The only time I ever heard Annette complain about you four was when you were at each other's throats. I know what she meant. My boys used to lay into each other.'

'Yes, I remember.' Lucinda smirked. But right now she could cope with her sisters' bickering a lot more than touchy-feely sharing moments. Moving over to the stove, she poured some oil into a pan, waited for the sizzle and then threw in the chopped onion.

Within seconds of the aroma drifting out to the rest of the house, Madeleine waltzed into the kitchen, heading for the near-empty bottle of wine first, topping up her glass and then acknowledging Mrs Sampson.

'Well, hello there.' She beamed a tipsy smile and threw one arm around the housekeeper.

'Hello, Madeleine.' Mrs Sampson kissed her on the cheek. 'Good to see you. Any jet lag yet?'

Madeleine lifted her glass. 'I'll worry about jet lag and hangovers tomorrow.'

Lucinda rolled her eyes as Madeleine crossed over and peered into the pan. 'That smells good, little sister.'

'It's just onion,' Lucinda snapped, thinking it would have been nice if her sisters had offered to help. They hadn't known that Mrs Sampson would be here, but since Abigail and Madeleine were the ones to decide they'd rather eat in the house than the restaurant, one of them could at least clear and set the table.

Madeleine took a long sip of her wine and leant back against the kitchen bench to watch. 'You'll make someone a good mum some day.'

Lucinda bristled. Shouldn't Madeleine of all people know that not everyone found it easy to breed? If she didn't feel like such a failure, maybe she'd be able to open up about her troubles and ask for some sisterly, or at least medical, advice.

'What are Abigail and Charlie up to?' Mrs Sampson asked, perhaps sensing Lucinda's irritation.

'Abigail got it in her head we needed to put up the Christmas tree, so we found the decorations and now she's busy directing Charlie where to put everything.' Madeleine didn't elaborate or share what else had happened during their quest.

That annoyed Lucinda—like her sisters had a secret they didn't want to share. She tried to laugh alongside Mrs Sampson's warm chuckle, but it didn't quite eventuate.

Oblivious, Madeleine dug her phone out of her pocket and started checking her emails or something. She laughed and smiled in a manner that looked out of place on someone usually so strait-laced and efficient.

'Message from a beau?' asked Mrs Sampson.

Madeleine looked horrified and put her phone away. 'As if. Anyway, fill me in on the local gossip,' she demanded.

Lucinda supposed she should be grateful that Madeleine and Mrs Sampson didn't feel the need to lure her into conversation. The way she felt right now, she was liable to snap at anything her older sister said. Silently seething, she moved around them as she proceeded to make the sauce and throw on the pasta. While it cooked, she poured herself an extra large glass of wine, deciding that today, and maybe even all this week, she'd forget about trying to eat healthily and stay off the vino. What was Christmas without a few drinks?

Besides, with Joe at work over two and a half thousand kilometres away, she was unlikely to hit the baby jackpot even if she was smack bang in the middle of her cycle.

The door from the motel opened and Dad appeared, carrying two bottles of wine and wearing a smile that looked as if it cost him an effort. 'Something smells good.'

'It's Lucinda working her magic,' Madeleine said, putting her wine down on the bench a moment to go over and take the bottles from him. 'Everything okay in the motel?'

He nodded. 'Where are the others?'

'They're putting up the Christmas tree.' When Dad didn't say anything, Madeleine looked worriedly to Lucinda and Mrs Sampson and then back to him. 'I hope you don't mind.'

'It's fine,' he said. 'I haven't had the time. I'll go freshen up before dinner.'

'And I'm going to see my other girls,' Mrs Sampson said as she bustled after him.

Lucinda watched Madeleine frown as they made their way out of the room. Mrs Sampson turned into the lounge room, but Dad didn't even pause to look as he made his way down the hallway and into the bathroom.

'I'm concerned about him,' Madeleine admitted.

'Me too,' Lucinda said, feeling a rare moment of affinity with her sister and relieved to be able to say so. 'But it's normal for him to be lost and still sad, isn't it? I know I am.'

Madeleine sighed. 'Yes, but there's a fine line between grief and depression.'

Chapter Three

Although Charlie and all her sisters had made the trek home for Mum's funeral, they'd been far too busy making arrangements, helping Dad with the motel and gracefully accepting sympathy from locals to sit down and eat a meal together.

'Do you realise this is the first time we've all eaten together since …' Abigail stopped without finishing her sentence.

No one said anything as chairs scraped back against the linoleum and Charlie snuck a glance around the table. It was plain from their expressions that they'd all been thinking along the same lines.

This was one of the 'firsts' experts referred to when they spoke about grief. Mostly they talked about the first birthday, first anniversary of death, first Christmas and so on, but Charlie reckoned the little occasions like this one were even harder. She swallowed as she sat down in the seat that had been hers for as long as she could remember. Dad was at the head of the table, Abigail was next to Charlie and Madeleine was sitting on the other side of the table. Lucinda was busy at the kitchen bench, where Mum had stood for so many years, serving the pasta. Mrs Sampson was in Mum's seat.

Usually confident and cheerful, the older woman looked uncertain tonight. 'Maybe I should leave you all to it,' she said, starting to stand.

'No,' Charlie protested. 'It'll be good to have you here.'

'Yes,' Madeleine agreed. 'You were as close to Mum as any of us.'

Dad remained quiet but the decision had been made. Wanting to deflect the attention from Mrs Sampson, Charlie looked to Lucinda. 'Do you want any help with that?' Once again, they'd left her to play Mum while the rest of them laughed and squabbled as they unpacked the decorations in the other room.

'I'm fine, thanks,' she replied, but Charlie thought her voice sounded tight.

'We've been putting up the Christmas tree, Dad,' Abigail said, an obvious attempt to make conversation. 'I rescued the angel Madeleine made in kindy; she wanted to throw it out. Remember how much Mum loved that angel?'

Dad smiled sadly and nodded slowly before taking a sip of his wine.

'It's ghastly.' Madeleine made a face that echoed her words. 'The only place for it is the bin.'

Charlie smirked. Ghastly was an apt word to describe the angel made with paper doilies, plastic cups and about a tonne of glitter. Although to be fair, it wasn't any more horrendous than the pieces the rest of them had made in primary school. Pieces that had been their mother's pride and joy, no matter how much they'd begged her to get rid of them.

'Maybe we should take a vote.' Abigail looked to the end of the table. 'Do you think it's time for a new angel, Dad?'

'Whatever you girls want.'

Charlie caught Abigail's eye across the table. The look on her face told her she too was worried about Dad's behaviour.

'So who's up for going to the Christmas Eve service tomorrow night?' Abigail asked brightly. It was something Mum had forced them along to every year and which they'd all complained about from an early age, although secretly Charlie suspected none of them hated it as much as they made out.

Madeleine rolled her eyes.

Lucinda, arriving at the table with two bowls laden with steaming pasta, said, 'I think that's a lovely idea. Will you come, Dad?'

'We'll see.'

'You'll be going, won't you Mrs S?' Abigail asked.

Mrs Sampson seemed quieter than usual and Charlie guessed it was because she didn't want to intrude on this family time. She wanted to say something to remind her that they all saw her as family anyway, but Lucinda placed a bowl each in front of Dad and Madeleine.

'Have you got anything special planned for tomorrow night in the motel?' she asked, trying again to lure him into conversation as Lucinda went back for the other bowls.

Surprisingly, Christmas Eve was always one of their busiest times in the motel restaurant. Many locals came for pre-midnight service dinner and drinks and in the past Mum and Dad had often hired a band for the evening. But Dad shook his head. 'Nah, didn't get round to organising anything. And besides, we're not very busy this year.' Then he went back to his pasta, pushing the fork around the plate but not actually putting anything in his mouth.

Lucinda looked to Abigail as she finally sat down next to Madeleine. 'Pity you didn't bring your violin. You could play a few tunes.'

'Oh, yes, that would be lovely,' remarked Mrs Sampson.

'Fuck, can you imagine?' Madeleine snorted at the same time. 'A violin would make Christmas carols sound like a funeral march.'

Abigail glared at Madeleine and then spooned the first mouthful of pasta into her mouth. She moaned in appreciation, then promptly changed the subject. 'Wow, this pasta is better than my favourite Italian restaurant in London. You are a domestic goddess, sis.'

Lucinda half-laughed. 'Don't know about that.'

'I bet Joe thinks so,' Charlie said, kind of wishing he was here. She'd always liked her brother-in-law. He had a mellow, fun-loving temperament that seemed to rub off on everyone around him and she felt like they could all do with a dose of mellow right now.

'Nothing I cook could ever compare to Rosa,' Lucinda said, an edge of bitterness in her voice. Picturing Lucinda's Italian mother-in-law, Charlie thought maybe she was lucky she hadn't found anyone to enter into the institute of marriage with yet.

'I guess that's true.' Abigail sighed. 'Remind me never to marry a man whose mum cooks better than me.'

'That rules out pretty much every man on the planet,' said Madeleine, laughing.

Abigail stuck her tongue out at Madeleine but there was a twinkle in her eye.

'Girls,' Dad said, his tone both warning and amused. 'Can you be nice to each other for five minutes?'

'No,' Abigail and Madeleine said in unison.

'Of course we can,' Lucinda promised at the same time, but awkward silence followed. The dynamics were all wrong without Mum sitting alongside them at the table. Even Mrs Sampson's usually chirpy presence did nothing to allay the melancholy mood.

'So,' Charlie said when she could no longer stand it. 'I've started teaching hula-hooping classes at the Brunswick Senior Citizens' Centre.'

Dad didn't appear to hear, but Mrs Sampson smiled again and her sisters all stared at her as if she said she'd just announced she'd volunteered to go on the space mission to Mars. Charlie wished she'd kept her mouth shut.

'That's nice,' Lucinda said after too long. Charlie reckoned Lucinda didn't really understand her any more than the other two. Madeleine and Lucinda were too conservative and although

Abigail had her music, her tastes were highbrow. She'd rather slit her own throat than listen to the reggae music Charlie liked. And their tastes weren't just different when it came to music.

'And are you still working at the café as well?' Lucinda asked, at least trying to show an interest.

Charlie nodded. Addicts of caffeine, her sisters had always been far more comfortable talking about her café job than they were about her passions for things like tarot cards, sculpture and aromatherapy. Sometimes she wondered if she was adopted. If Mum hadn't read her horoscopes everyday, Charlie would have been certain.

'Is that hot guy still working there?' Abigail asked.

Charlie rolled her eyes. A while back she'd sent a Facebook request for her sisters to like the café page and Abigail had messaged immediately asking who the bloke with the shaved head, rocking body and tattooed arms was. 'Yep. Unfortunately he's happily dating one of the waitresses.'

Abigail shrugged. 'What about you, Charles? You seeing anyone?'

'Not at the moment. You?' Charlie turned the limelight back the other way. 'Or are you too busy working as usual?'

'*Actually*, there's something I need to …' Abigail straightened but then went quiet. Charlie and the others, even Dad, looked up at the way she said that one word. It sounded … significant, like she was about to deliver an important announcement. Charlie noticed her hand was shaking slightly, which was very un-Abigail-like. Must be serious.

'Are you okay?' she asked.

'Yes.' Abigail came alive again, her eyes twinkling and a blush rushing into her cheeks. 'Actually, I am seeing someone. He's blond …' She paused and that look of a besotted-lover—all gooey distant eyes—came over her face. 'And gorgeous. And so damn nice. As it happens, he's an Australian also working in London. He's back to visit his family for Christmas too; we came over on the same flight.'

'And another one bites the dust,' Madeleine said dryly, taking another sip of her wine. 'That look you've got in your eyes is the same one Lucinda had when she told us about Joe. Remember?'

'Well, I'm happy for you.' Lucinda leaned across the table and patted Abigail's hand. 'That's great news, isn't it Dad?'

They all looked to Dad, who blinked as if he hadn't taken in a word of what they'd been saying. 'What? Yes, lovely.'

'Mum would have loved him, Dad.' Abigail reached out to take his hand. 'Tell us the story of when you met her again?'

'Ah, not tonight, love.' He extracted his hand and pushed back his chair. 'It's lovely to see you all, but I think the drive to Adelaide and back has got to me. Do you mind if I call it an early night?'

Charlie looked down. Aside from moving it around his plate, he hadn't touched his dinner.

'That's fine, Dad,' Lucinda said, 'but is there anything we can help with tomorrow? Motel-wise?'

He sighed, before glancing at each of them in turn. 'Actually girls, there's something I've been wanting to tell you and I guess there's going to be no better time than now.'

Charlie's breath caught in her throat as she imagined the worst. Was he sick? Did he have cancer? *Please no.* She couldn't handle losing him so close to her mother.

Finally, he spoke. 'I've decided to sell the motel.'

'Oh.' Abigail looked speechless, which had to be a first.

'Makes sense.' Madeleine nodded, but her expression was grave.

'Yes,' Lucinda agreed. 'It's a big job on your own, even with fabulous staff.'

Mrs Sampson stared down at her empty bowl as if this weren't a surprise.

Charlie didn't know what to think. She felt a tear bubble. The Meadow Brook Motel had been in Mum's family for generations. She couldn't imagine her life without it here to come back to, but she didn't want to make Dad feel guilty.

'It's not a decision I make lightly,' he admitted. 'Your mother loved this place. It was her life—and it was my life when she was here beside me—but I don't want to do it on my own. I've contacted a broker and we'll advertise in the new year. Of course, it could take a while to sell.'

They all nodded, each digesting this news in their own way.

'And there's one thing I would like your help with,' Dad admitted, staring down at his barely touched plate. Charlie struggled to recall a time he'd ever asked any of them for anything.

'Yes,' she and her sisters said in perfect unison.

He cleared his throat and looked down at the table rather than at any of them. 'It's your mother's things ... I don't know what to do with them. I tried to clear out her clothes and ...' His voice broke slightly. 'It was too hard. Do you think you girls could do this while you're home? The broker said it would be good if we could declutter the house a bit.'

'Yes.'

'Sure.'

'Of course'

'Definitely.'

Charlie thought of the clothes they'd seen in the wardrobe only an hour or so ago. She could understand why Dad hadn't felt able to deal with them. They still smelt of Mum and she guessed taking them off their hangers and boxing them up to donate to the Salvos or something was probably going to be one of the hardest things she'd ever done.

Chapter Four

Jet lag was the pits. Abigail hadn't slept a wink despite the wine she'd had last night with her sisters. Although to be honest, she wasn't sure she'd be able to sleep even if she hadn't just travelled halfway across the world. Sighing, she rolled over in the too-soft bed of her motel room and eyed the digital clock on the bedside table. It wasn't even 6.00 am but already the South Australian sunlight was blaring through the faded curtains and someone in the room next door was having a shower, singing loudly as the water pipes groaned their objection. She groaned hers as well and then sat up in bed, once again wishing she'd brought her violin. Playing music was her preferred method of stress relief, and she could have given Mr Shower Rockstar a run for his money.

She leaned over, peeled back the curtains and saw her sister emerging from a room along the verandah. Looked like Abigail wasn't the only one with sleeping issues. Although Madeleine was wearing tiny gym shorts, a tight little tank top and sneakers, suggesting she was going to make the most of her wakefulness.

Before she could think better of it, Abigail leapt out of bed and raced across the room to open the door. 'Madeleine,' she called. 'Are you going for a run?'

Madeleine raised one eyebrow and then indicated her attire. 'No, I'm going to the Opera House to watch the ballet.'

Abigail ignored the sarcasm. 'Can I come with you?'

Another raised eyebrow. 'I didn't know you were a runner.'

'There's a lot you don't know about me. Give me two minutes.' Total lie. She didn't even own a proper pair of running shoes but as she closed the door and went to get changed, she decided a t-shirt, her denim shorts and slip-on sandshoes would almost pass. When she went back outside, she spoke before Madeleine had a chance to comment on her bizarre running gear. 'So, you couldn't sleep either.'

Madeleine shook her head. 'Things on my mind.'

'Me too,' Abigail said, before thinking better of it. Thankfully Madeleine didn't appear inclined to ask and although Abigail was curious about whatever was bothering her sister, she didn't ask either just in case she turned the question back on her. 'Let's go then.'

Madeleine, who'd no doubt been stretching while waiting for Abigail, launched off across the car park and Abigail charged after her, hoping she wouldn't pull a ligament or anything. Then again, if she fell and broke her arm, she'd have a pretty solid excuse not to go back to London. And she could tell her family that the orchestra couldn't wait for her. That was much better than the truth. If only she wasn't a wimp with an extremely low pain threshold. If only she wouldn't die if she had to go for more than this holiday without playing her violin.

And then there was the boyfriend she'd invented last night. Geez, as if she didn't have enough to worry about trying to keep her failure a secret, now she'd invented a guy she'd need to keep track of as well. No wonder sleep had eluded her.

Five minutes later, sweat was pouring off Abigail's skin, her lungs were burning and her legs aching. She barely noticed the massive road trains roaring past them as she pounded along the gravel shoulder of the highway trying to keep up with Madeleine. Although her sister was likely fit enough to keep up a conversation while she ran, Abigail was not and both of them seemed happy for a bit of quiet contemplation. Was Madeleine thinking similar things to her? Wondering what their first family Christmas without Mum would be like? She'd naïvely imagined it would be good for all of them to be together but if dinner last night had shown anything, it was that her family simply didn't know how to interact without Mum at the helm.

Poor Mrs Sampson, having to sit at the table with a bunch of sour-faced Pattersons.

Dad was like a ghost, barely saying anything until he'd dropped his bombshell and then hurried off to bed, leaving them to digest the news. While he'd been present, Abigail had tried to cheer him up with memories of Mum, but each time someone had shut her down, riding over the top of her with some inane topic of conversation. As if her sisters knew better than she did how to deal with his grief.

As they turned off the highway on to a gravel road that bordered the perimeter of the town, Abigail slowed a little and tried to regulate her breathing. She wasn't actually sure the running was doing any good. All she could think about was the fact that maybe her sisters were right. Was she too young to know any-thing about anything? She'd certainly made a total balls-up of her opportunity in the London Symphony Orchestra. And that was part of the reason she was jittery, part of the reason she kept trying to make conversation—to ensure no one asked her about work. Since the initial shock about her missing violin, everyone appeared too consumed with other things to pay much interest but someone was sure to enquire sooner or later.

For the next few hundred metres, Abigail tried to come up with a plausible story, or better yet, a way to evade the situation entirely. She didn't want to lie outright but nor did she want to admit her failure. She couldn't bear to see the look on her sisters' faces—or worse, Dad's face—when she told them she'd been fired from her dream job. Her family had been so proud when she'd scored the gig as one of the youngest violinists ever to join the prestigious orchestra, and they'd be so disappointed if they found out the truth.

Hadn't they suffered enough disappointment lately?

'Crazy old bat.' It was the first thing Madeleine had said since they'd left the motel and it jolted Abigail from her thoughts. She looked up to see they were approaching an old, run-down fibro cottage, the garden (if you could call it that) overrun with purple flowers, chipped outdoor ornaments and cats.

Abigail jogged after Madeleine, glancing back at the house just in time to see an old woman glaring at them from the middle of her overgrown garden. Wearing a black skirt that brushed the ground, a dull grey saggy jumper—in this weather!—and a black scarf wrapped around her head, she looked like some kind of witch. As a child, Abigail had heard rumours about the woman. The centre of many a children's horror story, she was nicknamed 'Wacky Wanda' and the local schoolkids estimated her to be around one hundred years old—though no one knew her real name or age. Word had it she only ever ventured into the main street to buy cigarettes and the weekend paper. Lord knew where she bought other supplies, such as food.

But Abigail had always felt a little sorry for the old woman. Her sisters might drive her insane sometimes but she couldn't imagine what it would be like if she didn't have *any* of them. She lifted her hand and waved, calling out 'Merry Christmas' as she did so.

The woman's eyes narrowed and then she made a weird hissing noise, before mumbling something and turning away in apparent disgust. Although Abigail couldn't make out the words, whatever it was, it was obviously unpleasant. Her sympathy evaporated. *I was only trying to be nice.* A weird shiver scuttled down her spine like she'd just run through a spider's web.

She felt Madeleine's hand close around her arm as she urged her on. 'Come along, keep running.'

'Did you hear what she said?' Abigail asked.

'Fuck knows. She probably thought we were trespassing. I'm sure she's perfectly harmless though.'

Lucinda woke to the buzzing of her phone. She rolled over groggily and reached for it. Despite only having two glasses of wine last night, her head harboured the mother of all hangovers. Probably more the emotional stress of yesterday than the alcohol.

Smiling at the caller ID, she snuggled back into the pillows and pressed Accept. 'Hey gorgeous.'

'Babe.' Joe's incredibly sexy, deep voice seeped into her bones, acting like an instant pain relief. Things may have been a little tense between them lately but absence always made the heart grow fonder. 'Thought I'd get a quick call in before I start my shift. How was yesterday?'

'Draining,' she admitted. 'Dad's being really quiet and everyone's walking on eggshells. I think it's going to be a long week.'

'I'm sorry I can't be there.'

'It's fine. We both decided that it was for the best. Your mum will forgive you not attending Christmas if the reason is work, but if it's because you're spending it with *my* family instead, she'll probably excommunicate us.'

He laughed. 'Maybe that wouldn't be such a bad thing.'

But Lucinda knew he didn't mean it. Although Joe's mother had been dropping less than subtle hints that it was time he joined her other (five) children in providing her with grandchildren, he still adored her. He could say things like that but if Lucinda dared utter one mildly negative word about his *mamma*, she'd be given the silent treatment for a week.

'Dad has decided to sell the motel,' she said, not wanting to think about their failure to procreate.

'Really?' Joe was momentarily nonplussed. Then, 'I guess that makes sense. Must be a lot of work on his own. How do you feel about that?'

'It's weird to think of anyone else owning it but at the same time, I see where he's coming from. And I'm worried about him. I think we all are. He seems really sad. Hopefully not having the pressure of the motel will help.'

'His wife just died, of course he's sad.'

'I know.' Lucinda thought about that a moment. 'Maybe we expected too much of him. It was always going to be strange coming back here without Mum but I didn't think it would be this weird. I don't know how we're supposed to get through Christmas.'

'Will Aunt Mags be coming?'

'Yes.' Immediate relief rushed through her at the thought of Dad's eccentric older sister, Margaret—more affectionately known as Mags. She lived in a retirement home in Port Augusta, where by all accounts she was having the time of her life.

'Well, there you go,' Joe said, as if he'd just solved the problem of world peace. 'No one can be morose when Mags is around. She'll get you through it. What are you going to do today?'

'Dad asked us to help him start sort through the house, mostly Mum's things, so I'm going to try to get everyone focused on that. Lord knows I probably won't be able to rouse Abigail or Madeleine till early afternoon. Even without jet lag into the equation they've never been early risers. We also need to go shopping—there's nothing in the house and I guess I'll be organising Christmas lunch.' She sighed again, already mentally writing a to-do list. 'I saw Mitch McDonald last night and he reckoned Dad might be struggling a bit with the motel.'

'Charlie's old friend?' Joe asked.

'One and the same.'

'Maybe he's got a point. And maybe your dad knows, otherwise he wouldn't be considering selling,' he said, ever the voice of reason.

'I suppose,' Lucinda mused, 'but I also talked to Mrs Sampson and although she was less forthcoming, reading between the lines, I'm pretty sure she's just as tired and overworked as Dad.'

'You've got your hands full then. No time for missing your poor hardworking beloved husband.'

Lucinda laughed. 'I'll miss you all right, but don't pretend you're all hard done by. We all know nothing gives you more joy than blowing things up.'

'What can I say? I like excitement. But seriously, babe, you look after yourself. Try to have fun with your sisters and Brian. It's important for you all to be together at a time like this. Try and relax, okay?'

Lucinda suddenly choked up. She knew what he really meant. He wanted her to put aside her 'obsession'—he'd actually called it that last week in a moment of anger—with having a baby and concentrate on something else for a bit. Maybe she could do if it wasn't for his mother and his baby-machine sisters-in-law. Then again, probably not. She wanted nothing more than to have babies, to start a family with Joe like the one her parents had happily made together.

'I'll try,' she promised, wanting to end the conversation before she fell apart. 'You have a good day.'

'Will do. Love ya, babe.'

'Love you, too.'

Not sure whether she felt better or worse after her conversation with Joe, but thoroughly awake now, Lucinda climbed out of bed and ventured down the hallway. The house was still quiet—she guessed Charlie must be asleep and Dad would be in the motel kitchen, doing the breakfast service. She filled the kettle, then flicked the switch so it'd be ready to make coffee after her shower.

When she emerged from the bathroom, there was a loud discussion happening in the kitchen.

'What's going on?' She glanced from Madeleine to Charlie to Abigail. All dressed in exercise gear, Charlie looked serene but Madeleine and Abigail were drenched in sweat and Abigail looked like she'd seen a ghost.

'Madeleine and Abigail went for a jog and had a run-in with that old gypsy lady who lives on the outskirts of town,' Charlie explained. 'Remember Wacky Wanda?'

'It was hardly a run-in.' Madeleine crossed the room to the kettle and poured Lucinda's boiling water into her mug. She tossed in a tea bag and stirred. 'She just gave us an odd look and mumbled something unintelligible.'

Abigail ran her hands up and down her arms as if cold. 'I was trying to be nice and she looked like she wanted to put a hex on me.'

Lucinda laughed. 'You've listened to far too many schoolyard stories. I'm surprised that old hermit's still alive. She seemed ancient even when we were kids. And I'm sure she's not really a witch.'

'She might be,' Charlie said, 'but even if she is, real witches aren't like the one that poisoned Snow White, so I wouldn't stress about her. As Madeleine said, you frightened her.'

'Yes, I'm sure her bark is worse than her bite,' exclaimed Madeleine, laughing.

'Do you want me to make you a coffee?' Lucinda could tell Abigail was genuinely spooked. 'I was about to make a plunger.'

'Thanks.' Abigail smiled gratefully up at her.

Lucinda refilled the kettle.

'Right ... I'm going back to my meditation,' Charlie announced, before looking to Lucinda. 'Do you still want to get stuck into Mum's things today?'

'Yep. I think so. What say we all meet back here after lunch. I'm going to the supermarket to get supplies this morning. Anyone have any requests for Christmas cuisine?' Although they hadn't officially discussed it, Lucinda assumed that she'd be expected to play chef. Charlie would cook vegetarian food—which Dad abhorred—and Abigail and Madeleine were about as useful in the kitchen as a couple of blind wombats.

'Nah, but I'll come with you,' Abigail volunteered. 'It'll be good to get out. And this place needs some Froot Loops.'

Lucinda bit down on the impulse to tell her that Froot Loops were empty calories that would rot her teeth, and instead turned to make their coffee.

The three sisters came together in their parents' bedroom at precisely two o'clock. Abigail held up two packets of Tim Tams and a couple of bottles of Diet Coke (treats she'd bought on her shopping trip with Lucinda). Charlie brought carrot and celery sticks and a tub of hummus to the party. Madeleine had contemplated sneaking into the motel bar to steal a bottle of wine, but then thought maybe it was too early in the day. Lucinda brought a pile of empty boxes she'd picked up at the supermarket that morning.

To say their mum had been a hoarder would be a gross understatement, especially where her wardrobe was concerned.

Without a doubt this was going to be a mammoth and emotionally draining task. No wonder Dad had palmed it off on them.

'Where do we start?' Madeleine asked, looking to the others for direction.

'Before we do, there's something else I want to talk to you all about.' Lucinda looked back to the door as if to check they were on their own, then she lowered her voice. 'Last night I spoke to Mitch McDonald in the bar.'

'You saw Mitch?' Charlie's eyes widened in surprise. 'Why didn't you send him in to say hello?'

'I did.' Lucinda looked apologetically to Charlie. 'He said he wanted to let us catch up. I'm sure he'll make contact though; sorry I forgot to mention it.'

'It's fine. What is it you wanted to say?'

'Well,' Lucinda inhaled deeply. 'The restaurant was almost empty and Mitch was the only customer in the bar, which struck me as odd considering how busy we used to get on a Friday night. He said he'd been keeping an eye on Dad and that he was a little concerned he wasn't coping.'

'And you didn't think to tell us this last night?' Madeleine's jaw tightened.

'I wanted us to have a nice dinner. And after talking to Mrs Sampson I also wanted to nose around the books and stuff today.'

'And?' Madeleine didn't hide her annoyance. 'What did Mrs Sampson say?' She herself had gone back to bed after the jog and spent the morning catching up on sleep.

'She was a little cagey, but she admitted she's been shouldering a lot more of the motel responsibility since Mum died. She tried to tell me she didn't mind but I could see how exhausted she is. She hasn't had a day off in over a month. Apparently Dad got behind paying some of the staff wages and so a few of the casual cleaners and wait staff quit. Mrs Sampson and Rob have been doing the best they can but it's not fair on either of them.'

'Poor Dad,' Abigail sniffed. 'Maybe one of us should have stayed longer after the funeral.'

'Right,' Madeleine nodded, unable to rein in her sarcastic tone. 'And you would have given up your prestigious position in the London Symphony Orchestra to cook bacon and eggs for strangers?'

Abigail poked her tongue out but didn't say anything.

'Anyway,' Lucinda said with emphasis that demanded attention, 'this morning I told Mrs Sampson she needed to take a few days off over Christmas, maybe even go to Adelaide and spend it with her kids, and that from tomorrow until we leave we'll take on her duties.'

Madeleine raised her eyebrows. 'What about our holiday?'

'Oh for fuck's sake, Madeleine,' snapped Lucinda, cursing uncharacteristically, 'stop being such a princess. Do you have a better solution? Do you even care about Dad? Or do you only care about yourself?'

Madeleine wanted to yell something caustic back but Lucinda's words hit hard. The truth was she wasn't so much annoyed about having to help but about Lucinda making this decision without consulting anyone else. Sometimes she thought her sister should have been born first; she certainly acted like she was in charge of everyone.

'Look, let's not fight about this now. We can't change the past,' said Charlie, ever the peacekeeper. 'But Lucinda's right. We can at least give Mrs Sampson a holiday and take the pressure off Dad while we're here.'

'I'm happy to help,' Abigail said, her usual chirpiness grating on Madeleine's already tetchy nerves, 'but—'

'We know you can't cook to save your life,' Charlie said with a laugh. 'If I recall, neither can Madeleine.'

It was Madeleine's turn to poke out her tongue. *What am I, sixteen again?* Being around her sisters was making her behave like a child. 'Let me guess, we're on room cleaning duty then.' She knew she should have stayed in Baltimore.

'We'll work out a fair roster,' Lucinda promised. 'Now, shall we get started?'

'Yes.' The sooner they got started, the sooner they'd finish and Madeleine could escape to her room for a little sanity-restoring solitude.

'Great.' Lucinda gestured to the boxes she'd placed on the queen size bed. 'I thought maybe we could make three piles. Stuff that is still good enough to give to the Salvos, stuff that should be binned and … sentimental stuff that we can't bear to part with.'

'Like Mum's wedding dress?' Abigail suggested, glancing up at the big white box with a silver ribbon that lived on the top shelf of the walk-in robe. Madeleine could only recall one occasion when Mum had brought it out—she'd joked about being too fat to ever use it again—but they'd always known that dress was special. She and Dad had been almost sickeningly in love, often pausing to kiss like newlyweds as they passed in the hallway or in the bar.

'Yes.' Lucinda nodded. 'The wedding dress stays. It didn't fit for my big Italian wedding—' she rolled her eyes '—but maybe one of you would like to wear it when you get married.'

'Moving right along,' Madeleine said. If they agonised over every single item, they'd still be here next Christmas. She walked into the jam-packed robe and reached for a few shoeboxes. Their mother was a walking cliché where shoes were concerned—owning far more than she could ever possibly wear. Madeleine and Abigail had inherited this obsession. 'I'll start with these.'

Madeleine took the shoeboxes to the other side of the room, figuring that this would be a quick job. Unlike her sisters, she wasn't sentimental. She'd take a look inside and if they were broken or hideously out of fashion, she'd turf them. But the Salvos could think again if they thought they were getting any of the good vintage stuff.

'Okay,' Lucinda agreed, 'but we all need to be mindful of Dad and each other. If we're not sure about a decision, we consult.'

'Deal,' said Charlie and Abigail in unison.

'Deal,' Madeleine echoed, lifting the lid on a pair of pink tap shoes. Despite her desire to get through this as quickly as possible, she couldn't help showing her sisters. 'Remember Mum bought these when Abigail and Charlie started dance classes?'

'Yes.' Abigail shrieked. 'She used to be so embarrassing standing at the back of the hall, copying the teacher.'

'Possibly why neither of us lasted long in the class,' Charlie added with a wry smile.

The next hour was actually a lot more fun than they had anticipated. Madeleine relaxed despite herself and what could have been a very sad process became a kind of tribute to Mum's individual fashion sense; a tribute to her.

Every few minutes someone would exclaim, 'Oh my, do you remember when she wore this?' Then the sister in question would hold the gown up against herself and prance around the room imitating their mother as they shared memories. As with everything she did, Abigail took this to the extreme, actually removing her own clothes to dress up as their mother. She was wearing a nineteen-eighties blue taffeta ball gown—terrifying shoulder pads and all—when Madeleine found a shoebox that didn't contain shoes.

'Oh,' she said as she looked into a box bursting full of greeting cards. She picked up the first one and the tiered cake on the front immediately identified it as a wedding card. 'What do you think Dad would want us to do with these?'

'What are they?' Charlie asked, folding a fluffy white jumper as she spoke.

Lucinda emerged from the walk-in robe and came to stand alongside Abigail who'd stopped dancing like she was some eighties teenager.

'Wedding cards,' Madeleine told them.

'Ooh, let me have a look.' Abigail bounded forward and snatched the card out of Madeleine's hand. 'Dear Brian and Annette. True love is a blessing. Cherish it and each other always. Congratulations on your nuptials. Best wishes, Mr and Mrs Benedict.'

'Who?' Charlie frowned.

'Fuck knows,' Madeleine said, not giving a damn anyway. Was Lucinda actually crying? Good Lord, she should have kept her mouth shut and disposed of this box discreetly. Her sisters were too sentimental for their own good.

Abigail reached for another card and before Madeleine knew it, the others had abandoned their posts and were sitting on the floor blubbering like babies over the romantic sentiments in their parents' wedding cards.

She'd just decided it was time to go fetch that wine after all when Lucinda said, 'Hey, take a look at this one. A bit weird, don't you think?'

Curious despite herself, Madeleine leaned over Lucinda's shoulder and followed along as she read the card aloud. 'Darling Annette, it is a pleasure to welcome you to the Patterson family on this beautiful spring day. We truly hope you and Brian will be very happy and that you are right in your belief that the Patterson curse is a load of codswallop. Best wishes, Aunt Victoria and Aunt Sarah.'

'Who the heck are Aunt Victoria and Aunt Sarah?' Abigail asked.

'The names ring a bell,' Charlie said, biting her lip.

Lucinda and Madeleine looked at each other and Madeleine saw her own memory reflected in her sister's face. 'They were Grandpa Jimmy's sisters,' she said. 'I can barely remember them. They died just after Abigail was born—terrible head-on collision on the highway—so you probably wouldn't remember them much either, Charlie.'

'We didn't see them very often, did we?' Lucinda looked to Madeleine for clarification.

She shook her head. 'If I remember, Mum didn't like them much.'

'No wonder.' Charlie half-laughed. 'What kind of people write about a curse in a wedding card?'

'I wonder what the curse was?' A frown line creased Abigail's otherwise flawless forehead.

Lucinda scratched the side of her neck. 'Isn't Paterson's Curse that pretty purple flower? The one that's actually a noxious weed that farmers hate?'

Charlie nodded. 'Yep, but most people round here call it Salvation Jane.'

'You don't think that's what they were talking about, do you?' Abigail, never one with any interest in local agriculture, looked immensely disappointed.

'Does it matter?' Madeleine snapped, wishing she'd never found this dumb box. Knowing her little sister, she'd want to get to the bottom of what was probably nothing and, knowing the others, they'd go along with it to appease her.

'I'm a little curious,' Lucinda admitted, rubbing her lips together in the way she always did when deep in thought.

'Me too,' Charlie added. 'Maybe there's some big family secret we've never been privy to.'

Madeleine sighed, realising progress would be halted until they got to the bottom of it. 'It's probably nothing more than two silly women with a hyperactive imagination but if you're all so concerned, why don't we ask Dad?'

Hopefully he was in the motel and Madeleine could grab a glass of wine from the bar while they indulged this excitement. Surely if the curse was worth worrying about, they'd have heard about it before now.

Leaving the bedroom looking like a war had been fought between its walls, the four sisters hurried down the hallway and through the door to the motel.

[faint, illegible text from previous page showing through]

Chapter Five

Abigail had always thought of her family as boring. She boasted two happily married parents who'd lived practically their whole lives in small town Meadow Brook, and three reasonably normal sisters—if you didn't count Charlie's new age tendencies. Thus, the idea of a family curse intrigued her. Not that she actually believed in curses, but the idea was far more exciting than the other things going on in her life.

'Dad!' She waved the card in the air as they approached the reception desk where their father was doing something at the computer. 'Look what we just found.'

He looked up; his smile was weary but he was trying. 'Hello, my princesses. Sorry I've been a bit preoccupied today. How's the sorting going in the house?'

'We're making progress,' Lucinda told him.

'It's fine, Dad. We know you're busy,' Madeleine spoke at the same time. 'We can come back later if you like.'

'No.' He shook his head, plucked his glasses off his nose and put them down on the desk. 'What did you want to show me?'

'This.' Abigail opened the card and put it down on the desk in front of him. 'Do you know what they mean by the Patterson curse?'

She held her breath as he read, hoping that maybe this would create an exciting diversion from real life for him as well. A funny expression came over his face—like he was reading about the death of a loved one. She glanced at her sisters and from the look on their faces they'd seen it too.

'Dad?' Lucinda pressed.

'It's codswallop.' He stood and dumped the card in the waste paper basket beside him, avoiding their eyes. 'That's what your mother used to say and she was absolutely right. You girls are far too intelligent to believe a word of it.'

Madeleine laughed. 'Of course we are, but can't you at least give us something. I know the great aunts were a bit eccentric, but a curse? What kind of curse?'

Abigail held her breath. If anyone could get it out of Dad it was Madeleine. She hadn't seemed the slightest bit interested back in the bedroom, but they all knew their oldest sister didn't like being kept in the dark.

Dad, already on his way out of reception, paused. 'I'm sorry, but I promised Netty I'd never tell you. She didn't believe in it, and she didn't want you girls to ever have that kind of negativity affecting your lives. Just forget about it. *Please*.'

With a sad and slightly angry look on his face, Dad walked through to his office and closed the door behind him.

'Well,' Abigail blinked. 'Was that weird or was that just me?'

'Weird,' agreed Charlie and Lucinda.

'I need a drink,' Madeleine exclaimed, turning and heading to the bar.

The others followed and without asking she unscrewed a bottle of McLaren Vale chardonnay and poured four glasses.

'Okay, I'll admit,' Madeleine said after taking her first sip, '*now* I'm curious.'

Abigail smiled. 'So what are we going to do about it?'

'Maybe we should just leave it,' Lucinda suggested, twisting the stem of her wine glass between her thumb and forefinger. 'Mum and Dad obviously don't want us knowing. I trust their judgement and shouldn't we respect their opinion?'

Charlie nodded. 'I agree. If we hadn't stumbled on the cards we'd be none the wiser.'

'But we *did*,' Abigail pleaded, excitement thrumming through her veins.

'And I for one have better things to do than spend all eternity wondering if some curse is going to strike me down dead when I least expect it,' Madeleine said. Abigail couldn't tell if she was taking the piss or not, but at least she now wanted to know.

Charlie shot Madeleine a disbelieving glare. 'I didn't think you'd place any importance on things like curses? Aren't they in the same basket as palm reading, horoscopes and all the other things you take great joy in teasing me about.'

'Maybe.' Madeleine shrugged. 'But none of those things affect me personally. This one is a *Patterson* curse. I think we all have a right to know.'

Silence followed and Abigail guessed her sisters were all pondering the same thing as her. Did they have a right to know? And did she really want to know? What if the curse was something about death or bad luck or disease? She shuddered. Dad's brother, Uncle William had died long before his time when he was caught in a rip on a family holiday to Goolwa Beach. And as Madeleine had just informed them, Dad's aunts had died in a horrific car accident.

And what about Mum's bee sting?

Sheesh! Maybe there really was some ghastly Patterson curse.

'So how do you plan on finding out?' Lucinda asked. 'I don't think it's a good idea to keep pestering Dad in his current state.'

'Yes, Lucinda, thank you for that blindingly obvious piece of information.' Madeleine tapped her fingernails on the bar. 'We could ask some of the locals who've been in Meadow Brook forever. Someone might know something.'

Lucinda shook her head. 'You've been living in big cities too long. Word would get back to Dad and he'd be upset we'd gone behind his back. I seriously think we should just forget about it and concentrate on the important things, like sorting through Mum's stuff and helping with the motel.'

'What do you think, Charlie?' Madeleine asked.

'I think sometimes a little knowledge can be dangerous,' she replied, which Abigail guessed was her way of saying maybe they should let this go.

'But knowledge surely beats ignorance? Forearmed is forewarned and all.' Madeleine downed her wine and refilled. 'Ah, whatever. We're not going to find any more answers here. I'm tired. Shall we take the rest of this bottle back to the bedroom?'

Although the curse had been a bit of an anticlimax, Abigail was no longer in the mood to continue sorting. She feigned a yawn. 'Do you mind if we take a break? Come back to sorting later? To be honest, I'm feeling a little overwhelmed by it all.'

The others nodded and Lucinda wrapped her arm around Abigail's shoulder. 'Good idea. Let's reconvene after Christmas.'

'What does a bloke have to do round here to get a drink on Christmas Eve?'

Charlie looked up from where she'd been polishing glasses behind the bar and her heart halted in her throat. Mitch McDonald—her childhood best friend and the only person she'd really missed aside from her parents since leaving Meadow Brook eight years ago. Dumping the glass and polish cloth on the bar, she ran around it and launched herself at him.

'Long time no see.' He chuckled as he enveloped her in his muscular arms. She caught a whiff of his unique scent—a comforting combo of wood shavings and coffee—as they hugged in the way of long-lost friends. It had only been six months since she'd seen him at her mum's funeral, but it felt like a lot longer. After a few long moments, he peeled her off. She slithered to the ground and he looked into her eyes. 'Hey kiddo.'

She rolled her eyes and punched him on the arm. He was five months older than her but he'd called her that as long as she could remember. 'Lucinda said you were here last night. Why didn't you come into the house?'

'I was letting you have time with your sisters.'

Another eye roll. 'You know I'd rather hang with you over them any day.' At least Mitch understood her. He'd never made her feel lame because she chose to be a vegetarian, didn't have a university degree and had a few unconventional ideas. 'Can I get you a drink?'

He winked. 'Only if you'll have one too and come out into the courtyard with me.'

She grinned. 'Does that line work on all the ladies?'

He shrugged an I-can't-help-it-if-I'm-gorgeous shrug. 'Pretty much.'

Truth was Mitch had been the ugly duckling at high school and although he'd grown from a nerdy beanpole into a tall, dark-haired, muscular, hot truckie-cum-handyman of a guy, it still baffled him when women showed interest. He'd often joked to Charlie that aside from her and her sisters, he didn't know how to talk or act around women. But if the word about town was correct, he knew enough.

Grabbing two bottles of beer from the fridge, Charlie called through to the restaurant where Madeleine and Lucinda were folding napkins for tomorrow's breakfast service. 'Can you guys watch the bar for a few minutes?'

They looked up, nodded and then went back to their business. It wasn't a huge ask considering the restaurant was now closed and the bar empty besides Dad, a few of his old cronies, and Abigail who was playing pool with two young blokes in the corner. They either hadn't heard about the band on at the pub or had decided Abigail was better entertainment. Charlie wondered what her boyfriend would think about that.

She carried the bottles over to the door that led into the courtyard and Mitch opened it for her. As the door clunked shut behind them, they wandered over to the old cement picnic tables that had been the only furniture in the sparse courtyard for as long as she could remember. Although it was dark, the gentle breeze still held the warmth of the scorching summer day. Charlie perched on the table and Mitch straddled one of the benches. They each took a slug of their beers and then sat in silence a few moments, appreciating the time to just chill and be together again.

'So, what have you been up to lately, Donald?' Charlie asked, using the nickname he'd gotten in high school. He hated it and she'd never use it in public but when it was just the two of them, she had fun riling him.

'You call me that again and I'll throw you over my shoulder and run down the main street shouting, "You've been a bad, bad girl."'

He would too. She curbed her grin. 'Fine, what have you been up to lately, *Mitchell*?'

'The usual ... Driving, making stuff, helping Macca on the farm and visiting Dad in the nursing home.'

Charlie heard his voice hitch on the last bit. 'How is your dad?'

Rachael Johns

Mitch shrugged. 'He tries to keep his spirits up and so I try to be positive when I visit, but it's hell watching him slowly deteriorate. And I feel guilty that I don't get in to see him as much as I should. After everything he's done for me, I—'

'Aw, Mitch.' Charlie felt a lump swell in her throat. Mitch had been inseparable from his dad ever since his mum ran out on them when Mitch was only four. Rick McDonald was a truckie, and had often worked long hours, so when they were growing up Mitch had frequently come home with Charlie after school and hung out at the motel. 'You must get lonely at home on your own.'

He shot her a look. 'You can put away your violin, Charles. I find *company* when I need it.'

'Sex isn't the same as family.'

'Nah, but it's a pretty damn good substitute.'

Charlie felt heat rush to her cheeks and thanked the Lord it was dark so Mitch couldn't see it. She found she didn't like thinking about Mitch's carnal encounters, but maybe that was just because she hadn't had any of her own for quite some time. 'Lucinda also said you've been keeping an eye on Dad,' she said, wedging her beer bottle between her knees. 'Thanks.'

'Lucinda's a bit of a tattletale,' he said, taking another swig.

Charlie chuckled; Lucinda had always been the one to tell their parents if one of the sisters had done anything naughty. 'Maybe, but the fact remains we appreciate it.'

'It's nothing. Brian always treated me like part of the family. It's no hardship popping in and having a beer with him. It's my way of saying thanks for putting up with me all these years.'

She laughed, then sobered. 'So, how do you think he's doing?'

There was a moment's pause, as if Mitch was deciding between telling the truth or protecting her from it. 'Not that good. It's like he's on autopilot at the motel, and I'm not sure he's looking after his health that well either.'

'What do you mean?'

'I don't think he's eating much—although Mrs Sampson tries her best to feed him up—and he's drinking a fair bit.'

'Ah shit.' Charlie sighed. 'Maybe I should have come home after Mum died.'

'You did.'

'Not just for the funeral. I meant for an extended period. We left Dad to cope with his grief by himself.'

Mitch reached up and put a hand on Charlie's knee. 'Don't beat yourself up. Annette's death was a shock to all of you. I think your dad just needs a little more time. The stress of running the motel on his own probably hasn't helped.'

'Exactly,' Charlie persisted. 'I should have come home and helped with that.'

'Hey, what about your sisters?' he reprimanded. 'I didn't see any of them moving back either.'

'That's different. Lucinda couldn't very well up and leave her husband and Madeleine and Abigail have more important jobs than I do.'

'I object,' he said. 'Playing the violin is definitely not more important than making coffee or uplifting the spiritual wellbeing of others through fitness.'

She laughed.

'In fact,' he continued, 'I would pay Abigail *not* to play the violin. I'd rather listen to an orchestra of tomcats fighting in the night. But I'd be quite happy to watch you and a bunch of other hot women hula-hooping.'

Charlie whacked him playfully again. 'Don't let Abigail hear you saying that. She'll scratch your eyes out.'

'Noted. So, aside from the dad issue, any other Patterson family gossip I need to know about?'

Charlie opened her mouth to say 'nah' but the word died on her tongue. 'Actually,' she said, leaning forward slightly, 'there was a little bit of excitement this arvo.'

'Do tell.' He grinned the grin that made women's insides quiver.

'Apparently we have a family curse,' she announced, waiting for his reaction.

His hand froze on the way to his mouth, the bottle hanging there. 'A what?'

She loved the way his eyes widened in disbelief. 'Well,' she began, 'Dad asked us to sort through Mum's stuff and we found this wedding card that kinda warned her to be careful of the Patterson curse. None of us had ever heard of such a thing before and so we asked Dad. He got a bit weird and told us he'd promised Mum never to tell us about it.'

'Bizarre.' He cocked his head to one side. 'Do you believe in curses?'

She pondered this a moment and then shrugged. 'I think maybe I do, but I've never thought much about them. Madeleine and Abigail are desperate to find out but Lucinda thinks we should respect Dad's wishes and let it rest.'

Mitch pointed his bottle at her. 'What do you think?'

She shrugged. 'I'm vaguely curious but I don't want to upset Dad. And I'm not sure what good knowing would do anyway.'

'I wonder what type of curse it is? Do you want me to ask my old man if he remembers any local gossip about it?'

'Nah, it's okay.' Although she thought she believed in the possibility of curses, she'd meant it when she told Abigail that sometimes knowledge could be dangerous. Whatever the curse, it was unlikely to be a good one. How often did you hear about a curse that bestowed good luck upon its recipients?

They sipped their beers and over the next hour or so Mitch caught Charlie up on local gossip—who'd gotten married, had babies, left town, come back, run off with so-and-so's wife. Charlie sent birthday and Christmas cards and Mitch shot off the occasional text message, but they didn't see or speak to each other on a regular basis. Still, when they were together, it was like they'd never been apart.

Eventually the door to the motel opened and Madeleine appeared, her body a tall, slim silhouette against the light from inside. 'Are you guys coming to church?'

'Yes.' Charlie leapt off the table and grabbed Mitch's hand. 'Come on.'

He groaned. 'Do I have to?'

Before Charlie could reply, they heard the painful sounds of a very tipsy Abigail singing *Santa Claus Is Coming To Town*. Mitch snorted and laughed. 'If she's coming, this should be interesting.'

The three of them went back inside to find Abigail dancing on the pool table, her two drunken suitors getting their jollies every time she twirled and her skirt flew up.

Lucinda was trying to yell at them over the top of Abigail's noise. 'Closing time boys. Time to head back to wherever you come from.' She shooed them with her hands like they were a couple of pesky mosquitoes.

'We're not ready to go yet,' one of them moaned.

'Tough.' Lucinda glared at them. Her tone—the one Charlie imagined she used on naughty six-year-old boys—worked. Clutching each other for support, the young men staggered out to where Madeleine was now holding open the door.

'Night, boys.' Madeleine waved as they walked past.

When the door shut behind them, Lucinda looked up at Abigail. 'Get down,' she said sternly.

Mitch and Charlie exchanged amused glances. He leaned close to her and whispered, 'I'd get down if I was her. Lucinda has always made me quake in my boots.'

Abigail obeyed, but voiced her objections loudly. 'No one ever lets me have any fun. Those boys were cute.'

Lucinda grabbed hold of her elbow to steady her. 'And is your boyfriend cute as well?'

Abigail looked momentarily nonplussed and then said, 'Oh, yes, he is. Very much so.' She straightened up and dusted herself off. Her words were slurred when she asked, 'Are we still going to church?'

'Where's Dad?' Charlie realised he'd been quiet during the commotion. In years past if Abigail had even scraped a fingernail over the top of his pool table, he'd have burst an artery.

'Over there.' Madeleine pointed to the corner, where he was crashed out in an armchair, his chest heaving slowly up and down and his mouth wide open. His friends must have gone home.

'Do you think we should wake him?' Lucinda asked.

Charlie was torn. Midnight mass was their mum's thing and although none of them were very enthusiastic about attending, doing this together would be good for them. 'Let's try.'

'I think I'm going to be sick,' Abigail pronounced, rushing for motel's conveniences.

Lucinda frowned after her. 'Maybe we should leave her behind.'

Madeleine sighed angrily and rubbed the side of her forehead as if this was all too much.

Charlie crossed the room to their father, knelt down next to his chair and gently shook his shoulder. 'Dad, wake up. Do you want to come to church?'

Despite the softness of her voice, he opened his eyes, blinked. 'Must have dozed off a moment. What time is it?'

'Time to go to mass. Are you up for it?'

He took a moment and then nodded. 'Yes, I think your mother would expect us to.'

Halfway through the midnight mass, a chill ran down Lucinda's spine as she heard the piercing cry of a newborn baby in one of the pews behind her. What kind of parents brought a tiny baby out so late? She glanced along the row at the blank faces of her father and sisters—Abigail in her drunken stupor had fallen asleep—and past them at the families on the other side of the aisle. *Lots* of parents if the number of kids in the church were anything to go by. And none of those little cherubs looked comfortable. Half were fast asleep in their parents' arms, the other half were whining and squirming.

She let out a deep sigh. If only she and Joe would hit the pregnancy jackpot, she'd be such a good mum. As a good Catholic daughter-in-law, of course she'd take her children to mass regularly but she'd never bring them out way past their bedtime in the name of tradition. It would be a different thing if these people actually attended church regularly but, like herself, most of them were Christmas and Easter churchgoers.

She shook her head, disgusted at her judgemental thoughts and not wanting to feel like this tonight. Coming to midnight mass on Christmas Eve had always been a special occasion for her family and she'd wanted to feel the warmth of those memories, but being here without Mum only felt wrong. Although the five of them were almost squished into their pew, it still felt like there was a gaping hole where Annette had always sat.

'Are you okay?' Charlie nudged her in the side and Lucinda realised the congregation had stood to sing what she hoped was the final hymn. The sooner church ended the better.

'Fine.' She blinked and stood quickly, tossing Charlie a carefree smile.

Half her prayers were answered when the priest wished everyone a Merry Christmas before walking up the aisle, but her hopes of a speedy escape were dashed. They hadn't even managed to wake Abigail before they were ambushed by old 'friends', come to commiserate with them over their first Christmas without their mother—as if they needed reminding—and also enquire about their lives.

'Luci! So great to see you.' Kate McDonald, who'd been in the same year as her at school and was now married to Mitch's brother Macca, leaned over from the pew in front and gave her a massive hug.

'You too,' Lucinda said, smiling tightly as Kate pulled back and then absentmindedly patted the golden curls of the little girl standing on the pew beside her.

'I'm so sorry to hear about your mum. I was in Adelaide having number four when you came back for the funeral.' Kate gestured beside her to Macca, who was holding a sleeping baby. He smiled politely and then glanced at his watch.

'Thanks,' Lucinda said. 'And congratulations on your new addition. You have a lovely little family.' She hoped her voice didn't betray her shaky emotions. It's not that she wasn't happy for her old friend, but why couldn't she have that too?

'Will we hear the pitter-patter of tiny feet for you and Joe soon?' Kate asked, her eyes twinkling.

There were so many things Lucinda wanted to say to that question, but unfortunately none of them were socially acceptable—especially in a church. She was so sick of people asking her when she and Joe were going to start a family. They *were* a family. She summoned a smile and shrugged, 'We're in no rush; we're just enjoying each other's company at the moment.' Lies, all lies.

Kate frowned as if she couldn't get her head around this idea. 'Oh … well, all right then. Don't leave it too long. You're not getting any younger.'

'Honey, we really should go.' Macca, who looked asleep on his feet, touched her on the arm. 'The kids need to go to bed.'

Yes, listen to your sensible man, thought Lucinda, while still smiling through her teeth.

Kate ignored her husband. 'We should catch up for coffee and cake at Rosie Jean's while you're in town.'

'I'd like that,' Lucinda said, 'but it's a crazy time of year and I'm trying to help Dad at the motel while I'm home, I'm not sure I'll have the time.' As if to accentuate her point, she linked her arm through her father's. He too had been accosted and was nodding at something one of the old dears from the church was saying. 'We should get home too.'

'Yes, good idea.' Dad smiled apologetically at the woman who appeared to be coming on to him. Single pensioners could be vultures! 'Early start tomorrow.'

Finally Kate got the message, as did Dad's suitor, both of them heading off to pester someone else. Madeleine, Charlie and Mitch, who'd also been talking to old schoolfriends stooped to drag Abigail to her feet and the six of them started down the aisle towards the exit. More people stopped them on their way, asking after the girls. Two more old 'friends' asked Lucinda about future babies and one even dared to ask Madeleine if she was going to find the time to breed.

'Why?' she asked, peering down at the snotty nosed toddler attached to the woman.

'Well.' The woman looked flummoxed. She adjusted the child on her hip and smiled as he wailed. 'Kids are a delight, aren't they?'

'I'm quite happy delivering them,' Madeleine said, before dragging Abigail after her to the door.

That's the problem with small towns, Lucinda thought. They were populated with busybodies. But there were also good things.

When Mum died, these people had rallied around Dad, helping him with the motel, cooking meals and offering their support. She shouldn't be too harsh on them.

Waving goodbye to a few more people as they went, the Patterson clan climbed into the old van.

'Well, that was a riot,' Madeleine noted when the door was safely shut behind them.

Nobody replied and Lucinda only hoped that tomorrow, when it was just her sisters, Dad and Aunt Mags, they'd finally find a little Christmas spirit.

Chapter Six

Dressed in her orchestra black, Abigail held her violin against her shoulder, balancing her chin on the rest as she looked past the conductor and out into the audience of cultured people wearing their evening best. She still got a buzz before every performance, an all-over thrill that shimmered through her body. Rehearsing with her colleagues or even practising by herself made her happy but there was something magical about playing for an appreciative crowd. Thrillseekers or extreme sportsmen might disagree but as far as Abigail was concerned, this was as good as any bungee jump, and better than leaping out of a plane. Better than wine, better than sex, even better than chocolate. For as long as she could remember— since the moment she'd picked up her first violin—she'd known the orchestra was her calling. Playing music was like breathing.

If she couldn't play, she would die.

She grinned as the lights in concert hall dimmed slightly and Walter, their ancient conductor, lifted his baton demanding the attention of his musicians. Abigail gladly gave him hers, her excitement swelling to epic proportions as she waited for her signal. This would *never* get old.

And then it came. As natural as walking and breathing, her fingers slid across the strings as her other hand glided her bow across them in time with her fellow string musicians. She heard the deep sounds of the woodwind family coming to life behind her—her favourite, the bassoons—and the steadying beat of the percussion at the back. Whatever else was happening in the world didn't matter as she lost herself in the music.

It all went well for the first few concertos, Abigail silently congratulating herself for her outstanding effort, but then something awful happened.

Her mind went blank.

Her fingers froze on the strings.

The notes on the stand in front of her blurred and her hand holding the bow clenched so tightly that her fingernails dug into her skin.

Oh shit. Oh fuck. She glanced from side to side, hoping none of her fellow musicians had seen her falter, hoping their music was strong enough to cover her. But then the kettledrums grew louder, so loud she felt as if they were playing inside her head. She just wanted them to stop. She wanted to remember her music. She wanted to scream.

Why is this happening to me?

'Get your lazy ass out of bed,' came Madeleine's muffled shout, slightly tinged with a not-quite-American accent. 'We're supposed to be in this together.'

Abigail frowned. In *what* together? Her eyes blinked open and she sat up so fast her head spun. She slammed her hand against her chest, hoping to calm the erratic beating of her heart.

'It's just another dream,' she whispered, taking a deep breath. When would she stop reliving that god-awful day?

The door burst open. Madeleine, wearing a scowl, bright pink rubber gloves and jiggling the master key ring on her index finger crossed to the curtains and yanked them back, letting in the harsh morning sunlight. 'Merry Christmas, sleepyhead,' she sang faux-chirpily. 'It's time to get up and clean the rooms. I've already done one.'

Abigail groaned and flopped back against the pillow. She didn't know what was more of a nightmare—the dream she'd been rudely awoken from or her real life. So much for this trip being a holiday. So much for presents first thing on Christmas Day.

'My head hurts,' she whined.

'Hardly surprising considering how much you drank last night,' Madeleine said, not showing one ounce of sympathy. Abigail didn't think this was fair coming from the woman who seemed to have had a glass of wine in her hand constantly since they arrived, but she was too shook up to mention this. She'd hoped being intoxicated would stop the nightmares, but apparently not.

'Just let me have a shower and I'll be with you,' she promised.

'Fine. I'll see you in a moment.' Madeleine turned in her sneakers and marched back out of the room. If Abigail wasn't feeling so shite, she'd have found great amusement in the sight of Madeleine wearing cleaning gloves. She couldn't recall ever seeing her oldest sister anywhere *near* a cleaning product. Without a doubt, Madeleine paid someone to do her dirty work.

Despite wanting to crawl back under her covers and tug a pillow over her head, Abigail forced herself to get up. A grumpy Madeleine was one thing but if she didn't pull her weight she could add an irate Lucinda to her list of woes and that wasn't a happy prospect. She hurried her shower and then dressed in shorts and a t-shirt, ready to work. For the first time in her life she wished she could cook, because surely making breakfast would be better than scrubbing motel rooms. After tying her hair back into a high ponytail and pulling on her sandshoes, she went outside to find Madeleine.

'Stop laughing, you jerk. It's not funny.' Madeleine—with a rare smile on her face—was leaning against the cleaning trolley a few rooms along the verandah, talking into her mobile phone. 'How would you like to spend your Christmas changing sheets that smell of other people's sex lives? I just had to pick up a used condom.'

Abigail grimaced at the thought. Was there any way she could get out of this?

'Honestly,' Madeleine continued, 'you wouldn't believe what pigs people are when they don't have to clean up after themselves. Give me a nice hygienic maternity ward over this any day. I have a newfound respect for cleaners.'

Abigail approached the trolley and gestured that she was going to start on the next room. Madeleine barely acknowledged her, laughing at something whoever was on the other end of the line said. Abigail stripped the bed—thankfully she didn't find any nasty surprises—and then bundled the sheets up, tossing them in a pile by the door, ready to take to the laundry. Screwing up her nose, she returned to the trolley, pulled out a pair of plastic gloves—orange ones—took a deep breath and picked up a cloth and some spray. As she scrubbed the vanity of toothpaste and soggy hair, Abigail wondered if this was what her life would be like from now on. She would need to get some sort of job when she returned to London. Her meagre savings wouldn't last more than a couple of weeks but she wasn't trained to do anything except play music. Racking her mind for anything besides cleaning toilets for a crust, she worked quickly to clean the bathroom. She surveyed her handiwork and then went outside to get rid of the used linen and fetch the vacuum.

Madeleine was *still* on the telephone. Now who wasn't pulling their weight? Sighing her loud annoyance, Abigail marched past her sister on the way to the laundry and when she returned

Madeleine was finally finishing up her phone call. Abigail paused, no longer feeling any guilt about eavesdropping.

'Merry Christmas, Hugo,' Madeleine was saying, like it was the funniest thing in the world, and then she disconnected.

'Hugo?' Abigail raised her eyebrows. 'Significant other I should know about, dear sister?'

Madeleine scoffed. 'My only significant other is my iPhone. Hugo is a colleague and a friend. He rang to wish me a good Christmas. I think he must have had a few drinks.'

'He sounds like my type of guy,' Abigail said, peeling her lurid orange gloves off and retrieving a blue pair. Those orange ones stank of something she didn't want to think about.

'He's engaged,' Madeleine informed her with a smug smile. 'Not that you should care, since you are apparently coupled-off.'

'I didn't say I wanted to marry the guy. I was just making conversation. Must be a *good* friend if he rings you all the way over here.'

'He is.' Madeleine smiled in the manner of a dreamy schoolgirl. Abigail bit her tongue on asking if the guy's fiancée liked him making over-the-ocean phone calls to another woman.

'Anyway.' Madeleine snapped out of her trance-like state and picked a clipboard up off the trolley. 'We've got three more rooms to go,' she said, glancing down at the chart that listed rooms that were currently occupied and needed a freshen up and those that were being vacated today and needed the full overhaul.

'How about I take one room, you take another and we'll share the third?' Abigail suggested.

'Sounds good to me.' Madeleine shoved her mobile phone into the back pocket of her shorts, turned on her heels and headed towards room 19. In turn Abigail grabbed the cleaning equipment she required and took room 11.

The two sisters worked hard for another hour, scrubbing toilets, emptying bins, putting sheets in the massive commercial washing machine and making beds until all the rooms were ready for their guests.

'I'm utterly exhausted,' Abigail moaned when they were finished, feeling as if she could fall atop her bed and sleep for a month.

'Me too.' Madeleine nodded and then glanced at her phone. 'But it's almost time to collect Aunt Mags. Do you want to come with me?'

Abigail smiled at the thought of flamboyant Aunt Mags, who held court in a retirement village when she wasn't flitting to some far corner of the earth. 'Hmm, let's see, a toss up between a trip to Port Augusta to pick up Mags or being bossed around by Lucinda to help make Christmas lunch?' She grinned. 'Give me five minutes to get changed.'

Madeleine adored Aunt Mags—all the sisters did—and so she'd been more than happy to volunteer to collect her. And, like Abigail, she reckoned being well out the way of Lucinda's Christmas lunch preparations was a smart idea.

At almost ten years older than Dad, Aunt Mags was still very independent and capable, but her eyesight had deteriorated dramatically in the last few years. Last year after she'd had her driver's licence taken away, she'd surprised everyone by announcing that she was moving out of her tiny cottage and into an 'entertainment centre' (her words—she didn't like the word 'retirement') that had recently opened in Port Augusta. Meadow Brook itself was too small for such a development, so many of Aunt Mags's friends had chosen to make the move as well. Apparently it was quite a social hub—with events on almost every day of the week to keep the old folks amused. Indoor bowls, scrapbooking, card games, Bogan Bingo, you name it!

'You should put your name down,' Aunt Mags had told Mum and Dad when she'd first announced her decision.

'Over my dead body,' had been Dad's response, with a few more colourful words interspersed in between. Or so Mum had told Madeleine later on Skype. But apparently Mags was having the time of her life. She sent regular emails about her adventures and it sounded like she had many fans in the retirement village, including a few gentleman friends. Madeleine couldn't blame them; there was just something about Mags that uplifted all those around her.

It was a blessing for all of them that she'd chosen to spend Christmas at the motel instead of heading out to the farm to see her nephews. Hopefully with Aunt Mags knocking back the gin and tonics at the kitchen table, conversation would flow more easily than it had the last few days. If anyone could make Dad smile, it was his much-loved, eccentric older sister.

'I can't wait to see her,' Abigail said as they climbed the steps of the retirement village's reception. Neither of them had been here before so they needed directions to Mags's villa.

'Me too.' Madeleine pushed open the door and held it while Abigail stepped into the foyer.

'Wow, not bad.' Abigail's words echoed Madeleine's thoughts as they glanced around what seemed more like the reception of a five-star hotel than, let's face it, the entrance to what was essentially a dressed-up nursing home.

'Hello? Can I help you?' A terribly thin, tiny woman behind the desk stood up and peered at them over the top of her steel-rimmed spectacles. She didn't look pleased to be working on Christmas Day.

'We're here to pick up Margaret Patterson,' Madeleine told her.

The woman's face lit up at the mention of Aunt Mags. 'She's in villa 2B. Just outside this door—' She pointed to her right '—and across the courtyard, then turn left and you'll see it.'

They thanked the woman and then followed her directions, walking through what felt like a tropical oasis. If Madeleine didn't know better, she'd have thought she was in Bali. If all retirement villages were like this, she wouldn't mind getting old.

'It's quiet, isn't it?' Abigail noted as they approached the first row of little houses.

'I guess most people are off visiting their families.'

Before Abigail could reply they heard a loud, 'You-hoo, over here!'

They both laughed as they caught sight of Mags standing outside 2B waving her arms like someone needing to be rescued from the sea. She was dressed as Mrs Claus and wore a ridiculous smile.

'Oh, Aunt Mags.' Abigail launched into a jog, closing the distance between herself and their aunt. She threw herself into the older woman's arms and rested her head on her gigantic bosom. 'It's so good to see you.'

'Dear, dear child, enough of the theatrics,' Aunt Mags scolded, patting Abigail on the back. 'You'll embarrass me in front of my friends.'

'What friends?' Madeleine asked, looking around and seeing no one.

Mags gave her a look. 'Enough of your cheek, young lady, I have plenty of friends, but their families were less tardy about collecting them. I almost got heat stroke waiting for you two.'

Madeleine thought the costume might have something to do with that, but she knew better than to suggest such a thing to her crazy aunt. 'Let's get going now then,' she said instead.

Aunt Mags beamed and offered them each an arm. 'Grab my bag will you, Madeleine.'

She did as she was told and as they walked to the van they listened to Mags chat about a Christmas Eve party one of her neighbours had thrown last night. Apparently one of the residents had gotten so drunk on sherry that she'd sworn it was snowing.

'Esme went outside, lay down on the grass and tried to make snow angels and nobody could get her back up. In the end we had to call the nurses. But enough about me,' Mags barked as she clicked her seatbelt into place and settled her hands on the dashboard like she needed to hold on for dear life. 'What's new with you two?'

'Nothing much,' Abigail said from the back seat where she was checking her phone—no doubt on Facebook.

'I suppose you don't have much time for a life outside the orchestra.' Mags sounded only slightly sympathetic.

'She's got time for a boyfriend.' Madeleine laughed. 'She went all the way to London to find a man who comes from Adelaide.'

'No! Really?' Mags peered her head around into the backseat. 'You must tell me all about him.'

Happy to be the centre of attention, Abigail prattled on for the next little while about her boyfriend. Madeleine thought he sounded too good to be true.

'What about you, Madeleine?' Mags said, when Abigail seemed to run out of puff. 'Anyone warming your sheets these days?'

'My electric blanket. Better than any man. I can switch it on or off whenever I please.'

Mags snorted.

The truth was, the only man Madeleine could imagine putting up with on an ongoing basis was Hugo, and he was all set to marry someone else. She pushed that thought aside and decided it was time to enact the ambush she'd been planning since yesterday afternoon. Although she thought the whole curse thing a big joke, her dad's reaction had sparked her curiosity and she thought if she could drag the truth out of anyone it'd be Mags—she'd always liked spinning a good yarn.

'Aunt Mags, yesterday we started clearing through some of Mum's things to help Dad get the motel ready to put on the market.'

'Aw,' Mags sighed, 'what a horrid task.'

'Yes. But you'll never guess what we found.'

'Ooh, yes,' shrieked Abigail from the back seat. 'Tell her.'

'Sex toys?' Mags suggested, her tone wicked.

Madeleine blushed and Abigail giggled.

'Please, Aunt Mags. *No*.'

'We found a wedding card with something about a Patterson curse,' Abigail blurted.

Madeleine looked sideways just in time to see a weird expression cross Mags's face. She couldn't quite work it out. 'Know anything about that?'

'About what?' Mags asked, pretending to be a doddery old woman, which she most definitely was not.

'About the curse. Surely you've heard something about it before?'

Mags shook her head. 'Can't say it rings any bells. Have you asked your father?'

'Yes,' Abigail said. 'He said he promised Mum he'd never tell us.'

'That is odd. Did you say your father is selling the motel?'

Madeleine's fingers tightened around the steering wheel at Mags's less than subtle attempt to change the subject. Did she really know nothing about the curse? Or was she hiding something?

'Yes, but forget about that a moment,' snapped Abigail from the back seat. 'What do you know about this curse?'

Mags sighed deeply. 'I promised your mother I wouldn't say anything either. She swore us *all* to secrecy.'

Madeleine didn't like her aunt's uncharacteristically serious tone. 'Okay, now you're scaring me,' she said. And the truth was, nothing much scared Madeleine. 'If there *is* such thing as a Patterson curse, don't we—as Pattersons—deserve to know about it?'

'Probably; and after all, these things only have power if you let them.'

'What things?'

'Tell us, Aunty Mags,' Abigail pleaded.

'To be honest, I always thought Annette was a little precious about keeping it a secret. Especially since she swore black and blue she didn't believe a word of it.'

'A word of what?' Abigail asked, sounding more and more frustrated.

Madeleine gripped the wheel so hard her nails dug into her palms. 'Whatever it is, do *you* believe in it?'

Again Mags was quiet for a long while. Finally, she sighed. 'I wouldn't like to say either way.'

Madeleine's jaw clenched in frustration. What kind of answer was that? But before she or Abigail could say anything more, Mags spoke again. 'Do you really want to know?'

Charlie's words flashed into Madeleine's head. *Sometimes a little knowledge can be dangerous.* But Madeleine had never been the kind of person who could let something lie. 'Yes. I do,' she said and Abigail agreed.

Aunt Mags reached over and patted Madeleine's knee. 'If I tell you girls,' she began, 'you must promise never to tell your father. He'd never forgive me and the last thing he needs right now is more stress.'

A chill scuttled down Madeleine's spine. 'Agreed.'

'Promise,' came Abigail's reply from behind them.

'As I said, it's probably nothing, but the story goes that my grandfather, your great-grandfather, James Patterson, had a brief liaison with a girl from a gypsy type family before he met his wife, Laura. The girl—Doris was her name—fell head over heels for him but apparently she thought she meant more to James than she actually did. He just saw her as a friend. The girl's family were travellers, and when the others moved on, she and her sister stayed in town. I guess she hoped James would change his mind. But when he married Laura, the gypsy girl committed suicide.'

Abigail gasped. 'Oh God. Poor thing.'

Mags tsked. 'Poor James. Can you imagine the guilt? It wasn't his fault. You don't choose who you fall in love with.' Although initially reluctant to talk about the curse, once she started Mags got caught up in the tale, loving the drama of imparting some old family gossip. 'Anyway, Doris's sister got a real bee in her bonnet about it and blamed Laura for her death. The story goes that she visited Laura in hospital when she had her first child and cursed all her female descendants. Since that day …' She paused. For a second Madeleine thought she'd changed her mind, but then she finished, 'no Patterson-born women have ever had children.'

'Huh?' Madeleine tried to get a grip on what Mags had just told her. The cynic in her spoke first. 'Why curse the women when it was a man who broke her sister's heart?'

'Because,' Mags said dramatically, 'women get blamed for everything. Just look at Adam and Eve. Besides, who says curses have to make sense?'

Madeleine racked her brain, thinking back over their family tree. She'd never paid much attention to be honest, but if she thought hard enough, she knew Mags was right. Her dad and Aunt Mags had one brother—Uncle William—who'd had four sons. Going back a generation, their grandfather had been one of three children, hence the two aunts, who were widowed young and lived out their lives like a couple of spinsters. But that was only two generations of Pattersons and as far as she knew Aunt Mags had never wanted kids, never married, never tried for a family. So, her mum was probably right—coincidences and codswallop.

She felt a little let down. She was hoping for something a *lot* more exciting.

'What happened to the woman who gave the curse?' Abigail asked as Madeleine turned the car into the main street of Meadow Brook.

'Oh, she stayed in town,' Mags said, seemingly happy to tell all now she'd started. 'Drove Laura wild, following her, shaking her head and uttering mumbo jumbo whenever she could. In fact, her daughter still lives here. You probably know her. She lives out on the edge of town all by herself, well, except for her cats. There's been stories abounding about her for years.'

Madeleine almost swerved off the road and into the local Australia Post mailbox at this news. She recovered, brought the car back into the middle of the lane and then looked in the rear-view mirror.

'You mean Wacky Wanda?' Abigail asked. Her face had gone deathly pale.

Oblivious, Mags continued. 'Her real name is Lorraine. She was the same age as my father but never attended school. She and her mum kept to themselves until her mum died and as far as I know she's always lived alone. I feel sorry for the old girl. She must be in her nineties and I'm not sure she's ever left Meadow Brook. Some say she's not right in the head.'

Madeleine met Abigail's gaze in the mirror and saw her look of utter horror. 'Sounds like the *whole* family weren't right in the head,' she said.

Mags laughed. 'Mad as cut snakes I'd say.'

'But what if …' Abigail's question died on her tongue as Madeleine turned the van into the motel car park and saw an ambulance out the front.

'Goodness gracious, what's going on?' Mags asked, leaning forward as if doing so would give her a better view.

At that moment the front door of the motel opened and Charlie emerged, a stricken expression on her face as two men in ambulance uniforms wheeled out a stretcher, Lucinda bringing up the rear.

'Dad!' Abigail gasped.

Madeleine flung open the door and almost tripped in her efforts to get to him. 'What's going on?' she demanded to no one in particular as she stopped alongside the stretcher, glancing at the oxygen mask and defibrillator attached to him

'He had some kind of turn. They think it's his heart,' replied Lucinda, her voice shaky. 'They're taking him to Port Augusta.'

Madeleine looked from her dad's ashen face to the serious expressions of the volunteer ambulance officers. 'Mitch,' she said, recognising one of them. 'Have you given him Aspirin or a GTN spray?'

'Yes. We'll look after him, Mads.' He offered her what she guessed was meant to be a reassuring smile.

Mitch might be good at driving trucks and fixing *things* but what did he know about fixing people? And as for the other volunteer, he didn't look old enough to buy his own underwear. She puffed out a breath. 'I'm coming with you.'

Chapter Seven

'It can't be too bad or they'd have the lights and siren on, right?' Abigail asked, sounding like a five-year-old in need of reassurance.

It was the first time any of them had spoken since getting in the van almost ten minutes ago. Charlie took her eyes off the ambulance ahead of them and reached over to squeeze her sister's hand. 'I'm sure he'll be fine.'

'Us Pattersons come from tough stock,' Mags piped up from the passenger seat. 'It'd take more than a dicky heart to do Brian in.'

Lucinda, her knuckles white against the steering wheel, said tersely, 'It could be something as simple as indigestion. Let's not get carried away until we know the facts.'

She spoke with such authority that everyone went quiet again, leaving Charlie alone with her thoughts. She might not be a doctor like Madeleine or even trained in first aid like Mitch but she knew one thing. Whatever had happened to Dad, it was her fault. Lucinda was married, and there was no orchestra in Meadow Brook for Abigail or a hospital for Madeleine, but what had been keeping Charlie in Melbourne when Dad needed her?

Her stupid pride, that's what.

It had been unfair to expect him to cope on his own.

She should have stayed with him. She could have moved back to Meadow Brook when Mum died so she could help him with the motel. She'd known this, had seriously contemplated it, but something had stopped her doing what she knew was right. Something that had been a part of her for as long as she could remember. The little girl who'd never been as smart as Madeleine, as organised as Lucinda or as talented as Abigail had wanted—needed—to prove herself. She'd wanted to show her sisters that her life was as important as theirs. That she too had commitments she couldn't just abandon at the drop of a hat. But the price of that pride may have been her dad's health.

Please, she prayed silently to God or Mother Nature or anyone out there who might be able to help. *Please let him be okay and I'll come back.*

She loved her job at the café, her senior citizens hula-hooping classes were the highlight of her week, and she'd just signed up to do a diploma in naturopathy in the evenings. Yet none of these things were as important as Dad. Mostly it was the people that she loved at the café and she'd get plenty of interaction working at the motel. If she had some extra time maybe she could offer a yoga class in Meadow Brook. And the diploma would still be available in a few months or a year, whenever Dad sold the motel.

As they zoomed along the Eyre Highway towards Port Augusta Regional Hospital, Charlie mentally made plans—all the loose ends she'd have to tie up before moving home and how quickly she could do them. It was better than wondering about what could be happening with Dad in the back of that ambulance.

Finally, after what seemed like hours of driving rather than the thirty-minute journey it was, they arrived at the hospital. Lucinda parked in the first available car spot and they all escaped the vehicle as if it had just caught on fire. Even Aunt Mags, who wasn't always steady on her feet, walked towards the building with urgency.

They all knew where to find the Accident & Emergency waiting room. It was a smallish hospital and—as the queen of broken bones—Charlie had been there numerous times throughout her childhood. Someone had tried to make the place a little festive. Tinsel that looked liked it may have been new in 1973 was strung up across the ceilings, but it did little to cheer the place up. Mags settled herself on a plastic chair and picked up an ancient copy of *Women's Weekly* but didn't actually look at it. She tapped her heels on the hard floor and watched as Charlie, Abigail and Lucinda paced, their eyes glued on the door waiting for Madeleine or someone to come through with news. So much for making their first Christmas without Mum special.

'I'm going to call Joe,' Lucinda announced after about ten minutes, her mobile phone already at her ear.

As Charlie half-heartedly listened to Lucinda on the phone, she wished there was someone she could call, simply for something to do to occupy her hands and mind. But the one person she'd always turned to in an emergency—the friend she'd called when she'd first found out about Mum—was already in there.

Another ten minutes or so passed and then finally the door opened. Madeleine and Mitch appeared and the sisters rushed over. Mags heaved herself up and followed closely behind.

'What's going on?'

'How is he?'

'Can we see him?'

Madeleine held up her hand. 'The pain and tightening has eased in his chest. He's doing a lot better now, but they're going to do a few tests to try and work out what exactly happened and they'll keep him in overnight for observation. Once they transfer him to a ward, we'll be able to see him.'

'Thank God,' Charlie whispered as she reached out to hug Abigail.

'Told you so,' Mags said, squeezing Lucinda's hand. 'If it's going to be a while I might go see my friend Judith—she's in here with a ghastly UTI that just won't leave her be. Back soon.'

As Aunt Mags flitted off down the corridor towards the wards, Mitch grimaced. 'I think she means our old English teacher Judith Clarkson, and that was way too much information.'

Charlie laughed, a strange sound when she'd been so terrified only moments before, and then said, 'Thanks for everything you did for Dad, Mitch. That was really scary and I'm glad it was you that came.'

'Hey,' Mitch took her arm and the two of them stepped away from her sisters. 'You know I'd do anything for your old man. He's been doing it tough lately, overworking himself, but hopefully this will be a bit of a wake-up call.'

'Hmm …' Charlie was about to tell him the decision she'd made on the way here, but the other ambulance officer came up behind them.

'You ready to go?' he asked, obviously eager to get back to his Christmas lunch.

Not even glancing at the other bloke, Mitch met Charlie's eyes. 'Will you be okay? I can stay if you like. Paul can take the ambulance back.'

She shook her head. 'You should be with your family today. I've got my sisters.'

He gave her a look that said he knew just how reassuring they could be, which made her laugh again. She reached up and pulled him into a hug. 'Go. I'll call you later.'

'Okay.' With a reluctant sigh, Mitch lifted a hand to wave to the others. 'See you lot soon.' And then he followed his offsider back to the ambulance.

'How come I never noticed he's a bit of all right?' Abigail asked as Charlie turned back to them. 'Maybe it's the outfit. They're not wrong about a man in uniform.' She lifted her hand and fanned her face. 'Maybe I should see if he wants to take me out for a drink while I'm in town?'

Charlie felt her heart quicken. Mitch was *her* friend and the last thing she needed was one of her sisters complicating issues.

'Uh, boyfriend?' Madeleine and Lucinda reminded Abigail, and Charlie couldn't help but smirk.

'Oh, right.' She looked flustered. 'Is there a coffee machine in this place?'

'Probably, but it'll be vile,' said Madeleine.

Lucinda sighed. 'I don't care what it tastes like, I need caffeine.'

'Me too,' Abigail agreed, digging in her handbag for her purse. 'Who else wants one?'

Madeleine and Charlie both agreed that right now bad caffeine was better than none and Lucinda volunteered to accompany Abigail on the mission. As they hurried down the corridor, their shoes click-clacking on the floor, Madeleine and Charlie flopped down into plastic chairs.

Lucinda sat down and tried to do the impossible—get comfortable on a hard plastic chair and enjoy a polystyrene cup of lukewarm weak coffee while they waited to see Dad. Her sisters sat alongside her in complete silence, like four naughty schoolchildren in line to see the principal. She wished Joe was here. He could always make her relax and laugh in the grimmest situations and right now she was in dire need of one of his mammoth hugs. She'd spoken to him briefly, but although hearing his voice was good, it wasn't a substitute for having him here. She closed her eyes and tried to imagine his arms wrapped around her, her head resting on his strong shoulder.

'Hey, you'll never guess what?' Abigail exclaimed, bursting her fantasy.

Lucinda blinked and only just managed to avoid spilling her poor excuse for coffee. 'What?'

'Aunt Mags told us about the curse,' she said, her lips doing a weird thing between a frown and a smile.

Madeleine half-chuckled. 'Mum was right. Codswallop.'

Charlie leaned forward from the end of the row and looked to Abigail and Madeleine. 'Well, are you going to fill us in?'

Madeleine raised her eyebrows. 'I thought you and Lucinda were happy in ignorant bliss.'

'Oh, just tell us,' Lucinda snapped. At least it would give them something to focus on aside from Dad and the dilemma of what they should do once he was discharged. The others might have been too selfish to think about it, but it was blindingly clear to her that they couldn't leave him alone to fend for himself and the motel anymore.

'*Well*,' Abigail said and then paused for dramatics, 'apparently none of us will be able to bear children.'

Madeleine shook her head in disgust but Lucinda's heart turned to ice. 'I'm sorry, *what* did you say?'

Abigail recounted what Aunt Mags had told them about the curse and with every word she uttered, Lucinda felt more and more like the muesli she'd scoffed for breakfast and the few mouthfuls of dire coffee were going to make a reappearance.

'Luce, are you okay?' Charlie asked, placing a hand on Lucinda's knee.

Unable to reply, she slammed her hand over her mouth, leapt up and ran. She wasn't sure where the public bathrooms were so she made a mad dash for the exit, praying she'd make it outside in time. Almost crashing into a family coming inside, she tried to mumble an apology as she headed for the shrubbery off to the left.

Madeleine came up behind her as she was heaving the contents of her stomach all over a hydrangea bush. 'Was it something you ate?'

Lucinda gritted her teeth. Why couldn't Charlie have followed her? At least she'd have offered some sympathy or volunteered to hold back her hair. Sometimes she wondered about Madeleine's bedside manner. She retched again, but nothing more came since she'd been too busy cooking breakfast for the guests to eat much that morning.

'Can I get you anything?' Madeleine tried again, her voice softer this time, and then—shock horror—Lucinda felt her sister's palm on her back, moving in a soothing motion. That one tiny and unexpected gesture undid what was left of her self-control.

Tears poured messily down her cheeks, her body shuddering uncontrollably. She stumbled a few feet and then sunk onto the dry, brownish grass—obviously the hospital paid heed to South Australian water restrictions.

'Oh my God, Lucinda. What's the matter?' Madeleine, sounding uncharacteristically worried, dropped to her haunches beside her.

Lucinda felt mortified by this ugly display of the emotions when she'd been trying so hard to hold it all together these last few days, but found she could do nothing to rein them in. Like one of her students, hurt in the playground and inconsolable, she simply couldn't calm herself.

'Is this because of Dad?' Madeleine asked. 'I know he frightened us all, but if he's sensible and slows down a little, he'll be fine.'

Lucinda managed to shake her head. She felt guilty that she was so worked up over the baby thing when Dad was lying in the hospital with who knows what attached to him, but she couldn't help it. The baby thing consumed her.

'Are you sick then?' Madeleine barked, her tone a little impatient.

'Yes,' Lucinda snapped, finally turning and looking into her sister's face. 'I'm sick of not getting pregnant! I'm sick of seeing babies wherever I look! I'm sick of having to congratulate friends on their growing families! And now I hear this … that I'm cursed!'

'Whoa, let's backtrack a little. Are you having difficulties conceiving?'

Lucinda nodded as she swiped her cheeks with the back of her hand.

'How long have you been trying?' Madeleine asked and despite sitting on scratchy grass with the sun blaring down on top of them, Lucinda almost felt like she was sitting opposite her sister in her office.

'Eight months,' she confessed. And now she'd said it, she wondered why she hadn't confided in Madeleine before.

'Hmm.' Madeleine frowned. 'That's not an insurmountable amount of time. Are you tracking your ovulations? Making sure you have sex at the right time of the month.'

'Yes. Although a couple of months we've simply had to do it as close as we could because Joe was away during my peak conception time.'

'Getting pregnant can take longer for couples when one of them works away from home.'

Logically Lucinda knew this but she couldn't help feeling there was something else wrong. She was about to say so when Madeleine said, 'Still, if it's really worrying you, I know someone in Perth I can refer you to.'

'Joe's reluctant to get help yet. He thinks if we just relax, try to forget about it and enjoy each other, we'll hit the jackpot, but I just want to know. If there is something medically wrong with us, wouldn't it be better to find out so we can do something about it?'

Madeleine opened her mouth but Lucinda barrelled on before she could say anything. 'And now I hear about this curse.' She felt the tears that had only just started to subside welling up again at the thought of something so completely out of her control being her roadblock to motherhood. 'Oh God, what if there is something in it? What will we do then?'

Madeleine grabbed hold of Lucinda's hand and squeezed hard. 'I wish we'd never found that stupid card and I wish I hadn't pushed Mags into telling us. But you're far too intelligent to believe in something as ridiculous as a stupid gypsy curse.'

'Am I?' Right now she didn't know what she believed.

'Yes,' Madeleine said emphatically. 'I've been thinking back over the family tree since Mags told us about the curse and apart from us there have only been three Patterson-born women descended from James. The crazy great aunts—Sarah and Victoria—and Mags. Sarah and Victoria were both widowed young, probably before they had a chance to start a family, and Mags has never married. We shouldn't waste our time thinking about this. I can see now why Mum didn't want us to know. If there is some medical reason why you aren't getting pregnant, we'll almost certainly be able to find a way around it. But let's not get carried away with nonsense before we have any facts.'

Lucinda took a deep breath, wiped her cheeks again and summoned a smile. 'I know you're right,' she said. This was what she'd needed. Her smart, capable older sister to tell her that some stupid curse wasn't responsible for her inability to conceive.

'Of course I am. And who wears the trousers in your relationship anyway?' Madeleine gave her a mock-reproving glare. 'Tell Joe I've referred you both to a fertility specialist and he can shut up and attend the appointment if he knows what's good for him.'

Lucinda actually laughed. 'I will. And thank you.' She started to heave herself up off the grass and realised what a sight she must look. 'I suppose we better go back inside and see how Dad's going. I'll be in there as soon as I've cleaned myself up.'

Chapter Eight

The sisters left the hospital just after eight o'clock on Christmas night. They dropped Aunt Mags off at her 'entertainment centre' and then drove home in relative silence. Abigail tried again to bring the curse into conversation but Madeleine shut her down and by the time they pulled up outside the motel, she was almost asleep. It had been a long, exhausting, depressing Christmas and she couldn't wait to fall into the shower and then into bed.

The motel was in darkness except for a few lights on in the guest rooms and she considered how lucky it was that Dad's emergency had occurred on Christmas Day—the only day of the year when they didn't open the bar or the restaurant. When they'd left in a hurry that afternoon, Lucinda had scribbled her mobile phone number on a piece of paper and pinned it to the reception door but no one had bothered them for anything.

Abigail yawned as she climbed out of the van, calling over her shoulder as she started towards her motel room. 'Well, guess I'll see you lot bright and early tomorrow.' With Dad out of action and Lucinda having given Mrs Sampson the week off, there'd be plenty to keep the four of them busy. In a way she didn't mind—busy meant she'd have less time to think about her depressing life.

'Actually,' Lucinda's bossy voice cut through the still night, 'I was thinking we should discuss how we're going to help Dad.'

'Now?' Abigail couldn't help screwing up her nose. Why couldn't they have 'discussed' it during the journey from Port Augusta?

'You heard the doctor,' Lucinda said as she locked the van. 'Dad's been overdoing it and he has to slow down or next time he really will have a heart attack.'

Madeleine nodded. 'And now's as good a time as any. Lucinda can make us some of her awesome hot chocolate.'

'Good idea.' Lucinda smiled at Madeleine. Charlie also nodded her approval.

Abigail glanced from Lucinda to Madeleine and back again. Something bizarre was going on. She couldn't remember the last time her two oldest sisters had agreed on anything. Usually there was this tense vibe hanging in the air whenever they talked, because although Madeleine was the oldest, Lucinda always acted as if she were.

'Whatever,' she said eventually and headed towards the house. If she kicked up a stink and said she wanted to go to bed, they'd only tell her to stop acting like a spoiled child. Besides, she did care about Dad—he'd scared her today—and they needed to work out a game plan.

Lucinda unlocked the door and Charlie started flicking on lights as they all headed for the kitchen. They worked in unusual harmony to get hot chocolate and biscuits on the table before all sitting down around it. Abigail drew her mug into her hands and relished the comforting feeling of the warmth transferring from the china to her fingers. On a warm summer night, it wasn't like she needed actual heat, but it was soothing nonetheless.

'So,' Madeleine said, reaching across the table to pick up a Kingston biscuit, 'I think Dad's episode today proves it's a good thing he has decided to sell the motel.'

Abigail and the others nodded their agreement.

'But,' she continued, 'we need to be realistic. It could take months, even a year or two for a buyer to come along. Dad can't continue on his own the way he has been.'

'Can we employ some more staff?' Abigail asked, also reaching for a biscuit to dip into her Milo. Pity they didn't have any Tim Tams left. She could really do with a Tim Tam Slam right now.

Lucinda shook her head. 'I'm not sure that's really an option. Rob and Mrs Sampson are great, but Mrs Sampson said it's been hard to keep reliable staff. No one else is invested in the motel the way Dad is, the way we are.' She paused a moment. 'I think one of us needs to come home.'

'Are you volunteering?' Abigail blurted. Her heart beat hard and fast in her chest. She could do it. She could come home and help Dad because, unlike her sisters, she had no ties or commitments now. Hell, she didn't even have a job and if she didn't get one soon, she'd also have nowhere to live. But that would mean telling them that she'd cocked up. Big time. Could she bear that?

'Right now I'm just putting the problem out there,' Lucinda said. 'I don't know, maybe I could stay till the end of the school holidays and then one of you could take over.'

'No.' Madeleine put the biscuit she hadn't eaten down and tapped her fingernails on the table. 'You and Joe need to be together right now.' She looked pointedly at Lucinda. 'I could maybe do a couple of weeks but I can't see how Abigail and I can do this without serious ramifications at work.'

Which only left …

Abigail, Madeleine and Lucinda all looked to Charlie. She'd been quiet throughout most of the discussion but that wasn't unusual. Charlie had never been a big waster of words.

'I'll do it.' She voiced what they'd all been thinking. 'I don't need to give much notice at the café and …' Her voice drifted off as if there was no point listing her other little odd jobs.

'Are you sure?' Lucinda asked.

Charlie squeezed her lips together and nodded. 'It won't be forever.'

She didn't look sure and for one split second Abigail almost volunteered, but Madeleine raised her mug of hot chocolate and spoke before she had the chance. 'To Charlie, for saving the day. Thanks sis.'

And just like that it was sorted. Charlie would move back to Meadow Brook for as long as it took to sell the motel, Lucinda would go home to teaching and to Joe, Madeleine would continue the important task of bringing babies into the world and Abigail, well, she'd fly back to London and try to build something from the shattered pieces of her career.

'Charlie!'

At the sound of her name, Charlie slowed at the entrance to the motel reception. Because she recognised the voice, she turned and smiled. 'Hey, Mitch.' She waved as he jogged towards her. 'I've been meaning to call you. Thanks so much for saving Dad's life yesterday.'

He shook her compliment off with a wave, a shake of his head and a change of subject. 'Is it true what I hear on the bush telegraph? You're coming home?'

'Good news travels fast,' she said dryly. It was only Boxing Day, not even lunchtime. She'd barely gotten her head around the fact herself.

'I called to see how Brian was and Abigail told me you were moving back to help with the motel.'

She nodded, not brave enough to say anything for fear whatever she did say would sound bitter. Even though she'd already made the decision to come home, she hadn't liked how the conversation had gone down last night. Lucinda and Madeleine had made superficial remarks about trying to do their bit but Abigail hadn't even bothered. What would they have done if it was only the three of them? If they didn't have a sister with such an unimportant life that she could drop everything so that they didn't have to?

Mitch reached out and put his hand on her arm. 'Are you okay with this?'

A lump formed in her throat. He was the only one who wanted to know how she really felt. The only person who didn't take it for granted that Charlie would do whatever they needed her to do. 'Yes. It's easier for me to come home and I want to be here for Dad.' At least that last bit was true.

'Well, I think it's great.' He grinned down at her. 'I can't wait to have my best mate back in town. Movie nights, pool at the pub, drag races down the main street…'

She laughed, her head filling with memories of the crazy things they'd done together when they were younger. Hanging out with Mitch would be one of the positives about being back in Meadow Brook. Growing up, she'd always thought this would be her home forever but when Mitch had gotten serious with a local farmer's daughter named Lara Coates, Charlie had been like a third wheel. The coupling had changed the dynamics in their friendship and she'd found herself at home alone of an evening far more often than she'd liked.

Madeleine had been living in Melbourne by then and after visiting her for a weekend and falling in love with the eclectic city, Charlie decided maybe she should try something new as well. Broaden her horizons so to speak. If she stayed in Meadow Brook, she'd likely work in the motel with her parents until retirement. What kind of a life was that?

She'd gone home and announced that she was moving to Melbourne. That was seven years ago and although Mitch and Lara had lasted less than a year, Charlie had never regretted the decision to spread her wings. She felt like her own person in Melbourne, whereas in Meadow Brook she'd always felt overshadowed by her more ambitious sisters.

'So what's the plan? Do you need to sort some things out in Melbourne first?' Mitch asked.

'Yes. I need to book a flight and get one of my sisters to drive me to Adelaide so I can organise everything.' The sooner the better— the other three could handle the motel duties for the next few days because before long it would be all down to Charlie.

'I'll drive you.'

She blinked at Mitch's offer. 'Thanks, that'd be great. Will you be able to get a few hours off work?' She'd much prefer to share the three-hour drive to Adelaide Airport with Mitch than any one of her sisters, none of whom were her favourite people at the moment.

'No, I meant I'll drive you to Melbourne. We can take my ute or borrow one of the trucks from work if you think we'll need it. But you'll be able to bring more home this way.'

'Really? You have time to do that?'

'Charlie.' He gave her a mock-stern look. 'I'll make time for you.'

'Well, if you're sure.' She bit her lip a moment, thinking. 'I haven't got that much furniture and what I have I was going to put in storage, so the ute would be perfect.'

He grinned again. 'In that case … when do we leave?'

'How's tomorrow?'

Madeleine collected Dad from hospital the day after Boxing Day and brought him home just in time to wave Mitch and Charlie off on their trip to Melbourne. Lucinda hung back as Abigail and Madeleine hugged and kissed Charlie goodbye, thanking her profusely for what she was doing.

'This is ridiculous. You girls don't need to put your life on hold for me,' Dad grumbled as Mitch's ute faded into the distance.

'No arguments, Dad,' Lucinda said. Knowing their father, he wouldn't take kindly to relaxing but she intended to make sure he did.

'Doctor's orders,' Madeleine barked, before she and Abigail headed off on what was becoming their daily run. They were leaving in a few days' time and then it would be up to Lucinda to help with the running of the motel and to make sure Dad didn't overdo it until Charlie returned and Mrs Sampson was back from her much-needed break.

She didn't mind. In fact she embraced the thought of being so busy—cooking, cleaning, doing whatever else needed to be done—that she wouldn't have too much time to think. For the last two nights, sleep had been near on impossible and not only because she was worrying about Dad.

She hadn't said anything to her sisters because making arrangements for him and the motel had become everyone's priority, and there hadn't been time for anything else. Besides, they all thought it was a bit of a joke. As would Joe when—or rather *if*—she told him.

But she couldn't stop wondering … What if the curse *was* real?

Chapter Nine

As Charlie and Mitch drove away from her family, she didn't look back. The ute was loaded with an esky full of drinks and snacks packed by Lucinda, much of which consisted of leftovers from their ill-fated Christmas lunch.

'She'll make someone a good mum one day,' Mitch said, one hand on the steering wheel, the other wrapped around a roast turkey sandwich as he navigated out of town.

'She hopes so,' Charlie replied, not yet hungry enough to eat the salad sandwich packed for her. 'But apparently she and Joe have been trying for a while and nothing's happened yet. I think she's freaked about the curse.'

'Huh? What's the curse got to do with babies?'

'Oh God, with the dramas about Dad I forgot to tell you.' Charlie settled into her seat and as they started on the road to Port Augusta, she told Mitch what they'd uncovered.

'Surely Lucinda doesn't believe that nonsense,' Mitch exclaimed.

Charlie shrugged. 'We haven't had the chance to discuss it much but she got really upset at the hospital when Abigail told us what

Mags said. She thinks it might be the reason for her difficulties conceiving.'

'Do you think there's anything in it?' he asked

'Who knows? As I said a few nights ago, I don't know much about curses but I do believe in the power of the mind.'

'Well, that old lady has certainly always given me the heebie-jeebies. Remind me to stay well clear of her from now on.'

Charlie grinned at Mitch's words and then yawned, the physical and emotional upheaval of the past few days finally taking its toll.

'Why don't you try and get some rest?' he said. 'You can lean the seat back a bit and I've got an old cushion—promise it's clean—under the seat.'

'I can't sleep while you're driving; it'd be rude.' But she suddenly felt as if keeping her eyes open was going to take mammoth effort.

'Charles, I drive long distances for a living. You should rest while you can.' Left unsaid was that the moment they returned to Meadow Brook, she'd be busy from dawn to dusk, if not longer, cooking, cleaning and helping with all the other motel jobs. Her mum had made it look easy but Charlie knew she had big shoes to fill.

'If you're sure.' She failed to control another yawn.

He laughed, then leaned forward and switched on the stereo. 'You don't mind if I play a little quiet music, do you?'

'Of course not.' She shook her head as she reached under the seat for the cushion and then leaned it against the window, shifting about in an effort to get comfy. As the eternally popular sounds of INXS wafted over her—it wasn't exactly a lullaby but it was comforting—Charlie drifted into a peaceful slumber.

She slept through Port Augusta and Port Pirie and didn't even stir until Mitch returned to the ute after stopping at a servo just outside of Adelaide. She startled as he closed the door behind him and settled back into his seat.

'Hungry?' he asked, a boyish grin stretched across his face as he held up two Golden North Giant Twin bars.

'Oh my gosh,' she shrieked, all but snatching one out of his hands. 'I haven't had one of these in years.'

He laughed, leaned back in his seat and ripped the wrapper off his ice-cream. They sank their teeth into the chocolate-covered treat at exactly the same time and moaned in unison. Memories of sitting with him outside the Meadow Brook General Store on a wooden bench, stinking hot despite being under the shade of the verandah, came into her head and she couldn't help but smile even more.

'Remember that time you lost your pocket money and couldn't afford our after-school snack?' Mitch asked, obviously thinking along similar lines.

'Uh huh.' She cringed, her cheeks flaring in embarrassment. 'I cried because you'd be able to buy a Giant Twin and I wouldn't.' In her defence, she'd only been eight years old.

'It worked though. I gave you half of mine,' he said, his tone amused. 'You do realise I wouldn't share one of these—' he held up what was left of his ice-cream '—with just anyone.'

She swallowed her mouthful, loving the way the cold creamy sugar melted on her tongue. 'You are a true friend, Mitch McDonald.'

'And don't you forget it.' He screwed up the wrapper of his Giant Twin and held his hand out for hers. 'I'll go put these in the bin. Do you need to visit the conveniences before we get going again?'

'Good idea.' Handing him her wrapper, Charlie opened the ute's door, finishing her final mouthful as she climbed out. Truth was she could eat another but if she did, she'd probably feel sick. She didn't want to ruin a good thing. After freshening up in the less than fresh bathroom of the service station, she headed back to the ute to find Mitch leaning against the bonnet, basking in the mid-afternoon sun. His square jaw, roughened with dark stubble, glinted in the sunlight and he looked utterly gorgeous but she pushed aside the curl of heat that flickered in her belly. Most of the time she simply thought of Mitch as her oldest and closest friend, a bit like the brother she never had, but every once in a while she felt things she didn't want to feel. Things that would complicate and potentially jeopardise her most important friendship. She probably just needed to find someone temporary to scratch her itch.

She cleared her throat as she approached the ute. 'Want me to drive for a bit?'

He turned and raised his thick, dark eyebrows at her. 'I don't let just anyone drive my machine.'

She snorted, darted forward and ripped the keys from his hand before he realised what she was doing. 'Lucky I'm not just anyone then.' Swinging said keys on her index finger, she walked around and climbed into the ute.

Mitch chuckled but didn't put up a fight, instead swaggering round to the passenger's door and sliding in beside her. Charlie drove the next stint past Stirling, Hahndorf, Mount Barker and Murray Bridge and, although she assured him she could be trusted on the roads with his much-loved Ford F Truck and that he could get some rest too if he needed, he didn't nod off once. Instead he kept her amused with anecdotes of his daredevil niece and nephews, whom he obviously adored, and she couldn't help but think that one day he'd make an awesome dad.

Of course to become one he needed a woman in his life. 'Are you seeing anyone at the moment?' she blurted, suddenly thinking that perhaps she should have checked this before accepting his offer to drive her across the country. Not that she planned on doing anything untoward, but women could be funny about their boyfriends spending time alone with other women. Lara Coates had taught her that much.

'Nah.' He shook his head as she glanced over. 'The old dating thing is getting boring. You buy someone a drink, spend an evening making awkward conversation over dinner in the hope something will spark between you. Even if the spark is there, it never seems to last longer than a few months. I don't know … Maybe I'm ready to settle down but—'

'The right woman hasn't come along yet?'

He shrugged. 'Something like that. Maybe I'm too fussy, or maybe the dating pool in Meadow Brook is too small, but I don't want to go anywhere else. What about you? Anyone special back in Melbs?'

'Nope.' She didn't mind being single but her lady bits hadn't been exercised in quite some time and that was a little depressing. 'Maybe we need to take drastic measures. Try something like online speed-dating.'

'That's a thing?'

She laughed. 'Probably. Interested?'

'Hell no, it sounds worse than the in-person equivalent. I tried that once with a mate in Adelaide. It was the longest hour of my life. Besides, if I want to be set up, I only have to ask Mrs Willis at the Post Office.'

Charlie made a face. 'Isn't she a little old for you? You don't strike me as the toy boy type.'

Mitch laughed so hard Charlie worried he might choke. Finally, when his hysterics had subsided, he rubbed his eyes and said, 'She's always offering to set me up with her daughter.'

'Didn't her daughter have a sex change?'

'Yep. But Mrs Willis refuses to acknowledge it.'

That set them both off and Charlie had to slow the vehicle a little until she got her laughter under control. Man, it felt good hanging out with Mitch. He was so easy to be with and she never laughed as much in anyone else's company. He entertained her with more stories of potential set-ups and disastrous dates until they arrived at a truck stop just past Murray Bridge. She was quite happy to hold onto the wheel a little longer but Mitch insisted she pull over and let him drive.

'You're not a bad driver for a chick,' he said, 'but I'll take it from here.'

She glared and thumped him on the side of his arm. He feigned pain and she rolled her eyes, knowing he wasn't a chauvinist in the slightest. He just liked to drive. When they took off again, Mitch chomped on some homemade chocolate cookies and Charlie snacked on grapes and strawberries. Conversation flowed with old memories and new stories so that the time passed quickly on the uninspiring stretch of road between Murray Bridge and Bordertown where Mitch pulled into the car park of the local pub.

After locking his ute, they headed inside. Charlie was about to introduce herself to the middle-aged woman behind the counter and ask if they had any available rooms for the night, but Mitch spoke first. 'Hi there. I've got a room booked under McDonald.'

The woman looked down at a book on the desk. 'There you are. Twin beds?'

When Mitch nodded, she grabbed a key from a wall of hooks behind her and handed it to him. 'Do you have a credit card to pay for the booking?'

Charlie didn't know Mitch had booked a room ahead of time and while she appreciated the effort, no way would she let him foot the bill.

'I'm paying,' she said, whipping her purse out of her shoulder bag. She was quick but so was Mitch—their credit cards landed on the counter with a harmonised thwack. The receptionist laughed.

'In my day, we happily let the boys pay,' she told Charlie, obviously assuming they were together.

'Please.' Charlie looked to Mitch. 'I want to pay. You've already done so much.'

'All right,' he relented, 'but only if you promise to let me shout dinner.'

'Deal,' she said, knowing that wherever they ate, the vegetarian option (if there was one) was often the cheapest thing on the menu.

'We have a new chef and everyone in town is raving about him. Shall I reserve you a table?' the woman asked as she swiped Charlie's card through her machine.

Charlie looked to Mitch and they had a quick conversation with their eyes. 'Sounds good,' they agreed.

The woman gave them directions to their room, which they found to be clean and exactly what they needed for an overnight break. As the room was small with only the twin beds and minimal extra entertainment, they headed straight downstairs to the restaurant. Mitch ordered the beef and reef and Charlie a spinach and ricotta pasta, both of which they washed down with a few cold beers. Unlike the dates they'd recounted in the car, dinner wasn't awkward at all.

Charlie didn't feel the need to force conversation because they both knew this wasn't a precursor to sex or a relationship. This was an easy night between two old friends who knew each other as well, if not better, than they knew themselves. Although he professed to be so full he could burst, Mitch ordered dessert and Charlie stole the odd spoonful of his apple crumble when he pretended not to look. It was the most enjoyable night she'd had in a long while and despite agreeing they needed to turn in early, they somehow stayed up playing cards until the small hours of the morning.

When the alarm on Mitch's phone beeped at 7.00 am, Charlie groaned. She wasn't ready to wake up but it was another five and a half hours drive to Melbourne and she had a lot to get done in a short period of time once they arrived.

Mitch, seemingly not at all affected by lack of sleep, laughed and sprang from his bed opposite Charlie's. He was wearing nothing but a pair of black shorts and Charlie felt her body temperature skyrocket at the sight of him. She almost didn't hear when he said, 'I'll take the first shower.'

He took the few steps to the bathroom and the door clunked shut behind him. Seconds later Charlie heard water running. Images of Mitch—naked under the hot shards—flashed into her mind. She shook her head, bamboozled by the unexpected attack of lust that had hit her at the sight of his bare skin— the second of its kind in as many days. *Not good.* It wasn't like she hadn't seen him naked before. They'd skinny-dipped on the beach at Victor Harbor with a bunch of mates during Schoolies and had played strip poker with the same friends on another drunken occasion.

But both those times were almost a decade ago and Mitch had matured into a man since then. A tall, broad-shouldered man with a nice smattering of dark hair across a tanned torso that arrowed down to … *No. Stop!*

Overcome by these alien and unwelcome thoughts, Charlie threw back the sheet and leapt out of bed, throwing herself into the task of repacking the few things she'd used since they'd been here. The last thing she needed right now with the craziness of her dad and the motel was to complicate her life even more. And besides, even if she did feel something more than friendship for Mitch, even if he didn't laugh in her face if she confessed—and these were both very big ifs—her stay in Meadow Brook was temporary.

She loved Melbourne, had friends there, loved her seventies style flat in Brunswick, the different people she interacted with in her various jobs and their liberal ways of thinking. In contrast, Mitch loved Meadow Brook, where everyone knew everyone else's business and if anyone dared to think a little out of the box they became the fodder for the gossipmongers at the post office.

Mitch was traditional in many of the ways Charlie was not. He needed a woman who wanted to settle down, get married and have a family. While Charlie wasn't opposed to the idea of children, she didn't see the need for a piece of paper to prove two people's love and commitment to each other. And then there was the food thing. His love affair with junk food would drive her insane if she had to live with it on a regular basis.

No, she and Mitch were much better off being friends. In her experience, boyfriends and girlfriends came and went, but friends lasted forever. Her hormones would just have to get back in their box. No way would she ever jeopardise what they had for a quick roll in the hay. Likely it was stress, fatigue and maybe the few too many beers she'd had last night messing with her.

'Damn, that was a good shower.' Mitch emerged from the bathroom, rubbing a towel over his wet hair but thankfully now fully dressed in faded jeans, thongs and a t-shirt that exclaimed 'Hug a Truckie Today'.

Charlie raised an eyebrow and pointed to his chest. 'That t-shirt work for you?'

Mitch winked. 'Now that would be telling.'

Resisting the urge to pry, she picked up her wash bag and a change of clothes and headed into the shower, trying not to think about the fact that Mitch had been in the same spot only a few minutes earlier. But it didn't work. Annoyed with herself, she turned the tap to cold, blasted her mischievous libido into submission and then got out.

'That was speedy,' Mitch said when she stepped, fully dressed, back into the bedroom. He was sitting on his bed, leaning back against the wall and playing some game on his phone.

'I've got a lot to do once we get to Melbourne. Didn't want to waste any time.' To accentuate this point, she dumped her stuff back in her bag and then zipped it up. 'You ready to hit the road?'

'I was born ready.' He grinned, stood up and slipped his phone into his pocket.

Stopping only briefly to deposit their key in the box at reception, they headed outside to the ute. Charlie's stomach rumbled and at the exact same moment Mitch suggested, 'Shall we stop somewhere and grab some brekkie?'

'I'm in support of that plan,' she said, clicking her seatbelt into place.

They stopped at a little café on the main street of Bordertown and sat down long enough to refuel—Mitch with bacon and eggs and Charlie with avocado on toast. They'd long ago ceased commenting on each other's eating habits.

'You look stressed,' Mitch observed.

'No shit, Sherlock,' she said and then immediately regretted snapping. It wasn't his fault her mind had gone on some weird bender.

'What can I do to help?' he asked and her heart melted.

As if he wasn't already doing enough. She shook her head and pushed aside the plate of food she'd been unable to finish. 'I'm sorry. I'm just feeling a little overwhelmed at all I have to achieve the next couple of days.'

She thought perhaps her annoyance with her sisters was starting to garner strength and as they weren't here, she was taking it out on Mitch.

'All *we* have to achieve.' He reached out and placed his hand on top of hers and as warmth rushed through her at his touch, she wondered why some smart woman hadn't snapped him up. He was hot, hardworking, funny, smart and had the kindest, most generous heart of anyone she knew.

Before she said anything more, he took back his hand, retrieved his phone from his pocket and placed it in front of him. 'Why don't we make a checklist?' he suggested, opening his notes app. 'You hit me with everything that needs to be done before we leave Melbourne and I'll get it all down.'

Charlie swallowed, so grateful he was here to help her stay sane. 'Well, I need to call my landlord and see what we can do about my lease. Maybe help her find a new tenant. I need to go see Dave at the café. I already called to resign and he was so understanding, but I want to go say thanks in person. Then there's packing my stuff. I'll need to get some boxes from somewhere. Redirect my mail … '

Mitch's long fingers flew over his phone screen, keeping up with her jumpy train of thought. And when she finally ran out of tasks, she felt a lot better.

'Maybe you should make the phone calls during the next leg of our journey,' he suggested as he downed the last dregs of his coffee, which thanks to her were probably now cold.

'You know you're not just a pretty face, Mitch McDonald.' She smiled as she pushed back her chair. 'Ready to hit the road?'

'You betcha.' They left the café and before they'd driven out of Bordertown, Charlie was on the phone to her landlord.

They drove through Horsham and on to Ballarat, stopping only in Beaufort to use the public conveniences and raid Lucinda's container of snacks. By the time Mitch parallel parked out the front of the old warehouse that contained her apartment, she felt as if everything she needed to achieve between now and when they drove back to Meadow Brook was doable.

'Shall I go hunt down some lunch?' Mitch asked as she let them into her apartment and immediately crossed the room to pull back the curtains and open a window. Having been shut up for five days it felt a little stuffy.

'Do you think about anything but your stomach?' she asked, turning back to look at him.

He shrugged as if to ask, 'What else is there?' so she rolled her eyes and pointed to a pile of takeaway brochures on her hall side table. They were mostly from organic health food joints and likely wouldn't offer enough meat or grease for Mitch's liking, but she could do her bit to try and save his arteries. He walked over and flicked through them and she headed into the kitchen to put on the kettle.

Mitch might need food but Charlie was in dire need of a soothing cup of tea. She'd retrieved her favourite cat mug and was rifling through her collection of herbal blends when Mitch entered the kitchen, a frown on face and some A4 papers in his hands.

'Says here you're starting a course in February?'

Damn, another call she'd have to make. That cancellation had totally slipped her mind. 'Oh, I was,' she said, selecting a bag of Jasmine green tea.

Mitch stalked across the room and slammed the papers down on the bench beside her. She jumped.

'Do your sisters know about this?' he asked, firing another question before she had the chance to answer. 'Do they know what you're giving up to come home?'

She swallowed. 'I'm not giving up anything. I haven't started yet. You can't give up something you haven't started. And besides, I'm postponing it. Dad won't need me forever.'

Disappointment flitted across Mitch's face. 'You should have told them. They walk all over you and you let them.'

'I don't!'

He gave her a reproving look. 'Did anyone else volunteer to move back to Meadow Brook? No, they just expected that you would. Did you put up a fight?'

Charlie clenched her jaw. Mitch had no right to jump down her throat like this. 'I'd decided to come home before any of them even mentioned it. I want to be there for Dad. I consider it a privilege.' And that was true, she'd just have preferred it if her sisters had asked rather than assumed.

'I'm sorry. I'm not angry at you. You're doing a good thing, but they should know what you're sacrificing.' Mitch huffed out a breath and ran a hand through his scruffy dark hair.

'No. I don't want them to.' Her plan had been to have her diploma certificate in her hand before she ever mentioned it to anyone. That way if she couldn't handle the workload, no one would ever need to know she'd failed. Besides, it wasn't like any of her sisters would rate a diploma in naturopathy. Her eyes prickled with ridiculous tears.

Of course Mitch noticed. He reached out and grabbed her hand. Again a jolt of something hot and raw shot through to her core. 'Hey, it's okay. I promise I won't say anything.' Then he smiled. 'But well done, I'm proud of you.'

She laughed. 'I haven't done anything.'

'Yes, you have,' he said, before pulling back. 'Now, I'm off to hunt down a burger with the lot. Do you want a veggie one?'

Charlie shuddered at the thought of exactly what a veggie burger from the kind of burger joint Mitch liked would contain. She shook her head. 'I've got a pantry full of food.'

Mitch, who'd been standing in front of the pantry, opened the cupboard, peered inside and eyed the jars of seeds and nuts. 'None of that, my dear,' he said, raising his eyebrows, 'can be called food.'

'On that we'll just have to agree to disagree.' She laughed and picked up the kettle as Mitch swaggered back down the hall.

Chapter Ten

'What are you doing here?' Lucinda had just looked up from the reception desk to see Mrs Sampson standing in the doorway. 'You're supposed to be on holidays. In Adelaide. With your boys.'

Mrs Sampson stepped inside, the door banging shut behind her. 'I've been to Adelaide, I've annoyed my daughters-in-law and spoilt my grandkids and now I'm back where I'm needed. What's this about Brian having a heart attack? Is he okay? Why didn't you call me?'

Lucinda chose to answer the questions in reverse order. 'We didn't call because you are not on the roster this week and Madeleine, Abigail and I are managing just fine.'

Fine, that is, after a couple of days of bickering over who was in charge and who would do which jobs. Just when it was almost time for Abigail and Madeleine to leave again, they'd finally got into a solid rhythm.

'Dad's fine too,' Lucinda continued. 'He's taking it easy for as long as we can keep him pinned down but you can imagine how difficult that is. And it wasn't a heart attack. Merely a bad case of angina. Still, the doctor said if he doesn't slow down and stress less, it might turn into a heart attack, so they're sending him off to see a specialist.'

'Silly man.' Mrs Sampson shook her head and perched her hands on her hips. 'I'm always telling him he's doing too much, but he's as stubborn as an ox. He needs to learn when to take it easy for his own good.'

Lucinda raised her eyebrows. That sounded like the pot calling the kettle black but she bit her tongue. Thankfully, after a few days with her family, Mrs Sampson looked revived, almost like a new woman. 'I guess keeping busy keeps his mind off Mum. How did you find out anyway?' she asked.

'You've forgotten about the bush telegraph. I've lived in this town a long time—I have ears and eyes all over the place.'

Lucinda could well believe it. The bush telegraph even gave Facebook a run for its money. 'Right, so I suppose you know that Charlie and Mitch have gone to Melbourne to collect her things, and that she's moving back for a bit to help Dad.'

For a moment Mrs Sampson looked a little put out by this prospect. 'You girls don't need to disrupt your lives. Brian and I—'

Lucinda cut in. 'Are overworked, and as much as we appreciate everything you do, Mrs Sampson, things can't go on the way they have been.'

Mrs Sampson looked as if she were about to protest but then thought better of it. 'Fair enough. It'll be good for Brian to have one of his girls home. Is he in the house?'

Lucinda nodded.

'Very well, I'll go in and say hello, tell the other girls I'm back.'

'Madeleine and Abigail will be very happy to see you. They try their best, but neither of them are cut out for domesticities.'

Mrs Sampson chuckled and started towards the door, but she turned back to Lucinda at the last minute. 'You girls are all grown up now. Don't you think it's time you started calling me Sal? Mrs Sampson makes me feel like somebody's grandma.'

Lucinda didn't remind her that she *was* somebody's grandma and neither did she relent and use the housekeeper's first name. Enough things had changed in the last six months, so she needed to hold onto some normality.

Barely two seconds after she'd left, the door opened again and this time Aunt Mags appeared.

'Don't stand there looking like a stunned mullet, girl,' she barked as she stepped inside and closed the door behind her. 'I'm parched and I need a stiff drink.'

'How did you get here?'

'I hitchhiked,' Mags replied, as if it was the most normal thing in the world, 'and before you start lecturing, I'll have you know I've hitchhiked plenty of times before. I'm a very good judge of character. I'm still alive, aren't I? You young things are far too paranoid these days.'

Feeling a tension headache coming on and knowing there was no point arguing, Lucinda said, 'What can I get you to drink?'

'I'll have a Scotch on the rocks.' Aunt Mags stepped closer to reception and dumped her enormous handbag on the desk. She'd always had massive handbags—when the girls were little they'd thought her bag was like Mary Poppins's carpet bag as it always carried special treats. 'Where is everyone?'

'Dad, Madeleine, Abigail and Mrs Sampson are over in the house. It's a quiet time of day. I was just about to head in there and continue going through more of Mum's things.'

For a brief second a shadow crossed Aunt Mag's cheerful face. 'Well, I'll help then. I didn't have anything on today and since we missed out on our family get-together, I thought I'd come for a visit, check that my little brother is behaving himself.'

Smiling, Lucinda walked around the desk and pulled her into a hug. 'It's lovely to see you, but I do wish you'd called. One of us could have driven over to collect you.'

'Nonsense.' Mags waved a hand in front of her face. 'Where's the fun in that? The truck driver who gave me a lift was very nice on the eye.'

Lucinda couldn't help smiling. No wonder Aunt Mags had never married—there wasn't a man on the planet who'd ever be able to tame her. 'You go on inside. I'll bring your drink.'

'Bring the whole bottle,' Aunt Mags ordered as she went through into the house. 'I need to catch up for Christmas Day.'

Seconds later Lucinda heard the excited shrieks of her sisters. Truth was, they could all do with a dose of their aunt's special brand of crazy.

'I wish Charlie was here,' Abigail sighed. The three sisters, Mags and Dad sat around the kitchen table, enjoying afternoon tea as they pored over an album they'd found in a box alongside Mum's clothes, shoes and other keepsakes. It contained photos from before their parents had married and Mum looked so young, a little hippy-ish—like Charlie.

'I know,' Lucinda agreed, 'but we're keeping all these photos, so I'll make sure she sees them when she and Mitch come back.'

'Oh look,' Abigail shrieked, distracted by a photo of Mum in a tiny psychedelic patterned skirt, huge wedge platforms and a cowl-neck sweater. 'She looks like Marcia from *The Brady Bunch*.'

The others laughed and Lucinda had to concede there was a distinct similarity. Mum could have been Marcia's twin.

'She was far more beautiful than Marcia Brady,' Dad mused, staring wistfully down at the photo.

'Must be why she had so many admirers,' Madeleine noted, flicking through the next few pages in which Mum had a different man on her arm in each photo.

'Annette was always popular with the boys.' Mags laughed. 'But who could blame them?'

Dad smiled wistfully. 'I was the luckiest man alive. She had the pick of all the blokes in town and for some darn reason, she chose me.'

'Dad!' Madeleine exclaimed. 'Of course she chose you. You were the cream of the crop, still are. I blame you for me not being able to find a man. None of them live up to the high standards you set.'

'Is that your problem?' Abigail asked, unable to help herself. 'I thought it was just because you were such a bitch.'

'Abigail!' Dad chastised, but Abigail saw the amusement in his eyes.

'Joking,' she said and Madeleine laughed so no more was said on the matter.

Somehow they finished their coffees and dragged themselves away from the photos. Dad went back into the motel but Aunt Mags followed the girls down the corridor and into their parents' bedroom to continue on with the clothes. Abigail wasn't sure how much work they'd get done with their eccentric aunty buzzing about but she was glad of her presence. It was almost impossible to be glum when Auntie Mags was running commentary.

As they delved deeper into Mum's cupboards, arguments ensued over her shoes and accessories. Madeleine was all for throwing practically everything out or at least donating it to the local op shop.

Lucinda shook her head at this suggestion. 'I don't want all the locals walking around town in Mum's old clothes.'

Abigail had to agree. Although she wouldn't be around to see such a sight, she didn't like the idea of it. If they had to give away

Mum's stuff, she'd rather it went further afield, but the truth was, she didn't want to give any of it away.

'Doesn't this feel wrong?' she said, holding up a beautiful soft chenille jumper and touching it against her cheek. It still smelled of Mum's citrus perfume. 'It's like with every item we agree to throw away, we're getting rid of a little bit of her.'

She swallowed, knowing that any moment, she'd succumb to tears. She'd been strong the last few days—even when Dad had given them the scare of their life—but the emotional exhaustion of Dad, Mum and keeping her secret was starting to take its toll.

Her sisters looked stricken and neither said a word, surprising for two people who usually had plenty to say about everything.

'Now, now, girls,' Aunt Mags chided. 'Don't get so maudlin.' She heaved herself up from where she'd been perched on the bed, all but snatched the jumper from Abigail and shoved it into a black plastic bag. 'Your mother wasn't that jumper. Just like she wasn't those shoes or any of these dresses. I know you're all terrified about forgetting her, but that will never happen while you hold her close in your hearts. You need to hold onto the special memories—your individual ones and the ones you all share. No one can ever take those away from you.'

Abigail and her sisters nodded and she guessed their heads were probably as full of such memories as hers was.

'You're absolutely right,' Lucinda said, folding the blouse she'd been holding and placing it into the black bag.

Aunt Mags grinned, her ancient smile lines crinkling around her eyes. 'I'm not saying you need to ditch everything, but be sensible. Your father set you girls this task because he can't bear to throw anything away that belonged to Annette, but he trusts you to sort the special keepsakes from the rest. Now, let's keep going or you're not going to finish before you all fly away again.'

Abigail allowed herself one more quick sniff and then continued on with her aunt and sisters. Eventually they managed to divide it all into piles to throw and piles to donate, with certain items to be kept because they *were* sentimental, like the pair of Russian doll earrings Mum wore every year on her birthday. All the sisters were to go home with a pair of shoes or a special outfit that meant something to them. Although Charlie wasn't there, they were mindful of her and shot off the occasional photo message to keep her in the loop.

They slowed again when they started on the other boxes. Whenever they found something that made them a little weepy— like the baby scrapbooks Mum had lovingly crafted long before it was fashionable to do such things—Mags would say something funny to make them all smile again. She'd remind them that these books and all the other memories Mum had made simply proved what a special person she was.

'And don't forget to speak about her with Brian,' she said. 'Men typically don't like to wear their hearts on their sleeves but bottling up grief isn't healthy for anyone.'

'I think we've seen that first hand,' Madeleine mused, referring to Dad's ride in the ambulance and his short stay in hospital.

'Exactly.' Aunt Mags nodded once. 'It's up to us women to show him that talking about Annette is both healthy for the soul and necessary to keep her memory alive. Your mum was one of a kind, my lovelies, and she deserves to be remembered accordingly.'

On this the Patterson girls all agreed.

Chapter Eleven

Madeleine felt an uncharacteristic clench of guilt around her heart as she leant forward to hug Dad goodbye. Back on his feet now, although supposedly taking things easy, he'd insisted on driving her and Abigail to the bus stop in Port Augusta. Lucinda had stayed behind at the motel with Mrs Sampson, and Charlie and Mitch would be back tomorrow. She should have been over the moon that she was heading back to normality, back to her job at St Joe's, but she couldn't help but feel she was bailing out of other responsibilities.

'Promise to be sensible,' she said as she pulled out of her father's embrace to look at him. 'You scared us all the other day and I don't want the next time I come home to be your funeral.' It was blunt, but sometimes you needed to say things as they were. 'Let Charlie take on the load Mum used to carry. Maybe even take up a hobby or something. Didn't you used to play golf way back when the dinosaurs roamed the earth?'

'Just because you're as tall as me now, young lady, doesn't mean I'll put up with your cheek.' But he smiled as he said this and Madeleine felt satisfied he looked a little more rested than when they'd arrived a week ago. 'Who knows, maybe I will dig out the old clubs.'

'That's what I like to hear.' She gave him another kiss on the cheek as Abigail nudged her in the side. 'They're about to leave, we have to go.'

Madeleine stepped aside as Abigail threw her arms around Dad. 'I love you, Daddy. I'm going to miss you. Promise I'll come visit again soon.' She sniffed as she pulled back and Madeleine saw there was water in their father's eyes also.

'Come on, they'll leave without us,' she said before she too started blubbering. That was what she got for hanging out with her overemotional sisters for a week. Smiling inwardly, she thought she actually might miss them this time. Despite the odd disagreement and the stresses of dealing with Dad's heart scare, it had been fun spending time with them. After Lucinda had opened up to Madeleine, they'd felt closer than they had in a long time and she hoped she'd be hearing good news from her sister and Joe very soon.

One thing she wouldn't miss was cleaning the rooms. Rubber gloves did not for a good look make. Except in theatre of course.

With no time to stand around reminiscing, she grabbed hold of Abigail's hand and tugged her towards the open door of the bus. 'Bye, Dad,' they called over their shoulders.

He stood in front of the bus stop, waving as they climbed on board and settled themselves in the seats Madeleine had reserved right up the front. She couldn't recall the last time she'd travelled by bus—maybe in high school on an excursion—but they hadn't wanted Dad or Lucinda to have to drive them all the way to Adelaide. Hugo, who always teased her about enjoying the finer things in life, would laugh himself stupid if he ever found out. Not that he would. By the time she got off her flight at Thurgood Marshall airport, any horrors she might experience on this bus would have been overridden by the pleasure of flying international first class.

Abigail sighed as she slumped into her seat next to Madeleine. 'I feel like we only just arrived and now we're leaving.'

'And yet at the same time I feel like we've been home forever,' Madeleine said. Funny how she still thought of Meadow Brook as home, even though she never planned to go back there for good. 'It'll be good to get back to work though. I don't want to have to change anyone else's sheets for as long as I live.'

Abigail made a tiny noise as if she were trying to laugh but hadn't quite been able.

'You okay?' Madeleine asked.

'Yeah.' Her sister nodded and pasted on a clearly forced smile. 'I just ...' She shook her head. 'Maybe I should have stuck around a bit longer. It doesn't seem fair leaving Charlie to shoulder all the responsibility and—'

Madeleine cut her off. 'Don't be ridiculous. You can't give up your position in the orchestra and Dad would hate himself if you did. He's got Charlie *and* Mrs Sampson now; they'll keep him in line.'

Abigail exhaled slowly. 'I guess you're right.'

'Of course I am.' Then, as the bus veered away from the kerb, Madeleine asked, 'Is your boyfriend flying back to London with you? What's his name again?' Come to think of it, she wasn't sure Abigail had ever said.

'Um ... Jack. And no. He's spending another couple of weeks with his family.'

'You didn't want to catch up with him and meet the parents?'

'Lord, no.' Abigail sounded appalled. 'We're not at that stage yet.'

The bus driver's voice sounded through the overhead speakers. 'Welcome to those joining us at Port Augusta. A brief reminder that this is a non-smoking environment and if you choose to consume any food or drink on the journey, please take all rubbish with you when you leave. Our next stop is Port Pirie.'

At the mention of food, Madeleine's stomach turned a little. She tried to distract herself by talking to Abigail again. 'You must be excited about getting back to London. I still can't believe you didn't bring your violin.'

'I don't know what I was thinking,' Abigail admitted. 'I cannot wait to play. Do you ever go see concerts in Baltimore?'

'Occasionally,' Madeleine said. 'Although probably not the type you mean. There's a little bar not far from the hospital that has live bands on Friday nights. Sometimes a few of us go there for after-work drinks and end up staying until the early hours of the morning, when we're not on call of course.'

The two of them talked music and bands for a little while longer but halfway to Port Pirie, Madeleine's travel sickness arrived with a vengeance. It was all she could do for the rest of the journey to stop from throwing up, which made conversation impossible. Abigail played with her phone and finally, after what seemed like the longest bus ride in the history of bus rides, they arrived at Adelaide Airport.

After collecting their luggage from beneath the bus, the sisters went inside to check in. Abigail's flight was a few hours later than Madeleine's so after passing through customs they grabbed a couple of takeaway coffees and went to bide time at the gate. A couple of toddlers—twins perhaps—played not far from Abigail and Madeleine's feet, their harried-looking parents sitting in the row of chairs opposite. Madeleine laughed at their antics as they argued over an ugly looking doll with blue hair. There was also one with pink but neither of them wanted that one.

Her mind drifted. What would it be like to have a child of her own? To not simply bring other people's babies into the world, but have the whole experience for herself? It wasn't the first time she'd pondered these thoughts, but she usually pushed them aside for lack of a partner to have said baby with. As far as everyone else believed, she was a career woman first and foremost, with no desire at all to have a family. She'd managed to perfect this line and the persona that came with it so well that most of the time she believed it herself. After all, she was an experienced obstetrician at the top of her game, earning a more than hefty income and she loved what she did. Her apartment was gorgeous and her wardrobe one that other women envied. Shouldn't all this be enough?

'They're absolute ratbags,' laughed the young mum, noticing Madeleine watching as one twin reached out to yank the other one's pigtail.

'But oh-so-cute,' Madeleine replied, smiling as their dad reprimanded them. They looked up at him with their big, brown, angelic eyes and then promptly burst into tears. She couldn't help but stare as the parents gave each other a fed-up look and then each scooped up a child and pulled them onto their laps. The twins threw their arms around their parents' necks, snuggling in, one sucking her thumb and the other reaching up and bestowing kisses on the man, who tried his best to look stern.

Abigail dug her in the side. 'You're not getting clucky, are you?' she asked, sounding amused.

Madeleine scoffed and looked away from the little family. 'Course not,' she lied.

No way was she ready to admit such an alien thought to her sister anyway. Abigail would probably laugh, thinking she was joking. Lucinda had been the one to help their mother with her younger sisters, whereas Madeleine had been far more interested in doing her homework. From an early age, when a teacher at Meadow Brook Primary School had remarked on her being smarter than most of the other students, she'd known she wanted to do something that used her brains. She'd worked hard throughout school, thriving on achievement and positive reinforcement from her teachers, parents and peers. She liked learning and had aimed high, studying hard through high school to get the grades for Medicine. It was that or Law, but although she'd topped the class in all subjects, she'd always preferred science to humanities, so in the end her decision had come down to that.

A medical degree, although rewarding, was gruelling, as were the first few years as a young doctor on rotation. Choosing to specialise in obstetrics had added years on top of all that but she'd loved every moment of the study and the job, not once feeling as if she was missing out on a social life. She dated other doctors, people who like her didn't have time for a relationship but were happy to scratch an itch when necessary, going their separate ways without any heartbreak once the initial spark had worn off. If the thought of settling down ever visited, it was fleeting, something to consider later, when her career was established.

Well, that time was now, and she had to admit, since hearing about the curse and talking to Lucinda about her conception woes these last few days, she'd begun to sense a strange ticking coming from deep within her. She was thirty-five years old and medically she knew that if she wanted to have children, or at least a child, her window of opportunity would get smaller over the next few years as her fertility declined. How many couples did she see who were in their late thirties by the time they'd decided to try for a baby and had needed IVF to achieve it?

'Earth to Madeleine?' Abigail's voice jolted her from her thoughts.

She shook her head and smiled at her sister, noticing that the young family had moved on. 'What?'

'Your flight is boarding.' Abigail nodded towards the gate, then stood and heaved her cabin bag over her shoulder. 'You going to hug me goodbye?'

Madeleine also stood and held her arms open for her little sister. 'You look after yourself, okay? I guess I'll see you next Christmas.'

Abigail nodded. 'Unless I decide to come for a holiday in Baltimore before then.'

'That would be good.' Madeleine meant it—it would be fun to show Abigail around Maryland, introduce her to Hugo and Celia, although she doubted she'd come. Her youngest sister was as much of a workaholic as she was, so unless she travelled to the US with the orchestra, it probably would be next Christmas before they saw each other again. She wondered if Dad would have sold the motel by then and if so, where he might be living. Where would next Christmas actually be?

'Well, until next time.' Abigail pulled back from Madeleine's embrace. 'Have a good flight.'

'You too.'

Abigail breathed a sigh of relief as she waved Madeleine through the gate and onto her flight. Her week of playing charades and pretending her life was peachy-good was over. And it had been exhausting. She'd almost confessed her jobless state to Madeleine on the bus but once again hadn't been able to bring herself to do so. What good would it do? Charlie was already on her way back to Meadow Brook—having put her life on hold to help Dad. If she was going to say anything she should have done so the day she'd arrived, the day they'd all asked what she was doing travelling without her beloved violin. But pride had hindered that confession.

She'd planned on taking a quick walk around the tiny terminal before coming back to the gate, but even the effort of stretching her legs seemed too much. So instead, she slumped into the slippery plastic chair and let her bag drop to the floor beside her. It was time to head back to London and work out what the hell to do with her life. First thing would be hunting for a job and that prospect was about as appealing as jumping out of a plane without a parachute.

'Is this seat taken?'

Abigail looked up at the sound of a deep voice and felt her stomach do a tumble-turn. *Him!* The guy she'd met in the arrivals hall only a week ago. *It couldn't be!* The guy who'd been playing her imaginary boyfriend ever since. She ignored the pinprick of guilt that hit her at the thought of her lies and focused on him instead. If possible, he looked even more gorgeous than he had before. Perking up, she shook her head and hit him with a welcoming and perhaps slightly flirtatious smile. 'It's all yours.'

Mr Gorgeous dropped his backpack to the ground and lowered himself into the seat. Her insides tightened as his muscular thigh brushed up against her own. Although he wore jeans and she had on a pair of very comfortable black trousers, her skin flared at the brief connection and she couldn't help staring at his long legs as he stretched them out in front of him.

'This is a sweet coincidence,' the guy said, leaning back and resting his arm along the back of her seat. 'Did you have a good Christmas?'

From this over-friendly gesture to the easy smile on his face, he had cocky written all over him, but somehow it only made him more attractive. As did the fact he'd remembered her from their brief encounter the week before.

'It wasn't the best,' she admitted. But not wanting to tarnish any conversation they might have with the thoughts of her dad's heart thing and the emptiness of home without her mother, she offered her hand and promptly changed the subject. 'I'm Abigail. I don't believe we introduced ourselves last time we met.'

He took her hand and held it a tad longer than appropriate. The warmth that transferred from his skin to hers lit her all over her body, making her girly bits tingle in a way they hadn't since her last debacle of a relationship. 'Nigel,' he told her, and it was all she could do not to screw up her nose.

Nigel? How could someone that looked like him have a name like Nigel?

Still, she swallowed her disappointment. A person wasn't defined by their name and this guy had a lot of other things going for him. His height, his chiselled looks, his light-up-the-room smile, his outgoing personality to name but a few. 'Nice to meet you, Nigel.'

'And you, Abigail.' His tone matched hers—playfully suggestive—and the way he said her name made her want to whimper in pleasure. His gaze raked lazily over her body. 'I like your t-shirt.'

Her breasts suddenly felt heavy as if her bra had shrunk three sizes. What was it about this man? Despite the fact that he had a terribly unfortunate name and they were barely even acquaintances, she wanted to drag him off to the nearest corner and have her wicked way. She clamped her thighs together and smiled. 'Thank you. I bought it on Oxford Street.'

'I work near there. Where do you live and work?'

She gave him the basic facts—Islington and Barbican—but tried not to talk too much about herself. She mentioned she played the violin and worked in the music industry but quickly deflected the conversation back to him. And Nigel seemed more than happy to talk about himself, his love of surfing—which he'd indulged while home this last week—and his passion for his career in advertising. Although obviously a little arrogant, he also made her laugh.

Halfway through a story about a hair care company they'd recently created a campaign for, he leaned forward and slid his hand into her hair, twisting the long blonde strands around his finger before letting it work free. 'You'd make a gorgeous hair model,' he said, causing her cheeks to flush as he dropped his hand. 'In fact, you'd make a gorgeous anything model. Have you ever thought about it?'

She scoffed at his cheesy but undeniably pleasing line. 'No. I eat far too much junk food.'

'It doesn't show.' Again he unashamedly looked his fill but Abigail felt anything but annoyed. Every cell in her body felt heightened with awareness and she thought perhaps Nigel was her bright star in what had been a rather disappointing month.

When their flight was called twenty minutes later, he stood and offered his hand to help her up. That spark shot between his hand and hers again and as their gazes connected she knew he'd felt it too. She licked her lips, unable to remember the last time she'd felt such primal attraction to anyone. She wished she could somehow engineer sitting next to him, because the long hours ahead would be much more enjoyable with him cracking jokes and flirting beside her.

'Want to have a drink while we're waiting in Hong Kong?' Nigel asked as they made their way towards the boarding queue.

Abigail nodded, mentally punching the air. 'That'd be lovely.'

The truth was, after sitting with Nigel for barely half an hour she wanted to do a lot more than have a drink with him.

Abigail's bald-headed, ample-bodied, middle-aged travel companion tried to make conversation with her as the seatbelt light flashed off above their heads, but she couldn't be bothered playing her part. If she were sitting next to Nigel things would be quite different—she allowed herself a brief fantasy of the mischief they could get up to as they soared above the clouds—but she couldn't imagine finding anything this man might say of interest. She was about to try and get comfortable against the miniscule window in the hope of getting a little sleep, when a flight attendant stopped at the end of her row.

'Are you Abigail?' The perfectly polished woman smiled down at her.

Unsure what the attendant wanted, she nodded uncertainly.

The woman thrust out her hand and offered Abigail a tiny, folded up piece of paper. 'From your friend in business class,' she informed her before flitting off to attend to other duties.

Abigail's heartbeat picked up speed as she unfolded the paper. All it said was: *I'm in seat 4C. Log onto the in-flight messaging thingy and we can chat.*

Not even realising there was such a thing as in-flight messaging, it took a moment for her to work it out. When she finally got it up and running, she wasn't exactly sure what she should say.

She settled for: *Hi.*

Nigel's reply came almost instantly. *I'm sorry. I talked far too much about myself back there. It's something I do when I get nervous.*

Why were you nervous?

Don't play coy. Everything about you makes me nervous.

That made her smile so hard she thought her cheeks might split. *Oh?*

Yes, and hot. You made me so hot I had to loosen my shirt collar the moment I got to my seat.

She closed her eyes a moment, her mouth watering as she visualised Nigel unbuttoning the top few buttons of the sexy shirt he'd been wearing. His next message came before she recovered enough to send one of her own.

Too full-on? I don't want to scare you off.

Not at all. His candid confession gave her the confidence to offer one of her own. *I was just imagining you with your shirt off.*

LOL. Would I sound like a sleaze if I admitted I've been imagining you with your shirt off since we met in the arrivals hall last week?

She gasped at his suggestive words, but a tingling thrill rushed through her body. How to respond? *Possibly, but considering I was sleazy first, I'll let you off the hook.*

Phew. Didn't want this to be over before it started.

This? She bit her lip to stop herself from smiling like a crazy person.

Come on, sweet stuff, you can't say you didn't feel the chemistry between us?

Is that what it is? Abigail couldn't remember the last time she'd had so much fun flirting with someone.

The old man sitting next to me is snoring with his mouth open. Drool is running down and dripping off his chin, making an unfortunate stain on his trousers.

Eugh. Now that wasn't very sexy. She pushed Send before she realised she'd typed rather than thought that last bit. Whoops.

LOL. Exactly. I wish I was sitting next to you instead.

Maybe it was because he was far up the front of the plane, maybe it was because she didn't really know him, but Abigail felt bold. She was enjoying this and wanted to see how far she could take it. *What would you do if I was sitting next to you right now?*

Do you really want to know?

Yes. Abigail waited, her heart in her throat, for Nigel's response.

When it finally came, she slapped a hand over her mouth and squirmed in her chair. Was this a type of cyber sex? Plane sex? Whatever it was it was the most fun she'd had with her clothes on in a very long time and she could only imagine what fun she and Nigel would have with their clothes off.

Would you let me?

The messages that flew back and forth between them after that quickly went from hot and suggestive to blatantly dirty and Abigail knew all too well where her game-playing would lead.

They finally touched down at Hong Kong airport and as the other passengers filed off the plane, Abigail looked ahead for Nigel.

'Hey,' he said, smiling as she approached. He'd been waiting for her and gestured for her to go ahead of him, then placed his hand gently in the small of her back. It was the lightest touch, but it was full of intent and her skin burned as if he'd struck her with a match.

They didn't make it to the bar. Glancing around them to check for security, Nigel snuck Abigail into his frequent flyer club lounge and then pulled her into a private bathroom, locking the door behind them. Their bags had barely dropped to the floor before she was yanking Nigel up against her. Their bodies slammed together and his lips collided with hers in a hot, urgent kiss. Leaning against the wall for support, she wrapped her hands around him, sliding them down and into his jeans. He gasped as she felt the hot skin of his buttocks and then grabbed hold of her head to deepen their kiss even further. As his hands slid into her hair, caressing the nape of her neck, his delicious erection pressed against her body and she thought if she didn't have it inside her soon, she would combust. Their illicit messaging had felt like the longest foreplay in history and she was more than ready to take him.

His hands slipped from her hair and she let out a moan of pleasure as one landed on her breast. Damn the clothing between them. As if he could hear her thoughts, Nigel whipped her t-shirt over her head in one swift movement and then dipped his head to her breasts. His mouth covered one hot, already hard nipple and she felt the pull of desire tighten at her core. Fumbling, she worked at the waistband of his jeans, pulling them down and then freeing his splendid cock. Her hands closed around the silken length and he groaned.

'Abigail, you do much more of that and I won't be responsible for my actions.'

A little voice far back in her head whispered that what they were doing could in no way be described as responsible but she wanted to let go. To have fun. To feel good about herself again.

'To hell with responsibility,' she whispered, tightening her grip.

That seemed to be all the encouragement he needed. He tugged at her zipper, yanked off her panties and trousers, and then lifted her up as if she weighed nothing. Already dying from lust, she wrapped her legs around him as he drove his erection into her.

They'd barely begun when he froze. 'Fuck.'

'What?' she panted, feeling like a wanton hussy as she squeezed her inner muscles around him.

'Condom,' he groaned, pressing his head against her forehead.

'Shit.' Her heart slammed against her chest cavity. 'Have you got one?' She looked into his eyes, praying for an answer in the affirmative.

He shook his head and the expression that came over his face made her heart clench.

'Not a boy scout then?' Although at least it suggested he wasn't the type that did this kind of thing as a routine. If this was the usual way he put away time in transit, surely he'd have at least one rubber in his pocket.

'I'm sorry.'

So was she. Damn sorry. And she didn't want to admit defeat just yet. 'Are you safe?'

He nodded. 'I promise I've not done anything like this before and I always use protection.'

For some reason she trusted him.

Hope sparked in his eyes. 'You?'

In terms of STDs, yes she was safe. She wasn't on the pill or anything, but she could always see her doctor about the morning after pill.

'Yes,' she lied, before common sense had the time to ruin what was so far the most exhilarating sexual experience of her life. Maybe it was the stranger aspect or the public location, maybe it was him and the chemistry that had sparked between them since their first initial meeting at Adelaide airport. Whatever it was, she knew if she missed this opportunity she'd always regret it.

'Hallelujah,' Nigel hissed as he thrust back into her.

And her promiscuity was worth it. Despite his name, Nigel took her to heights she'd only ever dreamed about. He kissed her as they came together and then held her against him as their heartbeats slowly returned to normal. He didn't make her feel dirty or sordid, he made her feel strangely cherished and wonderful.

'Thank you,' he eventually said, his tone light as he gently let her go. 'I'll let you get cleaned up and then I think I owe you a drink.'

She smiled at him, amazed that she didn't have one iota of remorse about what they'd just done. 'That sounds good.'

Miraculously, there was no awkwardness as they showered and put themselves back together. And when they were ready, they picked up their bags and Nigel opened the door. They stepped out into the lounge as if they hadn't just been up to naughty fun and strode to the bar, looking like a couple who had known each other forever.

Moments later, Abigail was enjoying a chilled glass of top-of-the-range bubbly while Nigel sipped on a boutique beer. They both wore smug and satisfied smiles and every now and then shared a look acknowledging what had just happened between them.

Much to Abigail's surprise, the conversation flowed. She told Nigel things she'd been keeping secret all week and he offered sympathy at her embarrassing departure from the orchestra. He was a good listener.

'What will you do now?' he asked.

She shrugged and took another sip of her sparkling wine. 'Get a job I suppose. I grew up in a motel so I have some experience in hospitality and customer service.'

'But won't that bore you to tears? Won't you miss your music?'

She sighed, surprised that he got that. 'Probably. But what other choice do I have?' Busking? She shuddered at the thought.

'Have you thought about teaching?'

'No,' she admitted. Truth be told, she'd been too busy feeling sorry for herself to think of an action plan.

'It'd be better than busking,' he said, as if he were a mind reader. 'You can advertise in your local area, put the word out on Facebook. You are on Facebook, aren't you?'

She nodded, silently contemplating his suggestion.

'Hey, we should friend each other,' Nigel suggested, inadvertently changing the subject.

Abigail hadn't thought ahead to what—if anything—would happen between them after they landed in London, but she found she liked the idea of maintaining a connection, at least online. It made what had happened between them seem less seedy.

'Sure,' she said, pulling her phone out of her handbag.

'What's your last name?' he asked.

'Patterson.' By the time she'd switched her phone back on and logged onto Facebook, he'd already sent her a request. She clicked Accept and grinned at him.

'Abigail,' he said, his tone and expression now serious. 'I really like you and I've had a lot of *fun* today but I want to be upfront. I'm not looking for a relationship. I'm far too focused on climbing the career ladder to put in the time.'

'Oh.' She pursed her lips together, feeling stupid suddenly. It's not like she was expecting they get married or anything but ...

He took her hand. 'However, I'd like to see you again. That was fabulous sex and I can't let you go without saying I'd like to do it again.'

She blinked and then blurted. 'Are you asking me to be your *fuck buddy*?'

He had the good grace to look coy. 'No. Well, yes, maybe, but I prefer the term "friends with benefits". Are you going to slap me in the face?'

She thought about it for a moment and then laughed. The truth was she was in no place for a relationship either—she needed to sort her life out before letting another person in permanently. And she didn't know how much longer she'd be in London. She'd never had a casual partner before but she could see the advantages. On-tap sexual pleasure without the drag of a commitment. And didn't she deserve some kind of joy in her otherwise disappointing life? While she was teaching other people's children to murder music or—heaven forbid—busking, at least she'd have Nigel to call on whenever she needed a pick-me-up.

'You're making me nervous,' Nigel said, when she still hadn't answered. 'Look, forget I mentioned it, stupid idea.'

'Not so fast, mister.' She grinned at him and then leaned forward so that he had a perfect view of her cleavage. Then, she held out her hand. 'Fuck buddies it is.'

Chuckling, Nigel bypassed her hand and leaned in for a kiss. He wrapped one hand around the back of her head and pulled her towards him, covering her mouth with a possessive and slightly rough kiss. She loved it.

And she liked the way he made her feel—sexy and powerful instead of pathetic and vulnerable.

Chapter Twelve

By the time Madeleine landed at Thurgood Marshall Airport in Baltimore, she'd made a major life decision. Even though she had no husband, boyfriend or the slightest prospect of a partner, she was going to have a baby. Curse be damned! No crazy old gypsy woman was going to stop her procreating now that she'd decided that was what she wanted to do.

The more she'd thought about it, the more she wondered why she'd never contemplated it before. She was a modern woman, with a secure job and good savings. Just because Mr Right hadn't happened along, didn't mean she shouldn't experience motherhood.

And as with every decision Madeleine had ever made, once she'd made this one, she threw herself into it wholeheartedly. Unable to sleep on the plane, she'd used the twenty-plus hours of travelling time to think and to plan. In transit at Sydney Airport, she'd scoured the internet for everything she could find about single women deciding to have children on their own. There were forums all over the place and hundreds of heartwarming stories of other women who'd made the decision and gone ahead to have gorgeous kids. As a doctor of obstetrics she already had a good understanding of the options available to couples wanting to get pregnant and she was right in thinking it wouldn't be all that different for her.

Her major decision was deciding on a sperm donor, and there were three possible options. She could pay for an anonymous donor from a sperm bank, use a 'known' donor or find someone wanting to co-parent.

She ruled this last option out almost immediately. It involved looking for an unattached man who wanted to be a father—the male equivalent of herself, she supposed. There were positives of this arrangement; if she found a suitable candidate in Baltimore, they might be able to come to some kind of arrangement regarding childcare, so that their baby didn't need to attend day care when she was working. But as far as Madeleine could see, that was the only positive.

What if the biological father met someone else, got married and decided he wanted Madeleine's child to go live with them? What if they disagreed over important things like their son or daughter's education? And worst of all … what if she decided she wanted to move back to Australia? If her child's father was anything more than a sperm donor, he'd have a kind of power over her she didn't want any man to have.

If she wanted a man in her life, she'd put herself out there— go on dates with marriageable men so she could have a family the traditional way. Problem was, the only man she could imagine putting up with twenty-four seven was Hugo, and he was engaged to someone else. Someone she liked and respected.

No, there were too many problems with the whole co-parent deal and the idea of choosing a known donor didn't seem much different. Even if she could find a suitable candidate amongst her single, male friends, it had the potential to get complicated. When she was seven months pregnant, the friend might suddenly decide they wanted to be involved in the baby's life and then she'd have to enter into some kind of awful custody battle. She supposed they'd sign legal documents before getting that far but still, someone totally anonymous seemed the safest way to go.

There was one other option, which fell somewhere between ordering sperm off the net and asking the favour of a friend. Waiting in LA airport, she discovered an international sperm donor website linking wannabe parents with potential donors. Registering with this site was surprisingly easy and after entering a few personal details and agreeing to the site's terms and conditions, Madeleine found herself with access to thousands of donor profiles. The idea was that she could meet with a potential donor before agreeing to take sperm from them. She scrolled through the database, trying not to think about the fact that choosing her child's father off one of these sites was a little like ordering a meal from the local takeaway. Although the profiles were far more detailed than the dishes on your average menu—offering everything from baby photos of potential donors to current photos, family medical histories, education, occupations and hobbies. Each of the men offering sperm had included notes—some short, some very long and detailed—about why they wanted to sow their wild seed, so to speak.

Clicking through the donors was addictive. She'd been so consumed with trying to imagine what a child made with her egg and the stranger on the screen's sperm that she'd almost missed her connection. From LA to Baltimore she wrote a detailed checklist of everything she required in a donor. Good health, a university education and non-smoker were things she wouldn't budge on, but she wasn't that hung up on eye colour or hair. And there were so many other things to consider, such as whether the person already had children and how many more times they planned to donate. She found some interesting people with weird and wonderful passions and outlooks on life.

And before she knew it, the plane was touching down in Baltimore. She heard the cry of a young baby behind her somewhere in economy and smiled, thinking that this time next year it could be her travelling with a newborn. Excitement thrummed through her veins at the thought of taking her baby home to visit Meadow Brook. As she waited to exit the plane, she felt happier, more buoyed than she had in a long time. It wasn't that she'd been depressed or unhappy but more that her life had fallen into a bit of a rut. She'd get up, attend a gym class or go for a run and then head in to work, only to do it all again the next day. But suddenly she had a project, something new and exciting to focus on and look forward to.

This wouldn't happen overnight, but Madeleine felt confident that if she went about it the right way, it would happen eventually. She all but floated off the plane, smiling at the other passengers as they made their way to the luggage carousels and customs, feeling a strange affinity to those people carrying toddlers or pushing prams. She wanted to reach out to them, to ask them questions about how old their babies were and whether they were sleeping through the night. Things she previously hadn't thought much about suddenly seemed vitally important. Not wanting to appear like a weirdo or scare anyone, she bit her tongue, instead adding mentally to her checklist as she waited in the queue to re-enter the United States.

When her passport had been stamped and the customs officer waved her through, she lugged her suitcase out into the arrivals hall, hoping there wouldn't be a massive line for cabs. As the automatic doors opened in front of her, she looked up to see Hugo waiting behind the barrier, a cheery grin spread over his face as he held up his iPad, the name Patterson in big, bold print on the screen.

Madeleine laughed as she went around the barrier to meet him. 'What are you doing?' she asked, leaning forward to air-kiss him.

His eyes sparkled and he shrugged as he ran a hand through his strawberry-blond hair. He looked a lot like a slightly older version of Prince Harry. 'Celia forced me to come. I wanted to stay at home and watch reruns of *How I Met Your Mother* but she said since I wasn't working, I should pick you up. Apparently the last thing you need after a long flight is to wait in line for a cab.'

'Celia is an angel,' Madeleine said as Hugo tucked his iPad under his arm and reached out to take the handle of her mammoth suitcase.

'Although you look amazingly alive for someone who's been on an airplane for the best part of a day.'

It wasn't exactly the compliment of the century, but Madeleine felt a warmth flush through her veins. She pushed it aside, ignoring it as she had done numerous times in the past. 'That's why it's worth paying for first class. How was your Christmas?'

As they headed for his BMW, Hugo talked about his excruciating Christmas at Celia's parents' place in the Hamptons and how he'd spent the whole time wishing he was at work, or at least back in Baltimore. 'My liver will likely never forgive me, but I had to drink myself silly so I didn't kill myself. Every time I visit Celia's family, I'm reminded why she lives so far away from them. Honestly, I'm sure they're insane.'

Madeleine laughed. 'That accounts for the phone call on Christmas Eve.'

'Shit. Did I say anything too embarrassing?' Hugo asked as they arrived at his car and he beeped it open.

'I'm not telling, but I learnt some pretty interesting things,' Madeleine teased, shivering as the bitter winter wind cut through the multi-level hour-by-hour car park and sliced into her cheeks. The contrast in temperature between here and South Australia made it feel like she'd landed on another planet, not simply another continent.

Hugo opened the passenger door for her. 'Get in before you catch your death.'

She obeyed, sliding into his luxurious leather seats as he stowed her luggage in the boot—no, *trunk*, she was back in America now—and then came round and slipped into the driver's seat beside her. 'So,' he said as he pressed some buttons to inject instant heat into the car, 'what was your family Christmas like?'

'Fuck, where do I start?' Madeleine placed her hands in front of the heating vents, wishing she'd had the forethought to ask one of her neighbours to pop into her apartment and switch on the central heating.

'That good hey?' Hugo chuckled as he navigated out of the car park. 'Tell me all.'

So Madeleine sat back and relayed the debacle that was Christmas, with her dad's health scare and having to help out at the motel.

Hugo roared with laughter at the bit about cleaning the rooms. He'd obviously been very drunk when he'd called her because he couldn't remember any of it. 'Well, I know who to call next time our cleaner quits,' he said, when his hysterics had finally subsided.

She shot him a glare. 'You're lucky you're driving or I'd clock you over the head for that.'

'Sorry.' Although he didn't sound very sorry at all. 'So I guess we're both more than happy to get back to work.'

'Oh yeah.' The weekend would be good to relax and recover from jet lag but as usual, she was itching to get back to the hospital. She was also itching to get the ball rolling on her baby project.

'Madeleine? Are you all right?' Hugo's question startled her. She blinked, then looked out the window and realised she couldn't remember travelling the last few minutes.

'Sure. Why?'

'I asked you if you wanted me to stop at the shops for food or anything,' he explained, slowing as they hit a morning traffic jam. 'You didn't answer. It was like you were in some kind of trance.'

She pursed her lips together, rubbing them one over the other as she contemplated whether or not to tell him what was on her mind. Part of her was desperate to tell Hugo her news—to share her excitement with a friend—but another part of her thought maybe she should keep it to herself a little longer, until she'd had a bit more time to think about the logistics.

The desperate Madeleine won out. 'I'm going to have a baby.'

Hugo's shock was palpable. Normally a very confident and capable driver, he braked hard and fast, only narrowly missing a collision with the car in front. 'What? Who's the father?'

'That,' she said, 'is where things get interesting.'

Chapter Thirteen

'Are you sure you don't want me to stay a little longer?' Her voice shaky, Lucinda looked from Charlie to her dad and back to Charlie. She was waiting for Bob Tucker, the owner of the local hardware store, who'd volunteered to drive her to Adelaide for her flight home as he was heading that way for a meeting. On the one hand she couldn't wait to get home to Joe, but she was worried about leaving Dad and the motel with Charlie.

Her sister meant well but she didn't have the same high standards or attention to detail that Lucinda had and she was sometimes a little airy-fairy, which meant she might miss something important, like Dad not paying bills on time or worse, him not looking after his health or slipping into depression.

'We'll be fine,' Charlie assured her, wrapping one arm around their father. 'Won't we, Dad?'

'Yep.' He nodded.

Lucinda sighed. 'Don't overwork Mrs Sampson, make sure you take your medication, and—' A horn beeped behind her and she turned to see Bob leaning out the window of his crew-cab ute, Meadow Brook Hardware Supplies in big bold type on the side.

'You ready?' he yelled and then pressed the horn again for good measure.

'Stop stressing, love.' Dad stepped forward and wrapped his arms around her. 'I've been doing this for a long time, and I really appreciate the break you girls have given me this last week. Charlie and I will make a good team, but you need to get back to your husband. And those kids.'

For a second, Lucinda flinched, thinking he meant her potential babies, but then she realised he was referring to her schoolchildren. She still had a few weeks until term one started and she hoped she'd summon some enthusiasm for her job again by then. It was hard teaching other people's kids day in, day out when all she wanted was to have a baby of her own.

'Thanks, Dad. Please look after yourself.' She kissed him on the cheek. 'I love you.'

'I love you, too. Now be off with you.'

He patted her on the bum like he had when she was a child as she turned to Charlie. 'Bye, little sis. Look after yourself and call me any time you need to.'

'I will.' Charlie hugged her and then pulled away. 'I've just remembered something. Hold on a moment.' She turned to race back inside the motel and Lucinda exchanged a confused look with Dad.

He shrugged and then walked across the tarmac to chat with Bob, who occasionally came into the motel for a drink and a game of pool. Lucinda threw her bags into the back of the ute and was starting back towards the motel when Charlie came running.

'Here. I got this for you.' She handed Lucinda a tissue-paper wrapped parcel. 'Mitch and I saw them at the markets in St Kilda and I thought of you.'

'What is it?' The small package felt surprisingly heavy in her hands.

The horn beeped again before Charlie had the chance to answer.

'Hurry up, love,' Dad called. 'Bob has an appointment to get to.'

'There's a card inside that explains everything,' Charlie said, before pulling Lucinda into a final hug. 'I really hope it helps.'

Perplexed, Lucinda uttered her thanks and then, carrying the little parcel carefully, ran to catch her lift. She'd barely clicked in her seatbelt when Bob swerved away from the kerb and onto the highway.

'You don't mind if we listen to talkback?' he asked, leaning forward to turn the volume up on his old car radio.

'Not at all.' Feeling *blah*—she'd quite enjoyed the last few days of looking after Dad and being busy at the motel—she wasn't in the mood to make small talk anyway. As some monotone-voiced man drawled on about the Prime Minister needing a good kick up the bum, Lucinda zoned out into her own little world. She looked down at Charlie's present on her lap and started to unwrap it.

The white paper peeled back to reveal a shiny little bronze statue that looked like some female relation to Buddha. She frowned as she fingered the smooth surface and then noticed the little card attached.

'A fertility statue?'

'Huh?' Bob asked and she realised she'd spoken aloud. 'What's that?'

'Oh, nothing.' She quickly rewrapped Charlie's gift and then placed it on the floor by her feet. The last thing she wanted was to get into discussions about her fertility issues with Bob Tucker, who might discuss her woes with his customers—or worse, her dad. It had been hard enough confiding in her sisters, but she was glad she had. Madeleine had proved a big support discussing all things medical and she now felt confident to explain it all to Joe, which would hopefully convince him to agree to seek help.

Abigail and Charlie had also been supportive and sympathetic, all three of them promising to send her and Joe positive thoughts.

She smiled, thinking about her sisters. Although it hadn't been the easiest trip home, they'd been forced to deal with their dad's health, the motel and their grief together, and it kind of felt like all that had brought them a little closer again.

Thanks to the dry voices of the talkback show, Lucinda dozed during the rest of the trip, catching up on much-needed sleep. Once at Adelaide airport, she thanked Bob for the lift and then trekked inside to check in.

Just as she was about to board, she got a text message from Joe. *Can't wait to see you. Travel safe. x.* She messaged him back and then switched off her phone ready to fly.

The house felt quiet without her sisters flittering around, so Charlie and Dad decided to eat dinner in the motel. Post Christmas and a day before New Years' Eve, the restaurant was quiet and they took turns getting up whenever someone needed serving in the bar.

Rob, excited to have someone to experiment on, emerged from the kitchen and laid a plate in front of Charlie. 'Vegetarian Wellington,' he announced, putting on a weird accent and flourishing his hands in the air.

Charlie looked down at the immaculately presented dish and then grinned up at Rob. 'It looks amazing.'

He nodded and then stood there expectantly. Charlie realised he was waiting for her to taste it. No pressure or anything. She picked up her knife and fork and cut off a chunk, then lifted it to her mouth and slipped it between her lips. And *oh my*! The flaky pastry crumbled and the flavours exploded on her tongue. She swallowed the first mouthful and, already forking up the second, looked up to Rob. 'That,' she pronounced, 'is possibly the best thing I've ever tasted. Put it on the menu. Right away.'

A smile burst across Rob's weathered face and his chest puffed up proudly.

Charlie looked to her father. 'That is, if it's okay with you, Dad.'

'Of course it is.' He took a sip of his beer and then gave a satisfied sigh. 'You're back as my right-hand girl, sweetheart, so you can make executive decisions like that on your own.'

'In that case, I'm having this every day.' She put the second mouthful into her mouth and if anything it was better than the first.

Rob beamed. 'I've got plenty of other recipes to try out now you're here. I love making vegetarian dishes.'

'All well and good, but where's my steak?' Dad asked gruffly.

Charlie rolled her eyes and Rob laughed. 'Sorry, boss.' Then he turned and headed back into the kitchen to get it.

Once Dad's steak had arrived, he and Charlie talked between mouthfuls. It was the first time she'd had him to herself for as long as she could remember. They talked about her sisters and then moved on to how they would divvy up the duties in the motel.

'I'm thinking we need to put ourselves on the roster,' Charlie said, wondering if she should go grab a pen and paper. Lucinda would but then again, this was just a starter conversation and she didn't want to be pushy. 'We'll factor in Mrs Sampson and Rob's days off and then work out where we can take time out too. So Rob works six evenings a week and you cook on the seventh? Are you happy with that?'

'Yes, I like cooking,' Dad said, 'unless you'd like a turn in the kitchen.'

She shook her head. 'I'll do breakfasts in the mornings and then help Mrs Sampson with the housekeeping.' She cringed at the idea of having to cook bacon and sausages but it was better than a full-on juicy steak, which was the most popular choice on the motel's dinner menu. 'That way you can sleep in if you want and then have a free morning to do office work.' She paused when she realised Dad was grinning at her. 'What's so funny?

'You've got it all worked out. This forward thinking and organised side of you is one we don't see very often.'

She chose not to take offence, secretly pleased he was impressed. 'Don't tell the others. It's a lot easier being the dummy of the family.'

'You're not dumb, Charlotte.'

She blinked. 'I know, Dad.' And then she almost told him about her desire to study, but she thought better of it at the last moment. She didn't want him feeling guilty for holding her back. 'So what are you going to do when the motel sells? Given it much thought?'

He puffed out a breath and shrugged. 'A little. I think I'd like to travel. Your mum and I often talked about places we'd like to see. I joked about travelling round Australia in a caravan but she said she'd only do it if we could afford five-star hotels. As much as she loved the motel life, she said, when she finally gave it up, she wanted to enjoy a little luxury.'

Charlie smiled, both at the joy in her dad's voice as he spoke about his wife and at her own memories. They'd all been uncertain whether talking about Mum helped him or whether each time they tried to bring her into the conversation it broke his heart a fraction more, but since Aunt Mags's unexpected visit they were finding talking about her much easier. 'That sounds just like Mum.'

'Maybe I'll do the caravan thing to spite her for leaving me so early,' he joked. 'Take her ashes with me or something.' Currently they were sitting in an urn, pride of place on the mantelpiece in the house.

Charlie almost choked on her mouthful of soda water. 'Dad!'

'Hey, if I didn't laugh, I'd cry.'

'You're allowed to do both,' she said, reaching out and touching his hand. 'And we need to talk about Mum, hold onto her memories so she'll live through us.'

'I know.' He squeezed her hand. 'But still, I might put the caravan thing on hold for a bit and go visit my girls instead. I've always fancied going to the States and I'm itching to hear Abigail play in the orchestra.'

'Sounds good. Maybe I'll come with you.'

'Where are you two off to?' A shadow loomed over their table and Charlie looked up to see Mitch. She'd been so focused on Dad she hadn't even heard the bell above the door ring.

'Round-the-world trip,' she explained, gesturing to one of the empty seats at their table. 'Wanna come?'

'Now there is a tempting offer,' he said, pulling out the seat and sitting down. 'When do we leave?'

Dad glanced between the two of them. 'I thought you two might be sick of each other after the road trip.'

'Well, she is pretty annoying—' Mitch offered Dad a look of faux sympathy '—which is why I thought I'd better come check that you were managing to put up with her.'

Dad chuckled as he pushed back his seat. 'There's a bloke at the bar needs serving. I'll leave you kids to it.'

'You think you're so funny, don't you?' Charlie shot Mitch a glare, trying to stifle her smile.

He leaned back in his chair, stretched his arms up and linked his hands behind his head. 'Pretty much.'

'Does the funny guy want dinner?'

'Nah.' He shook his head. 'I was helping Macca out on the farm this arvo and Kate twisted my arm to stay on for a roast.'

'Bet it didn't need much twisting.' Although Charlie wondered why anyone would want to cook such a thing in the height of summer.

Mitch patted his stomach. 'I might be able to find room for some dessert though. What's on the menu tonight?'

'Apple crumble and ice-cream.'

Mitch groaned and his eyes rolled back in his head.

For one brief second, Charlie imagined that it was the same look he might get in the throes of sex, but she ignored the quivering feeling that sparked within and told herself to get a grip. Once she'd managed to overcome her errant hormones on the road, she and Mitch had had a fantastic few days together, reinforcing how much she valued his friendship. Above *all* else.

'I guess that's a yes,' she said, pushing herself back from the table. 'I'll go get you some.'

She returned a few minutes later and dumped his bowl on the table. Dad was now engrossed in conversation at the bar with an elderly gentleman staying at the motel. Mitch caught Charlie looking at him.

'How's he doing?' he asked, between mouthfuls.

'Good, I think.' She glanced around, speaking her thoughts as they came into her head. 'Although in theory it should be easier on him with me here, I think he's really ready to move on and I'm wondering if there's anything we can do to improve the chances of a quick sale?'

'Sick of Meadow Brook already?' Mitch teased.

She gave him a look and he apologised.

'Sorry. What kind of things were you thinking?'

She sighed. 'I don't know, only surface stuff because there isn't a big budget for renovations, but this place hasn't had a makeover since I was in primary school. It's stuck in the late nineties and I'm thinking a bit of paint, maybe some new carpet, fresh linen in the rooms, new tables and chairs?' Even as she listed all these things, she knew they probably couldn't afford half of them but it was good to dream, right?

As if reading her mind, Mitch said, 'It's amazing what a paint job can do to a place.'

'Yes, maybe we should start with that. I'll have a chat with Dad. How's the apple pie?'

He made a face. 'It's terrible. I think you should box the rest up for me, so as to not to upset any of the customers.'

'Funny guy.'

He shrugged. 'But seriously, do you think Rob would box me up a slice or two in a couple of containers? I'm off to Darwin tomorrow with a load.'

'I think we can manage that,' she said, thinking she'd miss his cheeky face. 'How long will you be gone?'

'Four or five days. And when I get back, you'd better have those paint colours picked out.'

She laughed. 'What for?'

He cocked an eyebrow. 'You don't think I'm gonna let you loose with a paintbrush on your own, do you?

Chapter Fourteen

Lucinda exited the plane to a sea of eager faces, but one stood out in the crowd. Her heart leapt at the sight of her gorgeous husband; his tall, rangy body, tanned skin and dark hair. His chiselled jaw and classic Italian good looks still made her swoon. 'Joe,' she whispered under her breath as she picked up her pace. Although their time apart hadn't been any longer than the stints he usually did away, it felt different this time.

Running now, she flung herself into his open arms, relishing the feeling as he closed them around her and pressed a kiss into her hair.

'Hey babe. Missed you,' he said when they finally pulled apart. 'For a while there, I was worried you weren't gonna come back.'

'As if,' she scoffed, linking her hand with his as they started towards the escalators that led to the baggage claim area.

'Well, to celebrate your return, I'm taking you out to dinner so that you don't have to cook.'

She turned and cocked an eyebrow at him as they stepped onto the escalator. 'You know, you could always cook, Joe.' Here she was thinking he'd missed *her*, when the truth was he'd probably only missed his domestic goddess.

He looked sheepish, digging his hands into the pockets of his work shorts. 'I could. But we both know how crap I am in the kitchen. I'm liable to poison you.'

This was true and for that she laid the blame solely at his mother's feet. A typical Italian *mamma*, Rosa Mannolini did everything for her husband and sons, from cooking and cleaning to buying their socks and jocks. She'd tried to keep this up for the first few months after Lucinda and Joe were married, but eventually Lucinda had laid down the law. If her husband couldn't buy his own underwear, she would do it herself. At least then she could buy sexy black boxer briefs, rather than the ugly Y-fronts his *mamma* preferred. Lucinda shuddered at the memory. But she was not going to let mother-in-law from hell ruin her first night back with her husband.

She forced a laugh instead and said, 'So, where are we going?'

Joe took her to a lovely Indian restaurant in Subiaco and they sat at an outside table on the footpath where they could enjoy the balmy evening air and watch the people pass by on their way to the theatre across the road. It was the same place he'd taken her over a decade ago when she'd first moved to Perth to be with him. They'd met on a Contiki Tour of Europe—she'd been on summer holidays from university—and it had been love at first sight. From their first kiss on New Year's Eve at the top of the Eiffel Tower, she'd known she'd happily move states to be with him.

Although everyone had said it would be impossible, she'd transferred her degree from Adelaide to Perth and finished her final year of teaching at Edith Cowan University. Joe had already been in his second year at the mines by then, which had been good for her studies. When he was home they spent long relaxing days on the beach or in bed together, drinking wine and eating fine food, content to live in a world that included only them. During his weeks up north at work, she'd knuckled under, getting ahead on reading, assignments or studying for exams.

Back then the only blemish in their perfection had been his mother. Now it was Rosa *and* the fact that no matter how much they enjoyed making love, they hadn't been able to make a baby.

She wondered if he'd chosen this restaurant to remind her of the good times they'd had together. Back before they decided it was time to grow up and get serious about the family they'd talked about for so many years, thinking they had all the time in the world.

'Are you going to have a glass of wine?' Joe asked, leaning across the table and taking her hand.

Her first instinct was to say no—after all, trying for a baby and everything—but she stamped it down, deciding to make an effort to enjoy their evening together. 'Yes, I think I shall.'

Joe's grin stretched across his face and she realised he hadn't been expecting her to answer in the affirmative. 'Excellent. You enjoy yourself. I'm driving.'

They ordered the drinks and then their dinner—butter chicken, beef vindaloo, spiced eggplant and a mouth-watering dhal with cream and coriander—and Lucinda tried hard to make conversation that didn't involve her menstrual cycle. 'Has Mrs White done anything crazy lately?' Their next-door neighbour was known for her peculiar habits.

'Well,' Joe grinned ridiculously. 'Where do I start? A couple of days ago I ran into her at Bunnings and she was very elusive about why she was there. Anyway, I went to the gym yesterday and came home to find her painting the front exterior of her house.'

'What colour?'

'That's just it. Not one colour, but about half a dozen. She seems to be painting a rainbow mural. She said there isn't enough colour in the world. There goes the neighbourhood, hey?'

Lucinda couldn't help but laugh, imagining what the rest of their straitlaced neighbours would think of that. Joe went on to talk about work—a couple of men who'd been sacked for misconduct—and then began on his family.

'Stella has been sneaking out at nights to see her boyfriend,' Joe informed her about their niece. 'When Ricardo found out, he told her she was grounded until she was twenty-one and she told him she'd be married by then. Apparently the moment she turns eighteen, they're eloping.'

'Oh boy.' Lucinda laughed again, feeling a little sorry for her in-laws who had raised a very strong-willed daughter. Maybe that was a Mannolini trait. She imagined Rosa would have been a force to be reckoned with at seventeen.

'Let's hope we never have daughters,' Joe said, before shovelling another forkful of beef vindaloo into his mouth.

Lucinda sucked in a breath. Right now she'd be happy with *any* baby, whatever the gender. Suddenly bored of talking about everything but their fertility issue, she put down her fork, gulped a mouthful of water and then reached into her handbag for the gift from Charlie. She placed it in front of her on the table and watched Joe's eyes boggle.

'What is that?' he asked, as if she'd just put a dead rodent in front of him.

'It's a fertility statue,' she told him, keeping her voice even. 'Charlie gave it to me.'

Joe didn't look impressed. 'You've been talking about our problems with other people?'

She shook her head. 'They're my sisters, Joseph. You make it sound like I announced it on Facebook.'

He sighed and nodded towards the female Buddha. 'And that thing is supposed to do what?'

Lucinda shrugged. 'Charlie thinks it might help us get pregnant. It's a miniature replica of the Venus of Willendorf, which was found in a village in lower Austria,' she said, regurgitating what she'd read on the accompanying card. 'It's believed she was a fertility goddess and lots of people who have had these in their houses have overcome difficulties conceiving.'

Joe made a noise that indicated exactly how much faith he'd put in something like that.

'It can't hurt,' she said, feeling tears prickle behind her eyelids. And then more quietly: 'Neither can seeking medical help, which is what Madeleine thinks we should do.'

Joe sighed again as if mourning the end of their carefree evening. 'But we've only been trying for eight months. And I've been away during some of those peak times.'

'I'm thirty-two, Joe.' Lucinda worked hard not to raise her voice or succumb to tears. He hated it when she cried and she wanted this conversation to be on an even playing field. 'I know that's not ancient, but we don't have forever. As Madeleine says, if there is something wrong, it's better to find out sooner, so that we can address the issue. Get IVF if that's what it takes. And that in itself can sometimes take years.'

Joe frowned, reached out and took her hand again. 'Do you want this *that* badly?'

Frustration clawed at her. Did he not know her at all? '*Yes*. I want something that is both of us, something that is you and me, something that we made together. With our love.'

'Aren't we enough on our own?'

Lucinda went quiet, because as much as she loved him, she didn't know if they *were* enough, just the two of them. 'Of course we are,' she said, wanting it to be true, 'but I've always wanted to be a mum. You know that.'

Joe's grip on her hand tightened. 'Okay. If it means that much to you, we'll do it. We'll go see a doctor. But you have to promise me something?'

Through tears of joy and relief, she nodded. 'Anything.'

'That if there is something wrong with either of us—' he took a deep breath and she saw that his eyes also glistened with moisture '—we'll work through it and we'll stick together. I don't want to lose you, Luci.'

'Oh, Joe.' She lifted his hand and palmed it against her cheek. 'I love you.'

'And I love you.'

Full of curry, they bypassed dessert and went home to make love in the manner of two people who had known each other intimately for a very long time.

Chapter Fifteen

The elation of Abigail's first sexual experience with a stranger started to wear off the moment she stepped out of Heathrow into the dreary, awful, freezing winter's afternoon and realised she had to catch the tube back to Islington. She'd almost splurged on a black taxi but caught herself at the last second, remembering that now she didn't have a job she needed to make her pennies stretch. By the time her body clock roused her at half past three the next morning, the afterglow had well and truly dimmed.

Feeling like death warmed up, she rolled out of bed, shrugged into her dressing gown and tiptoed into the kitchen of the apartment she shared with two other musicians. Sam and Pamela had both been home when she'd returned last night but instead of asking about her holiday and making jealous comments about her tan, they'd launched straight into an attack.

'Remember the rent is due at the end of next week,' Sam had snapped by way of greeting as she polished her black uniform shoes.

'I know,' Abigail said, thinking she also needed to give her shoes some attention but then remembering that no, she didn't.

That was why they were so worried about her ability to pay her share of the rent.

'So what are you going to do for a crust now? I hear the pub on the corner is looking for waitresses,' Pamela sneered and then looked to Sam, who sniggered. They'd always been nice when they were part of the same circle—musicians in London's esteemed Symphony Orchestra—but they'd changed the second Abigail had been sacked. Now they made her feel as if she were Cinderella and they were the ugly stepsisters. She'd been glad of the chance to get away from them and go home to Australia for a bit.

Why-oh-why hadn't she stayed there?

Ignoring the instinct to tell her so-called friends they could stuff their room and find the rent themselves, Abigail had yawned, pleaded exhaustion and headed off to her room. Due to the time difference between England and Australia and the fact she'd been on a plane for the best part of twenty-four hours, she'd collapsed into bed and fallen asleep within minutes.

Now, awake ridiculously early, she wished she'd fought fatigue a little longer. In the kitchen, she quietly made herself some toast and a cup of tea and then took the snack back into her bedroom, where she sank her teeth into the first slice and promptly burst into tears. Marmite just didn't cut it when it came to comfort food. She needed Vegemite and she needed someone to tell her that everything was going to be okay.

If only Mum hadn't gone and got herself killed by a stupid bee.

What would she have said about this big fat mess? If Abigail closed her eyes, she could almost imagine Mum pulling her into her arms, stroking her hair and telling her that everyone made mistakes, that life would be boring if they didn't.

Then again, sometimes boring was safe and she couldn't remember Mum ever making mistakes.

Pushing the plate aside, not caring when one slice flopped off onto her bedspread, she leaned over and dragged out her violin from under the bed. She desperately wanted to play it, to seek the comfort it had always brought, but she could just imagine what Pamela and Sam would say if she played her favourite concerto this early in the morning. Cuddling the instrument to her like a child would a teddy bear, Abigail lay back against her pillow and let the tears fall.

What had become of her? Motherless, jobless, soon to be homeless. And now the kind of person who fucked strangers in airport bathrooms. With that thought, she groaned, remembering that she might not have a job to go to but, after yesterday's tawdry episode, she needed to see a doctor for the morning-after pill. That thought appealed about as much as the prospect of begging Sam and Pamela to let her do their washing and ironing in lieu of rent. How many times had she come home late and watched a trashy reality TV show about the risqué sex lives of London teens? Now she was in the same boat, but she couldn't use adolescence as an excuse.

A few hours later, Abigail sat in the waiting room of her local medical centre, just around the corner from her Islington flat, dreading going into her appointment and putting forward her request. She glanced up and met the gaze of the receptionist and immediately squirmed in her seat. Although this wasn't a sexual health clinic and she was surrounded by all sorts of people—old men, young mums with toddlers, sniffling twenty-somethings— she felt as if she had a flashing neon sign on her head announcing why she was there. Maybe she could make up some excuse about how she'd been having sex with her *long-term* boyfriend and the condom had broken.

Fighting the urge to flee, Abigail dug her mobile phone out of her bag and checked Facebook. Madeleine had landed back in Baltimore. One of her old schoolfriends had got engaged on Christmas Eve and ... hang on a second, Nigel had posted something too. She'd totally forgotten they'd friended each other yesterday.

Back in London after a fabulous Christmas with the fam. Thanks to a special lady the return flight wasn't all that bad either.

A special lady? A warmth flushed Abigail's skin and she pressed the Like button. Then she clicked on Nigel's profile and did a little Facebook stalking. There were things she already knew about him, such as that he lived in Hackney and worked in advertising, liked surfing and keeping fit. But knowing and seeing were two different things. She'd been intimate with him and knew what he looked like naked (or at least with his shirt half off and his jeans bunched around his ankles) but flicking through his photos brought him even more to life.

She smiled at photos of his family Christmas. His looked to be a typical Aussie family, who'd had a barbeque and followed lunch with a game of cricket on the beach. They were all smiles and appeared to be enjoying their time together immensely. There were other photos from his week at home—one of him with his arm wrapped around an elderly lady and another of him on the beach, holding his surfboard alongside a couple of mates around the same age.

He looked even nicer than she'd given him credit for.

'Abigail Patterson.' She startled at the sound of her name being called by the doctor on duty. Dropping her phone into her bag, she stumbled out of her chair and hurried over to a door held open by a grey-haired doctor who looked to be about a hundred and ten years old. *Ugh.* The last thing she wanted to do was discuss her sexual misadventures with him.

The door thumped shut behind them and she crossed over to the plastic seat alongside the doctor's desk. Doctor Granddad sat down in his chair and folded his hands together as if he were about to pray. 'How can I help you, Miss Patterson?'

She swallowed, already cringing at the thought of what his reaction to her confession might be. 'There's a possibility I might be pregnant,' she whispered.

He nodded slowly. 'And would that be a good or a bad thing, my dear?'

'Well …' she began, placing a hand on her stomach because she suddenly felt sick at the thought of telling him the truth. 'You see …'

And then a thought landed in her head: If she was pregnant it might not be such a disaster after all. She felt as if a light bulb had been switched on. She'd always planned to have a family one day. Would it be such a bad thing if that dream was brought forward a few years? It wasn't like she was doing anything more worthwhile at the moment. Granted, she'd never planned on parenting alone but now she thought about it, having a baby could fix a lot of things.

For starters it would give her the perfect excuse to head back to Australia without having to tell her family anything about the orchestra. Suddenly, getting pregnant out of wedlock, to a stranger no less, seemed far less shameful than confessing her career failure. A giggle escaped her and she felt a weight lift off her shoulders.

Doctor Granddad looked at her, his forehead wrinkled in concern. 'Are you okay?'

'Yes, sorry.' She took a deep breath and focused. 'It would be a good thing if I'm pregnant.'

'Excellent.' The doctor's shoulders slumped and he leaned back in his seat. 'Shall we do a pregnancy test?'

'You can find out that soon?'

The doctor frowned again and rubbed the side of his grey-stubbled jawline. 'When do you think you may have gotten pregnant?'

'Yesterday.' She smiled, the idea blossoming.

'I see.' Was he stifling a smirk? 'When was your last period?'

Blushing, because she'd never before spoken about such intimate things with a man, she tried to think back to when she'd last required tampons. It had been shortly before she'd flown to Australia, because she remembered being happy she didn't have to deal with all that on the plane. 'About two weeks ago.'

He nodded. 'And your cycles? Are they regular?'

'Like clockwork.'

'And you had unprotected sex yesterday?'

'Yes. With my boyfriend.' She felt compelled to add this last bit because she didn't want this elderly doctor thinking she was some kind of wanton hussy. Her thoughts drifted to Nigel and she felt a pinprick of guilt at this new plan, but she pushed both the guilt and him out of her head. What he didn't know, couldn't hurt him.

'In that case, you very well may be pregnant.'

Joy! The thought of a tiny baby appeared like a spring flower in what had been a very dreary winter. What only hours ago she'd thought of as her stupidest moment ever, now had the power to be something monumental, something amazing.

Then there was that stupid curse. Lucinda had freaked when they'd found out about it and if Abigail were honest, she hadn't liked thinking about it either. Getting a positive pregnancy result would be the nail in the coffin of its ridiculousness.

'Here are some pamphlets for you about pregnancy health and nutrition.' Again Doctor Granddad interrupted her thoughts, but she paid attention because this was important. If she was going to have a baby, she would do everything she could to make sure it was healthy. 'You'll need to start taking folate supplements immediately.'

'Okay.' She took out her phone and made a note while the doctor scribbled something on a piece of paper.

'You're currently not on any medication are you? Don't have any long-running medical conditions?'

She shook her head.

'Good. In that case, eat healthily for the next couple of weeks, stay off the alcohol and cigarettes and maybe I'll see you back here soon.'

Realising she'd been dismissed, Abigail stood, thanked the brusque old doctor and then let herself out. She had a spring in her step that had been absent that morning and didn't feel jet lagged in the slightest as she headed off to Boots to get the folate tablets and other pre-natal supplements.

Once she had all she needed, she'd tackle the other issue—finding work to tide her over until it was time to go back to Australia.

Chapter Sixteen

'Are you okay?' Joe patted Lucinda's knee and she turned her head to look at him. They were sitting in the waiting room at the local doctor's surgery.

She gave her husband a smile and nodded. 'Yep, I'm good.' Truth was she felt nervous. Too nervous for conversation. She couldn't even flick the pages of the six-month-old copy of *New Idea* in her lap because her hands were shaking and she was sitting on them so Joe wouldn't notice. What if something was wrong? Maybe it would be better to know because then they could do something about it, but … what if nothing could be done?

Apparently oblivious to her inner turmoil, Joe removed his hand and then glanced at his watch. Lucinda swallowed the irritation that rose within her at this gesture, as if he had some place else he'd rather be. Still, considering his reluctance to even solicit help until recently, she was grateful he was here.

Just when she thought she couldn't stand the waiting any longer, a tall, skinny, female GP walked into the middle of the waiting room and called their names.

Smiling at the attractive doctor, Joe practically sprang from his seat and then as an afterthought looked back to Lucinda. 'You coming?'

She nodded as she walked past him into the doctor's room.

'So, what can I do for you lovely people today?' Dr Slater said chirpily as she shut the door and crossed the room. She gestured that they should sit. Her desk had the usual medical paraphernalia and also about a dozen photo frames with cute little toddlers smiling out at them. Dr Slater only worked two days a week because she had young children, so hopefully she'd understand Lucinda's desire for a family.

Joe made himself comfortable but Lucinda sat perched on the edge of her seat as if ready to flee at any moment. He looked to her and nodded his head, indicating she should say something.

'Well.' Lucinda took a deep breath, averting her gaze from the photos. 'We need a referral to see Doctor Lee Randall.'

The look in the doctor's eyes told Lucinda she knew exactly who Dr Randall was and what he specialised in. 'I see. Do you believe you're pregnant?'

Lucinda shook her head and tried to swallow the emotion that bubbled at the back of her throat. She'd promised herself, and Joe, she wouldn't cry. 'That's the problem. We've been trying to conceive and it's not happening.'

'I see,' Dr Slater said again, before leaning back in her chair. 'How long have you been trying?'

'Eight months,' Lucinda said, wishing the moment the words were out that she'd lied and said twelve months instead. 'But I'm thirty-two and Joe works away so if there is something wrong, we need to find out sooner rather than later. My sister is an obstetrician in America and she recommended—'

Dr Slater cut her off before she could finish her sentence. 'When did you go off birth control?'

'A year ago.' Actually it was only eight months but Lucinda wanted the doctor to take their plight seriously.

'I see, and how often have you been trying?'

She glanced at Joe, who was clearly finding this a little awkward. 'Joe works, two weeks on, one week off, so we've been having sex almost every day when he's home.'

Dr Slater made a note. 'Are you charting your ovulation?'

Lucinda nodded.

'And how often has ovulation coincided with Joe being away?'

'Only twice, and the second time I flew out to Kalgoorlie to spend those days with him.'

'Hmm.' Thank God the doctor hadn't said 'I see' again. 'Are your cycles regular?'

'Yes.'

Dr Slater fired off one question after another and Lucinda answered them, trying not to lose her patience or her temper. *Did either of them smoke or binge drink? Were they stressed at work? Had she ever had a miscarriage before trying to conceive with Joe?* And then the biggie … *Was there any family history of infertility?*

Joe chose this moment to speak up. 'No.' He snorted. 'My mum had six kids and my brothers only have to look at their wives to get them pregnant.'

Dr Slater laughed and Lucinda wanted to punch them both. Instead she said, 'And my mother had four children. No problems my side either as far as I know.'

But at that moment the curse popped into her head.

She'd tried to forget about it these last few weeks and hadn't told Joe because she already knew what he'd think, but it was part of her family history, right? Almost about to say something, she caught herself at the last moment. She was pretty sure that wasn't the type of history the doctor was interested in and she didn't want her mental state called into question.

'In that case,' began Dr Slater, 'my advice is to stop worrying so much about conceiving, make sure you have intercourse every day when Joe's at home, and come back to me in a few months if you still haven't had any luck.'

Joe chuckled. 'A guy can't complain about that medical advice.'

Dr Slater half-laughed, then pushed back her chair. Joe started to stand as if that was the end of that. *Do you think we're idiots?* Lucinda wanted to scream. It's not as if they weren't having enough sex already and she'd read every book on fertility and conception under the sun, so she knew their timing and everything else was right. And even though Dr Randall was a friend of Madeleine's, it still might take them months to get an appointment. How many friends' pregnancies would be announced or babies born while she waited? No, she couldn't keep going the way they were. She couldn't stand it!

'My sister has already spoken to Doctor Randall,' Lucinda said firmly, her hands tightly gripping her handbag, 'and he has agreed to see us. We just need a local referral.' She gave the doctor a look that she hoped conveyed her message: *I'm not leaving this surgery without that little piece of paper.*

Dr Slater sighed, turned to her computer screen without saying a word, opened a document and began to type. Lucinda tried to peer past Joe and read the words but she couldn't make them out. Joe looked to her questioningly but she looked away, peeved at his lack of support. Sometimes she seriously wondered if he wanted to have a family at all—oh, he said all the right things to his *mamma*, but he didn't take their efforts seriously the way she did.

Finally, Dr Slater stopped typing and reached over to the printer as it shot out a couple of pieces of paper. She folded the top one up, put it into an envelope then made a show of sealing it shut, before handing it to Lucinda.

'Here's your referral. And—' she picked up the other piece of paper and thrust it towards them '—since you're eager to get started,

I'm sending you for some blood tests so that Doctor Randall will have the results by the time you go to his appointment.'

Lucinda blinked. It was actually happening. She felt like the two bits of paper in her hand were winning lottery tickets. Despite the fact blood tests made her faint and this was only the first step in what might be a very long and arduous process, she wanted to fling her arms up in the air and dance around the doctor's surgery.

'Thanks,' Joe said, standing. 'We really appreciate it, don't we, Luce?'

'Yes.' Lucinda nodded, still smiling, willing to forgive Dr Slater's initial reluctance because now she had more important things to focus on. She couldn't wait to call Madeleine and tell her the news.

Chapter Seventeen

Taking a deep breath, Abigail placed her violin case down on the cold pavement beside her and prayed that the rain and the police would stay away long enough for her to make a few pounds. Although hopeful that next week would bring a positive pregnancy test and a reason to pack up her bags and head back to Australia, she had to do something just in case. Her credit card was almost maxed out and getting a job had proved a lot harder than she'd imagined.

Following Nigel's suggestion, she'd drafted a brief post for Facebook about being available to teach violin and piano to children or adults in their own home and had been about to publish her status when she'd realised the problem. Her sisters were on Facebook and although they rarely commented on anything she had to say, she'd bet her last penny they'd make a big deal about this. Disheartened, she'd gone to Plan B, which involved 'borrowing' Pamela's printer, Sam's paper and dusting off her old résumé. Despite the rain, she'd spent two days trekking around London, going into shops—she'd started with the music stores—asking if they were looking for workers.

Having to do this was demoralising in itself but the response she got from almost every potential employer made her want to scream. 'Bit over-qualified to work here, aren't you, love?' Just because she had a First Class Honours degree in classical music, didn't mean she wasn't prepared to stand behind a counter and learn how to use a cash register. Hell, she'd even try her hand at pulling pints if someone would have her. But it seemed no one was hiring right now. They'd all taken on extra staff for the Christmas period but now that was over, if anything, they were cutting back.

Which is why she felt she had no other option but to put herself out here for passers-by to take pity on. Her hands shaking—she'd never done anything illegal before in her life but couldn't afford the time or money it would take to get a busker's permit—she bent down and released the clasps on her violin case.

'I'm sorry,' she whispered as she tenderly picked it and the bow up out of its case. It felt like sacrilege to be playing her prized instrument on a dirty London street with the overcast sky frowning down at them, but the second she lifted it up and put her chin on the chin rest, she began to relax. She positioned her fingers on the strings, took a deep breath and launched into Tchaikovsky's Violin Concerto in D major.

Before long a small crowd had gathered around her and people were tossing money in her case at a pleasing rate. She smiled her thanks as the coins dropped and clinked against each other, thinking that perhaps she'd go out and splurge on a baby name book when she was done. And something delicious to eat. If she *was* pregnant, she needed to keep her strength up. She was so distracted by these thoughts and the actual glee of playing for an audience again that she almost didn't hear the shout from one of the onlookers.

'Pigs are coming!'

Her fingers faltered on the strings, as she wondered what farm animals were doing in central London, and then it clicked. *Police.* How the person guessed she didn't have a busker's permit she had no clue, but she called out her thanks as she shoved her violin and bow back into the case and fumbled to get it shut. A coin lodged in one of the clasps and a cold sweat erupted on the back of her neck as the crowd dispersed.

A menacing figure dressed in the Met's navy blue approached from about twenty metres away. Clutching her not-quite-shut case under her arm, Abigail launched into a run. She didn't know where she was headed, just that she needed to get away.

'Oi, Miss!' The policeman's angry voice followed her and she upped her speed as if she were running from a rabid dog. *No Abigail, nothing like that. Just the law.* Good Lord, what had become of her? She ran until her legs burned, her clothes were soaked through from an inconvenient downpour and she felt certain she'd lost her pursuer. And then she found an empty bus shelter and slumped down onto the bench. Her heart rate took a good ten minutes to return to normal and about the same time her body stopped shaking. She took a breath—wished she'd thought to pack a bottle of water—and then looked around, trying to work out where exactly she'd run to.

Just as she determined she was at least three or four Tube stations away from her flat, her phone pinged, alerting her to a Facebook message. Not ready yet to emerge from her hideaway and happy for a distraction, she pulled it out of her jacket pocket and glanced down at the screen.

Nigel. A warm flush came over her drenched body as she slid her finger along to unlock her phone and read the message. It had been four days since they'd parted ways at Heathrow and she'd pretty much given up hope of him contacting her. He'd been on her mind a lot because of the baby possibility but she'd told herself maybe it was a good thing he'd been silent.

Hey, how you doing? Hope you're all recovered from jet lag. Not sure if you're keen or not, but my boss has a daughter who's been learning the violin and her teacher just quit. I told him I might know someone. She's a bit of a brat if I'm honest, but she goes to a posh girls' school and might have friends who are also interested.

Hell yes, she was interested. If they went to a posh girls' school she could charge appropriately. *Thanks. I'm well,* she replied, *and most definitely interested in an intro to your boss and his delightful daughter.*

His reply was instant. *Great, but that wasn't the only reason I messaged. I have the ulterior motive of wanting to catch up. Interested?*

Abigail bit her lip. Catch up? Was that a euphemism for shag each other silly and then part ways again? And did she care if it was? That's what they'd agreed to after all. *Sure. When?*

Is tonight too soon?

The way she felt at that moment tonight wasn't soon enough. It would be good not to spend the evening hiding away in her room, trying to avoid Pamela and Sam. *Sounds good. Where shall we meet?*

Want to come to my place?

Abigail answered in the affirmative, happy that he hadn't suggested coming to her. She was curious about seeing where he lived. He sent her an address in Hackney and told her not to worry about dinner.

Somewhat buoyed by the exchange, Abigail opened her violin case, removed the stuck coin, closed it again and then went to catch the Tube home.

From the street, Nigel's apartment wasn't much to look at. It was one of those old, dirty brown brick buildings that went the length of the block and had white doors and windows every few metres, but the cars parked along the street indicated the residents were comfortable. Her hand shaking ever so slightly, Abigail raised the black steel knocker and made her presence known. Within seconds she heard the sound of hurried footsteps and straightened as the door swung open.

Nigel stood before her, wearing low-slung faded jeans, a plain black t-shirt and no shoes. Her breath caught in her throat. She'd forgotten how downright sexy he was and the bare feet thing made her think of home, which was comforting after the day she'd had.

'Hey,' he grinned, then leaned forward and kissed her on the cheek. 'I'm glad you found me.'

She smiled back, her nerves evaporating at his easy way. 'Me too.'

He stepped back a little and gestured into the house. 'Coming in?'

'Yep.' She nodded and stepped past him, catching a whiff of some divine male cologne as she did so. 'What is that smell?'

'You don't like it?' Nigel shut the door behind them.

'On the contrary. I like it very much.' So much it made her want to launch herself at him. That's why she was here, right? To have mad, no-strings attached, monkey sex. She squeezed her thighs together at the thought.

'Good. It's a sample from a client. We're putting together a bid for their next big campaign.' Nigel reached towards her and she sucked in a breath as his hands landed on her waist. 'Can I take your coat?'

'Yes.' A delicious fizz rushed through her as he unzipped her black waterproof jacket and gently eased it back and over her shoulders. Considering it was the middle of a freezing London winter, she had plenty more layers beneath, but this small gesture felt like a prelude to what was to come. She couldn't get there fast enough.

He turned and hung her jacket on a hook by the door and she noticed two more hanging alongside it.

'Do you live with anyone else?' she asked, wondering why the thought hadn't crossed her mind.

He nodded. 'Yes, but Chad—an American—is barely ever here. He travels a lot for work, so we've got the place all to ourselves tonight.'

'Good.' She smiled at him in a way that could not be misconstrued and in reply, he took hold of her hand and led her down the narrow hallway into the living room. It had a bright and airy feel considering outside it was already pitch black and drizzling again. An old-fashioned fire roared in the corner and stark-white, plump couches were angled towards it. A few black throw cushions adorned the couches, bookshelves lined one wall and the others held black-and-white photos of international landmarks.

'Those are Chad's photos,' Nigel informed her. 'He's a travel photographer. This is his place.'

'Uh huh.' Truth was she didn't give two hoots about the décor of Nigel's pad or who owned it.

'Can I get you a glass of wine?'

Abigail almost said yes, thinking that perhaps they could both do with a little Dutch courage to follow through on what had seemed like a very good idea when they were together in Hong Kong airport. And then she remembered that alcohol might not be a good idea. But she'd led Nigel to believe she was on the pill, so she couldn't exactly tell him she might be pregnant with his baby. 'I'll just have a glass of water if that's okay. I've got a bit of a headache.'

'You should have said.' Yet Nigel didn't look annoyed, he looked concerned. 'Can I get you some painkillers? Do you need something to eat?'

She thought maybe he needed to work on his playboy—by definition fuck buddies didn't play Florence Nightingale to one another—but his genuine concern warmed her heart. It only made him all the more attractive and she realised, if she was pregnant, that this might be her last chance to do something so reckless.

Considering he'd been the best sex of her life so far, she wanted this last hurrah.

'No, thank you. What I need,' she said, taking a daring step towards him, 'is for you to help me forget about my crap day. Any ideas on how you might do that?'

His lips curled into a wicked grin. *Much better*, she thought, as he closed the gap between them and yanked her against him. His mouth captured hers and his hands slid around her back and under her shirt. She felt the hard length of his cock against her belly. Part of her wanted to take it slower this time, to truly languish in the experience, but the other half overruled. Their tongues entwined and she pulled at his t-shirt, their mouths parting only long enough for her to get it over his head.

She palmed her hands against his hard, hot chest, loving the feel of him. He had a perfect splattering of blond hair and she followed the trail downwards, boldly sliding her hand into his jeans, groaning as her fingers closed around her heart's desire.

'Fuck me, Abigail,' he hissed, tearing at the buttons on her cardigan. It was a recent, expensive purchase from her favourite boutique and she heard two buttons pop off and fly to who knows where. She didn't care. She wanted them both naked. Yesterday.

'Hurry,' she whispered as Nigel removed the rest of her clothing and then shucked his own jeans and jocks.

He pulled them down onto the rug in front of the fire, his hands roving over her breasts and then, 'Oh *God*,' lower. Already hot and desperate, she almost couldn't bear it as he slid two fingers inside her. She gripped his shoulders, clinging to him for support as he worked her into even more of a state. She couldn't recall ever feeling this good in her life and her fears that maybe their second time together wouldn't be as mind-blowing vanished.

Just before her orgasm hit, she pushed him off, rolled him over and climbed on top. His fingers were magic but she wanted his cock inside her and she couldn't wait a second longer. As she sank down onto his hard length, he thrust upwards and his eyes stayed open, watching her intently as they rode the wave and then crashed together.

'That was …' Nigel didn't seem able to define it as she lay on top of him, her head resting on his chest as she tried to catch her breath.

'I know,' she panted.

Silence reigned for a few more long moments. And then Nigel said, 'We didn't use a condom again.'

'I promise I'm safe,' Abigail lied. It might have been the truth. If she were already carrying his baby, she could hardly get pregnant again.

Nigel chuckled and ran his fingers up through her hair. He clasped the back of her head and drew it toward him, kissing her hard. As his tongue touched hers, desire stirred again. He did things to her, made her feel and want things that no man had ever managed before. Maybe it was the newness of their situation, the naughtiness. Either way, she couldn't complain about feeling *this* good.

'So what was so bad about your day?' he asked, still holding her against him.

Abigail wasn't sure fuck buddies were supposed to get into detailed discussions about shitty days but she found herself confiding in him. She cringed as she told him about her busking debacle but he didn't laugh or make her feel stupid.

'It sounds like you could do with some pizza,' he said, when she'd finally finished. 'How's that head now?'

'Much better. And pizza sounds just about perfect.'

Deciding there were no rules to follow and they were adults and could work their situation however they wanted, Abigail cleaned up while Nigel ordered pizza. Once again, as it had at the airport, conversation flowed between them. As they shared their histories—discovering they'd been in London about the same length of time and that Nigel also had three older sisters—Abigail couldn't help thinking about what her life would be like if she was pregnant.

Would she tell him? Would he want to be involved? Would he tell his family? He might be angry at first, but despite his declaration that his career came first, she couldn't imagine him turning his back on a baby. Of course that might put paid to her moving back home, so maybe it would be better for everyone if he didn't know.

'I guess I'd better be going,' she said reluctantly after devouring three slices of pizza.

'I'll call you a cab.' Nigel pushed himself off the floor, where they'd been sitting while they ate and talked.

'No,' she argued, thinking that even the fare from here to her place would break her budget.

As if reading her mind, Nigel said, 'I'm paying and there's no arguments.'

She didn't really want to tackle the Tube this late at night—where she'd either freeze to death or have to put up with some drunken lout—so she relented. 'Thank you.'

Nigel helped her into her coat, zipped it up like she were a little girl and then kissed her again in a way that said she was most definitely not. Pleasant shivers skittered down her spine. 'I'll see you soon,' he said, not making any commitments about when as he opened the front door and then slipped a fifty pound note into her hand.

She frowned down at the note, feeling uneasy about taking his money after what they'd just done. As if reading her mind, he squeezed her hand. 'If it makes you feel better you can consider it a loan, but no way am I letting you take public transport at this time of night.' Then he dipped his head and kissed her again.

A black cab was already waiting a few metres away, its bright headlights piercing the dark. 'Thank you,' she whispered as she turned and ran out into the night.

Chapter Eighteen

Madeleine waited at the entrance of a little café not far from the hospital, glancing furtively at all the tables and wondering if the man she was about to meet was already sitting there. She pulled out her phone, clicked a few buttons and brought up his photo on her screen. Although the café was rapidly filling up with people coming from work to an early dinner, she was certain her guy wasn't here yet.

She sighed and decided to sit anyway. As she pulled out a seat at a table by the window, she silently prayed—something she didn't do often—that this man would be the one. Since returning from Australia two weeks ago, her life had been consumed with two things; work and her baby project. She was quite happy with this status quo but only wished things could happen a little faster. After signing up for the known donor website, she'd spent countless hours scrolling through possible biological fathers for her child. Using her detailed checklist, she'd narrowed down her options to a top five, all of whom lived in Maryland.

She had exchanged emails with all five men and from their correspondence, quickly ruled out a further three. Now it was time to assess the final two in person and hopefully make a decision so they could start trying in a couple of weeks. Although Madeleine knew women should ideally be taking folate supplements for at least three months before trying to conceive, she already ate a balanced diet and exercised regularly so felt confident in her body and health.

'Hello? Are you Madeleine?'

She looked up at the unfamiliar voice and took a couple of seconds to recognise the speaker as Potential Donor Number One. To say he looked different to his profile picture would be a gross understatement.

'Um, yes, hi,' she said, standing and offering out her hand, trying but failing miserably not to stare at the pink and blue streaks in his jet-black hair. In his photo, he'd been wearing a business suit; today he wore oil-streaked jeans and a torn leather jacket. And a weird smell was coming off him. 'And you must be …'

'Ross. Ross Clark.' He shook her hand so hard it hurt and then sat down in the seat opposite her. 'Pleased to meet you.'

'Yes.' She pursed her lips together, not quite able to say the same. First impressions didn't instil her with a whole lot of confidence.

They smiled at each other awkwardly across the table and then Ross joked, 'Maybe we should have met in a bar. That way we could have a drink to settle the nerves.'

'Shall I order us some coffee?' she asked, telling herself she needed to give this a proper chance. So, he had blue and pink hair and he'd gotten a nose ring since the photo, but that stuff was superficial.

'Good plan.'

Madeleine summoned a waitress, ordered their drinks and then turned back to Ross, trying to work out how to start their conversation. It felt oddly like a first date, except a) Ross wasn't her type, b) they had more important things to talk about than favourite movies, food and football teams and c) they'd already exchanged so many emails over the past week that she felt like they knew each other very well. At least, she had until she'd met him in person. He certainly didn't look like the lawyer he claimed to be.

'I must admit, I was a little bit nervous about meeting you,' Ross said, tapping his long fingernails on the tabletop. They matched his hair, alternating pink and blue nail polish. 'It's like I'm in some job interview or something. But it also feels like meeting up with a long-lost friend. How's your sister by the way?'

'Huh?'

'Lucinda.'

'Oh, right.' Madeleine nodded, remembering how in her first email she'd mentioned her younger sister was also trying to get pregnant. As it happened, she and Luce had had a lengthy conversation the other day—quite unusual for them—and she'd been pleased to hear Lucinda and Joe were going to see her friend in Perth about their fertility issues. 'She's good, thanks.'

'Excellent. So have you told her what we're doing?'

Madeleine blinked, wondering for a moment what he was talking about. 'Oh.' She shook her head. 'No, I've only told a couple of close friends. What about you?'

'Sure.' Ross beamed. 'I've told everyone I know. They can't wait to meet our baby.'

Madeleine's heart went cold. Alarm bells rang loud and clear inside her head. She made a funny noise in her throat. 'Um, Ross, that wouldn't be the agreement. We've already talked this through. You'd be a legal donor, that's it. We'd have an agreement drawn up, you'd bring me sperm at the right time of the month and then if it worked, we'd never see each other again. Well, not until the child was of legal age and could look for you—if that's what he or she desired.'

Ross frowned, reached across the table and took her hand. A shudder of revulsion shot through her as his thumb rubbed slowly against the tender skin of her wrist. 'I would come to you when the time was right and we would make love to conceive the child. I believe all children should be conceived in love.'

Madeleine blinked and yanked back her hand. Who was this nutter? Was this some kind of cruel joke? 'No, Ross, that was never on the agenda. I barely know you and I certainly don't love you.' The thought of 'making love' with him made her skin crawl.

At that moment the waitress arrived with their coffee and Ross suddenly burst into tears. The waitress looked at Madeleine like she murdered puppies in her spare time and other patrons in the café began to glance over at them as well. Another woman might have felt sympathy for the snivelling punk in front of her, but Madeleine only felt anger, frustration and annoyance that he'd wasted her time. She pulled out her purse, slapped a ten-dollar note on the table, then stood and stormed out of the café into the rain.

'Well, that was a total and utter waste of time.' She cursed under her breath as she opened her umbrella and then stalked down the sidewalk to the restaurant where she'd agreed to meet Hugo and Celia for dinner. The minute she got there she would get out her phone and report Ross Clark for breaching the terms and conditions of the known donor website. The man was a lunatic if ever she'd met one.

As Madeleine sat at the bar of one of the finest restaurants in Baltimore waiting for her friends to arrive, she eyed the row of bottles on the wall and almost succumbed to the urge to order a stiff drink. If Potential Donor Number Two was as dire as Potential Donor Number One had been, then it might be a while before she got to the sperm-meets-egg stage of the process. What harm would one little drink do?

'Evening,' the smartly dressed barman smiled at her. 'What can I get for you?'

She opened her mouth to ask for a vodka tonic, but changed her mind at the last second. 'Just a club soda, please,' she said instead, deciding that Madeleine Patterson wasn't the type to let one little setback keep her down. She wanted this baby more than anything and she wasn't going to let the likes of Ross Clark stop her.

Still, despite her bravado, when Hugo walked in, he took one look at her, cocked his head to the side and said, 'Disaster?'

She sighed as he leaned forward and gave her a quick hug. 'That is the understatement of the century.'

'Let me order a drink and then you can tell Uncle Hugo all about it,' he said as he took the stool beside her.

She tried to laugh at his words, but it didn't quite come out that way. Why couldn't she find a donor like Hugo? Someone who was smart, intelligent, not crazy and also just happened to be incredibly good-looking. She stared at his profile as he made small talk with the barman and couldn't help but imagine what her baby would look like if he were the father. He ticked all her boxes, except for one thing…

'Where's Celia?' she asked.

Hugo thanked the barman for his beer and then turned back to Madeleine. 'She just messaged to say she's running late and that we should go ahead and order without her. Apparently she got held up in surgery this afternoon.'

'Oh, okay.' Celia was a paediatric otolaryngologist, and often dealt with the ear, nose and throat problems of the children that Hugo and Madeleine had brought into the world.

Before Madeleine could say anymore, the maître d' approached them. 'Your table is ready, or would you prefer to wait for the third member of your party.'

Hugo shook his head and stood. 'No, unfortunately, she's running late.' He looked back to Madeleine and smiled, then gestured that she should go ahead.

She slipped off her stool, picked up her handbag (she'd never get used to saying 'purse' as they called it in the States) and the half-finished glass of club soda, then smiled at the maître d' as he led them to their table. Hugo gently pressed his hand against the small of her back as she passed him. It was such a simple, innocent gesture—he was only being a gentleman—but Madeleine's emotions were wreaking havoc with her body. A tingling shot up her spine from where he'd touched her and quickly spread all over.

They arrived at their table, a lovely private spot with views overlooking Inner Harbor, which shone and sparkled with the lights of boats and buildings on the other side of the Patapsco River. It still took her breath away every time she looked at it. The maître d' pulled back Madeleine's chair and once she'd sat, he shook open a napkin and laid it across her lap.

'Your waiter for the evening will be Hans and he'll be here with the menus in a moment, but can I get you something to drink to start with?' he asked, smiling first at Madeleine and then at Hugo.

'Shall we order a bottle of wine?' Hugo asked, opening the drinks menu.

Madeleine shook her head and tapped the side of her glass. 'I'm sticking to soda.'

'Right, I forgot.' He closed the menu. 'Maybe I'll wait and see what Celia wants.'

Madeleine looked up at the maître d'. 'Can I get a refill, please?'

'Of course.' The maître d' bowed his head and then took the drinks menu from Hugo. 'Hans will be with you in a moment.'

'Thanks,' Hugo and Madeleine said at the same time as he turned to walk away.

'So what happened?' Hugo asked, leaning back in his seat.

'I'm not sure I want to talk about it.' Madeleine sulked.

'Okay, whatever you want.' He nodded. 'You'll never guess who I ran into at the hospital this afternoon?'

But of course Madeleine could no more keep her disastrous meeting with Ross to herself, any more than she could her initial plan to have a baby. 'Oh, Hugo, he was awful,' she confessed, taking a sip of her soda and pretending it was champagne.

And then her sorry story spilled from her lips.

'Maybe the next guy will be better?' Hugo offered encouragingly once Madeleine had finished.

'Maybe.' She frowned. 'But he was top of my list. I was hoping I wouldn't have to get to Potential Donor Number Two.'

'Hey folks, sorry I'm late. What have I missed?' Celia landed beside them, her face radiant and her jet-black hair immaculately straight and hanging down her back. Heads throughout the restaurant turned to look at her as she unwrapped herself from her winter coat. Madeleine felt certain she never looked so amazing when she'd just emerged from a stressful surgical situation. It would be easy to hate Celia if she wasn't so damn nice.

Hugo leapt up, took her pale pink coat and then kissed her on the cheek and Madeleine felt a stab in her heart. Usually she managed to ignore her feelings for Hugo, but today, in her highly charged, extra-emotional state, it was an effort.

Hugo held out Celia's seat but before she sat she leaned across and air-kissed Madeleine's cheek. 'How are you, darling? Feels like forever since we caught up, although Hugo's kept me up-to-date.' She raised her eyebrows as she lowered herself into her chair. 'I must say I'm surprised but intrigued by your venture. How was your meeting tonight?'

Madeleine rolled her eyes and was halfway through rehashing the story when their waiter arrived.

'Good evening.' He grinned as he placed a gold embossed menu down in front of each of them. 'I'm Hans and I will be serving you this evening. Would you like me to run through the chef's specials?'

The three of them looked up and nodded, although Madeleine was in no mood for eating anything. Celia ordered the lobster bisque and Hugo the pan-roasted dorade. They both requested the suggested wine accompaniments and then Hans looked to Madeleine for her decision.

She scanned the menu once again. 'I'll have the baby spinach and frisée salad, please. No wine.'

Celia tsked. 'You'll have to eat more than that if you get pregnant.' She'd always been one of those women who could eat heartily and still imitate a beanpole. There was literally *nothing* not perfect about her.

'I'll worry about that when I'm actually pregnant,' Madeleine replied, perhaps a little too tersely. 'But I have a major hurdle to get over first.'

'Hmm?' Celia sighed and flicked her hair over her shoulders. 'I'm still struggling with why you would actually want to do this. Are you sure you know what you're getting yourself into?'

'Celia,' Hugo warned, reaching over and placing a hand on his long-time girlfriend's knee. 'This is Madeleine's decision.'

She gave him a look. 'I know and part of me thinks it's great— if she wants to have a baby, then why should she wait around for Mr Right? But—' she looked back to Madeleine '—I never saw you as the motherly type. What brought this on?'

Madeleine swallowed, inwardly thinking about the Patterson curse. Although she didn't believe there was any truth in such things, finding out about the curse had affected her more than she was willing to admit and she very much wanted to prove it rubbish.

Of course she couldn't tell her friends this—they were liable to laugh in her face, think she was joking and then, when they realised she was serious, start questioning her sanity. Besides, it wasn't just the curse. It went much deeper than that—to a yearning she'd been trying to ignore for years.

'My sister Lucinda and her husband are trying for a baby. Being back home, talking with her and also seeing the children of some of my old schoolfriends, made me realise I'm not getting any younger. I never consciously decided not to have children, but work always came first and I guess I always imagined that when I met Mr Right, I'd think about a family then. But I'm thirty-five years old and Mr Right is nowhere in sight.'

'So do you think you might go the anonymous donor route instead now?' Hugo asked.

She sighed. Initially the sperm bank option had seemed too cold, clinical and calculated, but if Ross Clark was an indication of the options on the known donor site, maybe an anonymous donor would be the best idea. At least then she wouldn't *know* if her baby's father was a lunatic. But that thought didn't sit well either.

'I don't know.' Madeleine ran her fingers through her hair in frustration as the waiter arrived with Hugo and Celia's drinks. She eyed them jealously. 'Let's talk about something else. Why were you delayed in surgery?'

Celia puffed out air between her lips. 'You'd think a tonsillectomy would be simple, right?' She launched into a description about her hellish afternoon in which her five-year-old patient had suffered an extreme reaction to the anaesthesia.

'Oh shit.'

Hugo and Madeleine offered their sympathies, having both experienced equally traumatic situations. They exchanged stories of operations gone wrong, both fascinated and horrified by the memories in a way that only other doctors could understand. When their meals arrived, talk continued in this vein, for which Madeleine was thankful. Although finding a donor had been her focus the last two weeks, she didn't want to lament on her disappointment all evening.

She thought her friends had all but forgotten her donor woes when Celia interrupted Hugo in the middle of a graphic description of one of his patients who'd haemorrhaged badly during a VBAC.

'I've got it,' she shrieked, as if she'd suddenly had a premonition of the winning lottery numbers.

'What?' Madeleine and Hugo asked at the same time.

Celia grinned, her eyes lighting up her whole face. She pointed between herself and Hugo. 'We're not planning on having children. Golly, I could never do that whole pregnancy and birth thing and I'd go insane if I had to take more than a week off work, but I must admit it'd be a pity to waste these good genes.' She leaned over and pinched Hugo's cheeks like he was a chubby little baby. He didn't look impressed. 'Hugo can be your sperm donor!'

Hugo dropped his fork and knocked over his wine glass. His mouth fell open.

Madeleine froze, shock paralysing her at Celia's candid suggestion.

'Don't look so appalled, you two.' Celia waved her index finger at them as if they were a couple of naughty children.

Madeleine felt drops of Hugo's wine dripping over the table and making a cold, wet patch on her favourite white trousers, but still she couldn't move. Hugo looked as frozen as her but Celia barrelled on. 'It's the perfect solution. He's good-looking, intelligent, funny, in good health, fit—' she went on and on listing all the reasons Madeleine had already thought of '—and best of all, he's available right now. And, you won't have to go through any more awkward pseudo dates trying to find the right candidate. You can just get straight to the fun part.'

Madeleine gulped. *Fun part?* Images of her and Hugo in bed, their limbs entwined in the throes of passion landed unbidden in her head. Her cheeks flushed. 'Actual conception would be done via turkey baster method,' she said, only just managing to choke the words out.

Celia laughed. 'By fun, I meant the morning sickness, swollen ankles and horrific food cravings.'

'Oh, right.' Her heart rate slowed a little but she couldn't bring herself to look at Hugo.

'So what do you think?' Celia asked, all but bouncing in her seat.

Madeleine braved a glance, hope sparking within her that he might share Celia's enthusiasm but Hugo looked as if he'd lost the power of speech. She honestly didn't know what to say. She couldn't tell the truth—that part of her loved the idea, that if Celia hadn't been in the picture she might have summoned the courage to ask him herself, that if he'd been the one to suggest it … she'd have done a celebratory jig around the restaurant.

'Really … can one of you just say something?' Celia picked up her glass of wine. 'You'd think I'd suggested a threesome or something.'

Hugo made a spluttering noise as if he were suffocating. Madeleine understood how he felt.

She would kill for a glass of wine now, anything to help her cope with this awkward situation. 'I understand what you're saying, Celia, but even if Hugo was willing, I wouldn't want to compromise our friendship and—'

Celia waved a hand in the air. 'We're all grown-ups. Nothing would be compromised. I have a very good lawyer friend who I'm sure would be happy to draw up contracts between you. He loves interesting cases such as this.'

'Celia, leave it.' Hugo rarely raised his voice or spoke sternly and Madeleine found it inappropriately sexy. 'Madeleine has already made her decision.'

'Fine. I was only trying to help.' Celia looked to Madeleine. 'You know that, right?'

She nodded and smiled at her friend, hoping her disappointment didn't show on her face. 'I appreciate the sentiment.' She took another sip of her club soda but it just didn't cut it. Ross Clark had ruined the evening and it had gone downhill from there. 'If you don't mind, I'm going to head home. It's been a long, disappointing day and I'm tired.'

'Of course.' Hugo stood to help Madeleine out of her chair and gave her a quick peck on the cheek but he wouldn't look her in the eye. She felt as if she owed him an apology, but she hadn't suggested this crazy idea. 'I'll see you at work.'

'Good night.' Madeleine smiled at Hugo and then at Celia. 'Hope you have a less stressful day tomorrow.'

'Thanks.' Celia wiggled her fingers in a wave. 'Keep us posted on Potential Donor Number Two. Fingers crossed.'

'Will do. See ya.' Madeleine all but stalked out of the restaurant, feeling a maelstrom of emotions as she hailed a cab in the rain. Would Celia and Hugo have words now that she'd gone? They'd always seemed so perfect but she guessed they must have disagreements behind closed doors. Didn't all couples?

Madeleine slid into the back seat of a cab, rattled off the address of her apartment in Towson and then sighed as she remembered the day she'd met Hugo. Fresh from Australia, she'd been excited about starting work at St Joe's and Hugo had been one of the first people she'd met on the maternity ward. He'd been so welcoming, offering to show her round and introduce her to everyone, telling her to come to him if she needed anything. Tongue-tied is what she'd been, totally blown away by his gorgeous Boston accent and sunny smile. Not to mention his handsome looks; her whole body had quivered with awareness when he'd shaken her hand.

She'd noticed he wore no ring on his finger and hoped that was a sign he didn't have a significant other. So many times she'd almost asked one of the nurses, but she hadn't wanted to give away her little crush. Then, a week after she'd arrived, he invited her for drinks after work on a Friday night. 'A whole bunch of us from the hospital go.' The group thing meant it wasn't a date, she got that, but she couldn't help hoping that maybe something would grow from the opportunity to see him outside of work. Surely the fact he'd asked her meant something. Unable to remember the last time she'd gotten excited about a man, she'd made an effort to change her outfit and reapply her makeup before walking the short distance to the bar.

Her head held high, nervous anticipation thrumming through her veins, she'd pushed open the door, walked inside and scanned the crowded venue. As Hugo stood a good head above most people, it took all of two seconds to locate him and in that moment, she felt as if someone had punched her in the gut. She actually stumbled backwards, ridiculous nausea rearing in her stomach at the sight of Hugo with his arm wrapped around the most stunning woman she had ever laid eyes on. She was living that old Alanis Morissette song—like meeting the man of your dreams and then meeting his beautiful wife.

Of course someone like him would be attached. It had been stupid to imagine otherwise, but the last thing she wanted was to stand around making small talk with the woman who'd just broken her heart. She'd almost managed to escape, but Hugo had seen her just as she was slipping back outside. He'd run after her into the bustling Baltimore street and although she'd tried to make some excuse about not feeling well, he'd refused to take no for an answer. He'd linked his arm through hers and led her back into the bar, where she met a number of other people who worked on other wards of the hospital. Including Celia Jameson, his fiancée.

Madeleine should have distanced herself then, but Celia had been as warm and welcoming as Hugo. The two of them sort of adopted her, always inviting her to things and making sure the Aussie didn't have any free time to miss home. As much as Madeleine wanted to hate Celia for being engaged to the man of her dreams, she couldn't. Celia and Hugo had become good friends over the past three years—her best friends—and she'd learnt to ignore, or at least handle, her attraction to him.

Chapter Nineteen

As promised, the day he got back from Darwin, Mitch turned up at the motel and reported for duty.

'Let me guess,' he said as he swaggered into reception, where Charlie had just finished welcoming two new guests. Wearing cut-off cargo shorts that made her more aware of his tanned, muscular thighs than she cared to be, another one of his silly t-shirts and a scruffy Adelaide Crows cap on his head, he leaned back against the reception counter and made a theatrical show of glancing around. Using his hands to assist, he said, 'Fire engine red for the walls, canary yellow for the ceilings and maybe the odd feature in ocean blue.'

She rolled her eyes but couldn't stifle a laugh. 'Thank God you're not an interior decorator.'

He feigned offence and crossed his arms. 'What's wrong with red, yellow and blue?'

'Nothing, if you're renovating a kindergarten.'

'Okay smart-arse, what colours are you thinking?'

Excited to be able to fill him in on all the plans she'd made while he'd been up north, Charlie grabbed a folder off the desk.

Most of her decisions had been made late at night, because during the day she'd been run off her feet with all the general motel jobs. How Dad and Mrs Sampson had ever managed on their own she didn't know.

'This,' she told him, gesturing to a soft off-white colour and then to a shade called *eggplant*, 'and this for the feature walls.' Although one of the design websites she'd looked at had insisted feature walls were a thing of the past, she believed they'd work in the motel rooms, where the rest of the furniture would still be plain.

Mitch shrugged. 'Whatever takes your fancy.' But then he grinned. 'And you're the boss. When do we start?'

She'd never been the boss of anything in her life and she didn't know when she was supposed to fit in painting between all the other tasks but she also couldn't wait to get the makeover under-way. And what kind of fool would turn away free labour? 'How about right now? Can you take me to the hardware store to collect the paint and stuff?'

'Does "stuff" include stopping in at Rosie's for a slice of carrot cake?'

Charlie glanced at the time on the computer screen: a quarter past two. She'd already checked in the last of today's arrivals and Dad was in the office doing paperwork, so she could probably spare half an hour. Her tastebuds all but moaned at the thought of Rosie's famous carrot cake. It was the one of the few foods she and Mitch agreed on. That and Golden North Giant Twin bars.

'I guess it can,' she said, picking up her bag. 'I'll just go tell Dad what's going on.'

On reflection, stopping at Rosie Jean's Country Kitchen was perhaps not the smartest idea. Within twenty seconds of Mitch and Charlie walking in the door, she was swamped with greetings and questions from locals. Snowed under at the motel the last few days, she'd barely been anywhere aside from a quick trip to the general store for some personal hygiene products, but apparently her return to town qualified as this week's big news.

'I heard you were back,' said Janie Lee, president of the local Country Women's Association and the third person to accost Charlie as she headed for the counter. Janie and her husband had retired from the family farm a few years back but unlike many others in the region, they hadn't gone farther afield to greener pastures, choosing instead to buy a house in town. Secretly Charlie thought it was probably because Janie couldn't bear the idea of living too far from her sons and she felt a little sorry for the daughters-in-law, one of whom had been in the same year at school as she and Mitch. 'Your father must be over the moon.'

Charlie smiled at the older woman. 'I hope so.' He'd started to smile more in the last few days and appeared to be sleeping better now that he didn't have to get up at the crack of dawn every day. Still, although she'd sent an email to her sisters telling them all this earlier that day, she wasn't about to share their private business with Janie Lee, known to be the local busybody for very good reason.

Mitch's hand came down on Charlie's arm as he tossed Janie one of his practiced grins—the kind that made both little girls and adult women swoon. 'We're in a bit of a hurry, Mrs Lee. Charlie has some fab ideas about renovating the motel and after cake, we're off to get paint.'

'Ooh.' Her eyes lit up and without another word to Charlie or Mitch she bustled off to the other side of the café, plonked her ample-sized behind down on a seat and leant forward to share the gossip with her fellow old biddies.

'Phew, that was a close one,' Mitch hissed as he let go of her arm and started towards the display cabinet laid out with Rosie's home-baked country goodies. They both knew Janie had been hoping for news of her dad, how poor old Brian Patterson the widower was coping without his wife.

'Charlie!'

Almost at the counter, she turned at the sound of her voice and saw Lisa, a girl from her class at school waving from a nearby table.

'Hey, Lisa. How are you going?' she asked, walking over to her.

'Oh, you know.' Lisa gestured to the pram beside her. It was one of those double ones and a plump baby was sitting on one side gnawing on a soggy bread stick. At the table next to Lisa, his mouth smeared with chocolate cake, was the cutest toddler Charlie had ever laid eyes on. She couldn't imagine what life would be like with these two in tow; she could barely manage to organise herself.

'Say no more.' She laughed. 'They're gorgeous.'

'They're monsters,' Lisa replied, but her eyes sparkled, telling Charlie they were her pride and joy. Then she looked past Charlie to Mitch. 'Are you and Mitch back on?'

Charlie blinked, then blushed. 'We were never on in the first place.'

'Oh …' Lisa grabbed a baby wipe out of her bag and started cleaning the toddler. 'Maybe we can catch up some time. I know you're probably run off your feet but if you do get a spare moment, you're welcome to come to my place for a coffee. That's if you don't mind mess.'

'Mum always used to say, "Dull women have immaculate houses," so I'm quite fond of mess.'

A sympathetic smile crossed Lisa's face. 'I was so sorry to hear about Annette. You hear about kids being allergic to bees, but … well, she's left a big hole in this community.'

'Thanks.' Charlie appreciated the genuine tone of Lisa's words. 'I'd love to catch up some time.'

'That's great.' Lisa grinned as she grabbed a serviette from under her coffee mug and found a pen in her bag. She scribbled down her mobile phone number and the address of a farm just outside of town. 'Call me.'

'I will,' Charlie promised, before heading over to Mitch who was now sitting at a table reading the local rag.

'I ordered for you,' he said, giving her a reproachful glare.

She slid onto a seat next to him. 'Not my fault I'm popular.'

He snorted and lifted the paper. 'I'm surprised you're not front page, but you'll be old news by next week, so don't go getting a big head.'

She poked her tongue out at him just as Rosie arrived with two massive portions of carrot cake. 'Thanks, Rosie.' Charlie smiled up at the older woman, who had the drive and enthusiasm of the Energizer Bunny.

'You're welcome, love. Good to see you getting out for a break. Sally Sampson says you'd been working like a Trojan since coming home.'

Bless Mrs Sampson, thought Charlie. As if she could talk. The woman went above and beyond most paid employees, but she guessed she didn't have much else to keep her busy. 'It hasn't been all hard work. I've had fun.'

'I'm glad to hear it. Enjoy your cake,' Rosie said, before heading back into the kitchen.

'And eat it quick.' Mitch picked up his dessert fork and stabbed it into the cream cheese icing. 'Next thing I'll be needing to book an appointment to see you.'

Despite Mitch's faux-grumpiness and Janie Lee's prying, Charlie felt good to be back in a place where everyone knew her and took the time to stop and talk. As much as she loved Melbourne, every-one there always seemed to be in a rush. The slower pace of life in Meadow Brook suited her. Not that she'd truly had the chance to experience it yet with all she wanted and needed to do at the motel, but that was okay—it looked like she might be here for a while.

Smiling, she picked up her own fork and scooped up the first delicious bite. 'Ahh … Now that was worth coming home for.'

Thankfully, the hardware store was mostly frequented by men, who although happy to see Charlie again and make small talk about the motel, didn't try and lure her into lengthy conversation. Bob Tucker, who had owned the shop for as long as Charlie could remember, helped Mitch carry the heavy tins out onto the back of the ute and then wished them well.

'I should possibly give this place a bit of a facelift too,' he said, leaning back against the tray of Mitch's ute and glancing at the fibro and tin building that housed his store. Charlie agreed that a coat of paint would be an improvement, but she wasn't sure if it would really make a difference to Mr Tucker's clientele.

Mitch chuckled as they both climbed into the vehicle. 'Better not do too good a job on the motel or you'll have everyone round here asking for renovation advice.'

Charlie shook her head as she clicked in her seatbelt. 'All I'm doing is a bit of painting.' But then her eyes caught on the display of potted colour on the verandah of Tucker's shop. 'What do you think about refreshing the old garden beds at the front of the motel? They could do with a good weed and you've got to admit they're looking a little tired.'

Mitch tsked. 'Give the girl a bit of power and she goes crazy.'

She shot him a glare. 'I'm only trying to improve things.'

'I'm joking, Charles,' he said as he reversed out their parking spot. 'I think all your ideas are awesome.'

'Thanks.' She relaxed at his words, hoping he was right and she wasn't taking on too much.

It took less than two minutes to drive back to the motel, because in Meadow Brook there was really only one street. At one end there was the motel and Shire buildings and at the other end the industrial area with the hardware store, agricultural supplies and mechanic. In the middle you could find a general store, chemist, post office and a hair salon that was open whenever its owner felt the need.

Dad and Mrs Sampson were outside having a cup of tea in the courtyard when they arrived. 'Good to see your dad relaxing,' Mitch said as they began unloading from the tray.

'It is,' Charlie agreed, but then frowned. 'Although Mrs Sampson was supposed to finish her shift a couple of hours ago.'

'Doesn't look like she's working to me,' Mitch noted, lifting two tins of paint. 'Now, where are we going to store all this stuff?'

Charlie gestured to the storage shed. 'I cleared a spot in there yesterday.'

'Excellent.' A tin in each arm, he started towards the shed. Charlie grabbed the box of other painting supplies and hurried after him.

'You kids want help with that?' Dad called from his position on the picnic bench.

'No way,' Charlie yelled back. It had barely been two weeks since he'd frightened them all half to death by imitating a heart attack. 'Keep him under control, Mrs Sampson.'

The motel's housekeeper laughed. 'I'll do my best.'

And Charlie and Mitch got back to task. Once they'd carried everything they wouldn't need right away to storage, Charlie already felt like she'd done a day's hard labour and she leant against the wall to catch her breath. 'I'm buggered.'

Mitch laughed as he stooped down to grab a bucket and some cloths. 'Toughen up, princess. We've barely started. And I promise you the end result will be worth the effort.'

Pushing aside the thought of how good his butt looked when he bent over, she gave him an evil glare and straightened. 'Why do I get the feeling I might regret letting you help?'

He raised an eyebrow at her. 'Why do I get the feeling you're going to drive me crazy with your moaning and complaining?'

She bent over, picked up a paintbrush and went to whack him with it but he dodged out of her way, laughing as he started towards the motel rooms. 'Which room's up first?' he called over his shoulder.

Jogging to catch up, Charlie overtook him and dug her master key out of her pocket. 'Number fifteen.' It was the one she and Mrs Sampson had agreed was most in need of a makeover and she couldn't wait to paint over the weird looking stains on the walls. Although she wanted to do the bar and restaurant as well, she'd decided to start on a vacant room while she worked out the logistics.

For the next couple of hours, Charlie and Mitch worked like pack horses, prepping the room for its first coat. This included moving the furniture into the middle of the room and covering it with drop cloths, scrubbing down the walls and then using special blue tape to cover up the light switches, cornices and power points. Halfway through, Mitch drove home to get his stereo. When he returned, talking and singing along to their favourite tunes made the time pass quickly. Although you still couldn't see much evidence of their progress, Charlie felt good about what they'd achieved.

At eight o'clock a knock sounded on the door and she looked up to see Dad standing in the doorway, holding two pizza boxes and a sixpack of beer.

'Hey Dad,' she said, putting the paint roller in her hand into its tray. She crossed to the door, kissed him on the cheek and took the boxes. 'You might be my favourite person in the world right now.'

'Oi,' Mitch protested, gesturing to the wall he'd been painting. 'I thought that was me.'

Dad laughed, stepped into the room and put the beer down on the pile of furniture. 'You kids have been working hard. Dinner is the least I could do.'

'Thanks, Brian,' Mitch said, coming over and picking up the sixpack. 'You having one too?'

'No thanks.' Dad shook his head. 'I'm heading off for an early night soon and the doc told me I should cut back on the grog anyway.'

'Harsh, but understandable.' Mitch put the beers back down. Charlie smiled at him, grateful he wasn't going to drink in front of Dad.

'Anyway, enjoy.' Dad nodded towards the boxes of pizza. 'And don't work too hard. Don't want you running yourself ragged, Charlie.'

'I'll look after her,' Mitch promised, sidling close and wrapping and arm around her shoulders.

Despite the fact he was a little sweaty from the hours of hard work, Charlie stilled at his nearness as her belly did a weird fluttery thing. She really had to get a grip on those errant hormones. Extricating herself from his grasp, she said, 'Thanks for your concern boys, but I'm a big girl and I can look after myself.'

Dad took that as his cue to leave. As he turned to go, Charlie opened the first box of pizza. Identifying it as meat lovers, she shoved it towards Mitch and then took the other box and sat down on the floor, leaning against the bed. Mitch joined her a few moments later with two bottles of Coopers Pale Ale. As he cracked them open, Charlie took her first bite of Rob's vegetarian pizza and moaned with pleasure. Back in Melbourne she rarely ate fast food, but she had to admit, this was good.

'Food tastes so much better when you've worked for it,' she said.

'As does beer.' Mitch handed her a bottle.

'Amen to that.' She took a satisfying sip, then alternated more between mouthfuls of pizza and beer.

'You and Lisa looked to be having a good chat today,' Mitch commented.

She nodded. 'Yes, she's still as sweet as she was in high school and her kids are gorgeous. She invited me over for coffee sometime.'

'That's nice. Although pray it's during her kids' naptime. I've seen her boy in action and he's a terror.'

'So she says.' Charlie smiled, unable to imagine those angelic little children causing any trouble. 'Do you catch up with any of the old crew?' She didn't have to tell him she meant the folks they used to hang out with in high school. Unlike her sisters, she'd gone to school in Port Augusta with the other kids from Meadow Brook whose parents weren't rich enough to send them to boarding school. The Pattersons hadn't had that kind of money either, but Madeleine, Lucinda and Abigail had all gone away to school on scholarships.

'Occasionally. Tom and Eric farm their parents' properties now, and since I help Macca out a bit, we often catch up for a celebration after harvest.'

'By celebration, I take it you mean piss-up?'

'You know me too well.' He grinned and then took a mouthful of beer. 'Of course I only go along to keep the others in line.'

'Likely story.' Charlie shook her head. Mitch had always known how to party.

'Maybe we should have some sort of reunion while you're back in town,' he suggested.

She screwed up her nose. The concept of school reunions had always terrified her. All those people spruiking their career and relationship success. 'By the way,' he added, 'Kate and Macca want you to come out for lunch one day. If you can take the time off.'

'Sounds like a plan, but right now, it's time to paint.'

Charlie pushed herself up and collected their rubbish. By the time she came back from delivering it to the bin outside, Mitch was back into it, bopping along to the music as he swept the roller up and down the wall. She could easily have stood there and admired the way his arm muscles bunched beneath the cuff of his t-shirt or the strong, tanned column of his neck, which for some reason she'd never noticed before.

Instead she averted her gaze, crossed the room to her own roller tray and got back to work, reminding herself she was here to help Dad with the motel, not to blur the friendship lines with Mitch.

Chapter Twenty

Abigail perched on the end of the closed toilet seat, her knees bouncing up and down as she stared at the little white stick on the vanity in front of her and waited. It felt like the longest one minute of her life. The instructions said results could sometimes be seen within forty seconds but that they could take up to five minutes, so she planned to wait at least a minute before checking. At thirty seconds, she had to sit on her hands to stop herself from reaching out and holding the test kit, staring at it while she willed two little blue lines to appear. Her mouth was dry and her heart palpitating—it actually felt as if the suspense might kill her—so at sixty-one seconds she leapt off the toilet, snatched up the stick and looked.

No! Her heart slammed into her stomach. Just one little blue line, indicating the test had worked but that she had not hit the jackpot. But … She forced herself to take a breath. There were still three and a half minutes of hope to go. Giving up on trying to think or do anything else, she leaned against the wall, staring at the stick as the seconds ticked down on her mobile phone timer. It seemed to take forever.

Finally her alarm went off and she glared at the stick. No matter how close she brought it to her face or how hard she peered down at it, there was only one distinct blue line. Abigail hurled the test kit into the bathroom wastebasket, cursing and muttering under her breath. Her period wasn't due for another two days but this was an early indicator test and although she'd had sore breasts and been a little nauseous, somehow she knew in her heart she wasn't pregnant, that her mind had conjured up those symptoms.

She kicked her foot against the vanity, remembered she wasn't wearing any shoes and then swore in pain as she collapsed onto the toilet seat again. *Dammit.* She'd been so certain this was it. Her sex education teacher in high school had made it sound like a girl could get pregnant simply by giving a guy a blow job and that unprotected sex was a one-way ticket to motherhood. The unprotected sex she'd had with Nigel in the airport had been so fine, it could probably have blown her all the way back to London. And she'd been smack-bang in the middle of her cycle.

If that kind of sex hadn't managed to get her up the duff, then what would? For one split second the Patterson curse entered her head, but she dismissed it immediately. Her mother hadn't believed it and either did she, no matter how much that freaky old woman gave her the heebie-jeebies.

But whether or not the curse had any bearing, one thing *was* certain. Her get-out-of-London-quick solution had failed. She'd put off calling Nigel's boss about giving his daughter music lessons because she didn't want to muck them around when she had to leave. Yet after two weeks of struggling to make ends meet, her situation was dire and Sam and Pamela wouldn't give her any leeway, so it was time to make that call.

Sighing, she leant forward and scooped her phone off the vanity, swiped it open and then clicked through Nigel's messages, looking for his boss's phone number. Nigel had been busy at work so they hadn't seen each other since that night at his flat but if anyone got hold of their phones, they'd need a bucket of ice over their head to cool down. The text-sex they'd been having was better than actual sex she'd had with anyone else and it suddenly struck her there was an upside to not being pregnant.

I can go back for more.

And this time, she'd be prepared. She'd buy one of those ovulation testing kit things she'd seen at Boots and somehow engineer 'seeing' Nigel a few times during her fertile window. A tiny jab of guilt pricked her heart at the unethical nature of this plan, but she reasoned it away. She might be using Nigel to have a baby, but he'd openly admitted he was using *her* for sex.

Slightly encouraged by that thought, she sent him a quick text. *Hey hot stuff, methinks you're working too hard. Need some help relaxing?*

The good thing about Nigel was that he seemed to be permanently attached to his smart phone and she never had to wait long for a reply. *Why sex kitten? You offering?*

She wrote back telling him exactly what she was offering and they made a date for later that night. Then, she picked the pregnancy test kit out of the wastebasket—she didn't want Sam or Pamela to find it—and took it to the rubbish bin to dispose of.

It was time to make some phone calls.

Within half an hour, she'd made contact with Nigel's boss, Daniel, and agreed to meet him and his daughter Livia that afternoon at their house in Chelsea for the first lesson.

Chapter Twenty-one

Lucinda had managed to avoid a Mannolini Christmas, so she knew there was no way she'd get out of the annual Australia Day barbeque at Joe's parents' place. She took a deep breath and clutched the bottle of wine on her lap as Joe turned their Nissan Pathfinder into the driveway of his parents' house in Gooseberry Hill. It was a gift for his dad as the national day of celebration coincided with his birthday, but Lucinda already longed for a drink herself.

If anyone could drive her to drink it was Joe's mother, but, wanting to be in immaculate health when they went to the specialist, she hadn't had a drop of alcohol since she'd come home from Meadow Brook.

Joe turned the key in the ignition, silencing the engine. 'You okay?' he asked, reaching out and brushing his thumb across her cheek.

She nodded and gave him a grateful smile. He'd been so caring and attentive since her near-meltdown in the Indian restaurant and had even started to eat better and reduce his alcohol intake as well. Not that he'd ever been a big drinker, but like most men he

211

enjoyed a beer or two at the end of the day. Even so, he'd given this up since their appointment with Dr Slater.

They climbed out of the car and even before they'd started up the path to the house, they were ambushed by a troop of children brandishing water guns.

'Got ya, Aunty Luce,' squealed Emil, one of Joe's nephews.

Lucinda laughed as a squirt of water landed in the centre of her back. She spun around and glared at four of her nieces and nephews lined up behind her.

'Hey!' Joe yelled as they aimed and fired at him. Then he thrust the car keys and his wallet at Lucinda. 'Get out of the way,' he hissed as he raced off towards the house.

'Where's Uncle Joe going?' asked little Isabella, who did a great job of keeping up with her older cousins and siblings.

'I don't know.' Lucinda shrugged, although she secretly had her suspicions and tried to distract them. 'What have you guys been up to these school holidays?'

'We saw *Submarines in Space* at the movies yesterday,' shouted Emil.

Why could little boys never just speak at a normal level?

'Yeah, it was awesome,' yelled his twin brother, Carlos. 'The aliens exploded and we saw their guts and everything.'

'Yuk!' Isabella squealed, just as Joe appeared behind them.

Seeing the hose in his hand, Lucinda stepped backwards onto the verandah and put everything she was holding out of harm's way.

Shrieks and squeals erupted in front of her as Joe blasted his nieces and nephews.

'Hey, that's not fair!' Carlos dropped his Super Soaker and perched his hands on his hips as water rained down on top of him. 'You've got a bigger gun.'

'Life's *not* fair, little mate.' Joe grinned wickedly as he lunged forward and scooped Carlos's gun off the ground.

He tossed it to Lucinda and she couldn't help herself. 'Come on Carlos,' she called, 'let's get him.'

The kids all laughed as Lucinda chased Joe around the front lawn. Her feeble attempts to get him must have looked ridiculous—within seconds she was drenched through from her pale pink t-shirt to her denim skirt. She wished she'd had the sense to take off her wedge sandals before embarking on this misdemeanour. She dropped the gun and held up her hands. 'Joe, I surrender.'

Laughing, he tossed the hose down on the lawn and swaggered over to her. 'I'm sorry, my love,' he said as he wrapped his arms around her and drew her wet body against him, 'but you look so damn hot sopping wet.'

So did he. But before she could say this or anything else, they felt the hose on them. Lucinda spun around to see little Isabella cackling as she soaked them even more. 'I can't believe you didn't turn it off.'

'She may look small, but she's dangerous,' Joe growled. 'We're going to have to tackle her.'

Thankfully, help came in the form of Joe's oldest brother Mario, who switched the tap off and yelled at the kids to go jump in the pool instead of wasting good water.

Joe and Lucinda exchanged glances and tried to stifle their smiles, but within seconds they found themselves alone again and succumbed to hysterics. She couldn't remember the last time they'd had laughed so much or had so much fun together. How much better would it be, mucking around like that with their own kids? Their own little family.

As if reading her mind, Joe pulled her into another hug. 'It'll happen, you know. Our time is just around the corner.'

'I know.' Since making their appointment with the specialist, Lucinda felt a lot more positive. It had been easier to get through the last few weeks of school holidays, going through the motions of preparing for the new term, knowing that they were finally doing something about their possible fertility problem.

'Now, we better get inside before Mum sends out a search party,' Joe said, starting towards the verandah and their pile of stuff.

As if she'd heard herself being mentioned, the front door swung open to reveal the domineering presence of Rosa Mannolini. She perched her hands on her ample hips but didn't look half as sweet as Carlos had when he'd done the same. 'Are you two coming inside?' she hollered.

'Hi Mamma.' Joe grinned and waved at her as he picked up his keys, wallet and bottle of wine. He spread his arms and made to hug her.

'Don't you come near me young man. You're soaking wet.'

Geez, point out the obvious why don't you, thought Lucinda, but she swallowed her annoyance. 'Hey Rosa. Happy Australia Day.'

'Hello, Lucia,' Rosa said, as if butter wouldn't melt. She'd always insisted on calling her that and each time she said Lucia instead of Lucinda was a gentle reminder that Lucinda would never live up to her expectations. She supposed that's what came of marrying an Italian mother's youngest son. 'It's lovely to see you.'

Which meant, *it's been a long time since you've bothered to visit*. Joe had seen his parents since Christmas, but Lucinda had come down with a sudden headache that night.

'You too,' she said, leaning forward to kiss Rosa on the cheek, careful not to lean against her with her wet clothes. 'I'm just going to go get dry.'

She slipped past Joe and her monster-in-law, figuring she'd change into her bathers and then hang her wet clothes on the washing line. In this summer heat, they'd be dry before she could stake her claim on one of the sun lounges by the pool.

As Lucinda changed in the bathroom, she could hear the shrieks and squeals of the kids outside, music blasting from the stereo and the chatter of the adults drinking and laughing on the verandah. She smiled. That was what family was about. Although each new pregnancy announcement from one of her in-laws felt like a knife twisting in her heart, she liked Joe's family—well, most of them—and she was glad she'd come.

Bundling up her wet clothes and making sure her bikini straps were tied properly, she walked down the hallway heading for outside, but stopped at the sound of Joe and Rosa talking. Something in their tone—not loud but almost aggressive—made her heart still as she cocked her ear to listen.

'*Mother*,' Joe said, and Lucinda could tell he was angry because he always called her Mamma to her face, 'stop pestering Lucinda and me about babies.'

'You've been married for years, Joseph, together for longer. It's reasonable of me to want grandbabies.'

'I've lost count of how many *grandbabies* you have,' Joe scoffed.

'You were such a beautiful baby, Joseph.' Lucinda dared to peer around the wall and saw Rosa leaning forward and cupping Joe's jaw in her hand. 'Don't tell me you don't want children?'

Joe pulled away and Lucinda snapped back into her hiding place. 'Of course I want children,' he all but growled at his mother. 'And so does Lucinda. But how do you think she feels every time you ask her if she's pregnant yet or every time you buy us something for the *nursery*?'

'I … um …' Miracles did happen, Rosa appeared to be lost for words.

'We *are* trying to have a family, Mamma—' Joe's tone was only slightly softer '—but it looks like we might have … fertility problems.'

'Pah,' Rosa spat. Lucinda should have known that nothing would make her back down. She didn't have a heart after all. 'Mannolinis have never had problems making babies. I've always said that Lucia is far too skinny. She doesn't have child-bearing hips. If there's a problem, I tell you it'll be with her.'

Lucinda's eyes prickled with tears and she gripped her stomach as if someone had kicked her there. The wet clothes in her arms tumbled onto the polished tiles. What if Rosa was right?

'I love you, Mamma,' Joe said, and now there was real anger in his voice, 'but don't you *ever* speak about my wife like that again. I mean it. If you hurt her, you'll lose me because I will choose her over you *every* time. And it's *Lucinda*, not Lucia.'

Lucinda gasped, shocked by his words, and then snapped her hand over her mouth, hoping neither of them had heard her. No such luck. She heard Joe's bare feet slap across the tiles and seconds later he appeared around the corner. He opened his arms and pulled her into his embrace, planting a kiss on the top of her head.

'I'm sorry you had to hear that, baby.'

'I'm not,' she said, sniffling into his already wet t-shirt. 'Thank you.' It was the first time Lucinda could remember Joe standing up to his mother—standing up for *her*—and it made her feel closer to him than ever. She squeezed him tight, never wanting to let go.

He must have mistaken her clinginess for distress because he pulled back slightly and whispered, 'Let's go home. We'll go get take-out and watch the sky show on the TV later.'

As appealing as curling up on the couch with Joe and her favourite Thai takeaway was, she wouldn't allow Rosa to ruin her night. She wanted to hang out with the rest of Joe's family and watch the fireworks over the Swan River from their vantage spot on his parents' balcony. She wanted to see the expressions of glee on her nieces and nephews' faces and for once just appreciate what she had, rather than dwell on what she wanted.

'No, let's stay,' she said.

'You sure?'

She nodded and took his hand. 'But let's get you out of those wet clothes first.'

Still holding his hand, she leant down to scoop her wet things up into her arms and led him back into the bathroom. Not caring that this was his mother's place—or maybe because it was— she turned on the taps in the shower and stepped inside.

'Come here big boy.'

Grinning, Joe tugged his t-shirt over his head, ripped off his shorts and jocks and joined her.

Chapter Twenty-two

Charlie was sitting in front of the computer and scrolling through online linen sites with Mrs Sampson when Mitch swaggered into the reception area and demanded the presence of her company for Australia Day lunch on his brother's farm. She hadn't even realised it was Australia Day. Since being back home at the motel and spending all her spare time painting, she barely knew one day from another.

'Can't you see I'm busy?' She feigned annoyance as she gestured to the screen.

He leaned over the desk, so close she got an unnerving waft of whatever body wash he'd used that morning. 'You're going to turn down an afternoon out in the sun, hanging out with me, Kate and Macca for what? Online shopping?'

Mrs Sampson giggled. Although she was old enough to be Mitch's mother, she wasn't immune to his charm.

Charlie shot her a glare. 'This is important. Now we've finished a few of the rooms, I want to at least replace the bedding and curtains.'

Looking blank, Mitch shook his head. 'I'm happy to talk paint colours and what kind of fertiliser to use in the garden beds, but

218

I draw the line at bedding. Next you'll be asking me about throw cushions.'

Charlie tried not to smirk. 'No one asked for your opinion, *Mitchell*.'

He straightened and then grinned his cocky, the-world-is-my-oyster smile. 'That's right, they didn't. Well, phew.' He theatrically wiped a hand across his brow. 'You coming for a beer and a barbie, then?'

Charlie opened her mouth to object. As much as seeing Kate and Macca and hanging out with Mitch sounded fun, she didn't want to leave her dad alone tonight. Australia Day could swing both ways; they might be run off their feet by folks wanting a drink out, or everyone could choose to party at home. As if reading her mind, Mrs Sampson spoke before Charlie had the chance.

'Go, have fun,' she said, standing and making shooing movements with her hands. 'I'll hang around here in case things get busy. I've haven't got any plans. Between me, Brian and Rob we'll manage, I'm sure.'

Charlie lifted an eyebrow—Mrs Sampson had already done her shift for the day—but her old friend crossed her arms and glared right back. 'You deserve a break as much as the rest of us, missy.'

'Okay, okay, I know when I'm beat.' She glanced down at her hands and grimaced. Straight after the breakfast service she'd gotten stuck into the painting again and her fingers and nails were filthy. The least she could do was try and scrub off some of the paint before she went out. 'Give me ten minutes to get ready and I'm yours.'

'The timer's on,' Mitch called as she opened the door that led into the adjoining house. She rolled her eyes and flipped him the bird.

It took twenty minutes to drive out to Kate and Macca's farm, which was off the Eyre Highway as you headed towards the

Nullarbor. Charlie and Mitch spent the whole time chatting in the way of old friends who always have something or other to say to one another. They talked about meaningless things, such as the rumours there was going to be another series of *Big Brother* this year, and both proclaimed their disgust at this possibility.

'It went downhill after Gretel Killeen left I tell you,' Mitch said, tapping along to the Paul Kelly album playing softly in the background.

'The new host not hot enough for you?'

'I wouldn't even know who she is.' Mitch chuckled and then moved onto something not quite so meaningless. 'Speaking of women, do you reckon there's something going on between your dad and Mrs S?'

'What?' Charlie straightened in her seat and turned her head to look at him. 'Where did you get that idea?'

He shrugged. 'They seem to get along well and hang out a bit. She jumped at the excuse to help him out tonight.'

Charlie frowned. She'd thought *she* was responsible for the improvement in her dad's health and mood but what if it was because something was going on with their housekeeper? She didn't know how she'd feel about that. 'I don't know … Maybe.'

'Would it bother you?'

'What? Dad finding someone else?'

'Yeah.'

Her mum had barely been gone six months, so … 'I haven't really given it any thought, but I suppose I wouldn't mind as long as he was happy. He and Mum were such a perfect couple that it's just something I never contemplated. Did your dad ever date anyone after your parents broke up?'

Mitch shook his head. 'If he did he kept it quiet from Macca and me. I think Mum burnt him pretty bad, but I kind of wish he had found someone. Everyone deserves that, don't you reckon?'

Mitch glanced over at her and for a second Charlie wondered if he was trying to tell her something. Her stomach twisted and her heart skipped a beat but then he turned back to the road. 'We're here.'

Charlie swallowed as they bumped along Kate and Macca's long gravel driveway. By the time the house appeared in front of them, her emotions were almost under control. Had Mitch been trying to tell her something? Was he developing feelings for her too? Or was spending so much time together wreaking havoc with her common sense?

There were three vehicles parked out the front of the old but recently renovated farmhouse. A number of scooters, bicycles and other kid clutter littered across the dry lawn, but it was the vehicles that piqued Charlie's interest. She recognised Kate's four-wheel drive from the few times they'd run into each other in town, and the ute had to belong to Macca. The other car—a Holden wagon—was Lisa's. 'What's Lisa doing here?' she asked as Mitch pulled up alongside it.

He tugged the key out of the ignition and grinned at her. 'She and Kate know each other from the Toy Library or something and when Lisa said she'd not seen you as much as she'd hoped, Kate invited them over as well. It'll do you good to relax a bit.'

'Them' had to include Lisa's husband, Tim, who was a local mechanic, and her two adorable little boys. Charlie hadn't met Tim yet but she'd be glad to see Lisa. They'd met a couple of times for coffee but neither time had seemed long enough.

'Oh, that's great,' she said, opening the door and climbing out.

Mitch went to the back tray of his ute and retrieved an esky, his arm muscles doing that arousing flexing thing as he did so.

Charlie averted her gaze. 'Do you need any help?'

'Nope. All good. Lead the way.'

Following the noise of children playing, she headed around the house to the backyard and found the four adults sitting around the pool and four children splashing in it. Lisa's preschool-aged son was wearing a flotation device and the baby was asleep in her arms. Kate and Macca's three older kids looked to be pro-swimmers already, and their baby was fast asleep in a rocker beside the adults.

Kate, Macca, Lisa and a blond-haired man Charlie guessed to be Tim all raised their hands and offered greetings. She waved back as Kate rose from where she'd been sitting with her legs dangling in the pool and rushed over to open the pool gate. 'Come on in.'

'Thanks for inviting me.' Charlie hugged Kate, noticing her bikini and colourful sarong. 'Mitch didn't tell me you had a pool.'

'Men.' Kate rolled her eyes. 'Don't worry, I have hundreds of pairs of bathers you can borrow.'

Charlie wasn't sure she'd fit into Kate's bathers—and she certainly wouldn't look as good—but she accepted gratefully. 'Thanks. That would be good.'

'What would be good?' Mitch asked. Having delivered the esky onto the verandah, he now held up two beers and offered one to Charlie.

Taking it, she enjoyed a long, satisfying sip before replying. 'Kate's lending me some bathers since you forget to tell me to bring them.'

'You're a big girl, Charles,' he said, tossing her a fake-reproving look. 'I can't do everything for you. Of course, you could always swim in your underwear. Or skinny dip.'

She glared at him. 'Go and make yourself useful and play with the kids or something.'

Kate laughed as he waltzed into the pool area, greeted the adults, dumped his beer on a plastic table, yanked off his t-shirt and then plunged into the pool to hassle his niece and nephews. Of course they loved it and Charlie heard their squeals of joy behind her as she followed Kate into the house, trying not to ponder the sight of a shirtless Mitch.

'You two seem to be getting along very well,' Kate noted, as she led Charlie into the laundry and opened a cupboard that overflowed with towels and swimwear.

Charlie didn't know how to respond. Kate's tone told her she thought something was going on between them and she hoped it wasn't vibes she was giving off. She and Mitch had the friendship thing down pat but over the last few weeks, the attraction she'd previously managed to ignore had grown stronger and stronger and she wasn't sure what to do about it.

Of course this realisation terrified her and the last thing she wanted was to admit it to his sister-in-law. What if it got back to him and he didn't feel the same way? 'Mitch gets along with every-one,' she said, pretending she hadn't understood Kate's undertone. Then she grabbed a pair of bathers from the plastic tub Kate had pulled out. 'These look great.'

Leaving no room for further interrogation, she turned and escaped into the toilet off the laundry. She closed the door behind her and called, 'I'll see you back out there.'

'Okay.'

Charlie breathed a sigh of relief as she heard Kate's footsteps moving away. She plonked herself down on the toilet seat, need-ing a moment to collect her thoughts and emotions. She laid her head in her hands and let out a little cry of frustration but she couldn't hide away in here all day. Sooner or later someone would come along and ask her if she were okay. Taking a deep breath, she took off her clothes and tried on the bright red one-piece. She wasn't sure red was her colour but it would do. Folding her clothes into a pile, she left them in the laundry and grabbed a towel from the cupboard, wrapping it around her before heading back outside.

She'd just stepped off the edge of the verandah when she felt a presence behind her. Before she could turn to see who it was

Mitch launched himself at her, scooping her up and throwing her over his shoulder.

'What are you doing?' she squealed, pummelling his back as he jogged towards the pool area.

'Mitch!' Kate used her stern mum voice as they approached.

'Put her down!' Lisa ordered. At least that's what Charlie thought she said, but she was laughing so hard who could tell?

And no one was leaping to her rescue. In fact Tim was holding the gate open and the kids in the pool were chanting, 'Go Uncle Mitch! Go Uncle Mitch!'

Despite not liking where this was heading, Charlie couldn't help but notice how nice his back was. Smooth, hard, tanned and fabulous. She feared her light-headedness wasn't from being upside down, but rather from being this close to Mitch. So close she could open her mouth and lick him if she wanted to.

Just when she thought he was about to hurl her into the water, he stopped and put her down on the hot paving. Her heart racing, she swallowed, disappointed that he hadn't followed through. She'd needed the water to cool her errant libido.

'You are a bastard, Mitch McDonald,' she hissed, lifting her hands and pushing them against the hard wall of his chest. She caught him unawares and he stumbled backwards into the pool, cheers of delight erupting all around them.

'Hah! Serves you right, little brother,' Macca called, clapping his hands as Mitch spluttered to the surface. Tim and the women roared with laughter.

Charlie couldn't quite believe what she'd done. That shove hadn't been simply about getting him back for being a larrikin; it had contained all her anger and irritation at how he made her feel. She summoned a smile, laughing along with the others to try and cover this up.

Emerging from the water and running a hand through his wet hair like some kind of sea god, Mitch shook his head as he looked up at her. 'I can't believe you just did that.'

'Believe it, buster,' she retorted, before turning, collecting her beer and heading over to sit with Kate, Lisa and the babies.

'You two are a crack-up,' Lisa said.

Charlie took a sip of her beer, not wanting to talk about Mitch right now.

'Not sure I'm buying the "just friends" thing,' Kate mused.

'Me neither.' Lisa shook her head. 'Mitch does not look at you like he does one of the boys.'

Charlie blinked, torn between wanting to ask more about this so-called look and not wanting to risk Mitch hearing their conversation. If she'd been on her own with Lisa, she might have confessed the less-than-platonic feelings she'd been having lately.

'Your kids are all good swimmers,' she said, in an aim to redirect the conversation.

Whether they guessed her plan or not, both women smiled proudly.

'Logan could swim practically before he could walk,' Kate said, gesturing to her oldest son who was diving into the deep end. 'And Leo and Laura are also fish. I guess it helps having a pool at home. I'm sure this one will be the same,' she added, pointing to the rocker.

And they were off. Charlie sat back and listened as her friends chatted about their kids. She enjoyed the conversation and kept having to rein in thoughts about what it would be like if she and Mitch ever got together and had a family. When the kids finally got fed up with swimming, the guys started the barbeque. Kate set a blanket under a tree for the kids to eat on and the adults gathered around the outdoor setting on the verandah.

'Wow, this table is amazing,' Charlie marvelled as she ran her hand over the smoothly finished wood. It didn't look like the kind of thing you picked up at Bunnings.

'Thanks.' Kate beamed and glanced at her brother-in-law. 'Mitch made it.'

Charlie looked to Mitch and an uncharacteristic flush spread up his neck and into his cheeks. He shrugged as if it was nothing.

She knew he did some cabinetmaking when he wasn't driving trucks but she hadn't seen any of his craftsmanship in years. 'You've been holding out on me,' she scolded. 'Maybe we should hire you to make some new tables for the restaurant.'

'You couldn't afford me,' he scoffed.

Sadly, he was probably right, but she rolled her eyes, happy that Mitch was still bantering with her and didn't appear to have noticed her earlier annoyance.

The rest of the afternoon and evening went all too quickly. Charlie had fun kicking a football with Mitch, Macca, Tim and the kids and then sneaking off to have cuddles with the babies. Kate asked her about hula-hooping and both women expressed their hope that she'd considering running some exercise classes in Meadow Brook. Although Charlie didn't know how she'd fit that in between her normal motel work and the makeover, she promised to give it some thought.

The only sombre moment in the conversation was when Tim asked after Macca and Mitch's dad, Rick.

The two brothers exchanged sombre expressions and then Macca shrugged. 'Who knows, really? He tries to put on a brave face when we're around, but it kills me to see him locked up like that. He loves it when we take the kids to visit though, doesn't he, love?'

Kate nodded as Macca reached out to squeeze her knee.

'I just wish there was more we could do,' Mitch mused. Charlie looked at him, wishing there was something she could do to ease his guilt and anxiety. She knew how much better she felt now that she was home and able to keep a closer eye on her own father. If only there was a care facility in Meadow Brook and Rick wasn't all the way in Port Augusta.

Finally, Lisa's kids started grizzling and she and Tim decided to make a move.

'Do you want to head home now too?' Mitch asked. As designated driver, he'd stopped drinking hours ago.

Charlie yawned, tiredness washing over her. 'Yes, we'd better. I've got the usual early start in the morning.'

Everyone thanked Kate and Macca for their hospitality and all agreed they should do it more often, then Lisa and Tim bundled their small people into the wagon and Charlie climbed into Mitch's ute beside him. She clicked her seatbelt into place, glancing at Mitch's gorgeous profile as she did so. Totally dry now, he was wearing the board shorts he'd swum in and a scruffy old t-shirt—but even in the daggiest clothes he'd still look hotter than any other guy on the planet.

Charlie sucked in a breath, suddenly experiencing an intense urge to lean across and touch his face. Guessing the alcohol was affecting her senses, she closed her eyes and sank back in the seat, trying to forget that Mitch was sitting mere centimetres away. It was ridiculous—they'd been friends for years and had been working alongside each other sometimes hours on end for weeks—but she couldn't deny it was getting stronger.

And she couldn't forget Kate's insinuations or Lisa's comment about the way Mitch looked at her. Could they be right? Something deep inside her tightened at the thought. As far as she knew he hadn't been seeing any other women since she'd landed back in town but it had only been a month and she'd kept him pretty occupied at the motel.

'You okay?' Mitch asked.

She blinked open her eyes, realised they were already halfway down the driveway and summoned a chirpy smile to her face. 'Yep. I had a great night. Thanks for dragging me out.'

'Anytime.' Mitch grinned and then reached up to turn on the overhead light. 'And I hope I'm about to make it even better.'

Charlie's heart stopped at his words, tingles racing up her spine. *Was this it?* Was he going to pull the ute over to the side of the road and confess he felt exactly the same way she did?

'Oh?' She only just managed to speak, licking her lips in anticipation.

'Check under your seat.' His hands still sexily caressing the steering wheel, he nodded towards her feet.

Confused, she leant over, felt beneath her seat and drew out a thick, yellow envelope. 'What's this?'

'Look inside.'

She slid her finger beneath the seal and then drew out the papers inside, frowning as she read over the first page. 'It's an application form. For an online course.'

'Yep. In naturopathy.'

'But I don't understand.'

Mitch reached over and grabbed her hand—she tried not to react to his touch. 'You've been doing amazing things in the motel, Charlie. I'm proud of you, and your dad's proud of you, but you gave up a big dream to come home. This way you can study towards your degree and be around for Brian.'

'I ...' Emotion clogged her throat at the thoughtfulness behind Mitch's gesture. She didn't know what to say. 'Do you really think I can do this on top of everything else?'

'Of course you can. Besides, I'll help.'

Her insides lit up with excitement and possibility. In less than a month she'd already achieved so much at the motel, so maybe this wasn't such a crazy idea. 'Oh, Mitch. I could just kiss you,' she said, hugging the paperwork to her chest.

His cheeks flared red and he scoffed, 'Steady on, Charles. Don't get carried away.'

The words were like a slap in the face—a bitter announcement of how he felt. He cared about her—he wouldn't have gone out of his way to find out this course information if he didn't—but as a mate, or like he would a sister. Just the mere idea of her kissing him had brought a horror-stricken look to his eyes.

That hurt, but she was the one to blame. Mitch had never given her any indication that he ever wanted more.

He might have grown from a skinny, nerdy boy into a strapping, gorgeous man—inside and out—but Charlie hadn't changed. Why would he ever find her plain mousey looks and nothing body attractive?

'It was a figure of speech,' she said quickly, hoping she'd hidden her dismay. 'Don't get your knickers in a knot, I'd rather kiss a toad.'

'That's not very nice, Charlie-Warlie.' But he didn't sound offended. He'd recovered from her mention of kissing him and was now tapping his fingers on the steering wheel along to the Australia Day countdown on the radio.

Charlie shoved the paperwork back in the envelope, then reached up and turned off the overhead light, making the ute dark again, just in case there was anything on her face that might give away her feelings.

'I was thinking,' Mitch said as he tore along the Eyre Highway towards Meadow Brook, 'that maybe next special day we should have some sort of party at the motel instead.'

'What type of special day?' she asked, something twisting inside her at the way he said 'we.'

'St Patrick's Day is the next big one, unless you count Valentine's Day—but that's only good for couples. We could decorate the bar and restaurant with green streamers and balloons, have a special green cocktail, green food and encourage everyone to drink Kilkenny and Guinness. What do you reckon?'

'Green food?' That didn't sound appetising at all.

'Hey, I thought you'd love the idea. Most veggies are green.'

She laughed because she couldn't help herself. 'Okay. We'll talk about it,' she promised as he turned into the motel car park.

'We could even dress up!'

Charlie rolled her eyes, picturing Mitch in a leprechaun outfit. 'Whatever.'

'I've got a trip the next couple of days, but are you up for beers and pizza this Friday night?' he asked as she reached for the door handle.

With her face turned away from him, she closed her eyes and took a moment. The way she saw it, she had two choices; either repress the feelings she had for Mitch and let things go on the way they were, or tell him how she felt and risk losing the best friend she'd ever had.

Fact was, option two wasn't an option at all.

'Yeah, that'd be great. I'll see you then,' she said and then climbed out of the ute.

Mitch waited until she was safely inside before driving off and Charlie stood in the doorway, watching until his lights faded to nothing.

Chapter Twenty-three

'It's a girl, a beautiful baby girl!' Madeleine held up the tiny, perfect, albeit slightly red and wrinkly newborn to the first-time parents and then handed the bundle to Mike, the paediatrician on duty. He took the kid across the other side of the room to be assessed. While Mike and the midwives fussed round the baby and new parents, Madeleine tended to the task of stitching up her latest caesarean section. She prided herself on immaculate stitching and got a thrill out of seeing a good scar when her patients returned for their six-week check-up. By the time she'd finished, Mike had proclaimed the baby a healthy little cherub and placed it into its mother's arms for the first time.

She couldn't help gazing down at the new family.

Although she wasn't an emotional person, this was the one time when tears sometimes caught in the back of her throat. In those first few moments after birth when two people in love are meeting a brand new person that they created between them, everything seems like a miracle. Usually she managed to control her emotions by turning away and going to clean up, but today her eyes were glued on the sight as she fantasised that one day in the not too distant future she might have one of those moments of her own. It didn't matter that she'd be on her own because she'd get all the joy.

And then she remembered the diabolical meeting she'd had a few days ago with Potential Donor Number Two. It had been so disappointing she hadn't been able to bring herself to go back to the known donor site since. Yet, without a donor, her dreams of motherhood were futile.

'Are you okay?' Madeleine felt Mike's hand on her arm and, as she looked into his face, she felt a tear trickle down her cheek. Embarrassed, she swiped her arm across her face to get rid of it.

'Of course. Fine. I think I have something in my eye,' she lied, bestowing her patients with a brief smile before turning away.

Her job done for this couple—the midwives would take care of mum and baby and deliver them to the ward—Madeleine left, quickly cleaned up, changed out of her scrubs and then returned to her office. This C-section had been her last patient for the day and although she still wanted to do a round of the maternity ward to check on her other new mums, she first had to pull herself together. This meant getting over the setbacks that had been Potential Donors One and Two and getting back in the saddle—so to speak. Closing her office door, she sat down at her computer and was just entering the website into Safari when there was a knock.

Frowning, she minimised the web browser and called, 'Come in.'

The door opened and Hugo stood there, so tall he almost touched the top of the door frame and looking way sexier than a tired doctor at the end of his shift had any right to look. 'Can we talk?' he asked.

She nodded, a shiver running through her at his serious tone. 'Sure.'

He entered the room and closed the door behind him. Although she'd been alone with Hugo more times than she could count, her heart hitched in her chest and she felt as if her office had shrunk around them like something out of *Alice in Wonderland*.

'How are you?' she asked, needing to fill the silence. She and Hugo saw each other at the hospital almost daily in a professional capacity but for some reason, they'd barely talked as friends since that night in the restaurant with Celia almost two weeks ago. She didn't know whether she'd been subconsciously avoiding him or if he was avoiding her, but something had shifted between them and she wasn't happy about it.

'All right.' He sat down in the chair on the other side of her desk, rather than leaning against it like he so often did when they were chatting at the end of a hard day. 'I've been thinking about your predicament.'

'Oh.' Heat flooded her body and she reached for a pen, needing something to fiddle with.

'How'd you go with Potential Donor Number Two?'

Madeleine frowned. She'd been updating Celia via text or email on the saga of her donor hunt. Had she not told him? Or was he simply pretending to be in the dark? Quite frankly, with the weirdness between them, Madeleine wasn't sure she wanted to talk about such personal and confronting things.

But the look in Hugo's eyes unnerved her and in lieu of anything else to say she confessed. 'Dismally. I'm seriously considering resorting to the anonymous donor thing.'

It was Hugo's turn to frown. 'But you're going ahead with having a baby on your own?'

'Yes.' If anything, the hassles of finding a donor had made her more and more convinced of her decision. With each disappointment, her yearning to have a child of her own grew stronger. The way she'd almost lost control of her emotions in theatre proved that she needed to see this decision through.

'I'll do it.'

'What?' She thought she must have misheard. Or perhaps the conversation had moved onto some other topic without her noticing.

Hugo leaned forward and planted his elbows on her desk, clasping his hands together in the way he always did when he was serious or focused on something. Her heart picked up speed as he opened his mouth.

'I'm offering you my sperm, Madeleine. That is, if you find me, as a donor, suitable.'

Holy shit! Was he kidding? He checked all her boxes for suitability a hundred times over.

She couldn't help the smile that burst on her face as she imagined what a baby made with their combined genes would look like. Would it have blonde hair like hers or the sophisticated copper of his? Until she'd met Hugo, she'd never imagined anyone with red hair could be sexy, but he defied this myth. They were both tall and sporty, so unless they shared some weird recessive genes, their child would have good body structure and excellent muscle tone. And they had high IQs—she imagined them sitting on the floor doing flashcards with their super bright baby.

The word 'perfect' popped into her head, until she remembered Hugo wouldn't be sitting on the floor sharing parental duties. He wouldn't be there for the good times or the bad. That wouldn't be the arrangement. Her bubble deflating, a voice in her head said she should thank him for the very kind offer but decline. It was the sensible thing to do. After all, a close friend donor was never one of her options. And also, this hadn't been Hugo's idea originally.

If Celia hadn't suggested it at dinner, he'd never have come to her on his own. Would he?

'Are you sure?' The question came out of her mouth of its own accord but it was a good one. *If*, and it was a big if, they did this, she wanted to make sure he wasn't feeling pressured by Celia or herself.

He nodded. 'I've barely thought about anything else the past few days. The idea of you going out and looking for a stranger to … to do this *mammoth* thing, just doesn't sit right.'

'But you don't want children?'

He lifted one shoulder. 'Celia doesn't want children. I'm indifferent, but I love her.'

Madeleine tried to ignore the stab in her heart at his confession. Of course he loved Celia. She *knew* he loved Celia. Everyone loved Celia.

But then he added, 'And you want a child and I love you too.'

A shot of adrenalin jolted her heart but somehow she managed to ignore it. He might love her, but not in the same way he loved Celia. Gripping the edge of her desk and thankful she'd been sitting down when he'd hit her with those potent little words, she forced a grateful smile, unable to speak yet.

'And anyway,' he continued, the hint of a smile creeping onto his face, 'this wouldn't be my baby, right? Biologically yes, but I'd be like an uncle, interested in the child but with no legal claims or responsibility. Would that work?'

'Yes. I guess.' She'd never given serious thought to the whole friend-as-donor thing but it might be nice to know her baby would have a male role model, especially if they conceived a boy.

'I've already spoken to Celia's lawyer friend and he says he can get a contract drawn up pretty quickly. Of course we'll both have to have some medical tests, but …' He leaned back in his seat, clearly relaxing now he'd said what he wanted to say. 'What do you think? Do you want to do this?'

Madeleine closed her eyes a moment, thinking. The little voice telling her this was a bad idea was getting quieter and quieter. Hugo was offering her an amazing gift. If she accepted it, she could begin the next stage of this journey. No more scouring the internet for suitable donors, no more pseudo-dates in cafes with lunatics. It would be time to move on to tracking her temperature and peeing on ovulation sticks instead.

And, then came the biggie. If she used Hugo as her donor and did get pregnant, she'd always have a part of him, even if she'd never be able to have *him*. Maybe that would be enough?

'Okay. If you're sure,' she said eventually, finally meeting his gaze.

His lips twisted into a fully fledged smile. 'I am. I most definitely am. Celia's suggestion just caught me by surprise but the more I thought about it, the more it seemed the perfect solution to your problem. And it will be good to know the Proudfoot genes are not going to end with me.'

She laughed. 'Yes, that would be a terrible pity.'

Still grinning that Prince Harry smile, Hugo stood and then offered out his hand. 'Shall we shake on it?'

Her tummy fluttering, her hands also a little quivery and uncharacteristic tears welling up in her eyes, Madeleine nodded as she leant across her desk and reached out to him. His hand closed around hers in a firm grasp and the tiny little hairs on her arms and at the back of her neck lifted. 'Thank you,' she whispered, before quickly retrieving her hand.

'I think this deserves a celebration dinner,' he said, shoving his hands in his pockets. 'You, me and Celia. What do you say?'

Strangely, she didn't want to toast their decision with Celia. Madeleine would have preferred to go home and languish in a warm bath, dreaming about what was to come. But she couldn't exactly turn Hugo down after what he'd just offered. 'That sounds good.'

'Great. I'll go make a reservation.' With a slight wave of his hand, he turned, opened the door and walked out of her office, a definite spring in his step.

And Madeleine sank back in her seat to reflect on what the fuck had just happened.

Celia held up her crystal champagne flute and grinned at Madeleine and Hugo who were sitting at a square table on either side of her at their favourite harbourside restaurant. 'I think we need a toast.'

Hugo raised his glass, which incidentally held club soda because both he and Madeleine were not drinking in the lead-up to attempted conception.

'To Madeleine's baby,' Celia said, clinking her glass first with Madeleine and then with Hugo.

'To Madeleine's baby,' Hugo echoed.

'To … to my baby!' Madeleine had almost said 'our baby' and took a long sip, hoping neither Celia nor Hugo had noticed. She was sitting here with the father of her future child and his future wife. Talk about complicated.

'I'm so glad you accepted Hugo's offer,' Celia said, putting her glass down. 'I couldn't stand the thought of you having to meet any more of those awful men. Having a baby should be an enjoyable experience. And although this isn't the traditional scenario, you should be able to look your child in the eyes and tell him that you actually liked their father.'

Oh, yes, she liked him all right. Unable to speak, she simply nodded and took another sip of her club soda.

Celia didn't appear to notice her discomfort. 'When do you think you'll be able to start? Have you had any thoughts about names?'

'Um … well,' Madeleine tried to get her head around Celia's questions. It felt odd to be discussing such things with her, but then again, if it wasn't for Celia she'd probably have spent the evening going back for another trawl through the known donor website. She shuddered at the thought and told herself that if Hugo's fiancée could handle this weirdness, then so could she. Celia was the one who'd have to watch her grow bigger and bigger, knowing she was carrying Hugo's child.

But the bottom line was she thought Celia was probably the better person, definitely a nicer one, and it was kind of odd she didn't want to have children of her own.

Chapter Twenty-four

'Good news.'

Lucinda's heart was pounding so loud and fast she could feel it in her throat. Joe reached over from his seat beside her in the specialist's office and took hold of her hand.

'The results of all your tests are now back,' continued Dr Randall, smiling, 'and I'm pleased to tell you we found no abnormalities with either of you. Joe, your sperm are great little swimmers and the tests show plenty of them.'

'Bonza.' Joe grinned at Lucinda as if the doctor had just given him the gold medal in a masculinity contest.

'Hang on a second.' Lucinda snatched her hand from his and leaned forward in her chair, convinced she must have heard wrong. 'What about me? Surely you must have found something?'

'Nope, you're in perfect health too.' Dr Randall beamed and then glanced at her watch as if she had more important patients—people with actual problems—to get to. 'Your general health is impeccable and your follicle stimulating hormones, luteinising hormones and estradiol levels are great too. You're ovulating regularly.'

239

Although Dr Randall went on a little longer, listing all the ways in which she was perfectly normal and healthy, Lucinda zoned out. She was in shock.

Joe had experienced a few minutes of awkwardness when he'd had to wank into a jar and drive his sperm across town to the pathology lab, but she'd been subjected to all manner of dignity-robbing tests over the last few weeks. And for what?

There'd been blood tests to check general health and evaluate her hormone levels. Something called an HSG, which although relatively minor had involved time off work and a day stay in hospital. She'd had to wear a gown and had her legs put up in stirrups while the doctor inserted a catheter to inject dye into her fallopian tubes to check for blockages. This was done in correlation with an ultrasound and she'd watched the dye move through her tubes and across the screen as if she were watching someone else's medical procedure on TV. She'd always imagined her first ultrasound would be of her and Joe's baby, yet instead of trying to identify arms and legs and little gender-defining bits, she'd been trying to make sense of her insides.

It had all looked pretty clear, pretty normal, to Lucinda. But then again, she wasn't a doctor and she guessed they'd be able to see things she couldn't. She'd been dead certain that either she or Joe or maybe even both of them had a fertility problem, so this supposedly good news felt like a semi-trailer had slammed right into her, then reversed and gone at her again.

Because problems had solutions, but if nobody knew what the problem was, then how the *hell* were they supposed to fix it?

She'd been ready for a bad result, expecting the tests to show she ovulated irregularly or something like that. She'd read oodles of books and personal experiences on websites by women who'd had to take drugs to assist their ovulation and had fully expected this would be her. She'd been prepared for the moodiness, nausea, headaches, fatigue and all the medical hoops they'd have to jump through to get pregnant. She'd even warned Joe, but she hadn't been prepared for this.

Lucinda held up a hand, begging Dr Randall to stop. Joe glared at her rudeness but she didn't care. She didn't care that she'd be raging if one of her students' parents ever dared do the same to her. She didn't care that Dr Randall was an acquaintance of Madeleine's. Someone had to have answers.

'There must be some sort of mistake,' she said. 'I'm sure I've read somewhere that in some cases a man's sperm is not compatible with the conditions of a woman's vagina. Maybe that's what's wrong with us.'

'I don't think so,' Dr Randall said, her tone condescending. 'I'm fairly certain in time you and Joe will conceive naturally. We'll give you another six months and then if you've still not succeeded, we'll start discussing options such as IVF.'

'Six months?' She'd be thirty-three by then. And if there was nothing wrong with them, why wasn't she bloody pregnant already? It had been two months since Joe had agreed to see a doctor and during that time his weeks at home had coincided with her peak days of ovulation. They'd bonked like wild animals, she'd lain in bed afterwards with her legs up against the wall while reading a copy of *What to Expect When You're Expecting*. They'd done everything right already. Why couldn't Dr Randall understand?

'Yes.' The doctor nodded and pushed back her chair, standing to indicate their appointment was over. 'But I'm fairly confident I won't be seeing you again.'

Damn straight, thought Lucinda, as she yanked her handbag off the floor, stood and stormed out the room, tears already prickling beneath her eyelids. She needed a doctor who listened to her, someone who would actually help.

'What's wrong with you?' Joe asked, storming out into the car park a few minutes later and over to where Lucinda stood leaning against their car. He must have stayed to pay the bill or maybe chat with Dr Randall; knowing Joe he'd have apologised for her rudeness.

'What's wrong with *me*?' She couldn't believe him sometimes. 'Open the car, Joe, I don't want to discuss it here.'

He dug the key out of his pocket and aimed it at the car like a TV remote. Lucinda yanked open the passenger door and slid into the seat, slamming the door behind her. She didn't know whether to scream or sob.

Joe got in beside her but he didn't start the car. He turned to glare at her. 'Dr Randall gave us the best possible news. Did you *want* her to tell you one of us was infertile?' He spoke with his hands like a typical Italian. So many times in the past she'd found this trait endearing. Right now, it infuriated her.

'Yes,' she screamed, clenching her fists so hard her nails dug into her palms. 'Because right now nothing has changed. I wanted her to be able to fix things.' She bit her lip, losing her battle against tears.

'Aw, Luce.' Joe sighed and then reached over and drew her into his arms. She loved those big, strong arms, had always felt safe with them wrapped around her, but right now she had to fight the urge to pull away.

'There's something wrong, Joe,' she sniffed. 'I don't care what the tests show, I don't care what Dr Randall says. I just know there is. Maybe we really are cursed.'

'Cursed?' He scoffed, pulling back and shoving the keys in the ignition. 'Now you're just being ridiculous.'

Every bone in her body told her not to say anything; that with things already on tenterhooks between them, she should keep her lips zipped. But she could no longer bear this burden alone. She'd been having nightmares about the curse—dreaming about that weird old woman who'd starred in so many schoolyard stories coming into her bedroom and casting spells over the bed while she and Joe slept—and now that Dr Randall had told them there was nothing wrong, well ...

She shook her head. 'No, Joe. We found something when we were back home for Christmas, when we were packing up Mum's things.'

It must have been the tone in her voice because he turned again to look at her, letting the car idle. 'What?'

She sucked in a breath, already anticipating his reaction. 'We found a wedding card that mentioned a family curse, a Patterson curse. Of course we were all curious so we asked Dad but he totally clammed up. Got weird and told us Mum hadn't wanted us to know about it. Charlie and I respected this, but Abigail was still desperate to find out about it and well, you know Madeleine, she couldn't have cared less until Dad told her he didn't want her to know. Then she was like a dog on a bone. We had the motel and Dad to worry about, so I'd forgotten all about it, but Madeleine confronted Aunt Mags.'

'Luce, cut to the chase.' Joe drummed his fingers on the steering wheel. 'Did you find out?'

'Yes,' she hissed, frustrated at the way he always rushed her. 'Mags told Madeleine that years ago a local gyspy woman killed herself because she was in love with our great-grandfather but he married someone else. Apparently the woman's sister blamed my great-grandmother for stealing her sister's lover away, thus break-ing her heart, so she put a curse on all the women in the family from that day forward.'

Joe snorted and she glared at him. 'The curse,' she continued, 'is that no Patterson-born female will be able to have children.'

'Uh ... if that was the case, how come there's been four generations since your grandfather,' Joe asked, rolling his eyes.

'You're not listening. The curse is on Patterson-born females, so the Patterson men can marry and have children, but any *woman* born into the Patterson clan is barren.'

'And you believe this?' Joe's tone was sceptical but before she could reply, he continued. 'Luce, if this was really worrying you, why didn't you tell me before?'

She sighed. 'Because I knew you'd react like this and to be fair, I'd never have believed it either if we weren't living it. But you heard Dr Randall—there's *nothing* wrong with us, yet we've been trying for almost a year now to no avail. What other explanation is there?'

Joe, who usually had an answer for everything, went quiet.

Lucinda looked over at him and for the first time in her life felt real panic. She'd never entertained the thought that Joe would believe the curse, but what if he did? They might not have a medical issue but if the curse had real power, then their fertility problem was hers. Would the pressure from his mum get too much? Would his desire for a family grow stronger than his love for her?

'Okay,' Joe said, interrupting her thoughts 'I'm pretty sure it's a load of bullshit, but let's say there is something in this curse business. There must be something we can do. Maybe we can get it reversed or something?'

It was her turn to scoff. 'What? Do you think we can just look up a witchdoctor on the net and ask them to make a potion or say some mumbo jumbo to make everything better?'

'Maybe. I don't know.' He shrugged. 'Or we wait the few more months Dr Randall says and then if we're still not pregnant, they'll do IVF. I don't reckon some ancient curse can best modern-day medicine.'

Lucinda wasn't so sure but his words got her thinking. Now that she knew there weren't any medical fertility issues, she would focus her efforts on researching curses. Maybe Joe was right and something could be done. They couldn't be the only family who'd ever had a hex on them.

'I was going to suggest we go out to dinner to celebrate our results,' Joe said, 'but I guess you don't think we have anything to celebrate.'

She was about to snap that he was a quick learner, but instead bit her tongue and shook her head. 'I'm sorry, I'm not really in the mood. Let's just get something at home.'

They drove the short distance to Mount Lawley in silence and Lucinda wondered if Joe was still thinking about the curse or if he'd moved onto something else, like dinner or what sport might be on the TV that night.

To his credit, although he'd wanted to go out and she hadn't, Joe offered to make dinner, which left Lucinda to escape into their study. She switched on her laptop, typed 'family curses' into Google, but then decided to go straight to the horse's mouth. Without knowing what exactly she was going to say, she picked up the phone and dialled her aunt in Port Augusta.

'Good evening, Margaret Patterson speaking,' said Mags regally, as if she were Queen Elizabeth herself.

'Hi Aunt Mags, it's Lucinda.'

'Lucinda!' her aunt exclaimed. 'Long time no conversation. How lovely to hear from you.'

'I'm sorry, I've been terrible at keeping in touch lately. Life seems so crazy.' It wasn't exactly true. Aside from her work, she didn't have much else other than trying to get pregnant to occupy her time—but that was all-consuming.

'Oh, don't be silly. We're all as bad as each other, but that doesn't mean we don't care. I think about you girls all the time. And how's that lovely Joe?' she asked, continuing on before Lucinda had a chance to answer. 'I got an old friend to drive me out to Meadow Brook the other day and had a lovely lunch with

Charlie and your father. I'm pleased to report he's looking much better, and Charlie is doing wonderful things with the motel. You won't know it next time you visit.'

'That's fabulous, Aunt Mags,' Lucinda cut in, knowing if she didn't her aunt could go on forever. Charlie had been sending them updates about Dad and also photos of the redecoration she and Mitch had been doing, but as happy as Lucinda was that things were going well in Meadow Brook, she had other things on her mind. 'I wondered if you could tell me anything more about the Patterson curse?'

There was an uncharacteristic silence on the other end of the phone line and then finally, 'What do you want to know?'

As much as she hated discussing her and Joe's private woes, she needed Aunt Mags to know how important this was. 'Joe and I have been trying to have a baby for almost a year,' she confessed before telling her about their latest medical results. 'I guess I'm clutching at straws but I feel so helpless and I'm beginning to wonder if there is something in the curse. How much do you know about your aunts? Did they ever try to have children?'

Mags sighed and Lucinda could imagine her settling back in the armchair near her telephone. 'Sarah never married. Apparently she had a sweetheart but he died in the war. But Victoria was married for a year before her husband was sent away to fight. The way she carried on about the curse, I'm pretty sure they tried to have children like you and Joe—but to no avail.'

Lucinda sucked in a breath. 'You never married though, did you?'

'I'm going to be completely honest with you Lucinda, because I'm a big believer in knowledge equating to power, although in this situation I'm not exactly sure how.'

Lucinda wished her aunt would stop talking in riddles and get to the point. 'What do you mean?'

'In my youth, I was a little like our Charlie. It was the late sixties, early seventies and the world was all about free love, peace and doing whatever made you feel good.'

An image of a twenty-year-old Mags wearing a miniskirt, bright flowery shirt and platform heels came into her head as she listened.

'I fell desperately in love with the drummer in a band, and followed him all around Australia. We were together five years, no legal ceremonies or wedding rings—we didn't believe in such things—but we both wanted to have children. I guess we tried like you and Joe but after years of no success, Bruce left me. I heard he got some groupie pregnant the first night they slept together.'

Lucinda gasped, her heart breaking for her aunt. 'Oh, I'm so sorry.'

Mags made a clicking noise with her teeth. 'I got over him years ago, had a good life, travelling the world, enjoying others when I felt the need but following my own way most of the time. I don't need your pity.'

'So, you think maybe there is something in the curse? That maybe that's why you and Bruce never had a baby?'

'I wish I had answers, my dear. It could all be a coincidence. All I can tell you is that life can be rewarding without children as well. I've had a good life and I have no regrets. Don't let this situation eat at you until there's nothing left inside you but bitterness. Joe is a wonderful man—don't let something you don't have ruin what you do.'

'Thanks for sharing your story, Aunt Mags.' Lucinda paused a beat, nowhere near ready to throw in the towel on trying to get pregnant. 'And for your advice. I promise I won't leave it so long between phone calls next time.'

Mags chuckled. 'Let's not make promises, Lucinda dear. Let's just try to do our best. I'm as guilty as the rest of you for not picking up the phone or sending an email. Are you on Facebook? My friend Marlene is trying to get me to join up.'

'Yes, I am.' Lucinda laughed. 'You should. I'm not on much, but it does help you keep in contact with people you don't see often.'

They talked for a few more minutes and then Mags promptly ended the call, stating she had to go watch her Friday night show. Lucinda didn't mind as she was eager to find out what Dr Google had to say about curses.

She looked at the entries on the screen. The first was an article about ten well-known families with creepy curses, including Monaco's royal family, the Kennedys, the Onassis family and the Guinnesses, who in addition to being Ireland's most famous brewers of beer were also extremely unlucky.

There were a number of rumoured origins of the Kennedy curse—some said it was caused by cursed stolen coins, others by an angry Jewish rabbi—but whatever the cause, a curse was blamed for a string of terrible events and the fact an unusual number of Kennedys had died young. The Onassis family apparently caught the curse from the Kennedys when Jackie Kennedy married Aristotle Onassis. This made Lucinda smile—as if you could catch a curse like you could a common cold. After an alarming number of accidental deaths and calamities in the Guinness family, it was decided they too were cursed, but she couldn't find any theories about the origins of such a curse.

Yet most of these curses seemed to relate to unfortunate deaths, nothing at all like their situation. Lucinda scrolled through the next few entries—most of which were biblical sites talking about people living under bondage because of the sins of their forefathers—but all these curses seemed wishy-washy, bad luck passed on through generations. The Patterson curse was more like a personal vendetta.

She refined her search to 'gypsy curse' and waited. There were pages and pages of information once she started clicking. There were articles, links to books she could download, forums for people who believed their family had been cursed by gypsies … it just went on and on and on. But had Wanda's mother been an actual gypsy?

'Dinner's ready,' Joe announced, popping his head around the corner of the study door.

She glanced longingly at the screen, riveted by an account of a woman in New Jersey who believed her miscarriages were caused by a gypsy curse bestowed upon her great-great-grandparents. Although different to the Patterson curse, it was the closest story she'd found so far. 'Be there in a minute,' she called back, deciding it wouldn't take long to finish reading.

When she emerged from the study almost an hour later, Joe shook his head at her and stood up, lifting his empty plate off the table. 'It was hot half an hour ago,' he said, gesturing to the plate of bacon carbonara in front of her seat. 'Heat it up in the microwave if you want. I'm going to watch TV.'

Lucinda could tell he was pissed off but her energies were too focused on thinking about the curse to agonise over Joe's anger. She waited until she heard the sound of the television in the front lounge room and then picked up her plate and took it back into the study. It didn't matter if the pasta was cold. She had more important things on her mind.

Chapter Twenty-five

'Are you all right, Abigail? You seem kind of distracted today.'

Blinking at the sound of the little voice, Abigail realised she'd drifted off into her own little world. She summoned a smile as she looked down at Livia, the daughter of Nigel's boss and her first ever music student. 'Yes, I'm fine,' she reassured her. 'I was just lost in that beautiful music you were playing.'

Turned out Livia was a total child prodigy. At eight years old, she'd only had violin lessons with another teacher for eight months but was already better than many people who'd been playing for years. Abigail had thought teaching might be a drag, but Livia was a super-bright delight who oozed enthusiasm for music in much the same way Abigail had at her age. Even the few other children she'd picked up through word-of-mouth, although not as talented as Livia, were still fun to teach, but she'd need quite a few more students before she could stop worrying about living expenses.

The little girl frowned and put down her violin on the padded window seat beside them. 'I stopped playing about thirty seconds ago, but you were off on some other planet. You know, if there's something you need to get off your chest, I've been told I'm a very good listener.'

Abigail swallowed. Caught by a gifted and highly empathetic child. She fought the urge to chuckle at Livia's grown-up offer, but part of her was tempted to sit down and spill her guts. Truth was she *was* distracted. Early that afternoon, she'd done her fifth pregnancy test in twenty-four hours. The fact that they were all negative shocked her perhaps more than that first negative result a month ago.

Although her encounter with Nigel in Hong Kong airport had been right in the middle of her menstrual cycle, they had only done it once during that time. But this last month, she'd gone all out. She'd bought an ovulation test kit and also, after much reading on the internet, been taking her temperature every morning before she got out of bed. Using these two methods, she'd been almost certain she'd predicted the accurate window for conception and she'd engineered seeing Nigel every night for those few key days.

Sex with him still blew her socks off so spending time together was never a hardship, yet despite her efforts, only one line had appeared on each of the five different tests she'd bought.

'Thanks, sweetheart,' she said, gesturing for Livia to pick up her violin, 'but we've only got a few more minutes of your lesson and I want to make the most of them.'

Livia sighed, still looking at Abigail with grave concern, but she picked up her instrument, got into position and turned her attention back to the sheet music in front of them. Abigail tried to focus on the music, ready to correct any slight errors, but she found it difficult to concentrate with the burden of disappointment.

A little voice in her head said maybe this was a good thing, a sign she should quit this ridiculous quest to get pregnant while she had the chance, but something had occurred over the last few weeks. The crazy concept of a baby that had once been her get-out-of-London card had blossomed into something else; a deep yearning need. Wherever she went—be it on the Tube or in the local Tesco—she saw babies and pregnant women everywhere. She'd caught herself looking at maternity clothes in Marks and Spencer the other day, and had been surprised at how fashionable some of the outfits were. And whenever she was with Nigel, she looked into his big blue eyes and wondered if their baby's eyes would be the same amazing colour. She simply couldn't help herself.

'How was that?' Livia asked, lowering her violin and bow and looking to Abigail for approval.

'Fantabulistic.' Abigail injected enthusiasm into her voice and grinned down at the child. 'Shall we try a duet before I go?' It was an ambitious suggestion despite Livia's talent, but Abigail hoped playing for a few moments would help stop the thoughts churning in her head.

'Really? Awesome,' Livia said, bouncing a little in her excitement.

Abigail flicked through the pages of Livia's music book and chose a piece the little girl already knew that they could play together. 'This one?'

Livia nodded and Abigail stooped to retrieve her violin from its case. She lifted it to her chin and gave the nod for Livia to start. It wasn't the smoothest she'd ever played but it felt good to be playing with someone else again, to be playing for purpose. Just before the end of the piece, she became aware of another presence in the room. Thinking it was Livia's *au pair* or the housekeeper, Abigail continued and Livia followed her lead.

The moment they finished, applause erupted behind them and they turned to see Daniel and Nigel standing there grinning. Abigail's heart hitched a beat at the unexpected sight of Nigel. He wore a dark navy suit and a crisp white shirt, loosened at the collar and looked like he'd stepped right off the cover of GQ magazine. As her hormones stood to attention she fought an intense urge to go over and snog him silly.

'Bravo,' Daniel said, stepping further into the room. 'That was brilliant, darling.' He beamed down at his daughter, patting her on the head like she was some kind of pet. 'Aren't we lucky Nigel found Abigail for us?'

Nigel sidled over to Abigail and put his arm around her. 'Not as lucky as I am.' He kissed her on the forehead and warmth spread from that spot.

She half-laughed, not sure how to respond. He said stuff like that often, stuff that caused her stomach to flip and made her question the casual nature of their relationship, but she couldn't help liking the way it made her feel. 'This is a pleasant surprise.' She slipped out of his arm and began packing away her violin.

Nigel grinned. 'We had a meeting in Chelsea and when Daniel said you'd be here with Livia, I thought I'd come see if I could whisk you away for an early dinner.'

As if it could hear him, her stomach rumbled quietly. 'I could be tempted.'

'Make sure he takes you somewhere good,' Daniel said with a chuckle.

'Oh, I will.'

They all laughed again and then Abigail and Nigel said their goodbyes. They emerged from Daniel's large terrace house in well-to-do Holland Park to find a black car waiting for them. For Abigail, who'd been taking the Tube more than ever lately, it felt like such a luxury to climb into the back seat with Nigel.

He barked the address of a restaurant in Knightsbridge to the driver and then slid as close as he could to her, placing one hand on her thigh and the other on her neck as he leaned over and drew her lips to his. Abigail sank into his kiss, pleasure rippling through her body. He was just the tonic she needed after those five disappointing tests.

'You are possibly the best kisser in the universe,' she whispered when they finally came up for air.

He inched his thumb seductively a little further up her leg, drawing tiny circles on her inner thigh. 'It's easy to be good when the subject turns me on as much as you do.'

Glowing, she glanced down at her thigh, something low in her belly tightening at his teasing touch. If only they were in one of those limos that had a privacy screen to hide them from the prying eyes of their driver. Her mouth went dry and her spine tingled at the thought. Suddenly the hunger she'd felt when he'd suggested an early dinner turned into another kind of hunger altogether.

'Shall we bypass dinner and head back to your place?' she asked, her voice breathier than she meant it to be.

Nigel chuckled and squeezed her thigh. 'Steady on, vixen. A man needs to keep his strength up for what you have in mind.'

She swallowed her pout and asked, 'Where are we going then?'

He named one of London's top restaurants and she thanked God she'd dressed up a little for the music lesson. If she was ever to teach violin back in Meadow Brook she'd likely wear yoga pants and a sloppy joe, but Livia lived in a fancy neighbourhood and she'd wanted to blend in.

'Wow, is it a special occasion?'

'I got a promotion.' He beamed at her. 'With a corner office and everything.'

'Congratulations,' she said, genuinely happy for him. 'What exactly does it entail?'

His fingers still trailing leisurely up and down her leg, he told her about the new role. Although she knew next to nothing about advertising, Nigel spoke about it with such zest and passion, she found herself hanging on his every word. At the restaurant, their driver leapt out of the car and opened the door for them but it was Nigel who offered his hand to assist her. Despite being a hot, smart, ambitious sex god, he was also a gentleman and the more time she spent with him, the more she liked him.

'What?' Nigel asked when she giggled at that errant thought.

'Nothing.' She bit her lip and shook her head. Nigel took her violin from the driver and they walked the few steps to the restaurant.

'You and Livia sounded amazing back there,' he said as they waited for the maître d' to seat them.

She blushed. 'Oh, that was nothing.'

'Will you play for me later?'

'What will I get in return?' she teased.

He rolled his eyes but then leant towards her and whispered exactly what he could offer.

'Hell … For that I'll play for you naked.'

'I'm holding you to that,' he promised as a man wearing a tuxedo approached them.

The man bowed his head. 'Good evening, do you have a reservation?'

Nigel nodded. 'Under Lewis.'

They were led to a table in a quiet corner of the restaurant and offered the drinks menu. When Nigel ordered a bottle of expensive sparking wine, Abigail decided as she was not yet pregnant, she could indulge this once. So far, whenever she'd been with Nigel and he'd offered her a drink, she'd either made up some excuse or taken the drink and then poured it down the sink or into a pot plant when he wasn't looking. She'd gotten quite skilled at the art of deception.

Once the waiter had retreated, Abigail lifted her glass. 'To your promotion.'

'And to your naked violin playing,' Nigel added.

'You're incorrigible,' she said, giggling before taking her first sip.

'But you like me.' He winked and then also drank.

Yes, she thought. *I do*. Perhaps a little too much for their agreement and definitely too much to be trying to have his baby without his knowledge. If only she could get a few more violin students, maybe she'd get enough income to live comfortably in London. Maybe eventually she could tell her family that being in the orchestra hadn't been all she'd imagined it to be and so she'd chosen another direction. They didn't need to know she'd been sacked.

Nigel gestured to the menu. 'I've been here before and I know what I want. I recommend the fillet of halibut. Anyway, back in a moment.'

He stood and headed for the restrooms, leaving Abigail to wonder with whom he'd come here before. Was it business or another woman? She didn't like the prick of jealousy that burned her heart at the thought of the latter. But that was ridiculous. It wasn't like she had any claim on him.

Her phone beeped, signalling an incoming email, and she snatched it up, eager for the distraction. She smiled when she saw Lucinda's name in her inbox.

Hi sisters

Hope you are all well and happy in your various parts of the planet. Thanks Charlie for all you're doing with Dad and the motel—your updates and your efforts are muchly appreciated.

I just thought I'd fill you in on what's happening, or rather not happening, in me and Joe's life. As you know, we've been trying for a baby for some time and recently saw the specialist Madeleine recommended. Well, we've had a number of tests and the apparently good news is that neither of us have any medical conditions that would hinder our chances of conception. The professionals

think it is only a matter of time before we get lucky. But I'm so tired
of waiting and I can't help feeling that there's more going on. I
can't help wondering if there is some truth to the Patterson curse.

I've spoken to Aunt Mags about it and she confessed she once had
a love affair and also tried to get pregnant to no avail. I'm honestly
at a loss. Could a near century-old curse really have so much power?
And if so, what the hell are we supposed to do about it?

A chill came over Abigail as she read the email. Lucinda rarely
swore and although 'hell' wasn't exactly a curse word, her use of
it showed how upset she was. Back home at Christmas she hadn't
really understood Lucinda's desire to get pregnant but now she
did. Until recently, she'd never failed at anything, but pregnancy
wasn't like an exam you could prepare for, and every one of those
negative test results had felt like a personal affront.

But she couldn't pick up the phone and tell Lucinda she'd also
been trying to get pregnant. Lucinda would want to know why
and then she'd have to tell her about the orchestra and that would
defeat the whole purpose. The bigger the web of lies she wove,
the more alone she felt.

'You okay?'

Abigail startled at Nigel's question as he sat back down opposite
her. 'I … Uh …' She didn't know what to say.

He gestured to the phone she was holding in a vice-like grip.
'Bad news?'

Before she could reply, their waiter returned. 'Excuse me, are
you ready to order?'

Nigel looked to her questioningly. She smiled, nodded and
rattled off the dish he'd recommended earlier as she didn't want to
admit she hadn't even glanced at the menu yet.

'What's wrong?' Nigel asked, reaching across the table and
taking her hand as the waiter retreated.

'I got an email from my sister,' she confessed. 'She and her husband have been trying to have a baby for a while and they just had the results of fertility testing. They both got the all-clear.'

He frowned. 'Isn't that good news?'

She shrugged. 'Yes, in theory but … Apparently we have a family curse and Lucinda is beginning to think that it's responsible for her infertility.'

'A curse?'

Although Nigel looked sceptical, Abigail nodded and the whole story fell from her lips. He listened attentively and they barely noticed when their beautifully displayed dishes were placed in front of them.

'And you believe all that?' he asked, finally picking up his cutlery.

'I honestly don't know. I kind of wish we'd never found out.' Abigail picked up her fork and poked at her food, but with all the thoughts plaguing her she'd lost her appetite.

Nigel took his first mouthful and she could almost see his brain ticking over as he chewed. When he'd finished, he asked, 'Do you want kids?'

The direct question shocked her and she took a moment to answer. 'One day.' She hoped the quiver in her voice didn't give away just how soon she wanted that day to come. 'What about you?'

He rubbed his jawline slowly as if deep in contemplation and said, 'Yes. I do. Definitely. One day, when I've made my mark in the advertising world and have something more to offer a family than a workaholic, mostly absent dad.'

Abigail opened her mouth but no words came out. She had no idea what to say. The tiny bit of guilt she'd initially felt about trying to get pregnant without his knowledge or consent was growing each minute she spent in his company. Yet, Lucinda's email only enhanced her desire to have a baby. One of them had to prove this damn curse wrong!

'Speaking of work,' he said, and she was glad he'd changed the subject, 'I have a big dinner coming up in a couple of weekends. It's a black tie thing and I get put up in a posh hotel afterwards. Would you like to be my date and help me devour the mini-bar?'

While Nigel's eyes glistened at the prospect of mini-bar mischief, Abigail did a quick calculation in her head. Two weekends from now she would be in the middle of her cycle, making the date perfect timing for conception. And who in their right mind would turn down the offer of a naughty night in a swish hotel with a hot guy?

'That sounds like fun,' she said, already mentally going through her wardrobe to select an outfit.

'We'll make sure it is.' Nigel offered her another wink as he reached out to take a drink.

By the time they got back to his apartment, she'd drunk one too many glasses of champagne, which made playing the violin— naked or otherwise—difficult. He shook his head and laughed as she stood at the end of the bed and attempted a concerto. And when she pouted, he rose and went to her, gently taking the violin and placing it back in its case on the floor.

'I think you need some sleep,' he said, pulling her into his arms and down onto the bed with him. Her body thrummed in antici- pation of his touch, but he merely tugged the blankets up over them and snuggled her up against him. Within seconds, she felt her eyes drifting shut.

Warning bells were sounding loud and clear in her head, but she ignored them. It would be the first time she'd stayed the night.

Chapter Twenty-six

Good luck. Thinking of you and fingers crossed that it works. xo

Madeleine pressed a hand against her stomach as she read Celia's text, unsure whether her slight nausea was the result of the weirdness of her situation or anxiety over what was about to occur. She typed back a quick thanks and then left her phone on the kitchen bench as she ran around her apartment, making sure everything was in order. This wasn't necessary—Hugo had seen it in a state of glorious mess on many occasions—but somehow today felt different.

The intercom buzzed and while her body froze at the sound, the butterflies in her belly went crazy. She took a deep breath and rushed over to the wall by the door, pressing the button before she had time to back out. 'Hello?'

'Hey, Mads, it's me.'

'Come on up,' she said, hoping she didn't sound as shaky as she felt. She pressed the button to let him into the lobby below and then swung open her front door, anxiously awaiting his arrival. It seemed to take forever for the elevator on her floor to beep open and for Hugo to emerge, but even with time to prepare, she couldn't help the spark of awareness that flared low in her belly at the sight of him.

'Hi,' she breathed, inappropriately overcome by how hot he looked in simple blue jeans, a grey light-knit sweater and a black leather jacket over the top. Did he have to be so perfect?

He strode towards her and leant forward, brushing his lips against her cheek before pulling back. He half-smiled. 'Hello.'

She laughed nervously at the oddness between them and then stood back, gesturing for him to go on ahead of her into the apartment. 'Can I get you a drink?' she asked as she closed the door behind them.

He glanced around as if he'd never been there before and then shook his head. 'I'd rather we got this over with.'

He didn't sound like someone overly enthusiastic about what they were going to do and she almost asked him if he'd changed his mind. But the thought of Lucinda's email earlier that week and the desire to have a child, which had grown within her like some kind of out-of-control weed since she'd made her decision, kept Madeleine from saying anything of the sort. This was something she needed to do.

'Okay then.' She nodded, her heart beating wildly in her chest. 'Would you prefer to use the bathroom or my bedroom?'

'The bathroom,' he answered quickly and she cursed herself for offering the latter. It sounded a little too intimate, as if she were inviting him into her boudoir. He shrugged off his jacket and flung it onto the couch.

'The specimen jars are in there waiting for you,' she added, pointing in the direction of the bathroom.

'Great.' He smiled warmly at her, which slightly eased her anxiety. 'Do you want to go and get yourself ready in your bedroom and I'll leave the sample outside your door when I'm finished?'

'Sure. Good plan.' What exactly did he think *getting ready* entailed? Of course she'd read the research that conception was more likely if she were aroused when the sperm was injected. Was he suggesting she pleasure herself? Her cheeks burned at the thought.

'I'll knock,' he said, already turning towards the bathroom.

As Hugo closed the door behind him, Madeleine wondered if she should have left some dirty magazines in there for him, like they did in the IVF clinics. Or maybe a picture of herself naked? Her cheeks heated even more at that illicit thought, the warmth spreading to other parts of her body as her mind ran away to a naughty fantasy land. Aroused? She was already more than half-way there.

And then she heard a noise—much like that of a man in the throes of pleasure—that jolted her into action. Although curious about how Hugo would sound during sex, she didn't want him to come out and find her listening like some kind of pervert, so she rushed off to her bedroom, her uterus quivering at the thought of exactly what he was doing on the other side of the wall. She lay down on her bed, closed her eyes and imagined Hugo lying beside her. Before she realised what she was doing, her hand had slid beneath the waistband of her black yoga pants and down between her legs. Her breathing altered as she imagined Hugo's fingers pushing in and out of her, teasing that tender nub until she could bear the pleasure no more.

Her heart raced and she bit her lip to stop from crying out as the first orgasm she'd had in a very long while washed over her. She was lost in her bubble of bliss when a knock sounded at her bedroom door. Yanking her hand out of her pants, she sprang off the bed as if she'd just been caught doing something illegal.

'Thanks,' she managed to call out—unsure whether she was thanking him for his deposit or for playing an unwitting role in her exquisite release.

'You're welcome,' came Hugo's reply. 'See you at work.'

He sounded so very normal, except this situation was anything but. She waited until she heard the apartment door close and then opened her door slowly and peered down at the little jar on the floor. He'd done it.

It looked small and insignificant but that tiny specimen jar could hold her future inside it.

Her hand shaking, she bent down to pick it up, clutching it against her chest as she retreated to her room and put it on the bedside table beside the other paraphernalia she had lined up and ready for the next stage of the plan. Still warm from the aftershocks of her climax, she stared at Hugo's generous donation.

Was she crazy to even consider this?

Chapter Twenty-seven

It felt like Groundhog Day. Another day at school teaching six year olds who seemed to do nothing but whine and dob on each other. *Mrs Manomano* (none of them could pronounce her name), *Jackson pinched me. Mrs Manoram, Sophie's using the wrong pencil.* Their endless jabs at each other were enough to drive anyone insane and quite frankly, Lucinda wouldn't care what pencils the kids used if they'd just shut up and get on with their work. She hadn't always been so impatient with the littlies and she hated it, but she couldn't seem to snap out of her funk.

And then she'd come home and spent another evening doing the washing and cooking dinner, planning for the next day and half-heartedly watching *Outlander* on the TV while she cut out cardboard clovers for the St Patrick's Day assembly tomorrow. Her friends in the staffroom raved about the show but Lucinda couldn't seem to get excited about anything these days, not even the actor playing hot redhead Jamie Fraser.

After smoothing night cream over her tired skin and brushing her hair, she climbed into bed beside Joe, who'd retreated to their bedroom just after dinner. Although she ruffled the sheets as she slid between them, he was so focused on the iPad screen on the pillow in front of him and whatever was happening in the land of Minecraft that he didn't even stir. She knew if she tapped him on the shoulder and told him it was *that* time of the month, he'd put the game down and give her some attention, but when had sex become such a chore? Something they *needed*, rather than wanted, to do. When had spending the evening with a little screen, doing whatever one did when one played Minecraft, become more appealing than hanging out on the couch with her?

She remembered a time when she would climb into bed wearing a skimpy nightie and find him naked waiting for her. Nowadays Joe's standard night-time attire was faded boxer shorts and an old t-shirt. Once upon a time, he'd have turned to her with lustful eyes and asked her how her day was. They would have talked for hours before slipping into each other's arms and making love. They used to have so much to say to each other, but these days they barely seemed to have anything at all.

Was buying him the iPad a mistake? It had come into their bedroom and occupied him during the times that use to be just for them. Or was this just what happened to all marriages after you'd been together for more than a decade? People who were lucky enough to have children probably didn't even notice because they had so much else going on. And of course couples with children always had something to talk about with each other. She sighed, giving herself a headache with all these woeful thoughts, and then reached over to her bedside table to grab her own iPad. She swiped her finger across the screen and the forum she'd been looking at last night appeared. She skimmed the new messages quickly to see if there was anything interesting, anything that might be the key to fixing her plight.

But as usual there was nothing out of the ordinary. Why the hell did she bother reading this stuff? None of her research had done any good. No matter what she found, what she read, it didn't change anything. In all the forums and articles, all the stories of gypsy curses, they kept coming back to the same thing. Going back to the source. But, like in so many of the stories shared, the source of her family curse had died years ago.

She'd stopped sharing the stories with Joe a couple of weeks ago because it only irritated him. No wonder he preferred the iPad to her these days. She was even beginning to irritate herself. Puffing out a frustrated sigh between her teeth, Lucinda dumped the iPad on the floor beside her, deciding to abandon reading all this useless rubbish. The thought of another day like the one she'd had today made her want to scream out loud. What would Joe do if she did? If she opened her mouth as wide as it would go and hollered until her cheeks went red and her throat went dry?

Maybe then he'd ask her how her day was. And she would tell him: *Today was crap, Joe. One of the year five teachers announced her pregnancy and two of the mums from my class were showing off their beautiful newborn babies in the school pick-up line.* Sometimes it felt as if everyone in the world could get pregnant except her. If one more friend or colleague announced their pregnancy, she would not be responsible for her actions.

'Are you okay?'

She jumped at the sound of Joe's voice and turned to see he'd put the iPad away and was leaning on one elbow, looking up at her as if she were a stranger in his bed. Sometimes she felt that way and she hated it. She hated her life at the moment, she was beginning to hate herself, and if things kept going the way they were then Joe would be next in the firing line. Something had to change.

'No.' She shook her head and looked down at her husband. 'I'm not. I want to quit my job.'

'What?' He pushed up into a sitting position. The expression on his face and the tone of his voice echoed her own surprise.

Until she'd said it out loud, she hadn't actually known this was what she wanted, but now it seemed like the obvious solution.

She rubbed her lips together, taking a moment to collect her thoughts before explaining. 'I'm tired, Joe. I'm tired of all the negative energy I'm carrying around because of the baby thing, and school only makes it worse. Every day I'm dealing with other people's offspring, wondering if I'll ever be able to have any of my own and it feels like a slap in the face. I'm taking out my anger and frustration on the kids. And on you.'

She went quiet a moment and he didn't deny it. 'You know things aren't the best between us at the moment and I don't want the baby thing to come between us. I want to stay at home, focus on you, on me, on us and our marriage again.'

He frowned a little. 'But what about the weeks when I'm away? Won't you get bored?'

'I don't think so.' She shook her head and smiled, reaching out to take his hand. 'And think of the benefits. I won't be so tired and grumpy when you come home from work now. I won't have any planning to do, so I'll have time to make proper dinners and those chocolate mud cakes you used to love. I know the baby thing has taken over our lives and that is mostly my fault, so I want to do something about it.'

'Well, if you're sure.' He squeezed her hand back. 'I thought you loved teaching?'

'I do. Rather, I did, but I'm not the same person I was when I started and I don't think I'm a good teacher anymore. I don't have the passion, the drive, and if we do have children, I wouldn't want our kids to have a teacher like me, a teacher whose heart isn't one hundred percent in the job.' Sure she felt bad about deserting her class in the middle of the school year, but it wasn't any different to what she'd have to do if she *were* pregnant. And her students would be better off without her—they'd get some young, fresh, first-year-out teacher full of enthusiasm and eager to prove him- or herself. Someone exactly like she'd been ten years ago.

'Okay then,' Joe said. 'It's gonna be tight with the mortgage and stuff and I don't know how we'll afford IVF if we need to go down that track, but that's okay if you think it'll make you happier. You know that's all I want, right? It's all I've ever wanted.'

'Oh, Joe.' Lucinda leaned across and kissed him on the lips, her heart fuller for him than it had been in a long time. Her mood already felt lighter now she'd made this decision. She'd type up her letter of resignation in the morning. It was time to put herself and her marriage first.

Joe's hands slipped behind her back and he pulled her towards him, crushing her breasts against his chest as he deepened the kiss and ran his hands down to cup her buttocks. She felt the hard pressure of his aroused cock against her stomach and rubbed herself against it, trying to encourage herself as much as him. But all she could think was that this wasn't the right time of the month, so what was the point?

He pulled back and then flipped her onto her back, pausing a moment to rip his t-shirt up and over his head. More than ten years after she'd met him he was still the most gorgeous man she knew—all tan and sculpted muscles looming above her. She reached up and skimmed her fingernails down his chest, smiling when he sucked in his breath at her touch. His hands then traced a path to the bottom of her nightie and she wriggled, assisting him as he eased it up over her head.

'My *bella* Lucinda,' he said, his voice rough as he gazed down at her and then dipped his head to take one nipple in his mouth. His tongue twirled around the bud in a manner that had once driven her insane and she waited for the need and desire to flare up within her. Waited and inwardly prayed. But she just couldn't summon the desperation she'd once had for him.

'*Yes*, Joe.' She moaned, faking her arousal as he snuck his hand down between her legs and did things to her that used to drive her wild, just wishing he would get it over with so she could go to sleep. Remembering Meg Ryan's famous fake orgasm in *When Harry Met Sally*, Lucinda gave it her everything, panting and squirming and vocalising apparent delight. When she could take it no more, she urged him on top of her and sighed with relief when he plunged deep inside. Joe read this sigh as one of pleasure and as he pumped and then came, she wished to hell it was.

Lovemaking wasn't supposed to be something you got over and done with, just like it wasn't only for the purpose of making babies. She loved this man more than anyone and anything in the world and she wanted to revive that passion again.

She only hoped that quitting work and taking some time out would help.

Chapter Twenty-eight

Charlie couldn't remember her life in Melbourne ever being as hectic as this. She'd done her sixth hula-hoop class at the local tennis club hall this morning and there'd been double the number of attendees as last week. Word spread fast in the country and young mums and pensioners alike appeared to be happy to have a new avenue for fitness.

After class, she'd showered and was just sitting down at the kitchen table to start an assignment for her naturopathy course when Dad came in and she rushed to hide her workbooks under the table.

He didn't appear to notice as he crossed the room and bent to kiss her on the head. 'Hello, my love.' He straightened and rubbed the side of his forehead. 'Would you be able to drive down to Port Augusta and collect Mags for me today? I've got a bit of a headache and thought if I have a nap I might be able to get rid of it before tonight.'

'Are you okay?' Charlie looked up at him, concerned. Tonight, at Mitch's suggestion, they were holding their first theme night—St Patrick's Day at the Meadow Brook Motel—and Charlie hoped she wasn't putting added pressure on Dad. She'd done most of the organisation with a little help from Rob and Mrs Sampson, but still.

'I'm fine,' he insisted. 'It's just a headache.'

'Well, if you're sure. I'd love to go get Aunty Mags. Have you taken any painkillers?'

'I'll take one now. You're an angel, my girl. Drive safe.'

'I will.' Charlie smiled at Dad as he turned and headed down the corridor to his bedroom, then she grabbed her books from under the table and took them back to her own room. If she needed to drive to Port Augusta and back, study would have to wait. Everything about the course fascinated her, but finding the time to get her reading and assignments done was proving difficult. There was always something or someone requiring her attention and she rarely got a moment to herself. For that reason it would be nice to take a drive.

The only problem with time alone was that it gave her mind the chance to wander. And, as always, it found its way to Mitch.

Since the barbeque at Macca's place, he'd been busy working and they hadn't seen much of each other. She'd hoped this would help get her errant hormones back in order, but she missed him so much. Painting was boring without him wielding a brush and cracking jokes beside her. But unfortunately, she couldn't afford to pay him for his company and he needed to earn a living. And it wasn't like she was lacking in human interaction. Her dad and Mrs Sampson were always available for a chat, Rob liked to have a natter in the evenings and she'd started meeting Kate and Lisa for a drink at the café after each hula-hoop class, but none of them made her feel like she did when she was with Mitch.

Despite warning bells sounding in her head, she was very much looking forward to seeing him tonight.

Before she knew it, she was pulling up in front of the 'entertainment centre'. Charlie chuckled at the sight of Aunt Mags waiting out the front, wearing a bright green sundress, green boots, a green hat and …

Good Lord, had she spray-painted her hair? Trust Mags to go all out. There was a tattered overnight-sized suitcase (red, not green) at her feet, which she stooped to pick up as Charlie approached.

'Leave it,' Charlie called, jogging up the ramp and then leaning in for a hug. She picked up the suitcase and stepped back to admire her aunt's outfit. Up close, she noted green shamrock earrings and a matching necklace. 'You look fabulous.'

'Well, St Pat's was always one of my fave celebrations. The Irish know how to throw a party.' She glanced at Charlie's denim shorts and purple singlet. 'I hope you're planning on getting changed before tonight.'

'Of course.' She held out her arm to assist her aunt and then led her towards the old van. 'I have a green cocktail dress and appropriate jewellery. And we've gone all out with decorations in the bar. It should be a great night.'

'I have no doubt. I recall some of the parties your mum and dad used to throw when we were young. Before your time of course, although lots of the locals who are still around used to come. Mitch's dad was always in attendance.'

'Really?' Charlie's heart did a little flip at the mention of Mitch but she managed to keep the expression on her face passive. The last thing she needed was Mags getting wind of her strange feelings. Aunt Mags would pester and question her until she admitted something she didn't want to admit.

'Yes. Mitch's mum and Annette were good friends, but after Therese left, Rick stopped coming around.'

'Well, he's coming tonight,' Charlie said, keeping her voice light as she assisted Mags into the passenger seat and then stowed her suitcase in the back of the van.

'Oh?'

Charlie slid into the driver's seat. 'Yes, Mitch gets depressed about his dad being stuck in care and him not being able to help much, so I suggested he break him out for a bit of fun.'

'What a good idea.' Mags made a tsk noise with her tongue. 'Ghastly disease he's got, especially for someone who was always such a strong, strapping thing. I had a bit of a crush on him myself but even after his wife left, he never looked twice at me.'

Charlie bit her lower lip to stop from grinning as she started the van and eased out onto the road. She imagined most men would find Aunt Mags far too overpowering. 'More fool him.'

'Speaking of men,' began Aunt Mags, and Charlie didn't like where this could be going, 'how are you finding being back in Meadow Brook? I hope moving home isn't cramping your style, if you know what I mean.'

Charlie's eyes boggled and she gripped the steering wheel. Of course she knew what Mags meant but she didn't want to discuss her non-existent love-life with anyone. 'I didn't have much style to cramp, but I'm loving being back. I'm enjoying working at the motel, doing the renovations, reconnecting with people I went to school with and getting Dad to myself for a bit.'

Aunt Mags chuckled. 'Yes, I can understand that. Your sisters can be a little domineering.'

'That's one word for it.' As much as she loved her sisters, Charlie could never quite be herself around them, but being back in Meadow Brook on her own was more fun and rewarding than she had expected.

'What will you do with yourself when the motel sells?' Mags asked.

Charlie frowned. 'Go back to Melbourne, I guess.' Although truth be told, she'd been wondering lately about maybe staying on in Meadow Brook. The reasons she'd left in the first place were no longer there and she'd made some good friends in a short time. And then there was Mitch.

'You haven't thought about taking on the place yourself? I'm sure Brian's only selling it because none of you girls have ever shown any interest.'

Charlie spluttered. 'Me? Run the motel on my own?'

'What's so ridiculous about that?'

'Well …' Where should she start?

But Mags didn't give her a chance to list any of the reasons. 'You should have more confidence in yourself, Charlie-girl. You can do anything you put your mind to. You're more like your sisters than you think.'

Then, again before Charlie could reply, Mags asked in an ominous tone, 'Have you spoken to Lucinda much lately? She called me a month or so ago asking all sorts of questions about the Patterson curse and she didn't sound in a good way. I can't stop thinking about her, worrying that something isn't quite right with her and Joe. I'm thinking maybe I should pay her a visit.'

'To Western Australia?'

Aunt Mags snorted. 'It's not on the other side of the planet, you know. It's barely more than a bus ride in comparison to some of the places I've been. But I can't go until July when my seniors' board games group has our winter break.'

'I'm sure she'd love a visit,' Charlie said. Truthfully she was worried about Lucinda as well. She'd been sending weird emails at all hours of the night, suggesting she wasn't sleeping too well. Charlie had meant to talk to Abigail and Madeleine about it, but she never seemed to have the time. 'She did tell us she'd spoken to you about the curse and about your old boyfriend. Bruce, was it?'

Mags snorted. 'I wish I'd kept my trap shut about that damn curse. I think your father was right, and your mother. I'd never have said anything if I'd known Lucinda was having trouble conceiving.'

'I guess we can only hope she gets pregnant soon. That'll put a stop to all the speculation. She and Joe would make such wonderful parents.'

'Hmm … that they would.' Mags was quiet a moment but Charlie could tell she was contemplating something. 'There is something else that would work.'

'Oh?'

'You or one of your other sisters could get pregnant.'

Charlie snorted, knowing that if she'd been drinking at that moment, she'd have spat her mouthful out in a most unlady-like manner. Had Aunt Mags finally lost her mind? As far as she could recall, neither Abigail nor Madeleine had ever even mentioned the prospect of one day having children. And as for herself? Well …

'Last time I checked, it takes two to make a baby,' she said. 'Abigail and Madeleine are way too busy making music and delivering babies for that kind of commitment. And anyway, Abigail is the only one of us in any kind of relationship.'

'That's not the word on the bush telegraph,' Mags said, her tone amused. 'Janie Lee came down to visit her mother-in-law at the entertainment centre last week and she said you and Mitch make quite an item. She said she'd seen you in the café together and that word about town is he's also been spotted leaving the motel in the early hours of the morning.'

'He's been helping me paint the rooms. And I think Janie Lee's news is dated as he hasn't done so for a couple of weeks.'

'More's the pity.' Mags sighed. 'You can't tell me you don't think the boy is hot?'

'Who? Mitch?' Charlie felt her hands sweating on the steering wheel. Of course he was hot, but it didn't matter what she thought as he'd never see *her* as anything more than a friend.

'No, bloody Father Christmas. Of course Mitch. He's a strapping young lad and you are a gorgeous girl. You're both delightful people and the best of friends. It doesn't take a genius to see you'd be perfect for each other.'

'Maybe you should tell Mitch that,' Charlie snapped, before she could think better of it.

Mags smiled and folded her arms over her ample bosom. 'Maybe I will.'

A cold flush crept over Charlie as if someone had dumped a bucket of ice over her head. 'No, Aunt Mags, you can't. I didn't mean that.' Panic caused her heartbeat to accelerate. 'Please don't say anything.'

'Do you like him, Charlie-girl?'

Charlie rubbed her lips together. Everyone liked Mitch—he was that type of guy—but she knew Aunt Mags didn't mean like that. And she'd never been much of a liar. 'Yes,' she confessed, her heart clenching at the thought.

'Then you have to tell him.'

'No.' Charlie shook her head. 'I can't. You don't understand. He doesn't see me that way. He's made that clear a couple of times and I don't want to ruin our friendship by putting my feelings on him. Maybe if I hang around longer, maybe if we keep spending time together, maybe he'll see me as more than a friend, but I can't confess and I beg you, please, don't say anything either.'

'Oh dear girl, don't get yourself in such a tizz.' Mags reached across and patted Charlie's knee. 'I won't say anything if you really don't want me to, but you young folks are such scaredy-cats. In my day, if we liked a boy, we told them.'

Maybe if Charlie simply liked a boy, she would just tell him. But Mitch wasn't any old boy, he was her best friend and she didn't want to ruin that. Vowing to keep a close eye on Aunt Mags throughout the night, she continued on along the Eyre Highway without saying much else. Mags, happy to natter about the goings on of her neighbours at the 'entertainment centre', didn't appear to notice and before long they were pulling up in front of the motel.

'Wow,' Mags marvelled as she glanced out the window at the garden beds Charlie had only just started working on. When she wanted a break from painting she'd been getting outside and weeding. 'You have been working hard.'

'Thanks,' Charlie said, climbing out of the van and going round to assist her aunt. 'I'll show you to your room to get freshened up. Head over to the bar when you're ready. Dad and Mrs Sampson will be there and I'll be along soon.'

Charlie led her to one of the newly renovated rooms, basking in the compliments Mags offered. 'Charlie-girl, you've done an amazing job. It looks like a totally new place.' And then Charlie snuck off to the house to have a quick shower and put on her St Patrick's Day outfit.

She gasped at her reflection in the mirror, wondering if the green miniskirt she'd found amongst some of Abigail's old things was too short, but she didn't have anything else green so she'd have to suck up the embarrassment. Next came the green eye shadow, the hair ribbons and the pair of vintage green stilettos that were her mother's.

Almost as an afterthought, she picked up her mobile phone and snapped a selfie. She cringed at the image looking back at her and decided if she was going to make a habit of this, she'd need to practise her smile, but sent it off to her sisters anyway. Their lives were so busy that they rarely made the time to chat, but Aunt Mags's conversation in the car had made her think about them. Mum's sudden death had proved life could be short and unexpected—they should make more of an effort.

All good here. Dad doing much better. Think there might be something happening with Mrs Sampson, although I could be totally off the mark. St Pat's party in the motel tonight. Hope you are all well. xo Charlie

She attached the ghastly selfie and pressed Send. Then she headed down the hallway and through the door that led into the motel. It wasn't even six o'clock but already she could hear the music coming from the local band set up in the corner. Humming along to an old tune by The Corrs, Charlie stepped into the bar and restaurant area and froze.

It took her all of five seconds to work out what was different and she reached out to steady herself on the bar.

'Who …? How …? Why …?' She stumbled on her words, glancing from the new handcrafted tables in the restaurant that had replaced the ancient formica ones to the faces of Dad, Mrs Sampson, Rob, Aunt Mags and … Mitch. And of course she knew the answer. There was only one person who could make furniture like that and he was standing in between Dad and Rob, looking half pleased with himself, half embarrassed. And totally gorgeous in black trousers, a green shirt and a tie with shamrocks all over it.

Her heart swelled with love for him. So that's why he'd been so absent these last few weeks. She'd thought maybe he'd simply become bored of hanging out with her, tired of painting wall after wall, maybe even found the company of someone else … But it looked as if he'd been spending every spare minute in his workshop, crafting these magnificent tables.

She was in total awe. She was speechless. They still had a heck of a lot of work to bring the motel into the twenty-first century but Mitch's gorgeous new tables went a long way towards this goal. She thought back to Australia Day on the farm when she'd joked about needing him to make furniture for the motel and he'd quipped back that she couldn't afford him. She didn't know how she'd ever repay him.

'Don't just stand there, love,' Dad said, gesturing to the furniture around him. 'Thank the boy. He's been working on these tables for weeks—got chairs coming soon too, apparently. He made me promise not to tell you what he was doing and to somehow get you out of the way this afternoon so we could arrange them all. You like it?'

'I ...' So the headache had been a ruse. 'Yes, of course. They are amazing. Mitch ... I don't know what to say.'

'Thank you would be a great start,' Mrs Sampson suggested, grinning warmly. 'And then maybe get him a drink. He's pretty much brought all these tables in on his own this afternoon. Brian tried to help but Mitch and I put paid to that pretty fast.'

'Thank you.' Charlie gave her dad a look of reproof before meeting Mitch's gaze. His dark brown eyes were full of warmth. 'You are very, very sneaky.'

He shrugged as if it were nothing.

Before she could say any more, the door of the motel opened and she turned to see Macca striding through, pushing their father in a wheelchair. Kate followed closely behind with the children and the pram. The tables were forgotten as Mitch and Mrs Sampson rushed over. Not wanting to overwhelm Mr McDonald, Charlie stepped towards the nearest table and admired Mitch's handiwork. Was there anything he wasn't good at? And how the hell was she supposed to curb her feelings for him if he kept doing things like this?

As Rob headed back into the kitchen to work on his special St Pat's menu, Charlie helped her dad pouring drinks. More people started arriving and Mrs Sampson, always one to lend a hand, joined them behind the bar even though she wasn't on duty tonight.

'This was a great idea of yours,' Mrs Sampson whispered, nodding towards the growing crowd as she pulled a beer. 'The band is awesome and it's good to see your father smiling again.'

Dad, busy at the other end of the bar, didn't hear but Charlie paused and raised one eyebrow. 'I think Dad's smile has as much to do with you as it has with me or anyone else.'

Mrs Sampson's cheeks flushed a sweet pink.

'You know,' Charlie said, pausing in her task a moment, 'if something should happen between you and Dad, you'd have my blessing. I know he loved Mum, but he's still got a lot of life in him and I want him to be happy. And you too.'

Mrs Sampson looked as if she were about to cry. 'We're just good friends, Charlie, but thank you. Your words mean a lot to me.' Before Charlie could say any more, Mrs Sampson turned to a local couple who'd approached the bar. 'Evening, Alice, evening, Pete. What can I get for you both?'

Charlie left her mixing a green cocktail—their special for the evening—and took a tray of Kilkennys over to where Mitch and his family had gathered around a table. 'On the house,' she said, putting a glass in front of everyone.

'Not for me.' Kate shook her head. 'I'm breastfeeding, driving and on kid duty.'

Charlie laughed. 'No worries, can I get you a soft drink?'

'I'll get something in a moment. Logan!' Kate hissed her oldest son's name and chased him across the other side of the restaurant. 'Come and do some colouring in with your brother and sister.'

'We don't want to draw,' Leo sulked, slumping on a chair.

'Yeah, we wanna play on the iPad,' piped up his twin sister, Laura.

Kate, already halfway across the restaurant, didn't hear their pleas and if Macca did, he pretended otherwise, leaned back in his chair, picked up his pint of Kilkenny and took a long, loud sip.

'Charlie, how are you?' Mr McDonald asked from his wheel-chair, which Macca had parked near the window.

Smiling, she walked around the table and leant down to hug Mitch's dad. He looked so much frailer than she remembered and it broke her heart that this disease was eating him up. 'Hey, Mr McDonald, so good to see you. I'm sorry I haven't visited yet.' She felt guilty about that but life had been so busy and if she were honest, she didn't want to face more heartache so soon after losing her mother.

'Don't be silly. And how many times have I told you to call me Rick?' He patted her on the back. 'Mitch has been filling me in on all you two have been doing here but it's great to finally see it for myself.'

'Thanks. I'll take you to have a look in the rooms later.' She plonked herself down on a chair between Mitch and his dad.

'What else has been happening in Meadow Brook lately?' Rick boomed, proving that although his body was slowly failing him, his voice still carried strength.

Kate, who'd returned with Logan in tow, started telling her father-in-law about a dispute between Irene the hairdresser and the Shire council, who'd put up a tourism sign in front of her shop. Apparently the local birdlife liked their new perch and had showed their appreciation by pooping all over the footpath beneath it. Already several of Irene's customers had been splattered after stopping to admire their new dos in the shop window, and she was threatening to sue if they didn't remove the sign immediately.

As Rick roared with laugher at the story, Charlie turned to Mitch. She just looked at him a while, searching her heart and mind for the right words. What she really wanted to do was confess her feelings—tell him that being home in Meadow Brook had taught her many things. One, what she could achieve if she believed in herself and put her mind to it. Two, that being part of this small community again and being near Dad felt more wonderful than she'd ever imagined it could. And three—most importantly—that she knew why her insides tingled and her skin puckered with goosebumps whenever Mitch came close. It wasn't just his oozing sex appeal, not even their deep friendship. It was love. Honest-to-goodness true love, more than she'd ever felt for anyone, and it made her heart tremble.

It was so goddamn huge it terrified the bejesus out of her.

'I know I'm gorgeous, Charles, but there's no need to stare,' Mitch said, startling her.

Lord, she hoped she hadn't been drooling. She glanced around and saw that the others were still deep in conversations, Kate talking while wrangling her children into silence, and Aunt Mags and Mrs Sampson had kicked off the dancing. A number of other patrons were edging closer towards the dance floor to join them. She smiled at the sight and then turned back to Mitch.

'Full of yourself is what you are.' She took a long sip of her Kilkenny and then wiped her hand against her mouth because she suspected she had a froth moustache.

He snorted, feigning offence. 'I'm insulted. Is that any way to thank the guy who just spent weeks of his life slaving away making tables for you?'

Oh, right … That's what she'd wanted to say to him. She put down her beer and shook her head. 'I don't know how to thank you for that.' She skimmed her fingers along the smooth edge of the table they were sitting at. 'They're beautiful. Far too good really for this old place. You must have worked day and night for a month.'

He grinned. 'Pretty much. Although I suppose this is where I should admit that it's not a busy time on the farm, so Macca helped. A little bit.'

'I owe you both. Although now the rest of the joint looks even more ramshackle.' To prove her point, she looked down at the floor and tapped her feet against the dull, mission brown carpet. She'd hired the carpet shampoo machine from the general store, but sadly, you could barely tell.

'Chin up, Charles,' Mitch said. 'We've only just started. You should see the chairs I'm making. And once we give this area a paint job, you won't recognise the place.'

'Mitch …' She thought of how much the materials alone must have cost him. 'I don't know how I'm going to pay you for all your work and … everything.'

'Relax.' He reached over and took her hand, his long, lovely fingers wrapping around hers in a way that both comforted and set her on edge. 'I didn't do this because I wanted payment or recognition, I did it because I love …' He paused a second and her heart hammered as she waited for the rest of his sentence. 'Because I love working with wood and you guys are like family to me. As for the supplies, I sweet-talked Bob Tucker into giving me a discount.'

Tears welled in her eyes.

'Hey, don't cry.' Mitch shook his head. 'I'm no good with girls and tears.'

Yanking her hand out of his to wipe her eyes, she tried to laugh but it didn't quite eventuate.

'If you really think you owe me something, how about you come dance. We can't let your crazy aunt and Mrs Sampson have all the fun.'

Before Charlie could object, she found herself being propelled through the tables over to the dance floor. The band was rocking a boppy number and she thanked her lucky stars it wasn't something slow that would require her to get up close and personal with Mitch. She barely used to notice if they accidentally touched, but the way she'd felt when he'd held her hand indicated that if their bodies were pressed against each other, she'd be a goner.

'Ladies!' Mitch grinned, his voice oozing charm as he sidled up beside Aunt Mags and Mrs Sampson. Their faces were flushed from exertion but their smiles were wide. 'You two have all the moves.'

'Mitchell,' Mrs Sampson warned. 'Are you mocking a couple of old ladies?'

'Who are you calling old?' Aunt Mags glared good-naturedly at Mrs Sampson.

Mitch laughed and Charlie couldn't help but join in as they all bopped along to the music. After a while Mrs Sampson announced that she'd better go help Brian behind the bar.

'I'll come with you,' Charlie said. 'After all, this party was my idea, and you're not supposed to be on duty.'

'No.' Mrs Sampson waved her hand in dismissal. 'You kick up your heels a bit. You deserve some fun.'

Before Charlie could object, Mitch grabbed her round the waist and spun her round like they were some kind of ballroom dancing duo. 'You're a terrible dancer,' she said, laughing through her words.

'Takes one to know one,' he retorted. Terrible or not, he persisted and it didn't take long for Charlie to relax.

'Thanks for suggesting a St Patrick's theme night,' she said, rocking her hands above her head. 'I can't believe the number of people here. Tonight's takings will sure help towards more redecoration.'

'No probs,' he shouted to be heard over the band. 'It was worth it—if only to see you in that dress.' Mitch dropped his gaze to her legs and verbalised his approval. 'You have great pins, Charles. You should show them off more often.'

She felt as if someone had set a match to her skin and had no idea what to say in response. Was he flirting with her? Or were his words merely those of a good friend, trying to encourage another?

'Will you dance with me, Uncle Mitch?' At the sound of the little voice, Charlie looked down to see Kate and Macca's daughter, Laura, tugging at Mitch's shirt. 'Granddad said you would.'

Mitch smiled down at his adorable niece as he let go of Charlie's hands. 'Why of course, angel. You don't mind, do you, Charlie?'

'Of course not.' As if she could object. Yet, although her heart and body mourned the loss of such close contact, she couldn't help but smile as he scooped up the little girl and twirled off around the dance floor with her. If Laura was older, she'd have been jealous of the way he gazed into her eyes, but as she was only seven and related, it made Charlie smile. And she wasn't the only one. Mitch had put Laura down now and he was twirling her under his arm and the sight captured the hearts of everyone—or at least everyone female—in attendance. There was just something about Mitch. He had charisma in spades, sex appeal to match and when he was around, you couldn't help but feel happy.

Not wanting to analyse her feelings, Charlie looked towards the bar to see if she was needed. Mrs Sampson and Dad were still behind the taps and looked to have everything under control. If the aromas wafting from the kitchen were anything to go by, Rob was cooking up a storm and keeping the three backpackers they'd hired as casual waitresses for the evening on their toes. Kate and Macca had joined the crowd on the dance floor, so Charlie decided to go over and sit with Rick, who looked content if not a little contemplative sitting at the table with his two grandsons. She chuckled as she realised Logan and Leo were only quiet because they were glued to tablet screens.

'Hi there,' she said, collapsing into the seat beside Rick. The few minutes of exertion had her heart racing, or maybe that was the proximity to Mitch. Either way, she was glad of the opportunity for a few moments of rest.

'You should be careful with him, Charlie.'

'Huh?' Charlie frowned at Rick, wondering if she'd heard him wrong.

'Mitch.' He nodded towards his son, who—*grrr*—had been absconded by a woman not much older than a teen, wearing a green dress even shorter than Charlie's. She felt like an old crone in comparison. Where the hell had Laura gone?

'Lord knows I love him more than anything,' Rick went on, 'but he's always been a player and I wouldn't want to see you get hurt.'

Charlie's cheeks flamed. 'I know what Mitch is like, Rick. We've been friends for years.' Truth was, Mitch *hadn't* always been a player. As a kid and a teen, he'd been shy and awkward around everyone but her. And she'd seen no evidence of him playing around since she'd come home either.

'I'm just saying,' he continued, 'being back home, hanging out together, might blur the lines for you both. But believe me, friendship is more important than ...'

Sex? Was that what he was going to say? *Eek!* She interrupted before he had the chance. 'You don't need to worry about us. Mitch's friendship means more to me than anything and I wouldn't sacrifice it by doing something stupid.'

Falling between the sheets with him was more than a little appealing but maybe Rick was right. Once the initial spark had worn off, what then? What if being a couple didn't work out and that left her without Mitch in her life at all? Because she couldn't imagine being able to go back to normal friends once they'd been naked friends.

Naked friends. Her whole body quivered at the thought.

'I'm glad to hear it,' Rick said, reaching over and patting her leg. 'I'd hate to see either of you get hurt.'

'Thanks.' Charlie tried to smile but her eyes caught on Mitch and the teenager, still dancing closely. 'Hey, do you want me to take you to look at the rooms now? Before dinner?'

Rick's eyes lit up and she forgave him his fatherly advice. She guessed he meant well, even though she wasn't sure whether he was protecting her or didn't think her good enough for his youngest son. 'I'd love that.'

Charlie stood and took the handles of Rick's wheelchair. They escaped into the balmy evening air and he sighed.

'You okay?' she asked.

'Ah, Charlie, I try to be, but it's the pits to be so incapacitated. I can barely even hold up a book to read anymore and believe it or not, watching telly day in day out really does start to rot your brain. Just breathing this fresh country air feels like a luxury. Back at the facility the air is thick with disinfectant trying to cover over the stench of rotting life.'

Glad it was dark and Rick couldn't see her face, Charlie screwed up her nose at his gloomy description. She had no idea what to say because nothing would fix his situation. It was only going to get worse. They walked in silence to the furthest motel room, the one she'd done the most work on. Charlie stopped to unlock the door and then pushed it open and flicked on the lights.

'Stone the crows,' Rick exclaimed, his mouth agape as he looked over the room. 'It's like a totally different place.'

Charlie couldn't help but smile. She still got a buzz every time she looked at the progress that they'd made in such a short time. This particular room had fresh paint, fresh carpet and the new linen even made the old bed look presentable. She had dreams of renovating the bathrooms too and ripping out the tiny green and white seventies tiles, but ... one step at a time. A local artist friend of Lisa's had donated a couple of her paintings to hang on the walls. They finished Charlie's efforts off perfectly.

'I wish your mum could see this,' Rick said, still grinning as he gazed around the place. 'She had such passion for this old joint. Loved meeting new people day in day out.'

Rick went quiet and Charlie found his words had created a lump in her throat that made it difficult to speak. She put her hand out and squeezed his shoulder instead, to show she appreciated his sentiment. She wished Mum could have seen this as well, wished she'd come home earlier and worked alongside her, spent precious time with her before she'd died.

But there was no point playing the 'if only' game.

They spent a few more minutes in the room, Rick commenting on every little thing Charlie and Mitch had achieved and Charlie sharing some of her other ideas about motel improvement, before she decided to head back to the party. The McDonalds would be eating dinner soon, and Charlie needed to play host.

'Come on, let's go get some tucker.'

'Thanks for showing me your work, Charlie.'

'It was my pleasure.'

When they returned to the restaurant, there were still a few people on the dance floor and a couple of blokes playing pool in the bar, but many of the patrons had sat down to dinner. Charlie wheeled Rick back to his family, secretly pleased to see Mitch had abandoned the woman on the dance floor and was now playing with his niece and nephews. Aunt Mags sat beside him, snapping directions over his shoulder about how to play the game he was engrossed in on the iPad.

'I have an elderly neighbour who plays this game,' Mags informed him, as if *she* were a spring chicken, 'and he's much better than you, Mitchell.'

Mitch looked up and grinned knowingly at Charlie as she parked his father alongside Aunt Mags. She smiled back, glad to see Mags engaged, and then went off to relieve Dad and Mrs Sampson.

'You two go have some dinner,' she said, practically pushing them out of the bar area. 'I'll be fine.'

They didn't object, wandering over to join Mags and the McDonalds at their table. The evening progressed even better than Charlie had imagined. She got such a thrill watching the busy restaurant, the waitresses rushing back and forth from the kitchen, the patrons lined up at the bar, the hum of happy conversation in the room. After the plates were emptied and more drinks guzzled, the band took requests and their younger patrons headed back to the dance floor, while the older generation sat back chatting.

Charlie sighed a happy sigh as she surveyed the scene before her, feeling a sense of accomplishment she couldn't recall ever feeling before.

'You look pretty pleased with yourself.' She jolted as Mitch crept up beside her.

'I am,' she said, turning to look at him. The only thing that didn't feel perfect in her life right now were her illicit thoughts about him.

'You should be.' He put his arm around her shoulder and pulled her close. Her body reacted immediately, her heart and hormones pumping fast, but she told them to get back in their box. This was merely the embrace of a good friend. If Mitch had other feelings for her, he'd tell her.

'I'm really sorry,' he said, 'but I'm going to have to bail. Dad's tired and I told Macca I'd drive him back to Port Augusta so that he can take Kate and the kids home. Do you want me to come back later and help clean up?'

She shook her head. The way she felt, if he came back, if it was late and they were alone, she might not be able to stop herself confessing her love. She couldn't bear the thought of his rejection and how things would inevitably change between them if he didn't return her feelings. 'No, we'll be fine. Anyway, don't you have to work tomorrow?'

'Yep.' He grimaced. 'Another trip up north for a few days. See you when I get back, okay?'

She nodded, the cells in her body jolting as he leaned forward and brushed a kiss against her cheek, making it hard for her to speak in reply. Luckily, he didn't seem to notice.

As Mitch swaggered off to fetch Rick, Charlie's phone beeped in her pocket. She took it out and glanced at the screen, noticing she had several messages. The first was from Lucinda.

Great news, Charlie. About the motel I mean. Not sure what to think of Dad and Mrs Sampson, but I guess if he's happy … Oh and I've put my notice in at work. Two more weeks and I'll be a free woman.

Charlie blinked at that news. What was Lucinda going to do with herself if she wasn't teaching? Who was she going to boss around?

The next message from Madeleine echoed Charlie's thoughts. *Do you think she's pregnant? Why else would she quit?*

Abigail and Madeleine had had quite a conversation while Charlie had been busy serving drinks. She scrolled through the messages, which were like a debate between her sisters second-guessing what Lucinda was up to.

I hope she is. This from Abigail. *It'd be good to prove the stupid curse wrong.*

Fuck the curse, retorted Madeleine. *It'd just be good for her and Joe to be able to start a family. That's probably why she resigned. To de-stress and focus on getting pregnant.*

Well, good for her. Whatever the reason. Charlie typed into her phone and pressed Send.

Oh Charles, nice of you to join the conversation, but I'm off to work now. Sweet dreams, Madeleine texted.

Sweet dreams? Abigail messaged Charlie. *What is up with the world? First Lucinda stops teaching and now Madeleine is being nice?*

LOL. I thought she was being sarcastic.

Oh right. Of course. How's you anyway? Are you really happy being stuck in the back of beyond?

Happy as Larry. How's the orchestra?

Same as always. Gotta fly. Catch ya later. xo

Charlie smiled wistfully as she slipped her phone back into her pocket. Her sisters all led such busy lives but it was nice to touch base every now and then.

Chapter Twenty-nine

'I'm sorry, I'm a bit tired tonight,' Madeleine said. Celia was on the phone, asking if she wanted to have dinner with her and Hugo that night.

'That's okay. It could be a good sign.' As usual Celia sounded unrealistically chirpy. 'Have you had any other symptoms yet? When are you due again?'

It wasn't a sign. It was a lie. The only thing making Madeleine nauseous was the thought of spending an entire evening in both Celia *and* Hugo's company. She was sick of being the third wheel. She didn't want to be the onlooker of someone else's relationship. She wanted her own life, her own relationship.

And as much as she tried to deny it, the only man she wanted was Hugo.

The last two weeks had been the longest of her life. Every waking hour she thought about Hugo's sperm swimming inside her. She got hot flushes just thinking about it. Which made her feel pretty awkward at work, like some kind of teenager with an inappropriate crush on her teacher. But he'd been so damn nice and attentive that it was hard to suppress her feelings. Yesterday morning he'd bought her a hot chocolate and a delicious cinnamon roll from her favourite café. She'd almost cried when she'd opened the paper bag and looked inside.

'Do you think you … Do you think you might be?' he'd asked, gently touching her on the arm, hope swimming in his eyes.

Yesterday morning she'd thought it a possibility—why else would she be such an emotional wreck, crying over baked goods of all things? But then today she'd woken up with stomach cramps, signalling the start of her period, and her dreams of carrying Hugo's child had died.

One month, that's all it had been. She knew she shouldn't feel so despondent but she couldn't help it. In the past, most things had come easily to her, but this felt out of her control.

Madeleine swallowed as she grabbed her handbag from her locker in the staffroom and replied to Celia's question about her cycle. 'Tomorrow,' she lied, not yet ready for sympathy. She wanted to go home and be alone, not spend an evening with Hugo's girlfriend offering pep-me-up advice, telling her she'd have better luck next time. Celia didn't want children, so how could she ever understand? To her this was some kind of experiment, a bit of fun, much like watching a drama unfold on your favourite TV show—but for Madeleine it was real.

'Ooh, I'm so excited I could burst,' Celia squealed, hurting Madeleine's eardrums, exasperating her already pounding head. 'You go home and get some rest. I'm working tomorrow but be sure to buzz me if you have news.'

'Will do,' Madeleine promised as she shut her locker and hooked her bag over her shoulder. She'd have to tell them eventually but not tonight; knowing Celia and Hugo they'd cancel their dinner plans and come around to try and make her feel better. They'd bring her favourite Chinese takeaway and a bottle of vino, but they'd come together and she couldn't handle the dynamic duo tonight. She disconnected the call and walked out of the hospital, relieved she wasn't on call that evening. She'd already delivered two babies that day and seen numerous pregnant patients, but one more could quite possibly push her over the edge. It was hard to be encouraging and excited for a woman in labour when you wanted the same thing. What she really needed was someone who understood her predicament, someone who knew the disappointment of not getting pregnant.

As she strode along the sidewalk towards her apartment building, letting the cool spring evening air wash over her, her mind drifted to Lucinda. She hadn't always seen eye to eye with her sisters. Quite often they drove her insane—and Lucinda more than any of them—but since spending time together at Christmas, she'd been missing them more than usual. What would Lucinda say if she called and confessed her plan to have a baby on her own?

She glanced up and saw she was passing a bottle shop—a sign if ever there was one. And the shop just happened to be next door to her favourite Chinese restaurant.

Ten minutes later, a bottle of chardonnay tucked under her arm and her dinner smelling delicious in a plastic bag in her other hand, Madeleine let herself into her apartment. She kicked off her shoes, shrugged out of her jacket and took her bottle and food to the couch, detouring only to collect a wine glass from the kitchen. After guzzling half a glass and shovelling half a container of fried rice into her mouth, she picked up her mobile and dialled Australia.

'Hello?' Lucinda sounded a little sleepy.

'Did I wake you?'

'No. I'm just getting ready for work. Only two weeks to go and I can sleep as late as I like.'

'That's right, you quit. What's that all about?' She took another long gulp, settling back to listen.

'It just felt like the right thing to do,' Lucinda confessed. 'I want to focus on my marriage and getting pregnant and I shouldn't be teaching unless I'm one hundred percent dedicated to the job.'

'I see. No baby jackpot yet, then?' Charlie and Abigail both believed that was why Lucinda had quit work—they'd been debating this over text and email ever since Lucinda had made her announcement. But Madeleine thought if that were the case, she'd tell them.

Lucinda exhaled deeply. 'No. So, what's new with you?'

Madeleine couldn't quite bring herself to admit her failure, so instead of being entirely honest with Lucinda, she said, 'What would you think if I decided to have a baby as well?'

There was a weird sound at Lucinda's end, then a pregnant pause in conversation. 'I'm sorry, I think there was interference on the line. *What* did you say?'

Madeleine laughed. And it felt good after the disappointment of the day. 'You heard right. All your talk of babies at Christmas got me thinking. Maybe I want that too?'

'I think I need to sit down,' Lucinda said and Madeleine heard what sounded like the toilet seat clunking shut. 'Are you serious?'

'Deadly.'

'Who with? I didn't know you had a boyfriend.'

'I don't.' She paused a moment. Lucinda would be the first person she'd told besides Hugo and Celia. 'I'm going to use a donor.'

Lucinda whistled. 'Wow, that's big.'

'You don't mind do you?' She'd been hoping for solidarity but realised Lucinda might be upset if she got pregnant first.

'Mind? Of course not, I'm just a little shocked. I'll be happy if you succeed. A niece or nephew might be the closest I ever get to children, but I wouldn't go getting your hopes up. After seeing your doctor friend and finding out Joe and I are perfect breeding material, I'm seriously beginning to wonder if there isn't something in the Patterson curse. But good luck to you.'

'Don't be ridiculous,' scoffed Madeleine, lifting her wine glass and taking another swig. Truth was the same thought had crossed her mind that morning when she'd been peeling the plastic off her tampon, but she didn't abide such stupidity.

One failed attempt did not a curse make. She'd allow herself the disappointment over not being pregnant—hence the takeaway and vino—but she refused to waste time dwelling on such things. If she placed any credence in the curse, she may as well start believing in unicorns, which she hadn't even done as a young child. Fairy tales and folklore had never held her interest. Madeleine was a woman of facts and science. Her worldview simply couldn't accept such mumbo-jumbo.

She told Lucinda this now. 'You've had tests and there's nothing wrong with you.'

'But what about Aunt Mags? What about Sarah and Victoria?'

'Forget them,' Madeleine said firmly. 'You'll go insane if you keep thinking like this. And then quitting work and focusing on you and Joe will be for nothing. Relax, try not to stress, and it'll happen.' She cringed the moment the words escaped her mouth because they were the last thing any woman struggling to conceive wanted to hear, but as a health professional she believed they had merit.

'I've got to get ready for work. Keep me posted on your efforts.' Lucinda disconnected before Madeleine could say anything else.

She put her phone down on the coffee table and sighed. Fabulous, now not only did she feel like shite herself but she'd likely put Lucinda in a bad mood. Her schoolkids wouldn't know what they'd done wrong. As she took another sip of wine, enjoying each bittersweet mouthful because tomorrow she'd be back on the wagon, her phone beeped, signalling a message. Not on call, she almost ignored it, but curiosity got the better of her and she leaned just far enough forward to see the screen.

Her heart did a pitiable somersault as Hugo's name flashed up at her. She snatched up the phone and swiped the screen to read his message.

Are you okay? Celia said you sounded weird when you talked to her earlier.

Madeleine swallowed. Did Celia have a sixth sense or something? *I'm not pregnant,* she typed back and pressed Send before she could think better of it.

'Fuck,' she muttered, immediately regretting telling him. Celia might have a sixth sense but Madeleine was psychic—her friends would never let her suffer in solitude. There'd be a phone call, or worse, the two of them would land on her doorstep, all dressed up, having cut short their fancy dinner to look after poor, pathetic Madeleine. Resigned to some kind of intervention, she picked up her dinner and began to eat, one eye on the phone and one ear cocked towards the door.

When her plate was empty and the phone still silent, she thought maybe she'd been wrong. Maybe a quiet night to lament her situation would be hers, but less than a minute later, the intercom buzzed signalling a visitor.

'So predictable.' Taking her sweet time, she heaved herself off the couch and went across to answer. 'Yes,' she barked into the wall.

Hugo: 'Buzz me up.'

Without replying, she pressed the button that would let him into the building and then opened her door to await her unwanted visitors.

It wasn't long long before the doors to the elevator opened and Hugo appeared. On his lonesome. And he wasn't dressed up—instead faded jeans clung to his muscular thighs and he wore a Red Sox sweatshirt up top. You could take the boy out of Boston but you couldn't take Boston out of the boy. 'Where's Celia?' she asked as he approached her door.

He leaned down and pecked her on the cheek, then stepped inside. 'She got called in to work.'

'I see.' Madeleine closed the door, unsure whether it was the truth or whether Celia had stayed away on purpose, but she couldn't help being glad. 'Can I get you a glass?' she asked, gesturing to her half-drunk wine bottle on the coffee table.

He shook his head and looked down her body. Her nipples tingled at the assessment and she turned away, hoping he didn't see her blush. 'Get out of those work clothes and put on something comfortable. We're going out.'

'Comfortable?' He couldn't be taking her to a restaurant or a club then. 'Where are we going?'

'It's a surprise.'

'What if I don't want to go out?' She crossed her arms over her chest.

He raised one eyebrow. 'Frankly, my dear, I don't give a damn.'

And at his terrible impersonation of Rhett Butler, she smiled for the first time that day and went off to slip into jeans, all the while trying to guess where they were going.

'Are we going to the movies?' she asked when she emerged.

He merely grinned and held open the front door. As they descended to the ground floor and then drove through the city, she kept firing possibilities at him and he infuriated her by not answering.

Then, he turned into a car park of a building with a bright flashing bowling ball on the top of it. 'No way,' she said.

'Yes, way,' he replied, still grinning.

Lacing up her shoes a few minutes later, she looked across at him and laughed. 'I cannot remember the last time I went bowling.'

'Me either. Celia refuses—says she wouldn't be seen dead in goofy clown shoes.' Sitting next to her, he stretched his legs and flexed his feet, modelling the shoes he'd just put on.

'She may have a point.' But, shoes aside, Madeleine couldn't imagine perfect Celia ever stepping into a place like this.

'Once you get past the terrible outfits,' Hugo said, 'bowling can be addictive. And very therapeutic.' This reference was as close as he came to mentioning today's disappointment. Then he stood, walked over to the ball chute and picked up a bright orange bowling ball. 'I hope you're not a sore loser,' he called over his shoulder as he launched his ball right into the gutter.

She was still laughing when it was her turn to bowl and she staggered to her feet, picked up her hot pink ball and hurled it down the alley, knocking down all ten pins in one shot.

'What the fuck!' Hugo roared. 'Do you come here and do this on your lunch breaks or something?'

She smiled smugly and shrugged. 'Beginner's luck.' They both knew doctors didn't get lunch breaks.

'I'm just warming up,' Hugo said, going forward for his next turn. And this time he hit nine balls and got the last pin on his second bowl. Both her balls went down the gutter, which sent her and Hugo into another round of hysterics. On either side of them were serious groups, dressed head to foot in goofy bowling outfits. They all seemed to have their own balls and special bags to carry them, each embroidered with their name. Larry, Wayne, Alvin and Dennis were clearly unimpressed with Madeleine and Hugo's silliness, but she was having the best time.

Hugo was right. Staring down an alley at ten little white pins and then trying to hurl a heavy ball right into them worked wonders for her mood. The two glasses of wine she'd gulped before Hugo arrived might also have had something to do with it, but either way she felt a million times better than she had a few hours ago. Between games they ordered hot dogs and chips from a pimply, gangly teenager at the café and then washed it all down with beer.

Although it was late and there weren't any kids around, Madeleine couldn't help imagining Hugo taking their child bowling and that made her smile. Just something else to add to list of why he'd be the perfect donor; another argument for ignoring the reasons he was not.

'What are you grinning at?' Hugo asked, taking another slug of his beer.

She blinked. 'Nothing. Just happy I guess.'

'It's fun, isn't it.'

'Yes. Thank you for dragging me out. I needed it.'

'No worries. Now, drink up, we have another game to play. And tomorrow, we're both back on the wagon.'

Madeleine guessed that meant he was still happy to be her donor, but she decided not to mention that right now. Tonight wasn't about babies. It was about letting loose and having fun with a good friend. They played another game and if anything they were getting worse, but neither of them cared and when they were finished he took her home and saw her right back to her door.

'Would you like to come in for coffee?' she asked, and then blushed in case he thought she meant something else.

He shook his head. 'I better not.'

'All right. Good night then.'

He smiled and turned to go but then turned again when he'd gone only a few steps. He walked up to her and grabbed hold of her hands. Her heart, pounding uncontrollably, shot up to her throat.

'It'll be all right, Mads,' he said. 'We can do this. I promise.'

It sounded like the kind of pep talk Joe would give Lucinda—one partner bolstering up another. As if they were in this together, as if Hugo wanted this as much as she did.

'I know.' Madeleine forced a smile, inwardly reminding herself that he was not her partner and they were not doing this the traditional way.

No matter how much she wished they were.

Chapter Thirty

Don't forget your violin!

Abigail laughed at Nigel's message and then typed back, *Maybe.* Her naked violin recitals were becoming a bit of a thing for them and she had to admit they turned her on as much as they did him. Her dad would be appalled if he knew how she was putting all those years of tuition to use but she couldn't summon one iota of guilt. What he didn't know couldn't hurt him.

Tease, came his reply. *I'll see you soon.*

Putting her phone down on the dresser, she turned back to the mirror to finish scrutinising her outfit. 'Do I look ready for a ball?' she asked her reflection. The bathroom light glinted off the gold silk of her floor-length dress. Her legs may have been covered, but the way the fabric hugged her figure and dipped low at her back left little to the imagination. She couldn't wait to see the look on Nigel's face when he picked her up.

Okay, so it wasn't exactly a ball, but the way Nigel had described it, this advertising awards dinner sounded pretty flash and she didn't want to let him down. She applied the finishing touches to her makeup and then went back into her bedroom to grab her evening bag, overnighter and violin.

'You going out *again*?' Pamela asked from her position on the couch as Abigail trekked through the tiny living room to get to the front door. It was a lovely spring evening out; waiting outside for Nigel would be preferable to making small talk with Sam and Pamela for the next ten minutes.

'Yep,' she replied, her voice light to match the spring in her step. 'Don't wait up.'

They probably thought the violin a ruse, and that her frequent late nights were because she was stripping in a bar or something. How else could someone who'd been expelled from the orchestra possibly be earning money?

They could think what they like. Abigail didn't give a toss.

She closed the door behind her, walked down the front steps and then killed time catching up on Facebook while she waited. Charlie had dragged the Meadow Brook Motel into the era of social media by creating a page on which she regularly uploaded photos of her redecorating progress. Abigail had to hand it to her. The improvements made the old place look better than she'd ever imagined possible. In some photos, it almost sparkled. Of course it would never be able to compete with the kind of hotel Nigel was whisking her away to tonight, but it wasn't fair to make such a comparison.

At the sound of a car approaching, she looked up and smiled as a sleek, black limo slid to a stop just in front of her. When the chauffeur walked around to open the door for her, Abigail couldn't help glancing back at the townhouse. Sure enough, Pamela and Sam had their beady eyes pressed up against the window. Nosy parkers. She waved her immaculately manicured fingers at them, passed her violin case to the driver and then uttered her thanks as she climbed inside.

'Hey, good looking. Can I tempt you?' Nigel greeted her with a crystal flute of pink bubbly and patted the plush leather seat.

'Do you mean with the champagne or with something else?' Because he looked very temping in that swish, black tux. She slipped in beside him and kissed him firmly on the lips.

He placed the champagne glass in the holder and pulled her up against him. 'Vixen,' he murmured before recapturing her lips.

She loved it when he called her that. She loved it when he kissed her too. She couldn't recall a night they'd been together when she'd done anything but smile. And it wasn't just the earth-moving sex. He made her laugh all the time, and she could talk to him about anything. Well, almost anything.

She slipped her hands inside his jacket, loving the way his firm abs tightened beneath her touch.

Nigel groaned and pulled back. 'We can't. Not now. Not here. Not before…'

Reining in her disappointment, Abigail nodded and tried to catch her breath. 'Sorry.'

'Never apologise for turning me on,' he whispered, smiling as he reached out and brushed aside a few strands of flyaway hair that had fallen across her face. 'Just try not to do it for the next few minutes. I can't turn up at the Awards with a boner jutting out the front of my trousers.'

She snorted and glanced down at his groin, which sure enough boasted a rather impressive tent. 'I'll do my best.'

Grinning, he reached over and grabbed the two champagne flutes, handing one to her. 'Maybe we should talk about something boring, something safe, something that doesn't make me want to jump your bones.'

'Like …?' Glowing from his hot words, she racked her brain— conversation with Nigel was never boring.

'My grandma sent me a picture of her new slippers yesterday. It's apparently getting cold Down Under and she thought I'd like to see them.' He pulled out his phone to show her, chuckling. 'They are green with yellow dots, not those silly fluffy pink ones in case you were wondering. She likes keeping me up to date.'

'She sounds like quite a character. She'd probably get on like a house on fire with my Aunt Mags,' Abigail said, taking another sip and relishing the way the bubbles felt on her tongue. Imagine if she fell pregnant and had to go without this deliciousness for nine whole months? Or was it ten? The timing had always confused her.

'My whole family are characters. Why do you think I chose to live all the way over here on the other side of the world?'

'I was thinking it was because you were ambitious.'

He chuckled. 'Maybe a little.'

As they drove across London sharing crazy family stories (of which Abigail had plenty as well) they remarked on the various landmarks they passed. They'd both seen the main tourist sights— Big Ben, the Tower of London, Buckingham Palace, Westminster Abbey and the like—but Abigail admitted to wanting to go further afield and explore some of England's famous castles.

'I'll come with you,' Nigel said, squeezing her hand. 'Maybe we could hire a car and make a long weekend of it some time.'

Abigail wasn't sure fuck buddies went away to the country to see castles together, but then again, the more time she spent with Nigel, the less she wanted to be *just* fuck buddies anyway. 'That sounds great.'

Before they could plot their weekend getaway, the limo pulled into the grand entrance of one of London's finest hotels. The footmen were dressed in such finery (tails and top hats, no less) that they looked as if they could work for the queen herself. Once they'd checked in at reception and left their luggage with the concierge, they made their way to the ballroom.

'I don't think I've told you how amazing you look tonight,' Nigel whispered, drawing her close to him as they waited to go in. 'Let's hope this thing doesn't go too late.'

Desire rippled through Abigail at Nigel's words and all she could think about was ripping off his tux and getting down and dirty. A waiter passed with a tray of alcoholic beverages and Abigail snatched one, lifting the glass to her lips and taking a long sip. She wasn't pregnant yet, so she may as well enjoy herself that night. Besides, she needed the coolness of the expensive champagne to lower her rapidly rising body temperature.

'Nigel! Abigail!'

At the sound of their names, she turned to see Daniel and his wife, Liane, behind them.

'Hi.' She smiled as Nigel's boss leaned forward to kiss her on the cheek. Nigel did the same to Liane and then the men shook hands.

'Lovely to see you again, Abigail,' Liane said. They'd already met through her daughter's music lessons. 'Livia won't stop raving about you. She's loving music since you've taken over the teaching.'

'Yes,' Daniel agreed. 'We used to have to bribe her to practise; now we almost have to tear her away to do other things.'

'She's an absolute delight,' Abigail replied, basking in their compliments.

'She's certainly come on in leaps and bounds since you started with her,' Liane said, grinning. 'Now, tell me, where did you get that fabulous dress?'

'Oh, this old thing? It's actually my mother's.'

'I love vintage dresses,' Liane gushed. 'She has impeccable taste.'

'*Had*,' Abigail said before she could help herself. She absent-mindedly brushed a hand over the silk. 'Mum died six months ago. This was one of the dresses my sisters and I couldn't bear to throw out.'

Liane reached out and squeezed Abigail's hand, sympathy in her eyes. 'I'm sorry for your loss. I can see why you wanted to keep it.'

'Thanks.' Abigail swallowed, not wanting to cry here of all places. The loss of her mother hit her at the oddest moments, sometimes completely taking her by surprise.

When they finally made it into the ballroom, Liane stayed close to Abigail, introducing her to the other partners sitting at their table.

'Lovely to meet you,' smiled a woman with a blonde bob sitting directly opposite Abigail. 'Are you in advertising as well?'

'No.' Abigail laughed, shook her head and nodded to Nigel who sat beside her. 'I'm here with him.'

'What do you do for a living, then?' asked the blonde.

Liane answered for her. 'She's a music teacher. A brilliant one.'

'Really,' said another woman. 'What instrument do you teach?'

'The violin, although I could do piano as well,' Abigail replied, imagining what everyone was thinking. That old saying 'Those who can, do, and those who can't, teach,' popped into her head. But the women surprised her. Instead of looking at her with pity or distaste, they rushed to express their interest. In less than half an hour, she'd lined up five potential new students.

'And do you enjoy teaching?' they wanted to know.

Abigail found she didn't need to think about the answer. 'Yes. I love it.'

The realisation made her giddy. She thought back over the last couple of months. Besides the stress of wondering how she'd pay the next bill, her life was less pressured than ever before. She'd always gotten a buzz from striving to achieve, but she was learning that taking each day slower, appreciating the little moments rather than rush, rush, rushing to get stuff done, also had a special kind of appeal. Then there were the kids. They were much more fun than her stuffy old colleagues in the orchestra had been. They reminded her that music was supposed to be enjoyable. They reminded her why she'd wanted to play in the first place.

'How you going?' Nigel whispered, squeezing the hand he'd been holding since they sat. Although he'd been talking shop with his colleagues, she'd felt his glance on her every few seconds.

'Great.' She leaned over and kissed his cheek, inhaling the subtle but intoxicating scent of his cologne. It smelt a little like the herbal teas Charlie always drank. 'This is fun.'

'I thought that night would never end,' Nigel said as he slipped the room card into the slot and pushed open their door.

'I thought you were—' She'd been going to say 'enjoying yourself' but the words died on her tongue as she clocked eyes on the massive bed. She could tell how soft the sheets were without even touching them and in all the corners of the room vintage-looking lamps added a sensual glow. 'Wow,' she breathed.

'I know.' Nigel kicked the door shut behind them, tore her evening bag from her clutches and dumped it on an old-fashioned writing bureau. He put his hands on her waist and then spun her round. She gasped with glee as he all but ripped the zipper down the back of her dress and slipped his hands under the shoulder straps so the garment slithered to the floor. The gown hadn't warranted a bra and she closed her eyes, moaning in ecstasy as Nigel reached up and cupped her breasts. As his fingers toyed with her already hard nipples, his lips landed on the side of her neck and the burning desire she'd fought in the limo returned with a vengeance.

She spun around, yanked off his jacket and then started on his shirt. He kicked off his shoes as she worked the buckle of his belt. She couldn't get his trousers off quickly enough. Foreplay was overrated—simply sitting next to him all night had been enough. And to think she'd once thought playing the violin was better than sex; she hadn't known how good sex could be.

'You've turned me into a hussy,' she hissed as he lifted her up, her butt resting on the writing thingy. He rolled her knickers down her legs, but left her Manolo Blahnik heels on.

He thrust into her. 'And that's a problem how?'

'Christ!' she yelped as her body accommodated him. She bit down on his shoulder to stop from making more noise. They were in a posh hotel but who knew how thin the walls were.

'You know, we really should use condoms,' Nigel panted as he took them both closer and closer to release.

Abigail heart's slammed into her chest and she raised her eyebrow. *Really?* He wanted to talk about that now? In the middle of, ahem … things? 'Do you like using condoms? Do they give you a better experience?'

'Hell, no,' he scoffed, gripping her buttocks as he drove harder and further.

'Well, then,' she shrugged as she looked into his eyes. They were such a beautiful piercing blue tonight, and she could easily get lost in them. She was already halfway to losing her heart. 'Don't you think it's a little late to be sensible?'

Chuckling, Nigel thrust again, dipping his head and kissing her deliciously on the lips.

Abigail couldn't think about condoms or anything serious as they came together in a hot, messy, breath-stealing climax, but afterwards while they were relaxing in the giant claw-footed bathtub and later, when they took things slower—but equally as pleasurably—in bed, she started to worry. Why had he raised the issue of contraception now? They'd been sleeping together for a few months. Did it mean she wasn't his only fuck buddy? Her stomach lurched at the thought. All of a sudden she didn't find the term as amusing as she did when he'd first propositioned her.

'Are you all right?' he asked, once again brushing away errant hair that had fallen across her eyes.

'More than.' She hoped she sounded believable, as she didn't want to ruin this magical night with her silly insecurities.

Nigel lifted himself up onto his elbow and gazed down at her. 'I'm just going to come right out and say this, and before you ask, no, it's not the alcohol speaking. I was too busy talking and networking to drink much anyway.'

She frowned. Was this his way of telling her he'd had enough? Thanks for a fun few months but I think it's time we ended this?

Her insides twisted—she'd thought things were great between them; they'd rarely spent a night apart lately and she loved the times they simply hung together chatting or watching TV. But maybe Nigel was bored with that.

'You're scaring me,' she said, immediately wishing she could take it back. Maybe she was overacting. He wouldn't like it if she suddenly became all needy.

'That is not my intention.' She watched his Adam's apple slowly move up and down before he finally spoke again. 'When we met I told you I wasn't looking for a relationship ...'

Oh God!

How awkward. How horrible. How heartbreaking. She couldn't bear to cry in front of him. 'It's okay, Nigel.' She sat up straight, pulling the sheets up to cover herself. 'You don't have to—'

He cut her off. 'Yes, Abigail. I *do*. I know I said I didn't want commitment, but—' he blinked and took her hand '—that was before I found you. And now ... Now everything has changed.'

A sound a little like a cat's mewling slipped from her lips. Her heart grew three sizes. 'Oh?' she asked, not daring to say anything more.

But he nodded, his expression more serious than she'd ever seen it before. 'I think I'm falling in love with you. In fact, I'm terrified I already have.'

'Terrified?' Uncontrollable happiness bubbled within her.

'Yes. Terrified that my admission will make you flee from the bed, snatch up your sexy stilettos, run from this room and never contact me again.'

She laughed, then grabbed his ears and pulled him towards her, kissing him in a way that hopefully indicated exactly how she felt. But just in case, when they came up for air, she added, 'I'm not just a pretty face you know. I know a good thing when I'm shagging it and I've fallen in love with you as well.'

'Praise the Lord!' Nigel drew her into his arms and she snuggled against him, resting her head on his chest. Beneath her ear, his heart beat, and it was the most beautiful sound in the world. Somewhere in the back of her mind, she realised then that she hadn't done any naked violin playing for him yet, but she set the thought aside. They'd have all the time in the world for stuff like that now.

Wearing a grin so big it almost hurt her face, she drifted towards sleep with the sound of Nigel breathing deeply beside her. She was almost there when suddenly she jolted awake.

What if I'm pregnant?

Tonight had been prime timing for conception. She tried to swallow the lump that had appeared from nowhere and threatened to hinder her breathing. Nigel thought she was on the pill, so how would she explain that one? She couldn't bear the thought of what he'd do if he found out what she'd been planning.

What the hell was I thinking?

The crazy curse, the lack of an income and her utter disappointment in herself had skewed her brain, but now that things were almost back on track, her get-out-of-London pregnancy plan seemed more than stupid. It had been irrational and immoral. She only hoped Nigel would never find out. First thing tomorrow, she'd head back to that doctor and request the morning after pill.

Chapter Thirty-one

At the sound of each car approaching, Charlie looked up from where she was yanking weeds in the front garden to check for Dad and Mrs Sampson. They'd gone to Port Augusta that morning for Dad's medical check-up and she'd expected them back by now.

'You missed one.'

She jumped, her heart slamming into her chest cavity at the sound of Mitch coming up behind her. 'Where did you come from?'

'*Well*, Charles, when a man and a woman love each other—or at least lust strongly after each other...'

Pushing off her knees and into a stand, she shook her head at him. 'Can you ever be serious?'

He pretended to think a moment, then shook his head. 'Nope. That would be boring.'

She rolled her eyes, dusted the dirt from her hands and glanced at the motel car park. 'Where's your ute?'

He frowned. 'Didn't your dad tell you? He borrowed it for his trip to Port Augusta today. Said he had something to pick up.'

'No. He didn't.' She racked her brain for what it could possibly be and came up blank.

'Maybe it's a—' But before he could speculate, they turned at the unmistakable sound of his ute coming up the road.

Charlie's mouth fell open and her eyes widened at the sight of a caravan being towed along behind it.

'I was going to say "boat" but I think we have our answer,' Mitch finished.

Charlie was speechless. She knew Dad wanted to get a caravan eventually, but she'd thought he'd wait until he had the money from the motel. It wasn't like he could trek off on his big trip before then. Unless…

What if he decided he could? What if he leaves me in charge?

Her heart rate accelerated at the thought. Granted, things were going well here, and she was enjoying her work and the challenge each day brought, but she couldn't do it on her own.

'Relax.' Mitch put his hand on her arm as Dad turned the ute and caravan into the car park. 'Caravans don't bite.'

'I just…'

Reading her mind, Mitch said, 'This doesn't mean Brian's running away. It's just a step towards achieving a future dream. I think it's a great sign. It shows he wants to get on with life—find a new way of living.'

Charlie nodded. Silently telling herself to get a grip, she tried to smile as she went to greet them. 'I thought you were going to the doctor's.' She raised her eyebrows at Dad as he climbed out of the ute.

He exchanged a sheepish look with Mrs Sampson as she emerged from the passenger side. 'I did,' he said. 'And good news is, I've been given a clean bill of health. My blood pressure is down and my cholesterol too. All those ghastly vegetable juices you've been making me for breakfast have obviously done me good.'

'That's fabulous, Dad.' And it was, but right now Charlie was more interested in the caravan. Close up, it looked like he may have gotten it for a bargain. At least, she hoped so because there were a few dents in the side and it needed a new lick of paint. 'Looks like you also went shopping.'

'Oh. This?' Dad looked to the caravan as if he'd only just noticed it. Beside him Mrs Sampson laughed.

'Can we have a squiz inside?' Mitch asked, his tone amused. 'I've always loved the way these vans look so small yet fit so much.'

'Sure. Come on in.' Mrs Sampson dug a key out of her pocket and started towards the door.

Mitch and Dad followed and climbed up into the caravan after her, but Charlie had questions.

'Whose caravan is this exactly?' she asked, battling a queer feeling in her stomach as she hurried after them.

Mitch feigned interest in the fridge and the cupboards above the tiny kitchen, opening all the doors and closing them again as Dad and Mrs Sampson gave him the tour. Finally they met her gaze.

Dad spoke first. 'When I told Mrs Sampson my dream of owning a caravan and travelling around Australia, she said she had the same dream, so we decided to pool our savings and buy one together.'

'I see.' Did this mean they were *together*-together or were they going into this venture purely as friends? Charlie couldn't quite bring herself to ask, but was comforted by the fact that the van had two single beds instead of one double. Not that she didn't want Dad and Mrs Sampson to be an item—she'd all but given Mrs Sampson her blessing—but she wasn't quite ready to think about what that might actually entail.

'But we have some work to do before we can hit the road.' Mrs Sampson beamed and gestured around the confined space.

'And we wouldn't do that before the motel is sold,' Dad added.

'No, of course not.' Mrs Sampson shook her head. 'We'd never ask you to look after everything all on your own, but—'

'The things you've been doing here inspired us,' Dad explained. They were already finishing each other's sentences. 'Neither of us could justify spending so much money on our own, but then Sal found this old girl in *Caravans and Motorhomes*. We thought if you could orchestrate the redecoration of the whole motel, together we might be able to manage one measly caravan.'

'This fold-out table is a little loose.' Mitch had moved on from the cupboards. 'I'd be happy to fix it for you.'

'Thanks, Mitch. That would be great,' Mrs Sampson said and then looked back to Charlie. 'What colour scheme do you think we should go for in here?'

'Uh ...' Charlie recognised the attempt to draw her in, to make her feel part of this new addition to the Meadow Brook Motel family, and perhaps also to make sure she was still okay with Dad and Mrs Sampson getting closer ... if that was indeed what was going on. Although the caravan was a surprise, as she looked around, she felt her anxiety easing. It was cosy—or would be once they'd finished fixing it up—and Mrs Sampson was a woman of her dad's vintage with a lot of love and warmth in her heart.

She wondered, if Mum could look down from above, what would she think of Dad and Mrs Sampson together?

She didn't have to ponder the question for long. Somehow she knew Mum would approve. The two women had always been good friends, and she was sure Mum would be glad there was someone else—aside from the girls—looking out for Dad. To make sure he bought new socks when his old ones got holes in them, force him to the doctor when need be and to keep him company on the nights that would be long and lonely without his wife.

A lump formed in Charlie's throat as she fought happy–sad tears. 'It depends what kind of look you want. You could either embrace the retro theme or you could give it quite a modern feel.'

'Retro,' said both Dad and Mrs Sampson at the same time.

Charlie nodded her approval, thankful the tears hadn't eventuated. 'That would be my choice also.'

'And of course, you'll have to throw a party when it's finished,' Mitch suggested, rubbing his hands together in excitement. 'I'll be happy to break a bottle of bubbly against this baby.'

Charlie rolled her eyes but smiled all the same. 'I think that's for ships, not caravans.'

'I don't see why caravans should miss out on all the fun,' he said, his expression sober. 'That's a little prejudiced if you ask me.'

Dad and Mrs Sampson laughed and Charlie tried to resist but eventually couldn't help herself. No matter how hard she fought her attraction to Mitch, she couldn't help the way he made her feel—all warm and gooey inside.

'Well, I've gotta go help Macca moving sheep on the farm,' Mitch announced.

'Thanks for lending me your ute, son,' Dad said, clapping Mitch on the shoulder. 'Why don't you come have dinner in the motel tonight, on the house?'

'Thanks, that'd be great.' Mitch looked to Charlie and grinned. 'You up for a few episodes of *Breaking Bad* after?'

She nodded. He mightn't exactly be proposing a romantic evening, but at least while he was scoffing popcorn and watching telly with her, he wasn't out getting up to mischief with anybody else.

Chapter Thirty-two

Madeleine lounged back on the couch, reading a medical journal article on influenza in pregnancy while she waited for Hugo to arrive. This would be their second attempt at conception and this time she hadn't spent the last three hours madly running around the house swiping and wiping every mark and every spot of dust. Nor was she anxiously listening for the intercom to buzz like she had been the first time she'd summoned him for donor duty. This time she knew what to expect. Since the bowling night, they'd discussed what they were doing a lot more and both of them were more relaxed about the process.

Madeleine hoped this relaxed state would heighten their chances of success.

She sighed and tossed aside her iPad on which she'd been reading the journal. Who was she kidding? She wasn't stressed or nervous, but she still couldn't focus on anything except what they were about to do. Excitement thrummed through her veins at the thought of having Hugo to herself, even if only for half an hour. At work they talked, but they were never truly alone and if they socialised outside of work, Celia was usually in chirpy attendance, invariably wanting to talk about the baby that didn't exist yet. Her weird enthusiasm was beginning to get on Madeleine's nerves and sometimes it took all her self-control not to tell Celia to butt out. For someone who professed not to want kids herself, she wanted to talk about them a lot.

Before she could think any more about this, the intercom announced Hugo's arrival. Smiling, she all but flounced across her apartment to buzz him up.

'Evening,' he said with a cocky grin as he emerged from the elevator thirty seconds later. 'Sorry I'm late, got caught up in the labour ward.'

'Maybe that's a good omen.' Madeleine leant against her front door as he strode into her apartment. The scent of his cologne wafted past her and she tried to be subtle as she checked out his cute ass. The way his navy-blue trousers hugged his butt made her mouth go dry. Then again, she found him equally sexy in scrubs.

'Let's hope so.' He dumped his wallet and phone on the side table in the hall. 'Are you ready?'

She nodded, almost able to feel her ovaries jumping up and down in excitement. An illicit thrill scuttled down her spine and she had to squeeze her legs together at the thought of how it would be to try for a baby with Hugo the old-fashioned way. To have *him* inside her—not just his sperm.

'Madeleine? Are you okay?'

She blinked and nodded again. 'Sorry, just …' Her voice drifted off again because she couldn't confess her thoughts. 'The bathroom's ready for you. I'll be in my room again like last time.'

'Okay.'

And although she felt cheated at having such a short time with Hugo, she turned and fled, almost slamming the bedroom door behind her. She sat on the edge of her bed, her hands beneath her, determined this time to simply wait it out. No saucy shenanigans and no self-pleasure. She wasn't doing herself any favours thinking such naughty things about Hugo.

It seemed like an eternity and her fingers were almost numb when she finally heard the knock. Despite waiting for it, she startled at the sound.

'Good luck,' Hugo called through the door.

'Thanks,' she replied and then waited another five minutes until she was sure he was gone, before standing and creeping across the room to the door. She picked up the little container as if it were a pot of gold, closed the door and then returned to her bed, where she had all she needed ready to go.

She unscrewed the lid on Hugo's sample, filled the syringe and then laid it down on the bedside table.

'Please, let this work,' Madeleine whispered to no one in particular as she toed off her shoes and then slipped her jeans and panties down her legs. As she lay back, propped up slightly by pillows, and reached for the tiny tube that held Hugo's sperm, it struck her how clinical this felt. She wanted the conception of her child to be a pleasurable occasion, even if she were the only one involved.

Maybe it was an excuse to do what she'd wanted to do ever since Hugo strode into her apartment looking all edible and manly. Or maybe it was the research she'd read that indicated conception more likely if the woman achieved orgasm during the act. It hadn't worked last time but it couldn't do any harm.

And ... she couldn't help herself.

Madeleine put the syringe back on her bedside table and sucked in a breath as she moved her hand slowly down her torso and between her legs. She closed her eyes, taking herself away to an alternative reality where Hugo's fingers were stroking her intimately. And boy did he have magic fingers. Her breathing grew jagged as the pleasure built down below, satisfaction swamping her whole body when she came.

She took a few moments, breathing deeply and trying to gain back some kind of control, before she reached over and grabbed the syringe. Spreading her legs again, she positioned and aimed, praying for success. After the deed was done, Madeleine swung herself around and lifted her legs so they were high up, resting on the bedhead. She felt ridiculous but this was also in the literature she'd read about enhancing chances of conception.

Ten minutes passed and the abstract painting on the wall behind her bed could no longer hold her interest. Her stomach rumbled and she had an intense craving for something bad. Doubtful there was anything in her kitchen that would do the job, she climbed out of bed, slipped on her panties and went to find out. Lost in thoughts of Ben and Jerry's ice-cream, she crossed behind the couch on her way to the kitchen, completely oblivious to the ginger head resting against the back of it.

'All done?'

It was only when Hugo spoke and she had herself a near heart attack that Madeleine realised he hadn't left. Heat rushed to her cheeks at the knowledge that she hadn't bothered to put her jeans back on, and her hands went to the bottom of her t-shirt to try and yank it down.

'Yes,' she spluttered.

The expression on Hugo's face as he turned his head to look at her told her that her efforts to achieve decency were futile. 'Nice legs,' he commented, letting his gaze drift down. His head was at the same level as her girly bits.

An illicit thrill swept over her, warming her from head to toe. As if her naughtiness in the bedroom hadn't made her hot enough. Had she cried out? Oh fuck, what if he'd heard her?

'What are you still doing here?' she asked, flustered.

He shrugged. One of his arms was draped lazily along the back of the couch as if he wasn't finding this awkward at all. 'It felt wrong leaving you after … You know. Celia's working late again tonight and I thought maybe we could keep each other company or something.'

Madeleine's imagination ran away with her at what the 'or something' could be but she told herself she wasn't that kind of woman. Although maybe she could be if Hugo wanted her to be. Still gripping the bottom of her t-shirt like grim death, she shook her head to try and rid it of that thought. Celia was her friend; what kind of person did that make her? 'What did you have in mind?'

'Thought we could get some takeout and watch a movie.'

Well, that was better than spending a night alone pining after him, right? 'Okay, just let me …' Unable to verbalise the fact she was near naked in front of him, she simply gestured to her bare legs.

He nodded. 'Shall I order Chinese?'

'Sounds good,' she called over her shoulder as she fled back into her bedroom.

'I was thinking,' Hugo said, when she returned a few minutes later, 'maybe we should do this again tomorrow or the next day.'

She frowned. 'What? Takeaway and a movie.'

He chuckled. 'No. I meant have another shot at insemination. Last month we only did it once, but we'd increase our odds if we got in another try. What do you think?'

Madeleine flopped down on the couch beside him. It made sense indeed but she didn't know if she could handle the process again so soon after today. Although what they were doing was all above board, the faux-intimacy fatigued her. But damn, she wanted that baby. And the sooner the better if her lustful feelings towards Hugo were anything to go by.

Maybe once she was pregnant, she'd be able to distance herself from him and regain a little more control over her emotions. The whole situation was messing with her head. 'Yes, good idea. What about Sunday, lunchtime?'

It sounded like they were arranging a date.

'I'll have to check with Celia but it should be fine.' He picked up her remote, turned on the TV and then clicked a couple more buttons. He must have put in a DVD while she'd been getting changed, because the opening credits of *Skyfall* flashed onto the screen. Making himself at home, Hugo toed off his shoes, stretched his legs and put his feet up on the coffee table.

'Celia's still okay with all this then?' Madeleine asked.

'Yep. She hates Bond movies.'

That hadn't been what she meant and she guessed Hugo knew this but she let it slide, thinking instead about him and Celia as a couple. Sometimes she wondered what they had in common besides their medical degrees, love of expensive things and their rich, complicated families. On the other hand, Madeleine and Hugo were friends because they clicked on so many levels, not the least of which were their favourite movies. Celia liked movie adaptations of the classics, whereas Madeleine, like Hugo, had always preferred her entertainment with more action.

Half an hour into the movie, they were interrupted by the buzz of the intercom. 'That'll be the Chinese.' Hugo leapt to his feet.

While he went to collect their dinner, Madeleine paused the DVD, her mind drifting to what it would be like to come home to him every night. To be able to share their workday happy news and horror stories and then fall into bed together. She imagined having pregnancy cravings and Hugo rushing out in the middle of the night to buy her what she wanted. Although she knew these thoughts were wrong—that they were an emotional betrayal of her friend Celia—she couldn't help herself.

Hugo returned to the room and put two large plastic containers on the coffee table, along with some chopsticks and a couple of club sodas. 'I hope you're hungry.'

'Famished.' She all but fell upon the feast, grateful to have something to occupy her hands and mind.

Hugo un-paused the DVD and also began to eat. They sat in comfortable silence, chewing and watching the familiar scenes of a movie they'd watched so many times before. At some point Madeleine fell asleep, waking later to the sound of Hugo's voice and the feel of his hand gently shaking her arm.

'Mads, time to wake up.'

Taking a moment to come to, she blinked, gazing up into Hugo's eyes before realising her head was in his lap. She shot into a sitting position. 'Oh, I'm sorry,' she gushed, hoping she hadn't been snoring, or worse, drooling.

'It's fine,' he said, meeting and holding her gaze a few long moments. 'But I'd better be going. Celia will be home now.'

She nodded, unable to speak for fear she might say something she'd regret. Was it her imagination or was Hugo as reluctant to leave as she was to let him go?

Chapter Thirty-three

Joe was waiting at the school gate when Lucinda walked out for the final time, her arms laden with the last of twelve years of teaching resources and also presents from her students. Over the last few weeks, she'd slowly stripped her classroom bare of all the posters and banners and charts she'd made in the course of her career and had been boxing it all up and bringing a bit home each night.

'What are you doing here? Aren't you supposed to be at work?' she asked, scanning the nearly deserted car park. It was the last day of term and most of the teachers had zoomed away almost as soon as the bell rang. 'And where's my car?'

Grinning like a kid who'd just been given a year's supply of lollypops, Joe stepped up to her, relieved her of the box and then kissed her firmly on the lips. 'Surprise! I took some time off and I got Mum to drop me off to pick your car up this morning.'

'Why?' Once upon a time, she'd enjoyed surprises. But now … things like this just irritated her. It was like she had no control over anything anymore.

'To celebrate you becoming a lady of leisure,' he said, heading towards a red sports car that was parked a few feet away. He

322

heaved open the boot and shoved the box inside. She noted two small suitcases in there as well. From the outside, it didn't look like it could fit a shoebox.

'You didn't buy that, did you?' She couldn't keep the horror out of her voice.

'With you quitting your job?' Joe laughed and shook his head. 'I don't think so. It's on loan from a workmate. I told him I wanted to take my wife away for a dirty weekend down south and he was more than happy to oblige.'

At the cheeky, boyish expression on Joe's face and the mention of a weekend away, Lucinda felt the annoyance draining from her body. She'd made plans for the first weekend of her holidays—most of them involving flopping on the couch and eating copious amounts of cookies and cream ice-cream—but she appreciated Joe's effort. It would be good to do something special together. 'Where down south?' she asked, smiling.

'Where else but Bunker Bay?'

That won her over completely. She threw her arms around Joe and kissed him. They'd gone to Bunker Bay on their honeymoon and their first few anniversaries, but somehow the tradition had lapsed these last few years.

'Steady on, sweet pea. There'll be plenty of time for that when we get to the resort.' Then he pulled away and patted her playfully on the bum. 'I've packed clothes for you for a few nights away, but do you want to check in case I've forgotten anything?'

Lucinda shook her head and opened the passenger door. 'I trust you.' Then she slipped inside the luxurious interior. She'd already clicked her seatbelt into place by the time Joe lowered himself into the seat beside her.

'Let's hit the road.'

For the first time in what felt like months, they talked to each other on the three-and-a-half hour drive south. Without the distraction of their iPads—for Joe to play Minecraft or Lucinda to google stuff that only made her feel worse—they made proper conversation, not simply stuff like whose turn it was to put the bin out for collection. She was careful to steer clear of their fertility problems or anything that might bring them back to the baby issue. They didn't even talk work. Instead, they reminisced about other holidays and made plans for the next couple of days. The Margaret River Chocolate Factory was high on Lucinda's wish list. Joe added a few of their favourite wineries and a brewery and also suggested canoeing along the coast as they'd done years ago.

'And of course we'll want to spend a bit of time at the resort,' he said, reaching over and squeezing her thigh so she could not mistake his intentions.

She put her hand on top of his and stroked her thumb over his warm, smooth skin. 'Of course.' She didn't mention that it was a good time of the month—the ovulation kit had said so that morning—but maybe he'd been taking more notice than she thought. Maybe being away from home would be a good thing. They could relax in the lap of luxury and even spice up their lovemaking a little. Maybe that would be the key to success.

Joe pulled over at a roadhouse between Bunbury and Busselton and grabbed them each an ice-cream to eat in the car. Those few minutes munching were the only quiet moments during the whole trip.

Excited by the weekend ahead, Joe suggested maybe they should plan an even bigger holiday. 'We could go overseas for Christmas, to Europe or Canada maybe?'

'That sounds good.' Lucinda stopped herself asking what Rosa would think about him missing another Mannolini Christmas. Hopefully she'd be heavily pregnant by then and such a trip would be impractical anyway. Instead, she encouraged his enthusiasm, adding her two bob's worth about cities and places she'd always wanted to visit. By the time they arrived at the five-star resort, they had a whole fantasy itinerary planned out .

Joe had ordered a welcome basket with a bottle of top-of-the-range fizz to be in their room on arrival, and he insisted on running her a spa bath and pouring her a glass. As she sank into the warm bubbles, she felt special, cherished. When she'd walked out of her classroom that afternoon, she'd wondered if resigning was a mistake, but now she felt sure it had been the right thing to do—for herself, for Joe, for their marriage and future family.

Knowing Lucinda didn't like sharing baths, Joe perched himself on the toilet seat and also sipped champagne as she relaxed. 'I could stay here forever,' she said, before taking another sip of her drink.

Eventually the water went cold and Joe lured her out with the promise of dinner and something chocolate for dessert. She climbed out of the spa, he wrapped the resort's fluffy white robe around her and then led her into the bedroom. There he untied the robe he'd done up only a few seconds before and slipped his hands inside, palming them against her wet skin.

She sucked in a breath as his fingers inched upwards, one hand cupping one of her breasts while the other twirled circles around her other nipple. Maybe it was the champagne, maybe it was their opulent surroundings, but her body relaxed under his touch in a way it hadn't done for a long time. She leaned forward and pressed her lips against his, relishing his familiar taste as he eased the robe off her shoulders and let it pool onto the floor.

He gazed down at her nakedness, appreciation evident in his adoring smile. 'I love you, Lucinda Jane.'

Her eyes began to water. 'I love you too, Joseph Roberto.' And then she took the initiative, lifted her hands and pushed him down onto the enormous king size bed.

Afterwards they lay in each other's arms, sometimes talking, sometimes simply being, until their tummies began to rumble.

'I don't want to leave the comfort of this bed,' Joe groaned. 'Shall we order room service?'

'Good idea.' Lucinda nodded, already reaching for the in-room menu.

Half an hour later they were gorging on gourmet cheeseburgers and the most delicious sweet potato fries either of them had ever eaten, washing it all down with a crisp fruity chardonnay from a local winery.

It was a magical night, reminding her of what their relationship was like before they had started trying to conceive and the stress and pressure had taken over. She slept well and—judging by Joe's contented snoring—so did he. After waking later than usual with the autumn sun shining in through the window, announcing a beautiful day, they had fabulous morning sex and then showered together before hitting the road. They drove along the spectacular Indian Ocean coast and through the forests, stopping at wineries and cheese factories along the way.

Although she'd almost raised the fertility thing a couple of times, Joe was the first to mention children. They were sitting down for lunch at the Eagle Bay Brewing Company and, much to Lucinda's dismay, found themselves surrounded by young families. He reached across and took her hand as a gorgeous little girl who looked to be only about one year old started bellowing at the next table. Her older brother, maybe by two or three years, clearly wasn't happy about the attention her outburst brought so he started hurling his French fries across the table.

As Joe ducked to avoid a flying piece of deep-fried potato, he chuckled. 'See? Having kids isn't all it's cracked up to be. We'd never have another peaceful weekend like this again. Not to mention this morning's luxurious lie-in.'

He was probably only trying to make her feel better about their situation, but she bristled anyway. How could he think like this when he was so good with his nieces and nephews?

She smiled tightly and took a sip of her wine. 'They're probably just tired or something.'

Joe nodded and they turned their attention to the menu. Lucinda ordered a coconut chicken salad and tried to tune out her surroundings. But the squeals and happy laughter made her heart ache. No matter what her husband said, she couldn't think about babies as anything less than a blessing—one she wanted desperately. She and Joe weren't like the loved-up young couples that sat out on the balcony staring into each other's eyes; still so new and into each other that they didn't need another soul. They'd been there, done that and were ready for the next stage of their lives.

Joe kept up the talk of things they might do on their European holiday, but although Lucinda played her part, her heart wasn't in it. Thankfully, he didn't seem to notice.

'Shall we go hire a canoe now?' he asked, when he'd hoovered up the last of his chocolate mud cake dessert.

'Yep. Sounds great.' Maybe the fresh air would do her good.

He drove them down the coast to a little bay with a rustic looking shack that hired out canoes. The one good thing about this place was that it didn't seem to be overrun with young families. Although they'd canoed a number of times before, they pretended to listen as the boathouse guy rattled off rules and instructions as he handed out their life jackets. Her zip was a little stiff, so Joe helped her yank it up and then kissed her on the forehead. 'Fluoro orange suits you.'

She laughed, feeling herself loosen up a little. 'Pity I can't say the same about you.'

'Come on,' he said, giving her a wounded look, 'I look hot in any colour.'

She rolled her eyes, but it was true. If only being good-looking could help them with their fertility woes.

'You kids have fun,' said the guy as Joe held Lucinda's hand while she stepped into the canoe. They were almost old enough to be his parents.

'Thanks.' Joe waved as he pushed the canoe out into the water and then jumped in. The boat rocked and Lucinda squealed like a teenager as they glided out towards the open sea. Joe laughed and then started paddling like they were in the Olympics. Lucinda half-heartedly made an attempt to do her bit, but he had it under control and as they travelled slowly along the coastline, she gave him her oar and relaxed back to enjoy the ride. The afternoon sun beat down on them but thankfully Joe had remembered to pack their hats. He was responsible like that. If they had children, he'd be a great dad, remembering things like sunscreen without having to be reminded.

'Ah … isn't this the life.' Joe lifted the paddles into the boat, splashing a little water onto her legs. He sat back and they floated awhile, letting the gentle waves rock the canoe.

Lucinda couldn't remember feeling this relaxed for a very long time. Her eyes grew a little heavy and she guessed if she wasn't sitting upright, she'd likely fall asleep, but then something Joe said snapped her out of her serene state.

'It wouldn't be that bad, would it?'

'What?' she asked, stifling a yawn.

'This. Being out here with you, just the two of us, surrounded by such beauty, is magic. I'm having the best weekend. Would it really be so bad if we couldn't have children?'

Her heart froze, but he went on, oblivious.

'It'd be a different life, sure, but it could be just as good, just as full. Think of all the things we could do together.'

Lucinda tried to rein in her frustration. 'I'm not ready to give up just yet, Joe.'

'Course not.'

She couldn't understand why he didn't appear to care as much as she did about their conception problems.

And then as if he'd never brought up the baby issue, he picked up the oars and started paddling again. 'What do you want to do tonight? We could go out for dinner or we could head up to Busselton and go to the drive-in.'

'Do you know what's showing? After that lunch I'm not sure I could eat much for dinner.'

They decided to check the movie schedule as soon as they got back to the shore.

After another half hour on the water, Lucinda's arms grew tired and they turned back. They returned their canoe, oars and life jackets, thanked the boathouse guy and then trekked over the dunes to their car. Just as they were climbing inside, Joe's mobile rang.

He glanced down at the caller ID. 'It's Matt,' he said.

'Go on, answer it.' Lucinda smiled, telling him she didn't mind. Matt was a long-time friend and had been best man at their wedding. He worked on the mines too but a different one to Joe and they rarely managed to coordinate their schedules.

'Hey, buddy, how you going?' Joe said, turning the key in the ignition so he could wind down the windows while he talked.

Lucinda could hear Matt's voice but couldn't make out his side of the conversation.

Suddenly Joe's face lit up in excitement. 'Yeah, I'm off that weekend too. That'd be great. I can't remember the last time we went out fishing. Who else is coming?'

She got her phone out of her bag and checked Facebook while she waited for Joe to finish up. She was enjoying Charlie's updates of the hotel redecoration—they made her feel like she was a part of it, even though she was far away. On Charlie's personal page, there was also a photo of Dad's new caravan, which she 'liked' while pondering Charlie's suspicions that he and Mrs Sampson were becoming an item. Lucinda wasn't sure how she felt about that possibility, but she did want Dad to be happy.

'Okay, can't wait. Talk soon.' Joe disconnected his call and Lucinda slipped her mobile back into her handbag.

'You and Matt planning a fishing trip?'

His nodded, his grin stretching right across his face. 'It'll be ace to catch up.'

'When?'

He named a weekend four weeks away, the next time he'd be home from work. An alarm bell rang in Lucinda's head and she did a quick mental calculation, confirming what she already suspected.

'You can't go that weekend.'

Joe frowned. 'We haven't got anything on, have we?'

'That will be the right time of the month.' She tried to control her irritation.

Joe rolled his eyes and gripped the steering wheel. 'Luce, we can't let this rule our lives. I'm not going to tell Matt and the boys I can't go fishing because my wife will be ovulating that weekend.'

She blinked. *Why not?* It sounded perfectly reasonable to her. 'How far away will you be? Maybe you can come home in the evenings.'

'No way.' Joe sounded angry now. 'I'm not coming home to *service* you. It's one weekend and I'm going.'

'That's it? No discussion? Sometimes I really don't think you care at all about having children.'

'And sometimes I don't think you care about anything else,' he snapped, banging his fist on the steering wheel. The horn sounded, an echo of his fury.

She blinked, fighting back tears. He'd only get more annoyed if she cried.

'I can't live like this, Lucinda.'

'What are you saying?'

He sighed angrily and ran a hand through his hair, glaring at her as if she were the enemy. 'I'm trying damn hard to be patient.

I know how much this fertility thing is upsetting you. I planned this weekend for us, to give you a break and to show you just how much I love you, but it's not enough for you. Is it? I'm not enough, am I?'

She wanted to say that he was, but she couldn't bring herself to lie. She couldn't live like this anymore either, not unless they were one hundred percent on the same page. No matter what he said, he *didn't* understand how much this meant to her. 'I want it to be,' she whispered.

She glanced across at Joe. He looked broken. She'd done that. The invisible barricades holding back her tears ruptured and they flowed freely down her face. For the first time in their marriage, he didn't reach over and pull her against him. He didn't stroke her hair, whisper sweet nothings and then kiss away each teardrop one by one. He was less than a ruler's width away from her but she'd never felt so disconnected. So distant.

They sat in silence for a few long minutes, the car idling, both of them staring out at the ocean ahead. The beautiful view and the warm autumn weather seemed to be in direct opposition to the feelings inside her.

Joe looked at her again and shook his head, his eyes full of defeat. 'You know what I want? I want the Lucinda I fell in love with to come back. When you look at me, I want you to see more than a potential sperm donor. I want you to want me, *me*,' he roared. 'You don't want to have sex anymore unless it's the right time of the month and even when we do you go on about the curse and how it probably won't do any good anyway. That's not a marriage, Lucinda.'

'What are you saying?'

'See? You can't even deny it.' He made a scoffing noise. 'I dunno, maybe you should go home for a bit. Maybe you can help your dad and Charlie at the motel.'

'What?' Her heart cramped. 'Are you asking for a divorce?'

'I'm asking you to take some time away from me. To work out your feelings, to work out what really matters, because I can't take much more of this.'

She felt like he'd kicked her in the gut. But maybe he was right. Maybe she did need to get away—not just from work but from everything. Still it broke her heart that he was the one asking, that he couldn't put himself in her shoes and understand.

At least if she went home to Meadow Brook she could be some use. And working at the motel she wouldn't be surrounded by children, constantly reminded her of her barren state like she was at school.

'If you think it'll help,' she whispered.

'I don't know what will help. I still want to make this work, Lucinda, but if this goes on, I'm scared my anger will be stronger than any other feelings I have for you.'

Ouch. She simply nodded. His words hurt so much she found it impossible to speak.

Joe put the sports car into drive. Dinner didn't happen that night, nor did the drive-in at Busselton. They went back to the resort, collected their things and drove to Perth in absolute silence.

That evening, Lucinda packed her bags.

Chapter Thirty-four

Charlie's hand dived into the popcorn bowl, brushing against Mitch's as he did the same thing. Her heart stilled and a delicious fluttery feeling shot down her spine at the accidental connection, but he quickly pulled his hand back.

'Sorry,' he muttered, his gaze trained on the screen.

Inwardly Charlie sighed.

It was just another Sunday night. Dad and Mrs Sampson were manning the bar, no doubt talking caravan plans, and Mitch had come over to watch a few episodes of *Breaking Bad*, something that had become a ritual these past few weeks. Other nights when he came over, they'd head into one of the rooms to paint, but Sunday night was dedicated relaxation time. Lisa and Kate had started calling them an unofficial item because they hung out like an old married couple, but Mitch seemed oblivious to this.

While Charlie continued to struggle with her growing attraction to her best friend, he went on as if nothing had changed. He sent her photos of funny things he saw when he was on the road and often enquired how her study was progressing. It was going well. She could only find a few hours a week to study, so during that time she worked hard. Ironically, it was only when she lost herself in her naturopathy books that she managed to get him out of her head. Mitch occasionally referred to her going back to Melbourne, saying that he'd make more of an effort to visit her than he'd done in the past. But despite ample opportunities during the time they spent alone, he'd never offered any indication that he wanted anything more than friendship between them.

Unrequited love sucked.

'Do you want a drink?' Charlie asked, shoving the popcorn bowl towards him as she pushed herself up off the couch. She needed a few moments not in such close proximity to the object of her affection. Before he could reply, the front door to the house flew open and a gust of cool, April evening air shot inside.

Both of them looked to the door, shocked to see Lucinda standing there, a suitcase at her feet.

'Hello,' she said, looking from Charlie to Mitch as if they'd been expecting her. 'Is the kettle on?'

Charlie looked down at Mitch. He raised a questioning eyebrow and she shrugged one shoulder before turning to her sister. 'I can put it on.'

Questions crowded her mind: What the hell was Lucinda doing turning up unannounced on a Sunday night? She wanted to ask how she'd gotten here, how long she planned to stay, why she was on her own—but the look on Lucinda's face told her now was not the time for an interrogation.

'Good. I'll go dump my things.' Lucinda grabbed the handle of her suitcase and began dragging it inside, walking past Charlie and Mitch and continuing down the corridor to the spare bedroom.

'You didn't mention she was coming home,' Mitch said, slight accusation in his tone.

'You found out the same moment I did,' she hissed and then quickly lowered her voice. 'I wonder if this is just a holiday or if she's here to stay?' She shook her head at this last thought. 'No, it must just be a visit. She wouldn't leave Joe, would she?'

Mitch shrugged. 'I don't know, but Lady Muck wants the kettle on, so we'd better hop to it.'

Stifling a smile at Mitch's words but still in shock, Charlie nodded and started towards the kitchen. She'd just filled the kettle and was locating three mugs when Lucinda emerged again and slumped into a chair at the table.

'Actually, shall we have wine instead?'

A look of discomfort crossed Mitch's face and Charlie read his mind: wine meant girly talk. 'You go ahead, I was leaving anyway,' he lied. 'I guess I'll see you around, Lucinda.'

Charlie didn't want him to leave but before she could say so, Lucinda spoke. 'Yes, you will. I'm moving back home. You may as well know; Joe and I are taking a break and as I'd already quit my job, I thought I could make myself useful here. I guess you can go back to Melbourne.' Lucinda smiled as if delivering Charlie the news that she'd just won Lotto or something; she obviously thought she was doing her a favour, but Charlie's chest constricted at the declaration.

She didn't want to go back to Melbourne.

'I'm sorry to hear that, Lucinda. I hope you and Joe can work it out. Still, I'll leave you lovely ladies to catch up.' Mitch, already retreating, spoke easily but Charlie found she could barely breathe. What exactly did Lucinda mean by 'break'? Her head spinning, she yanked open the fridge, snatched a bottle of white wine and grabbed two glasses.

'Bye,' she managed to call out as she unscrewed the lid and filled the glasses. Without even passing Lucinda her drink, Charlie lifted her glass and gulped a few mouthfuls.

Lucinda raised her eyebrows. 'Has living in the motel turned you into an alcoholic?'

'No,' she spat. 'You coming home is just a shock, that's all.'

Lucinda's eyes widened as if a light bulb had lit up inside her head. 'Oh, did I interrupt something between you and Mitch?'

'No,' she said again, disappointment filling her heart at this admission. 'Don't be silly. I …' How could she explain to Lucinda how things were when she didn't really understand them herself? 'It's just I've been working so hard with the redecoration and I thought I'd have at least a little longer to get things in order.'

'I can't wait to see what you've done. The Facebook photos looked awesome. I'm not that great with a paintbrush but I'll do my best to continue what you've started.'

Knowing Lucinda meant well, Charlie tried to smile but it didn't quite work out that way. She didn't want anyone else finishing her special project. And she didn't want to leave Meadow Brook. In the last few months, she'd become part of the community—she ran her hula-hooping classes and had made friends outside of the motel. If she left, she'd miss Lisa and Kate more than she'd missed anyone in Melbourne. And she'd miss Mitch too. Again her heart tightened.

As if sensing her hesitation, Lucinda said, 'I thought you'd jump at the chance to go back to Melbourne?'

But now Charlie realised leaving Melbourne had never been a hardship. Her reluctance had been much more about her sisters expecting her to do so, rather than asking her. And Lucinda's return felt like deja vu. She was fed up with other people calling the shots in her life.

'I'm not sure,' she said, taking another sip of wine. 'I'm quite enjoying myself here.'

'Oh.' Lucinda looked taken aback. 'Well, that's great. We can work together, helping Dad. You don't mind, do you?'

It was the first time Charlie could ever recall her sister sounding uncertain about something and her heart swelled with concern as she remembered the reason for Lucinda's sudden return. 'Of course I don't mind. It'll be fun working together.'

But maybe she should leave, take a break while she had the chance. Was her renewed affection for this town more down to Mitch than anything else? Would staying put and allowing her feelings to grow be like watering a weed? Was Lucinda turning up a sign? An omen?

She could finish the room they were currently working on and then return to Melbourne, get on with the life she'd been happy leading until Dad's health had brought her back to Meadow Brook. Dave had promised her a job at the café whenever she returned and she could always camp on his couch while she looked for a new place to rent. He was cool like that, very easygoing and usually had at least one backpacker living with him. But then again, if she hung around, maybe Mitch would eventually catch on to the fact that they were meant to be together.

Or maybe she was a sad, lovesick girl clutching at straws.

'So, what's going on with you and Joe?' she asked. Talking about her sister's marriage had to be better than going insane with the thoughts churning through her own head. Besides, the idea of Joe and Lucinda splitting up broke her heart almost as much as the thought of Mitch never seeing her as more than a friend. Some things in life were meant to be and, like Mum and Dad, she'd always thought Joe and Lucinda were one of those unshakeable partnerships.

Lucinda let out a big sigh and shrugged her shoulders. 'I don't know. Things haven't been great for a while and Joe thinks we need some time apart.' She squeezed her lips together as if trying not to cry.

Charlie glanced towards the motel, considering going and getting Mrs Sampson for backup. She had life experience and would be much better at consoling Lucinda. But instead, she reached over to take her big sister's hand, silently telling her it was okay to be upset. 'I'm sorry.'

At these two words, Lucinda's lower lip quivered and within seconds tears were spilling down her cheeks. Charlie pushed their wine glasses out of the way and then wrapped her arms around her sister, holding her in a way she never had before. Lucinda had always been the mother hen, the strong, no-nonsense one who looked after everyone else. Charlie racked her brain for what to do besides pat her back and let her sob. She felt so helpless.

'I'm a mess,' Lucinda sniffed after a few minutes, finally pulling back and wiping her eyes with the bottom of her t-shirt.

'No you're not,' Charlie said. 'Hell, anyone in your situation would be falling apart. I wish there was something I could say to make it better. Do you want to talk about it? Or would you rather we just get drunk?'

A flicker of a smile appeared on Lucinda's face. 'I thought that was Abigail and Madeleine's answer to everything.'

Charlie shrugged. 'Maybe in some situations they have a point.'

Lucinda nodded, reached over and pulled her wine glass close. She lifted it up and downed the entire contents in one big gulp.

Charlie looked on, her eyes wide. 'Is it working? Do you feel better?'

'I might need another glass.'

Chuckling, Charlie did the honours and poured Lucinda another drink.

She downed that one too. 'I think I do feel a little better. Thank you.'

'Hey, I've not done anything except supply the grog.' Charlie took a sip of her own wine. 'How'd you get here anyway?'

'I hired a car at the airport.'

'I'd have come and collected you if you'd called ahead.'

'I know. Thanks.' Lucinda smiled but it seemed a pale imitation of her usual full-faced grin. 'I needed the time to think.'

'Of course. And did it help? Did you come to any conclusions? How long are you planning to stay?'

Lucinda held up her hand, her head starting to spin. 'Please, one question at a time.'

'Sorry.' Charlie looked down into her glass.

'It's okay. Joe and I went away this weekend.' She sighed again and told Charlie all about the beautiful surprise he'd arranged to celebrate her finishing work. About the sports car, the gorgeous resort, the pink champagne and the way he'd made her feel like his princess again on that first night.

'Sounds so romantic,' Charlie said, her tone wistful. 'I wish someone would organise something like that for me.'

'It *was* romantic, but he kept making these little pointed comments about how our lives could be okay without children. He says he wants a family and he says he'll do whatever it takes to get there, but I'm not sure he really cares. He's organised this boys only fishing trip for the next time I'm due to ovulate and when I found out … I lost it.'

Charlie raised an eyebrow and Lucinda could guess what she was thinking.

'I know. Me?' She knew she had a reputation amongst her sisters as being the level-headed one. Even in the classroom she barely ever raised her voice or lost her patience. 'Maybe I've been hanging around hot-headed Italians too long.'

Charlie laughed. 'When you say lost it—'

'Oh, I didn't throw things or hit him or anything, but I basically voiced my disapproval that he would choose a drunken fishing trip over the chance of getting pregnant. He got angry. I said he didn't care about kids and he said I didn't care about anything else.' Lucinda swallowed and grabbed hold of the glass again as she felt her control slipping.

The thought that she and Joe had separated made her feel as if someone had hacked out her heart.

'Oh, I don't know. Maybe I *was* overreacting but—' she paused a moment and pursed her lips tightly, trying not to cry '—I'm scared. Although he says he doesn't mind if we can't have kids, I'm terrified that he'll want them eventually ... with someone else. He's so great with children. You should see him with his nieces and nephews. They all adore him. And I'm scared that the Patterson curse is real and that's why the medics can't find anything wrong with me, with us. It's the only thing that makes sense, which means it's *me* keeping him from having that family.'

'I'm sure that's not true,' Charlie said, but Lucinda could tell when her sister was lying. Charlie believed in star signs, numerology, astrology—all that hippy stuff—so it wouldn't be a stretch for her to accept a gypsy curse.

'It doesn't matter. True or not, it's in my head and I can't think about anything else. Joe's right; I am obsessed. I was obsessed with getting pregnant before but since we found out about the curse, I've been unable to focus on anything else. That's why I quit work. I was doing a diabolical job because all my preparation time was spent on researching curses.'

'And did you find out anything useful?'

She shook her head. 'Nope. Nada. Apparently the only possible chance of a reversal is going back to the source. But the source of our curse died decades ago.'

'I wish we'd never found out about it,' Charlie said.

'It doesn't matter now anyway. I can't get pregnant without a husband and as much as it breaks my heart, Joe's right. Things have changed between us. The curse merely added another layer to what was already a stressful situation. If it wasn't for the stupid curse, maybe when we were told there weren't any medical problems, I'd have rejoiced. Reclaimed hope. Instead, I focused on something we don't even know is true and self-destructed. I refuse to give it another thought.'

Charlie nodded. 'Good plan. And no matter what you're going through, you're still my wise big sister. I know you and Joe can make this work.'

'Thanks.' Lucinda forced a weak smile. 'I hope you're right.'

Chapter Thirty-five

After the late night with Lucinda, Charlie found it hard to get up the next morning. Usually her body clock woke her just before dawn, but today she slept later than usual and almost died when she saw the time on her phone. The first guests would be arriving for breakfast any moment. She threw back the covers and leapt out of bed. There was no time for meditation or a shower, but she did splash water on her face and tie her hair in a high ponytail before yanking on her uniform polo shirt and a pair of jeans.

The greasy smell of bacon assaulted her the moment she stepped inside the motel. *Lucinda.* Charlie could have stayed in bed. Heck, she could have indulged in a long, hot shower. She continued into the dining room where she found her sister bustling around, placing serviette swans on every table.

Swans? She stopped and raised her eyebrows. Origami napkin creations had never before graced the tables of the Meadow Brook Motel. 'Did you even go to bed?' she asked.

'Morning!' Ignoring the question, Lucinda smiled too brightly, making it clear she didn't wish to be reminded of her meltdown last night, or her marriage situation.

Fair enough. At least her presence meant Charlie wouldn't have to deal with the sausages and bacon. 'Morning,' she replied, making a beeline for the tea and coffee making facilities. 'Thank God you've already put the kettle on. Do you want a cuppa?'

'I'd kill for another coffee,' Lucinda said.

Charlie made a strong coffee for her sister and a herbal tea for herself. Usually her tea went cold before she had the chance to drink it, but as Lucinda had everything under control, she managed the whole cup before their first guests arrived.

The sisters fell quickly into the routine they'd established when the two of them had been on breakfast duty over Christmas. Lucinda snuck back into the kitchen to finish the cooking and Charlie greeted the guests as they trickled in. She made small talk, refilled the jugs of orange juice, made sure there was enough milk for the tea and coffee, and then cleared the plates when the mostly grey-haired guests were finished. When the last diner had departed, they washed up together.

'Thanks for your help this morning,' Lucinda said as they were putting away the last of the cutlery.

Charlie felt a flicker of irritation inside her and was just about to remind Lucinda that she'd been doing this by herself since Christmas, so if anyone should be thanking anyone it was the other way around, when the door burst open and in marched Mrs Sampson.

'My darling girl, I've just heard. I'm so sorry.' She opened her arms and pulled Lucinda into her embrace before she could protest. When the bar and restaurant had shut last night, Dad had come into the house to find his daughters near trolleyed at the kitchen table. Through slurred voices, they'd given him the short version of why Lucinda was home and it appeared he'd relayed the information. 'It's lovely to see you, but I wish it were under better circumstances. Is there anything I can do to help?'

Lucinda sniffed and pulled back a little, summoning what was clearly an attempt at a brave face. 'Thanks, but I think this is something Joe and I need to get through on our own. We just need some time.'

Mrs Sampson smiled back. 'Well, if ever you need an ear or a shoulder to cry on, I'm here for you.' She glanced behind at Charlie. 'We all are.'

'Thanks.' Lucinda bit her lower lip, that one word shaky and full of emotion. It was clear she was barely holding it together and Charlie decided to cut her some slack.

'Hey, you want to come see what I've been doing in the rooms?' she asked, offering a distraction.

'That'd be great.' And then Lucinda looked to Mrs Sampson. 'Or should we do the housekeeping first?'

Mrs Sampson shook her head. 'Steady on, the rooms are my domain. You two will do me out of a job soon. I'm going to make myself a cup of tea, have a quick glance at the headlines—' she gestured to the newspapers they had delivered to the motel for the guests each morning '—and then get started.'

'Mrs Sampson hasn't been working too hard, has she?' Lucinda asked as they went outside and crossed the tarmac to the row of rooms.

'She's fine,' Charlie replied. 'We've got a good routine going on. She, Dad, Rob and I work together. Mrs Sampson mostly handles the housekeeping side of things, I've been doing the breakfasts in the morning, manning the desk till lunchtime and then squeezing in as much redecoration as I can while Dad gets the paperwork done. He and Rob generally run the restaurant and bar in the evening, although Mrs Sampson is often still here then too—she and Dad have been spending every spare minute talking caravanning.'

'I must admit,' Lucinda said, 'Dad looks a lot better than he did at Christmas. Is that because you've taken some of his workload or is there really something going on with Mrs Sampson?'

The sisters exchanged a look of slight horror.

'Well, he gets more sleep now, because he doesn't have to get up at the crack of dawn, but—' Charlie grinned knowingly '—I'm thinking it's a combination of both. You wouldn't mind if there *was* something going on between them, would you?'

Lucinda sighed. 'My love life is such a mess, so if Dad's got one, I'm staying right out of it. Don't you think I've got enough problems of my own?'

Before Charlie could reply, Lucinda added, 'On second thoughts, don't answer that. Let's see what you've been doing in your spare time.'

Charlie dug the master key out of her pocket and slipped it into the lock. She turned the handle and pushed the door open, holding it so Lucinda could go in ahead of her. 'Tada!'

'Holy Mackeroli!' Lucinda exclaimed as she stepped inside.

Basking in her sister's approval, Charlie pulled back the curtains to give her the full effect. 'It's not finished yet. We still have to put in new carpet and hang the pictures up on the wall but—'

'This is amazing. The photos on Facebook looked good, but … just … wow. You should be proud of what you've done here. It's so fresh, so inviting.'

Charlie's cheeks flushed at the compliment as a shadow appeared in the open doorway. Even before she turned to look, she sensed Mitch, but the expression on his face shocked her. His usually carefree, boyish grin was nowhere to be seen; in its place were bloodshot eyes and a furrowed brow. He still looked illegally gorgeous, but Charlie's heart leapt to her throat.

'What's the matter?' Lucinda's praise forgotten, she rushed over to Mitch. 'Is it your dad? Did something happen?'

He shook his head but the stern expression on his face didn't soften. 'I need you to come with me, Charlie.'

'But …?' She looked to Lucinda, torn between leaving her sister alone in her tender emotional state and going with Mitch, who was acting very bizarrely indeed.

As if reading her mind, Lucinda said, 'I'm fine. Go. I'll find Mrs Sampson and see if she needs any help.'

Lucinda let out a sigh of relief as she watched Charlie climb into Mitch's ute. She hoped nothing too serious was wrong but at the same time she welcomed the few moments to herself. She closed the door of the almost-renovated motel room, grabbed a glass from the bathroom, filled it with water and then guzzled it down, almost as fast as she'd guzzled last night's wine.

She groaned at the pain in her head—caused by a combination of said wine, lack of sleep, this whole awful situation and self-loathing. As unlikely as it seemed, the possibility of her being pregnant had never crossed her mind while she'd been bemoaning her troubles to Charlie, but now the thought of how all that wine might affect an unborn child made her want to throw up. It would be just typical that the moment she let everything go, the moment her life totally fell to pieces, that's when she'd strike it lucky.

Maybe it was good that she hadn't had babies on the brain last night. But then again, maybe Joe was right; maybe she was simply losing the plot.

'Oh, Joe.' She sighed and put the glass down with a thunk. What had he been doing yesterday while she'd been travelling or last night while she'd been crying? Playing Minecraft on the iPad? Drinking beer with his mates? Watching mindless television?

Or had he felt like her—utterly lost—wondering how the hell their lives had come to this?

How many times during the night had she picked up her phone, this close to calling home? She'd been desperate to hear his voice, but his final words were on constant replay in her head, like some nightmare she couldn't wake up from. The fear that all she'd hear was anger and resentment held her back.

Now, she leant against the bathroom wall and touched her pocket, feeling for her mobile. It felt like the only connection she had to Joe right now, and yet ...

Her life was like an impossible logic puzzle. She wanted to call him and apologise—to beg him to let her come home—but could she really tell him what he wanted to hear? She did love him and maybe she'd let her desire for a baby overshadow that, but she couldn't pretend it wasn't important to her. He wanted her to live their lives as if having a family didn't matter, but it *did* matter.

The noise of an incoming text message jolted her out of her thoughts and she ripped the phone from her pocket, thinking it might be Joe. Her heart sank as she read Madeleine's name on the screen.

What's this I hear about you leaving Joe?

So Dad, Mrs Sampson or Charlie had filled Madeleine in and likely Abigail as well. It's not that she didn't want them to know but the more people who did, the more this separation felt real.

I haven't left him. We're merely having a break.

It sounded so high school, like an old episode of *Friends*, not like her life.

Her phone started to ring. She didn't need to check the screen again to know it was her sister.

'Hey,' she said as she lifted it to her ear.

'I'm sorry.' At Madeleine's heartfelt sympathy and concern, Lucinda's eyes prickled again. Dammit, she couldn't even blame pregnancy hormones for her recent tendency towards waterworks.

She swallowed. 'Thank you.'

'I've never been good at saying the right things, not like you,' Madeleine said, 'but I just want you to know I'm always on the end of a phone line if you need to talk. Any time, day or night. The only time I won't be available is if I'm in the delivery suite, but I'll always call you back. Oh shit, I shouldn't have mentioned the delivery suite, should I? Not with you and Joe wanting … Argh … see, I've done it again. I'm terrible at this comforting business.'

Lucinda laughed through her tears. Despite Madeleine thinking she'd put her foot in it, by just being herself she helped. Lucinda had never felt much in need of a big sister's guidance before but now—maybe because Mum wasn't there to call on anymore—she wished Madeleine wasn't so far away. 'No, you're not,' she said, when she'd recovered. 'I needed that laugh.'

'Well, phew, I was about to order a box of chocolates and a crate of wine to be delivered post haste as an apology.'

'Maybe you should do that anyway,' Lucinda said, walking out of the bathroom and sitting down on the bed. 'How are you going? Any progress on the baby-making?'

'You don't want to talk about that.'

'Yes, I do.' Granted, she'd probably feel like she'd been kicked in the gut by a Clydesdale if Madeleine ended up pregnant now, but her older sister was trying hard to play the supportive role and so could she.

Madeleine sighed. 'We're in the waiting zone. Period due in a week. I swing between being hopeful and pessimistic.'

'I know what that's like. And is the donor okay about continuing until you succeed?'

'Hugo? Yeah, he's been great. So encouraging and supportive. He was a good friend before this, but …' Madeleine's voice drifted off.

'But?'

'Oh, it's just that things are a little weird with his girlfriend. She's a good friend too and has been really supportive—believe it or not this was her idea—but I feel as if the dynamics of our friendship have changed since we started this. I'm not quite sure how to act around her and...'

'And?' Lucinda had to prompt her again.

'Never mind.' Madeleine abruptly changed the subject. 'So, what are you going to do today?'

Lucinda guessed Madeleine wasn't telling her everything but she didn't have the energy to pry further. 'Well, Charlie's going great guns on her redecoration efforts, so I guess maybe I'll take over some of her load in the motel so she can focus on that.'

'I thought she might go back to Melbourne now that you're there.'

'Yes, I thought so too, but I suppose we don't have any idea how long I'll stay and she's really thrown herself into this project. She doesn't want to abandon it midstream.'

'Good for Charlie,' Madeleine said. 'Maybe she's finally found her calling.'

'Yes, maybe.'

'Look, I'd better go, but I meant it about calling me, any time.'

'Thanks. And good luck. I hope you've got good news to share soon.' Lucinda disconnected, thinking that just as Charlie had found direction, she herself had lost her way.

Chapter Thirty-six

Charlie barely had the chance to click her seatbelt into place before Mitch shot out of the car park, the wheels screeching as he turned onto the road. She glanced backwards through the rear-view window to check if he'd left skid marks on the tarmac and then turned to look at him.

'Have you got a death wish? What's this all about?'

'How's Lucinda?' he asked, ignoring her questions.

'She's fine. Understandably upset about the state of her marriage, but she'll be okay. I'm sure she and Joe will get through this.'

'That's good.' Yet his gruff tone didn't match his words. 'So, you don't think she'll stay long?'

'I don't know about that. They've got a bit to sort through, but …' She paused and let out a sigh. 'This isn't about Lucinda and Joe, is it?'

'Nope.'

'Then what?'

'You'll see.'

What the heck was going on? Short, brusque answers were very un-Mitch-like and his hands were jittering on the steering wheel as if he'd overdosed on caffeine. He seemed nervous but she couldn't for the life of her think why. She tried to recall a time she'd known Mitch to be apprehensive about anything and came up blank.

'Are we going to visit Kate and Macca?' she asked as they turned to the road that led to his brother's farm.

'*Please.*' This one pleading word was hissed through his teeth. 'Stop asking so many questions. Just be patient or you'll ruin everything.'

'So this isn't something bad? No one has died or been in an accident?'

'No. I promise. Nothing bad like that. At least, I hope you don't think it's bad.' He kind of groaned this last bit and Charlie noticed he'd turned a pale but definite shade of green.

Worried about Mitch's agitated state and not wanting it to get worse while driving, she zipped her lips and held on tightly to the seat as they zoomed along the gravel. About a kilometre before the turn-off to Kate and Macca's place, he turned into another driveway.

'Who lives here?' she asked.

'No one,' he said. 'It's part of Kate and Macca's land and they promised I could build a house out here one day if I got sick of living in town.'

'Okay,' was all Charlie could think of to say. He'd never mentioned anything about building a home. This trip was getting weirder and weirder by the second.

Mitch slowed a little as he drove further off the road. They climbed a slight hill and in the distance she saw a massive old Eucalypt tree with something bright beneath it. She squinted, trying to make out what it was but before she could, Mitch stopped the ute and climbed out.

'Where are you going?' she called as he started walking around the front. She unclicked her seatbelt and had her hand on the door to open it but he got there first.

'I don't want you to go back to Melbourne,' he blurted and then he took hold of her hands and pulled her out of the ute.

'What?' She frowned in confusion as a soft breeze blew against them.

'I know Lucinda's home so you're free to go back to the city and start your life again, but I don't want that.' His voice cracked a little and Charlie noted his eyes were glistening. 'You're my best friend in the world, Charles, and I want you to stay here and start a life with me.'

'What?' she said again, struggling to get her head around his words.

In reply, he grabbed hold of her shoulders, drew her towards him and kissed her hard on the lips. It was a no-holds-barred lip lock. The kind that made every inch of her body shiver deliciously. He slid his hands up her neck and into her hair, drawing her even closer and deepening the kiss with raw possessive tenderness.

So this was how Mitch kissed.

She'd gone to sleep imagining this every night for the last few months, but her fantasies had nothing on the reality. For the first few seconds she was frozen, but then heat shot through her, awakening every cell and bone in her body as if lit by an inner flame. Nothing she'd ever experienced before could match it. Not one tiny bit of her wanted to miss out and she snuck her hands around his waist about to grab hold of his buttocks and draw them even closer together.

And then Mitch abruptly pulled back.

Charlie let out a little moan as he disconnected himself from her embrace. The skin on her face tingled from the scrape of his stubble.

'I'm sorry, I didn't plan to do that,' he muttered, 'but I had to. I had to know what it felt like to kiss you, even if now you want to slap me in the face.'

'Why would I want to do that? That was the best damn kiss I've ever had in my life, Mitchell McDonald.' Despite her candid admission, she blushed, because ... well, this was Mitch—*Mitch!*—and they'd never done anything like that before.

'Really?' He looked a little sheepish. 'In that case ... do you want to do it again?'

'Hell yes.' This time she wasn't sure who grabbed who, which tongue led the way or whose hands went where first. It didn't matter. They were so tightly pressed together she could barely tell where she ended and Mitch began and that was exactly the way she wanted it. Soon she felt something hard pressing against her stomach and the knowledge of its existence caused the simmering desire within her to reach boiling point.

She tugged on the bottom of Mitch's shirt, hitching it up and over his head. They fumbled at each other's clothing. There wasn't any finesse, no cute striptease on either side, but it was quick and that was all that mattered. Before long their boots were kicked off in the dirt and their clothes scattered at their feet, both of them starkers in the paddock. The cool air didn't bother them because their bodies were radiating enough heat to send a hot air balloon into space.

Mitch slipped his hands between her legs and the feel of his calloused fingers touching her most intimate part almost made her combust. She fell back against the passenger seat, half in the ute, half out as he drove her to the brink.

'Oh. *Yes.* Mitch. *Wow.*' She sounded like a floozy. She didn't care. There was no one to hear them but a few sheep and maybe some cows and if the animals needed therapy after bearing witness to this, well, so be it. She'd been waiting for this moment for so long.

Just when she thought she might actually die from orgasm, she somehow found strength. Wanting Mitch inside her more than she'd ever wanted anything before, she clambered out of the ute and literally jumped his bones. Half-chuckling, he caught her as she wrapped her legs around his waist. He swivelled to lean against the ute and they both cried out as he thrust into her, taking on both their weights. He was so strong, so incredible, so … hers. And the thought made her heart want to burst with joy.

Afterwards, he slowly lowered her feet to the ground and then cupped her face with his hands, gazing into her eyes. 'Well, that's not exactly how I planned our first time.'

'Oh?' she said, still coming down from the effects of total ravishment. 'You were planning this?'

'I was hoping.' He slowly turned her round so she was looking towards the gum tree she'd noticed on arrival. 'I had a surprise set up down there, a confession to make, but I simply couldn't wait a moment longer.'

He stooped to pick up their clothes, handing hers to her one by one. They dressed and then he took her hand and they walked towards the tree. As they approached, she saw he'd laid out a large picnic rug scattered with what looked like pink and red rose petals.

'I feel a lot more confident about admitting how I feel now we've got the sex thing out of the way,' Mitch admitted as they came to the edge of the rug. A big esky sat off to the side and he let go of her hand to open it. Like a magician conjuring rabbits from a hat, he pulled out a bottle of bubbly, two glasses and a whole host of other treats. Charlie thought of her words to Lucinda last night about wishing someone would do something romantic for her. And she smiled.

'Sit,' he said.

She dropped to her knees and on closer inspection saw that the nibbles he'd chosen were all her favourite things. Among them were olives and a hummus dip that looked suspiciously homemade. 'Did you make this?' she asked, grabbing a carrot stick and dipping it in.

He nodded as she slipped it into her mouth. 'I wanted to do something special.' He sat beside her, opened the champagne, poured two glasses and then handed her one.

She took a sip, savouring the bubbles on her tongue, already light-headed from what they'd just done. 'I wasn't going to go back to Melbourne,' she confessed, 'but if it took you thinking that I would for this to happen between us, then I'm glad you did.'

He shook his head and took her hand in his. 'I love what we have going on—our playful banter, our movie nights, hell, I even love painting walls when it's with you—but I'm greedy. I want so much more.'

'So do I.' Charlie couldn't help but smile. 'But we've been together almost every day since I came home. Why didn't you say something?'

He sighed. 'Why didn't you?'

It was a good question.

'I've been trying to psych myself up for weeks,' he admitted, 'but I've been shit-scared you'd laugh in my face and tell me to quit mucking around. We've been friends for so long and I've always wanted more, but you've never given me any reason to hope.'

'*I've* never given *you* any reason to hope?' she exclaimed, unable to believe her ears.

He shook his head. 'You have your glamorous life in Melbourne and I'm nothing but a country truckie content to live in the sticks.'

'Oh, you're a lot more than that, Mitchell. And why do you think I went to Melbourne in the first place?'

He cocked his head to one side and frowned.

'I was tired of playing the third wheel to Mitch-and-Lara.'

'We've been broken up a long time. I think it was when I was with her that I realised no one would ever measure up to you.'

She shook her head in disbelief. 'What about all the women you dated between Lara and now? According to local gossip, you've been quite the playboy. Were you just wanting to be sure?'

He laughed at her outrage.

'You've been giving me mixed signals for months,' she continued. 'Hanging around constantly, yet when I joked about kissing you, you reacted like I'd given you herpes or something.'

'Now, now, Charles,' he said, sounding like his old cocky and loveable self again. 'Let's not argue about this. I think it's fair to say we were both stupid and slow, so how about we start making up for that right now.'

He reached out and stole the glass from her fingers, placing both their glasses on top of the esky.

'What exactly did you have in mind?' she asked, feeling more wanton than she ever had in her life.

'This,' he said, gently pushing her backwards until she lay flat on the rug. And then he covered her mouth and kissed her.

Chapter Thirty-seven

Madeleine was late. Since she'd started having periods at age twelve, her menstrual cycles had been like clockwork. She remembered joking with her schoolfriends in her teens that if she ever got pregnant, she'd know about it because of her never-deviating twenty-eight day cycles. Well, yesterday had been day twenty-seven and this morning ... nothing.

She'd leapt out of bed and rushed to the bathroom to make sure and then squealed in a manner most unlike her. The people in the surrounding apartments would be wondering what was going on. She didn't care. The last week had felt like a decade. Despite knowing that physical pregnancy symptoms were rarely reliable before the first missed period, she'd been second-guessing every little twinge or flutter in her body. The smells in the hospital cafeteria, which usually made her hungry, had made her nauseous instead. And she was tired, so damn tired. Hugo had been her rock, checking in with her every day. She even found herself sharing intimate things with him—like how her breasts were a little more tender than usual—things she'd have discussed if he was her husband and they were trying for a baby in the usual way.

Rachael Johns

It would be a relief that she hadn't been imagining all these symptoms.

If she were at the hospital, she'd get Hugo to take her blood or she'd pinch one of the pregnancy tests there, but as she wasn't at work today, she did what any normal wannabe mum would do. She showered and dressed quickly, scoffed a cold bagel and a cup of foul decaf coffee and then trekked the few blocks to the nearest Walgreens. A couple of teenagers were perusing the condoms and she glanced approvingly at them—adolescent pregnancies were a nightmare—before continuing on to the section that held pregnancy tests. Not one to be fooled by fancy packaging, she grabbed two boxes of the brand she recommended to patients and took them straight to the counter.

There was a spring in her step as she walked home, breathing in the fresh morning air, smiling at the vibrant colours of the maple trees that lined the streets and listening to the tweet of the birds above. May in America seemed the perfect time to be pregnant—new life abounded everywhere. And the baby would be born in February, in late winter, also a lovely time of year in Baltimore.

But would she still be in America then? The thought briefly crossed her mind that it might be nice to be back in Australia, nearer her family when she had the baby. She wanted her child to know its aunties and grandfather and crazy great-aunt, but then … she thought of Hugo. He'd helped her through so much in the last few years and she couldn't imagine entering motherhood without him beside her. And Celia of course—they'd *both* been there for her since she moved to Baltimore. She pushed this last thought aside as she approached her apartment building and felt anticipation once again pulsing through her veins.

Fumbling to get her key out of her pocket, she couldn't get inside fast enough. She headed straight for the bathroom, tearing the plastic wrapper off the pregnancy testing kit as she went, not caring where she dropped the rubbish. Although there were two pages of instructions, Madeleine didn't read any of them. It didn't take a rocket scientist to know how to work a pregnancy test and she had a degree in obstetrics. Lightheaded with excitement, she sat down on the toilet and peed on the stick.

As she waited for the result, she pondered how she'd changed in the last few months since deciding to have a baby. She certainly felt like a different person. Had she softened? In a few minutes the test would be finished. Everything would be confirmed. Once upon a time she'd thought the idea of people saving their positive pregnancy test disgusting—and unnecessarily sentimental—but now she harboured insane ideas about doing exactly that. Maybe she'd even take a photo and post it on Facebook.

Wouldn't so many of her friends, family and acquaintances be shocked by that announcement.

Still smiling, she reached over, plucked the test off the vanity and glanced down at the result.

'No!' Her heart felt as if it had been jolted with defibrillator paddles.

Only one line.

Negative.

She shook the stick as if that might alter the result. She'd been so certain.

'It has to be faulty.'

Hurling the defective test into the trash, she grabbed the second kit and ripped it open even more fervently than she had the first. This time she read the damn instructions, but as suspected she'd done everything right the first time. Madeleine closed her eyes and peed again, then put the stick down on the vanity and left the room. She paced her apartment for the specified wait time and then trekked back into her bathroom, her heart already heavy with suspicion.

Negative.

She may have been hopeful of pregnancy symptoms but she wasn't a fool. Two negative results meant her period was on its way, cruelly late for the first time in her life. Shoving the second test in the bin alongside the first, she marched into the kitchen, yanked open the freezer and glared at the lack of ice-cream. There was no chocolate in the cupboards either. This was the problem when you tried to live a reasonably healthy existence.

Wine, she needed wine. Who cared that it was barely noon, how else was she supposed to drown her sorrows? Thankfully, she had plenty of expensive vino languishing in her wine rack and wasn't on call this weekend. Something else to be grateful for. She was halfway through pouring herself a glass when her phone beeped.

Are we going to be parents?

A massive sob escaped her at Hugo's message. She'd wanted to be able to give him good news. Deep down she felt he wanted children, despite saying he didn't mind that Celia didn't, and the thought that she might give him something Celia wouldn't had made her feel special somehow.

No, she sent back, unable to bring herself to say anything else. She waited for his phone call—or at least a reply—but nothing came. And then it hit her. He was on his way over. This made her smile. Hugo's company would be a far better tonic than wine.

Then again, there was the very real possibility he'd also bring Celia.

Not wanting to be off her face when her friends came around, she poured her wine down the sink and put the bottle into the fridge. She plonked herself on the couch and waited. And waited and waited.

Hours passed and still the intercom didn't buzz. No phone call, no more messages. What was going on? Was he as gutted as she was? Maybe she should call or go round and check he was okay? This damn situation was so bloody complicated.

Confused and disenchanted, she decided to make herself some toast and was in the middle of spreading pâté over the thick slices when the intercom finally buzzed. She rushed over to answer it. 'Hello?'

'It's Hugo.'

'I'll buzz you up.'

Madeleine abandoned her snack and waited at her door. Her heart gave a little leap when he appeared alone. 'Hey there.'

'I'm sorry, Madeleine,' he said as he approached her. He didn't look too good.

'It's okay.' She grabbed his hand and yanked him into her apartment. 'It's not your fault. Maybe it'll be third time lucky.'

Closing the door behind them, she finally looked into Hugo's eyes and something she saw told her he wasn't apologising for the negative result. Had something else terrible happened between now and when she'd sent that text?

Her stomach twisting, she frowned. 'What's wrong?'

'Can we sit?'

'Sure,' she said, leading him through to the living room and gesturing to the couch. 'Do you want a drink? I have wine.'

He shook his head and gestured to the space on the couch beside him.

Her heart beating nervously, she sat.

'I can't be your donor anymore.'

He may as well have punched her in the head, such was the shock and pain and recoil at this words. 'What? *Why*?' Her voice cracked a little, which annoyed the hell out of her because although she didn't know what was happening, she knew she didn't want to cry.

'Fuck.' Hugo ran a hand through his hair. 'This is so difficult.'

No kidding, Sherlock. Someone nicer than her might have offered some soothing words of encouragement, but she just sat there silently waiting for an explanation.

'You know how Celia said she doesn't want babies?' It was a rhetorical question. 'It's not true. She broke down today after we got your text and told me the truth. She can't have children.'

'What? And she never told you this before?'

He shook his head. 'She was scared she'd lose me or that I'd see her as a lesser woman or something, so she came up with the story that she didn't want kids instead.'

Madeleine couldn't believe what she was hearing.

'When you decided to have a baby on your own,' Hugo continued, 'Celia got this nutty idea that this way I could still father a child. She confessed she thought maybe you'd struggle on your own with a child and get sick of it, and that maybe we could step in and help.'

'What?' Madeleine didn't care if she sounded outraged. 'She hoped I'd fail at motherhood and then she'd swoop in and take my baby?'

'*Our* baby,' Hugo reminded her, as if Celia's plan wasn't evil and insane.

'So what happened?' she asked through gritted teeth, resisting the urge to pick something—anything—up and throw it at him. 'Why has she suddenly changed her mind?'

'She's scared you and I are getting closer because of all of this. She's afraid something will happen between us and she'll lose me anyway, so she begged me to stop.'

Madeleine's breath halted as she waited for Hugo to confess that this was indeed the case, that he *did* feel closer to her and that this whole process had made him realise he loved her, not Celia. But of course he said nothing of the sort.

Somehow she managed to speak past the lump in her throat. 'So, you and Celia? You're staying together after all this?'

'Of course,' came his instant reply, as if he couldn't see why she'd imagine otherwise.

So many times she'd chatted with Hugo at work or on nights when Celia was working and they'd indulged their action movie habit. They'd talked about fun stuff and deeper things too; she thought she knew him better than she knew almost anyone. But now she felt like the man sitting next to her was a stranger.

Suddenly she didn't feel like she knew Hugo or Celia at all.

How could he not be angry at Celia? She'd lied to him for years and made him a pawn in her sick game without his knowledge.

But the answer was obvious. He loved her. And, like the age-old saying, he was blind to her faults.

The truth was that love had blinded Madeleine as well. She'd spent the last few months imagining that Hugo's bond with Celia wasn't actually all that strong. She'd conveniently forgotten that he was only her donor and had fantasised about him being a major player in her baby's life. She'd thought of him being there at the birth and then all the significant events that would follow.

Maybe in her own way she was as guilty as Celia.

But no, she'd never have asked Hugo to do this if Celia hadn't suggested it. A terrible cocktail of anger and sadness swept through her.

'I'm sorry,' Hugo said again, reaching out to squeeze her hand. 'We can still be friends, yeah?'

She flinched at his touch—the hand she'd imagined delving into intimate parts of her body so many times over the last few months now only made her feel cold, empty and alone. 'Please, just go,' she whispered, slipping her hand out of his, wanting him out of her apartment before she succumbed to any kind of emotion.

'Okay. I understand.'

I don't think you do.

Madeleine waited until she heard the click of her door shutting behind him. Then she stood and headed back into the kitchen.

Now she needed that wine.

Chapter Thirty-eight

Abigail had just finished microwaving a bag of popcorn, planning a night in her room with one of her favourite movies—possibly *Dirty Dancing*—when the doorbell rang.

'I'll get it,' she said to Sam and Pamela, who were making themselves something nutritious for dinner. Popcorn would do Abigail, and maybe a packet of chocolate biscuits for dessert. Neither of them replied so she flounced to the door, expecting it to be someone selling religion or wanting money for charity, but she was pleasantly surprised.

'Nigel,' she exclaimed. 'What are you doing here?'

Not that she wasn't over the moon to see him. He'd been working late on an energy drink campaign every night this week and had predicted the office would be his home all weekend as well, and she missed everything about him. In the course of a few weeks, she'd gone from not thinking herself in the market for a relationship to being head-over-heels in love. From being quite content in her own company to craving his whenever they were apart.

He stepped inside and they kissed in the manner of lovers who hadn't seen each other all week.

'It was a crap day at work,' he said when they finally pulled apart, 'and I had an urge to hear you playing the violin.'

Which really meant he needed some sex therapy and she was cool with that. He enjoyed listening to her play, but she guessed he liked what it usually led to even better. Her insides were already flaring with desire at the thought. She smiled and grabbed his hand, closing the door behind him with her foot because she still had the big bowl of popcorn in her other hand.

'I think I can manage that.' She led Nigel past her flatmates and couldn't help a smug smile as they looked him up and down, obvious surprise and appreciation in their gazes. *Eyes off girls, he's all mine. Officially.*

She still had to pinch herself sometimes when she thought about it—how just when she'd almost hit rock bottom, he'd come unexpectedly into her life and taught her to embrace her passions again. If it hadn't been for him she'd likely be pouring pints in some seedy bar, but instead she was blessed to work with enthusiastic children every day.

'So those are your roomies,' Nigel said, when they'd barricaded themselves in her bedroom.

'Yep. Total nannas both of them. I'll probably get a lecture later about having a man in my room with the door closed.'

He chuckled, dumped his laptop bag onto the floor and then pulled her roughly towards him. She dropped the bowl of popcorn and it spilled all over the floor but neither of them cared about the mess. 'In that case, we should really give them something to frown about.'

Their lips came together in a hungry clash and hands went everywhere as they tore at each other's clothes, making up for the time they'd lost over the last week. When they were naked, Nigel pushed her down onto the bed and licked his way up her body, starting with her toes and driving her to the brink of ecstasy as he travelled up her legs and inner thighs.

'I. Haven't. Even. Played. One. Tune. For. You. Yet,' she panted as his mouth landed on her most intimate part.

'Later,' he mumbled before doing something with his tongue that made her unable to think anymore.

Much later, when they'd sated each other's hunger for the time being, Abigail slipped out of bed and tiptoed across the floor to her violin case. As she removed the instrument, Nigel propped himself up in bed with the multitude of cushions she owned and linked his hands behind his head as he sat back to watch. He looked so damn sexy, sitting there like that—his impressive package hidden beneath the bed covers but his chest with its perfect smattering of blond hair visible for her to admire.

Smiling at him, Abigail took her position at the end of the bed and lifted her violin to her chin. Her breasts thrust upwards as she did so and she felt Nigel's appreciative gaze on her naked body as she began to play. If she told anyone about this thing they did, it might sound seedy but playing for him made her feel more beautiful and talented that she'd ever felt performing in one of the world's finest orchestras. She loved the way he listened intently, his head cocked to one side and an expression of awe on his face as her fingers moved across the strings.

He was the best damn audience she'd ever had and the most appreciative too. Usually she got applause, but Nigel gave her so much more. Although she'd just had one of the best orgasms of her life, having him watch her as she played always turned her on. By the time she'd finished a couple of pieces, she was hot and needy for him again. Nigel clapped and roared his praise and Abigail laughed, imagining the looks on Sam and Pamela's faces right now as she put her violin to bed and then crawled back in beside this incredible man. They made love with less urgency than they had earlier, but without sacrificing passion or pleasure.

Afterwards, feeling thoroughly sated, Abigail lay in Nigel's gorgeous arms—she'd always had a thing for nice arms and his were perfect—and they talked. The lovers she'd had in the past had never been interested in post-coital conversation, but Nigel liked talking with her every bit as much as he enjoyed sleeping with her. He stroked her hair and her fingers played idly across his chest as they caught up on what they'd both been up to the last few days.

'Are you making progress on the campaign?' Abigail asked, rubbing her toes teasingly up and down his calf.

'God, I hope so,' he said. 'I'm not sure I can take another week of this. I don't think we've had a client as difficult as this one in years. Just when we think we're close to what they're after, they change their *vision*.'

Abigail smiled at the way he said vision. If his arms weren't full of her, he'd likely have made inverted commas in the air with his fingers.

'I'd love to help but I wouldn't know where to start. I'm not good at anything apart from music.'

'I wouldn't say that,' he said, sliding his hand cheekily down her body.

She laughed and caught his hand with hers, bringing his fingers up to her lips and kissing his knuckles.

'What about you?' he asked. 'Any updates on your crazy family?'

'Hey, they're no crazier than yours,' she said, feigning annoyance. His big clan were far more interesting than hers as far as Abigail was concerned, but he loved hearing about her family and her Aussie life as much as she enjoyed hearing about his. They both adored London but were happy to have found each other because it meant they could talk about things like Vegemite, the Adelaide Crows and backyard barbies without people looking at them weirdly.

'True,' he said, 'but I hope your dad doesn't sell the motel before I get the chance to see it. It sounds like such a fun place to grow up.'

'I don't know how you got that idea.' Inwardly Abigail glowed at the thought of Nigel wanting to meet her family and see the place she used to call home. Her sisters would all fall in love with him and he liked AFL so her dad would approve.

'How's Lucinda doing?' he asked.

Abigail sighed. 'Not sure.' Her heart ached at the thought of Joe and Lucinda not being together. Lucinda herself hadn't said much apart from a quick email announcing that she'd moved home to help Dad and Charlie for a bit, but Charlie had sent a couple of updates. 'Charlie says she's driving everyone wild with cleaning regimes and reorganisation of everything from Dad's filing cabinet to the linen cupboard, which is Mrs Sampson's domain.'

'Mrs Sampson's the hotel housekeeper, right?'

'Right.' Abigail nodded. 'Although Charlie reckons she might be a little more than that to Dad.'

'So you're not the only one in the family getting up to no good?' Nigel said, once again sneaking his talented fingers down her body, this time lingering on one breast.

'Don't,' she squealed. Not because she didn't like his touch but because she was still getting used to the idea of Dad finding love again after Mum and she certainly wasn't ready to think about him and Mrs Sampson doing the horizontal mambo.

Nigel laughed and Abigail made a move to climb out of bed. 'Bathroom calls, back in a second.'

She grabbed her dressing gown from the edge of her bed and slipped it on before opening the door and hurrying down the hall to the bathroom. The television in the living room was on louder than usual and Abigail grinned at the thought that Sam and Pamela had turned it up to cover the sounds of her and Nigel making love.

Jealous prudes, she thought as she slipped into the bathroom and closed the door behind her. She did her business, freshened up a little and then checked her reflection in the mirror before heading back to Nigel.

'Are you hungry?' she asked as she re-entered the bedroom all of three, maybe four, minutes later.

He met her question with a glare and she froze as the door banged shut behind her. Her stomach clenched as her eyes zoned in on her open bedside drawer. The ovulation prediction kit she'd bought months ago lay on the bed in front of Nigel.

'What the hell is this?' he asked, gesturing to the box as if it were a rotting rodent.

She swallowed, her heart pounding so hard she swore he'd be able to hear it. 'What were you doing going through my drawers?'

Nigel sighed. 'Thinking about your dad and his new love gave me this great idea for a campaign for this client we're pitching to and I needed a pen and paper to write it down.'

She raised one eyebrow. 'And you couldn't use your phone?' Lord knows he used it for everything else.

'I always scrawl down my ideas on paper first, they just …' He halted mid-sentence and shook his head. 'I don't think it's me that needs to be explaining myself right now. What have you got this for? Is it yours? You told me you were on the pill.'

She opened her mouth to tell him no, it was a friend's, but she found she couldn't look into the eyes of the man she loved and blatantly lie. And what kind of friend would leave that in her bedside drawer? Abigail didn't want to start their relationship with such deception, but what exactly should she tell him? That she was on destitution's doorstep when they met and having a baby seemed a good way to go home without having to tell her family about being sacked from the orchestra? Or that she and her sisters had uncovered a family curse and somewhere in the back of her mind, trying to get pregnant and prove it wrong had seemed like a good idea? Whichever way she tried to explain it, he wouldn't care. And could she blame him?

There was no excuse for what she'd attempted to do.

'I'm sorry, Nigel,' she pleaded. 'When we met I was messed up and I thought having a baby might give me a renewed purpose in life. I didn't know what to do or how to *be* without the orchestra and I couldn't bring myself to tell my family the truth. I decided if I got pregnant, I'd go home and use that as an excuse for why I'd left.'

'And what? I was just some pawn in this sick plan?' He was already out of bed, yanking on his jeans.

'Yes. I mean, no!' She shook her head, tears prickling as she desperately searched for a way to make this right.

'I take it you didn't succeed,' he spat.

'No. I'm not pregnant.' She'd just finished her period, and after two months of hoping it wouldn't arrive, she'd never been so pleased to see it.

'Thank fuck.' Yet despite his words, Nigel kept dressing. He was doing up his shirt now and she knew she didn't have long to beg his forgiveness.

'Please don't leave. You need to understand, I gave up this idea a month ago. I think subconsciously it gave me a reason to keep on seeing you without admitting to myself it was love. The day after the hotel I went and got the morning after pill and I've been taking contraception pills ever since.'

'How am I supposed to believe you?'

'Because—' she swallowed, the words tripping on her tongue as tears threatened to barrel down her cheeks '—I love you. I may have been a mess when we met but I'm sure I'd never have done what we did in the plane if I hadn't felt an instant connection. I was fooling myself that it was just sex but all along it was more, you know it was.'

She reached out to grab his hand but he shook her off violently.

'I don't know anything,' he said, looking at her in a way that made her feel like the smallest thing in the world. 'My judgement is obviously totally skewed because as well as being the prettiest woman I'd ever laid eyes on, I also thought you were a good sort. But I can't love anyone who would go to such lengths to deceive someone. Did you ever think about the poor baby that might have been born from your irresponsibility?'

She opened her mouth to reply but he shouted over the top of her. 'No! You only thought of yourself. You didn't think about how it might affect a child or me? When I have a baby, I want it to be conceived in love with someone who is ready and willing to give that baby the best family life possible. And I want to be part of the decision.'

Picking up his laptop bag and shoes as if he couldn't be bothered with the time it would take to sit down and put them on, he gave her one last scathing look. 'Move aside, Abigail.'

In shock, she did so without thinking. He wrenched the door open but as he stormed down the hallway something snapped inside of her.

'You might think yourself all high and mighty, Nigel,' she shouted, 'but next time you fuck a stranger on an aeroplane, maybe think with your brain rather than your dick and bring condoms yourself!'

In reply, the front door of the house slammed shut. Abigail noticed that the sound on the television had been muted. No doubt her hideous flatmates found the dramas coming out of her bedroom far more exciting. She wanted to scream something at them too, but she started to shake instead as the realisation of what had just happened washed over her.

Stumbling backwards, she somehow found the strength to slam her bedroom door before she sank onto the floor and sobbed.

Why-oh-why hadn't she thrown away that kit? Truth was, since the desperation to get pregnant had gone, she'd not given one more thought to it languishing in her bedside drawer. Her heart burned as if it had been torched as she thought of the scathing way Nigel had looked at her while spitting his accusatory words.

How could she face even leaving her bedroom after Sam and Pamela had witnessed all that? She wasn't a bad person but he was right, she'd done a very bad thing. Shame washed away her anger at the things Nigel had said, leaving nothing but sadness and aching inside her.

'I want my mum,' she whispered into the silent room as she curled up in the foetal position and cried. She felt so alone and her mind drifted to her sisters—to Charlie in particular, who wouldn't judge her stupidity but would find something to say to make her feel a little better. But it was early morning in Meadow Brook and if Charlie were awake, she'd be in the middle of the breakfast service.

Despite this knowledge, Abigail heaved herself off the floor and over to her tiny desk where her laptop sat open and permanently on. Almost without thinking, she clicked on the little blue *Skype* icon at the bottom of the screen. As predicted, Charlie wasn't online but Madeleine's immaculately made-up face smiled from her avatar and a green tick sat alongside her name.

Maybe her oldest sister's advice could drag her out of this black hole. She made the call and was just about to give up when Madeleine's avatar came to life and her face appeared on the screen.

'Hey.' Madeleine sighed, before lifting a can of Diet Coke to her mouth and taking a sip.

'Can you talk?' Abigail asked, hoping she hadn't caught her in the middle of something.

'Yep. What can I do for you?'

Abigail took a deep breath and opened her mouth to speak but all that came out was a gut-wrenching sob.

'Oh shit, what's the matter?' Madeleine put down her can and leaned closer to the screen.

Tears now cascading down her cheeks again, Abigail took a few moments to pull herself together. She grabbed a box of tissues, wiped her eyes, blew her nose and then looked back at the screen, wishing she could reach into it and touch her sister. Even if Madeleine'd think her pathetic and stupid, Abigail needed the connection with someone who would still love her, no matter what.

'I'm an idiot.' She sniffed and blew her nose again.

'Right.' Madeleine nodded as if Abigail were on drugs. 'A very successful idiot who has more talent in her little finger than most people I know have in their whole body.'

'Yeah,' Abigail scoffed. 'So talented I got fired from the orchestra.'

'What?!'

Abigail nodded glumly.

'What happened?'

'I made a mistake during a performance. A pretty big one. I lost my place in the music and my mind went blank for a while. It was awful.'

'You poor thing. No wonder you're a mess.' Then Madeleine frowned. 'Hang on. They fired you for one mistake?'

Abigail shook her head. 'Anyone else would probably have got a warning and a good talking too, but … but I had a fling with the assistant manager last year, and only later found out he was married. I think he was looking for a reason to sack me.'

'That's outrageous! You should sue them for unfair dismissal. You can't let jerks like that get away with stuff like that. What happens to the next innocent young woman he preys on?'

Abigail took another deep breath. 'It was months ago—before Christmas. It feels like a lifetime ago. I didn't say anything because I didn't want you all to know what a failure I was, and besides, everyone had enough to worry about with the motel and Dad and everything. Honestly, I just wanted to forget about it.'

'Hang on a minute? You're telling me you lost your job almost six months ago.'

Abigail nodded again.

'What the fuck have you been doing all this time? Busking?'

'Well …' She told Madeleine about her disastrous attempt at busking and they both had a much-needed giggle, which helped Abigail get the rest of her sorry story out. How she'd been lying at Christmas about having a boyfriend, how she'd returned to London without a clue how she was going to make a living, how she'd met Nigel in the airport and been instantly attracted to him.

'We slept together in Hong Kong, no contraception.' Abigail cringed as she admitted this, knowing that Madeleine—as a medical professional—would be appalled she'd take such a risk with a stranger. Credit to her sister, she merely raised an eyebrow. 'And when I went to get the morning after pill, it struck me that if I was pregnant, I'd have a fab excuse to go home. I wouldn't need to tell anyone that I'd lost my job.'

Madeleine made a *tsk* noise with her teeth. 'You'd rather we all thought you got *accidentally pregnant—to a stranger*—than made one mistake at work?'

Abigail sighed. When Madeleine put it that way it sounded ridiculous, but it had made perfect sense at the time. 'Music is my world, it's what defines me. I couldn't bear you all thinking I'd failed. Besides, it struck me that if I got pregnant I'd prove the curse wrong and so everyone would be happy about that and—'

'That damn curse.' Madeleine spoke over the top of Abigail, shaking her head in anger.

'Relax. I realised it was stupid when I fell in love. I went on the pill and I've been making a new life for myself teaching, but it was too late.' She pursed her lips together, unsure if she could tell Madeleine about how Nigel had found the ovulation kit and the carnage that had erupted from that discovery. Her heart shook at the thought and she felt the tears welling up again. 'I've made a mess of everything. Nigel found out what I was up to and now he doesn't want anything more to do with me.'

'Why don't you just go home?' Madeleine suggested.

'To Meadow Brook?' Abigail half-laughed, half-sobbed. 'Because I don't have enough money. I like teaching but it barely covers my living expenses, I haven't saved a penny.'

'I'll give you the money for the ticket. Charlie, Lucinda and Dad will be stoked to have you back home and if you enjoy teaching music so much, well, you can do that in Australia just as well as you can in London. I'm sure you'll be inundated once word spreads that you're offering lessons. You know how hard it is to find music teachers in the country.'

While Madeleine's words made sense, Abigail couldn't get over the feeling of defeat and the anxiety over what everyone would think about her. 'But everyone's going to talk about me. Everyone is going to know what a failure I am.'

'No one needs to know why you came home. And anyway, you made one mistake. We all do.'

'Oh, yeah ... And what mistake have you ever made?'

'I fell in love with the wrong person. And that is the greatest mistake of all.'

Huh? Abigail realised while she'd been ugly-crying and lamenting her terrible life to Madeleine, she hadn't once thought to ask how her sister was. 'What are you talking about?'

'You're not the only one who's been trying to get pregnant,' Madeleine confessed, her tone more uncertain than Abigail had ever heard it before.

'What?' Her own shaky emotions took a back seat as she tried to get her head around Madeleine's words.

'I guess the curse got me thinking too,' she admitted, pausing to take a sip of her Diet Coke. 'And once I started I couldn't stop. I saw babies on the plane, in the airport, everywhere—and I decided that if I wanted to have a family, I couldn't sit around waiting for Mr Right. I decided to have one on my own.'

'Oh Lord. Did you find a fuck buddy like me? Or indulge in a string of one night stands?' Maybe they were more alike than Abigail had imagined.

'No.' Madeleine sneered. 'Of course not. Think of the risks. I chose to go the donor sperm route and to cut a long story short, I found a friend willing to be my donor.'

'Oh.' Abigail blinked. Yes, that did sound like a much more sensible, grown-up way to go about things. Why hadn't she thought of something like that? She pushed the thought of her own stupidity aside to focus on her sister's situation. 'And?'

'And for the last few months we've been going through the motions, attempting insemination. The problem was, I was stupid enough to choose a donor who I was actually in love with. I'd been fooling myself that I wasn't but we got even closer during the process and the lines started to blur for me. As much as I tried to remember this was a legal arrangement, I started to yearn for more than just Hugo's baby. I wanted Hugo. I wanted a family with him. The whole damn shebang.'

'Hugo?' Abigail racked her brain for why that name rang a bell. 'Isn't he the friend that drunk-called you at Christmas? Wasn't he engaged? What did the fiancée think of your arrangement?'

'It was her idea.'

'What?' Abigail couldn't conceal her shock. The phrase 'only in America' popped into her head.

Madeleine took another sip of Diet Coke. 'Exactly. And now it's a big fat freaking mess.'

Abigail listened as Madeleine told her how Hugo's fiancée had been all gung-ho and positive about the idea to start with and had then had some kind of mental breakdown because apparently she couldn't have children herself.

'Geez, it sounds like some kind of daytime soap opera,' she said, thinking of all those years she'd raced home from school to watch *The Bold and the Beautiful*. There'd been something perversely addictive about the way everyone seemed to be hooking up with everyone else's exes.

Madeleine laughed without amusement. 'I suppose in hindsight her excessive enthusiasm was a little bizarre. What woman wants her man to have a baby with another woman? But all the potential donors I'd met with were shocking and Hugo would be the perfect father in absolutely every way. I let that and my feelings for him blind me to Celia's weirdness. I told myself she was simply a really nice person, someone who wanted the best for her friends, but I was stupid. In the end, it was all about her.'

'Shit.'

'That's not what I said when I found out.' Madeleine chuckled. 'I felt like a pawn in her game of chess, but it's woken me up to one thing. I have to get over my feelings for Hugo. He loves Celia, whether she can have children or not, and nothing is ever going to change that. I've got to move on or risk killing myself with unrequited love.'

'What a mess we are.'

'Again, you are kinder with your words than I would be,' Madeleine said wryly. 'Maybe it's a good thing Mum isn't around to see what stuff-ups we've become.'

Abigail grinned. Her heart still felt raw from her bust-up with Nigel but talking to her big sister was kind of like putting a bandage on the wound. 'Speaking of family,' she said, 'do you think all this is somehow to do with the curse?'

'Huh?'

'Well,' Abigail began, 'I tried for three months to get pregnant and didn't. You had, was it two attempts, and didn't either? And Lucinda and Joe couldn't even manage it after a whole year.' Her throat tightened and the tears that had eased while listening to Madeleine threatened to return as she thought about the demise of Lucinda and Joe's relationship. She'd always thought they were the perfect couple, just like her parents had been.

If those two couldn't work things out, what hope did anyone else have?

Madeleine looked as if she'd just eaten something way past its use-by date. 'It's just a coincidence. I don't know what the deal is with Lucinda and Joe—that's weird, I'll admit—but you and I haven't been trying long enough to make any such assumption.'

Abigail wanted to believe this wisdom, but couldn't ignore the uneasiness that sat in her gut like a big ball of dried cement. She thought back to that day they'd had that run-in, or whatever you'd call it, with the old hermit woman. Something about Wanda, or Lorraine or whatever her name was, had chilled her to the bone. 'Maybe,' she said, knowing if she spoke her thoughts Madeleine would think her silly. 'So were you serious about lending me the money for a plane ticket home?'

Madeleine didn't say anything for a moment and Abigail hoped she hadn't changed her mind. 'On one condition.'

'Anything.' If Nigel told Daniel what a fruitcake she was, he probably wouldn't want her teaching Livia anymore and word would spread pretty fast to the rest of her students. And besides, what was there for her in London if she didn't have him?

'You'll fly home via the States and pick me up on your way. We'll fly from here together.'

'What? You're coming home again too? For how long?'

Madeleine shrugged. 'Maybe indefinitely. I'm going to hand in my notice. If you and Lucinda can be unemployed for a while—besides the motel—why can't I?'

'Uh … because you are the biggest workaholic I've ever met in my life.'

'Pot-kettle-black.' Madeleine smiled. 'You were pretty damn close, Abigail.'

'Yes, but I got sacked. I didn't quit.' Abigail wondered if there was something alcoholic in Madeleine's can of soft drink. 'Are you sure you know what you're doing?'

'Look, I'm not saying I'm going to move back to Meadow Brook and change bed sheets for the rest of my life, but I think a little holiday between jobs—a time to hang out with my sisters again—could be just what the doctor ordered.'

Abigail snorted with laughter. 'I give you a week.'

'You're probably right, but there are hospitals in Adelaide. I'll put my feelers out and see if there's anything for me over there. Losing Mum and then this fiasco with Hugo and Celia has made me realise what's important in life. It's you, Charlie, Lucinda and Dad. Family is what matters. And it sounds like Lucinda needs us right now, or at least Charlie needs us to help with Lucinda.'

Abigail allowed herself a tiny smile as she thought about the emails Charlie had sent concerning Lucinda. 'Wow. You're really going to do this.'

Madeleine nodded. 'Yes, I really am.'

Chapter Thirty-nine

Lucinda sat on the floor in the middle of the bar, all the motel's glassware surrounding her. She picked up a shot glass and scrutinised it, frowning at the smear marks around the rim and the dust that had collected in the bottom. Mum would turn in her grave if she saw the state of these glasses and Lord knew who would buy the motel in such a state. The only ones that looked clean were the few beer and wine glasses they used regularly. Dad and Mrs Sampson had been keeping things ticking along and Charlie had thrown herself into sprucing the place up a little, but Lucinda couldn't help but think it was a good thing she was here to take proper control.

If Dad was serious about selling the place, they couldn't just rest on their laurels and wait for someone to come along and throw money at them. She sighed and stood, picking up the first crate of glasses and taking it into the kitchen to start washing. She turned Rob's radio to a local station that was playing mostly eighties songs to try and drown out her thoughts, but no matter what she did, her mind kept drifting to Joe.

They'd spoken once in the two weeks she'd been away and it had been terrible. Simply needing to hear his voice, she'd called to remind him to put the council bin out and ask the neighbour to bring it in because he'd be heading off to work.

'I'm not an idiot, Lucinda,' he'd snapped.

'I would never think that; I just wanted to make sure you're okay.'

He snorted. 'I'm not okay. Are you?'

'No.'

'Well then ...' Silence had followed as Lucinda waited for Joe to ask her to come home, but he didn't and as much as she'd wanted to beg him to take her back, she knew their problems still loomed large. Although she missed him as she would a limb, she couldn't truthfully tell him she didn't still crave a baby. Part of her believed this was a flaw and that she was in the wrong; she wished she *could* push aside the dream and just get on with her life, but she hadn't yet worked out how to do that.

'I've gotta go,' Joe had said eventually and neither of them had called each other since.

Should she suggest marriage counselling? Joe still sounded so angry; maybe he needed this time apart as much as she did. She only hoped the old saying 'Absence makes the heart grow fonder' was true. And not 'Out of sight, out of mind'. Worried about this possibility, she'd taken to emailing instead. So far he hadn't replied—he was away at work again so she didn't even know if he was checking his emails—but she felt a little better keeping some kind of communication lines open.

She didn't write about anything serious, nothing about babies or their marital woes or even instruction about house matters; instead her nightly emails were a little like writing in a journal at the end of the day. Sometimes it was only a couple of lines, other times she wrote pages, filling him in on the jobs she'd done in the motel, attaching photos of Charlie's improvements and speculating on the relationship between Dad and Mrs Sampson. She imagined Joe reading her ramblings and laughing in the manner he used to do every evening when she told him about her day at school. He'd always loved hearing about the funny things kids said. Well, she had none of those things to pass on now but the patrons that came into the bar at night and the guests at the hotel provided fodder enough.

Writing to him felt like a kind of therapy. It made her feel closer to him and eased her anxieties about whether he was coping. She didn't need to worry about what he'd be eating or whether his clothes would be washed, because Rosa would take care of all of that. That's if Joe had told his family about their separation. She could just imagine Rosa's dramatic response, as if their rift was a personal insult. No doubt she'd said a few Hail Marys over the possibility of the first-ever Mannolini divorce and then started plotting Lucinda's replacement with a nice Italian girl. One with child-bearing hips.

'Hello, love, what are you up to?' asked Mrs Sampson, coming into the kitchen and jolting Lucinda from her depressing thoughts.

'Oh, just cleaning,' she said, pushing up her sleeves that had fallen again and were at risk of getting wet in the water. 'I've made a list of all the things that need spring cleaning and I'm tackling them one at a time.'

Mrs Sampson frowned. 'I didn't think the place was a *complete* dump.'

Lucinda felt immediately guilty. To Mrs Sampson, who worked hard and did her best to keep everything in order, her words must have felt like a slap in the face. But although she was a great housekeeper, one woman could not be expected to handle the day-to-day cleaning as well as the nitty-gritty stuff. 'It's not. I just thought I should do my bit while I'm hanging around.'

'You're more than doing your bit.' Mrs Sampson chuckled, not appearing to have taken the slightest offence. 'After your spring clean in the office yesterday I'm not sure your father knows where to find anything.'

'I'm being a pain, aren't I?' Lucinda sighed, her shoulders slumping.

'No, you are most definitely not. The office has never looked so good and Brian will get used to it.' She tugged Lucinda's hands out of the water, drying them with a tea towel as if she were a little child. 'But I think you deserve a break. Why don't you come down the street with me and have some coffee and cake at Rosie's?'

The thought of Rosie Jean's delicious homemade creations made Lucinda's tastebuds dance a jig, but she wavered. Since returning to the motel, she'd barely stepped outside, never mind made an appearance in town for fear of the field day the local gossips would have over her return. Although she'd asked Charlie, Mrs Sampson and Dad to tell everyone she'd simply come back to help for a while, she guessed tongues would be wagging with speculation. Then again, they'd talk more if she barricaded herself in the motel as if she had something to hide.

'Who will look after the motel?' she asked.

The older woman chuckled. 'Brian's in the office and Charlie's around somewhere. It'll be fine.'

'I don't want to talk about Joe,' Lucinda warned, worried that once her old friend asked a few pertinent questions or offered any kind of sympathy, she'd completely let loose. And she didn't want the local gossips hearing about the Facebook stalking she'd been doing the last few nights. Thankfully Joe's status still showed him as married.

'It's a deal,' Mrs Sampson promised. Then, as if she'd been reading Lucinda's mind, she added, 'We can *listen* to local gossip instead.'

'Guess who?'

Charlie startled as large, warm, lightly-calloused hands covered her eyes and a familiar body pressed itself up against her back.

Slowly, her lips curled into a grin and she turned her head and planted them on Mitch's. She'd been working hard retiling one of the bathrooms and had the music up as loud as she could while still being mindful of motel guests. But she was glad to see him and she made sure he knew that as she discarded her tools and wrapped her arms around him.

'I thought you were away for another night.'

'I pulled a few strings so I could come home early.' He leaned his head against her forehead. 'Missed you.'

'Missed you too.'

'Looks like you've been busy though.' He gestured to the new tiles lined up along the vanity.

'I'm hiding from Lucinda,' she explained. 'She's on some insane cleaning crusade. Nothing is safe. If I sit down for a second, she'll give me a job to do. I'd rather choose my own.'

He chuckled. 'Her way of coping, I guess.'

'Yep.' Charlie sighed sadly. 'I keep trying to talk to her about Joe, but she shuts me down and starts talking about something else that needs cleaning or fixing.'

'Give her time. She'll come to you when she's ready.'

'That's what Madeleine and Abigail say—I've been emailing them updates—but I feel so helpless.'

'I dunno, I reckon you feel pretty damn fabulous.' Mitch grinned wickedly and skimmed his hands over her breasts, squeezing gently. Desire flared within and she let out a little sigh of bliss. To think of all the years she'd missed out on this. Well, they were making up for lost time now.

Dipping his head to kiss her again, he ripped off the bandana that had been holding back her hair and she squealed as it floated to the floor. It was impossible to misread his intentions and she loved where this was going, but…

She nodded towards the open door. 'What if someone finds us?'

Mitch tugged her out of the bathroom, shoved her playfully onto the bed and went over to shut the door. 'It's locked.' He turned back towards her and ripped his hoodie and t-shirt up over his head.

For a second she forgot to breathe. He really was a thing of beauty, his upper body perfectly sculpted from all that lifting of heavy wood and wielding of big machinery. Yet, as he lowered himself onto the bed beside her, she shot up into a sitting position. 'There's a master key.'

'Live a little, Charles.' He whispered the words as he put his hands on her shoulders and gently eased her down onto the pillows. There weren't many but her libido gave no thought to comfort as it kicked into overdrive.

She gazed up into his beautiful brown eyes, skimming her hands over his lightly stubbled jaw and inhaling the raw male scent of him as he covered her body with his. Despite his jeans and all her clothes between them, she could feel his erection pressing against her belly and she wanted it more than she wanted to breathe. Totally in tune with her needs, he stripped her of her clothing, teasing, touching and tasting her all over as he did so. When he too was naked and they were both aroused beyond belief, he rolled over to the edge of the bed and pulled a condom from the back pocket of his jeans.

They'd done this so many times now that they knew exactly what each other wanted, yet each time felt new and even better than before. Charlie felt an intimacy with Mitch that she'd never had with anyone else before and it wasn't just the sex. Their souls were in tune as well. He completed her. For years she'd drifted, job to job, one guy or girl to the next, without feeling much purpose, but realising her love for Mitch had changed all that. She still had to pinch herself occasionally to make sure it wasn't all some lovely dream.

'Have I told you how much you rock my world?' Mitch asked, running his fingers through her mussed-up hair as he stared down at her.

Their hearts were still racing, their bodies still slick and he was still inside her, exactly where she liked him.

'Maybe once or twice.' She ran her hand up and down his bare back, savouring the feel of his hot, smooth skin. There was something quite intoxicating about creeping around behind everyone else's back.

Although Mitch had made it clear he wanted to tell the world about their hook-up—take out an advertisement in the local rag, throw a party, shout it from the rooftops or at the very least tell their families—Charlie had convinced him to keep it secret for the time being. If he told his dad, or Kate and Macca, someone would slip up and this was a small town so pretty soon everyone would know. And she didn't feel right about flashing around her happiness when Lucinda's relationship was on the rocks.

All that aside, this thing between them was so new that she wanted to enjoy it before she invited everyone else to the party. She was certain most people would be thrilled; even Mitch's dad, who'd kind of warned her off, would come round when he realised how serious they were about each other, that this wasn't some passing fad. They weren't planning on breaking each other's hearts—in fact it was totally the opposite. In the couple of weeks since they'd admitted their love and consummated their union, they'd made some grand plans for a future together. Mitch had said he'd move to Melbourne if that's where Charlie saw her life being, but she'd made it clear that Meadow Brook with him was where she wanted to be.

Chapter Forty

Dearest Nigel

I know I'm not your favourite person at the moment and I know you don't owe me anything, but please read this to the end. There's nothing I can say to make up for what I did. You were right, trying to get pregnant without your knowledge was unthinkable and unforgiveable. And although I regret what I did and how our wonderful time together ended, I will never regret being with you. Without knowing it, you lifted me out of a dark, dark hole and helped me see the hope in my life again. You encouraged me to take up teaching and because of that push, I've discovered a love of something I'd never have imagined. I'm even thinking about doing further training and getting my teaching degree. You brought the passion back into my life in so many ways and I hope with all my heart that you'll find happiness again with someone who truly deserves the good person that you are.

Love always,
Abigail.

After a number of attempts at writing to Nigel, Abigail folded this piece of pretty writing paper in half and slipped it inside a large envelope that also contained a CD of some of her favourite violin pieces. Tunes that, should he ever listen to them, would take him right back to their naked violin sessions. She wasn't stupid enough to think that listening to the music or reading her feelings on paper would change anything, but she couldn't bear to leave without giving it one last shot.

Over the last week, she'd tried to call him a number of times, gone round to knock on his door twice and messaged him maybe ten or fifteen times a day. Despite Madeleine's generous purchase of a ticket back home, leaving Nigel behind was proving to be the hardest thing she'd ever done. Much more painful than walking away from the orchestra. When he hadn't responded to any of her attempts at communication, she'd even contemplated storming into his workplace and demanding he listen to her until she made him see sense.

They shouldn't let one little mistake—okay, one giant mistake—ruin what could be a lifetime of happiness together.

But then she'd stumbled upon an article someone had shared on Facebook about people being stalked by crazy exes and she'd finally admitted defeat. No matter how broken her heart, she needed to walk away with as much dignity as she could cobble together from this horrible situation. She didn't want Nigel thinking she was even more of a nutcase than he already did.

With a sigh, she pushed back her seat and stood, slipped the envelope into her massive shoulder bag and surveyed the room. Balls of scrunched up paper littered the floor but aside from that you could barely tell anyone had ever slept here. The bed was stripped, her linen and cushion collection given to Oxfam, her trinkets and wall hangings already shipped back to Australia. All that remained was the bare furniture that came with the room, her violin and her two suitcases packed and ready for her flight in a couple of hours.

A lump formed in her throat at the thought that her time in London could be erased so easily. She'd been there almost two years, half of that with the orchestra, but it was memories of the last six months with Nigel that would stay with her forever. And, surprisingly, the time she'd spent teaching her eager little students. Telling her kids and their parents that she was heading back to Australia for 'family reasons' had nearly broken her heart all over again. Little Leila cried and Daniel and Liane refused to take the refund she'd offered on Livia's tuition fees, making her suspect that Nigel hadn't told them the real reason she was fleeing London.

The kindness of all the students' families had almost made her rethink her decision to go, but then she thought of Nigel and knew if she stayed, she'd be at risk of turning into that crazy stalker ex. Every time she went anywhere she'd be on the lookout for him and all the sights they'd visited together would make her want to cry. Thank God they'd never gotten around to that weekend away in the country, because she liked to think that one day she could come back to Britain and fulfil her castle dream, even if she didn't do so with him.

With another sigh, Abigail glanced at her watch; if she didn't want to miss her flight she needed to get going. She called for a cab because she wasn't going to struggle with all her luggage on the tube and then checked once again that the envelope was in her bag, ready to post at Heathrow Airport.

Although Pamela and Sam knew she was leaving, they'd gone off to work that morning without so much as attempting to knock on her bedroom door and say goodbye. She didn't care; actually, she was pleased. She left her key and final rent payment on the kitchen table without having to make polite small talk about how great they'd been to live with. Because that would have been a big fat lie. How she'd managed to live with their judgemental looks and snide remarks the last few months she had no clue.

As she wheeled her suitcases behind her, her violin case tucked beneath her arm, and maneuvered it all out the front door and down the steps, she tried to garner excitement about seeing her sisters again.

Yet, no matter how great it would be to be back home in the familiar surrounds of the Meadow Brook Motel, eating, drinking and laughing with her family, Abigail couldn't ignore the gaping hole in her heart at the knowledge that leaving London meant never seeing Nigel again.

Chapter Forty-one

Madeleine had all but cleared her desk of her personal possessions when Hugo appeared in the doorway. She glanced up and her insides twisted in the manner they always did when he was around, but her brain quickly shut the response down.

'What's this I hear about you leaving?' he asked, a slight frown marring his gorgeous features as he folded his arms across his broad chest.

She'd ummed and ahhed about telling him face to face but in the end she'd left it to the hospital grapevine—she didn't owe him an explanation. She'd been scared of what might come out of her mouth if they were alone—recriminations definitely, but also possibly confessions of a love she no longer wanted to feel. He didn't need to know she'd spent the last three years secretly lusting after him, stupidly hoping that one day he'd fall as hard for her as she'd fallen for him.

She was an educated, thirty-five-year-old woman. Her feelings for Hugo were unforgivable.

'I'm surprised it took you this long to find out,' she spoke evenly, feigning interest in something on her computer screen.

391

He took a step further into the room and closed her office door behind him. She flinched, unsure whether she could handle being in such close proximity in such a confined space. 'Everyone probably thought I already knew. We are friends after all.'

Were friends, she silently corrected. 'Well, you know now.' She summoned a saccharine smile to her face, the kind she could never abide in other people.

'When do you leave?'

'Tomorrow morning.' Although there wasn't much left to pack, she continued the charade of clearing her desk as if she didn't have time for this conversation. She certainly didn't have any enthusiasm for it.

'What about your patients?' Hugo asked, his tone outraged.

What right did *he* have to be angry at *her*? As if the patients weren't the first thing she'd thought about as soon as she'd disconnected her Skype call from Abigail. Yet, after a few hours agonising about whether leaving was the right thing to do, she'd made her decision. There was nothing left for her in Baltimore. Everyone in her social circle also knew Hugo and Celia, so she couldn't avoid them, and continuing the way things had been was impossible. She needed to take herself out of this unhealthy situation. Her patients wouldn't suffer. There were plenty of other fabulous obstetricians at the hospital, Hugo included. No matter what she now thought of him personally, he was good at his job.

She'd given her manager the necessary four weeks notice and asked if she could take the last three in holiday pay, citing family reasons as the impetus for her sudden departure. Thankfully he hadn't asked any questions.

'I'm sure some of them will be lucky enough to get you instead,' she said through gritted teeth. Hugo didn't appear to pick up on her sarcasm.

Instead, he pulled out the seat on the other side of her desk and sat. Her skin prickled with the knowledge his feet were mere inches from hers. The physical pull she felt towards him hadn't simply vanished because she wanted it to, which only confirmed that her decision to leave was the right one.

'I'm sorry.' He sighed, planted his elbows on her desk and folded his hands together as if in prayer.

'I don't really want to talk about this. Nor do I have the time. I'm leaving in two hours and I want to see my new mums and babies before I go.'

'Celia feels terrible,' he went on, ignoring her request. 'She wishes you'd answer her phone calls.'

Madeleine raised an eyebrow. 'Celia wouldn't like what I had to say if I did. My mum taught me if you haven't got anything nice to say, then don't say anything at all.'

Hugo chuckled. 'My mom says that too, although I'm not sure she ever listens to her own advice.'

Madeleine glared at him. He was acting so blasé. Sure, he'd attempted a pathetic apology, but if he could laugh when all she felt like doing was slitting someone's throat, then … She shook her head and stood. 'I've really got to go now. Nice knowing you.'

'Please, Madeleine, don't be like this.' He raced her to the door and blocked her exit. 'Celia and I just want to put it all behind us. It was a bad idea to offer you my sperm but that doesn't mean we can't support you as you look for someone else. We've been friends too long to let something like this come between us. Celia and I have decided to adopt and—'

'Shut up, Hugo!'

She didn't know why he couldn't just leave it. He and Celia hadn't been that good friends if they could have done what they did to her. Was he trying to ease his conscience? Well, too bloody bad because she didn't have the energy to worry about how he and Celia were coping; it was taking all her strength just to hold herself together.

He blinked as if he couldn't believe she'd just yelled at him. That gave her the chance to slip past and open the door. It would have felt good to evict him but she didn't want to risk him prolonging the agony.

So instead, Madeleine took a deep breath, pushed back her shoulders, raised her chin high and went to do her final rounds of the St Joseph's maternity ward.

Chapter Forty-two

'You girls from round here, then?' asked Abigail and Madeleine's jovial taxi driver as he headed along the Eyre Highway. The guy looked as if he singlehandedly kept FruChocs in business.

That thought made Abigail's mouth water. She hadn't had those chocolate-coated fruit snacks in years, but they were a South Australian speciality and now she was back on home turf she suddenly craved them.

Knowing Madeleine found doing anything—even talking—hard while travelling in a car, Abigail leaned forward from the back seat to reply. 'Yep, we both grew up in Meadow Brook. Our parents own the motel there.'

'Ahh …' Their driver drummed his fingers on the steering wheel. 'I know the place. My wife used to have friends out that way and we occasionally went there for meals. Was always good value.'

'Who are your wife's friends?' Abigail asked, guessing she'd probably know of them—Meadow Brook wasn't a big place.

In the rear-view mirror Abigail saw the driver's forehead furrow as if he was trying to remember. 'It's been a while. The couple broke up and my wife was friends with the woman, so we haven't been there in twenty-odd years. What was her name? She lost contact with us when she left her husband. Somebody McDonald I think.'

'Theresa McDonald.' Madeleine half-laughed, half-snorted. 'We used to know her too. Her husband Rick is a friend of our father's, and those sons she abandoned are like brothers to us.'

'Oh.' The driver sounded slightly chastised.

Abigail felt sorry for him. Madeleine's words had sounded like a reprimand but it wasn't this man's fault that Mitch and Macca's mother had left them. 'The boys are doing really well for themselves,' she said. 'Macca, the oldest, has a farm and he and his wife have three great little kids. And Mitch is good too. He drives trucks and also makes this amazing furniture. He recently crafted new tables and chairs for the motel's restaurant. I've only seen them on Facebook but they look awesome.'

'Ah, well, that's great to hear. I always wondered what made Theresa leave. Couldn't understand how she could walk away like that. It's one thing to leave your husband, but to leave two little boys …' As he shook his head, his voice drifted off and he abruptly changed the subject. 'You girls travelled a long way then?'

'Yep.' Abigail nodded. 'I've come from London and my sister from America.'

'Geez, global travellers. I've got a dream to take my wife round the world one day but we don't seem to manage to save much on a cabbie's income.'

'You'll get there, I'm sure,' Abigail encouraged. 'Does your wife work?'

They spent the rest of the journey listening to the taxi driver's life story, Abigail interjecting with occasional comments and Madeleine (Abigail suspected) napping in the front seat. The time went fast and as the driver slowed in front of the Meadow Brook

Motel, Madeleine stirred and Abigail felt excitement kick up inside her. Despite the fact that soon everyone would know about her dismissal from the orchestra, she couldn't wait to see her family and be back in the familiar and comforting surrounds of the motel.

'Thanks for the drive,' Abigail said as she put her hand on the door handle while Madeleine paid their fare. It was six o'clock and dark already but the lights were on inside the restaurant. It was good to see the car park near full, considering the motel had been almost empty at Christmas.

'No worries, ladies. Nice to meet you. Enjoy your time back home.'

'We will,' Abigail promised, wondering how long she'd last in the tiny town.

'Thanks,' Madeleine added as the driver helped them haul their luggage out of the boot.

As the taxi pulled back onto the road, the sisters carried their suitcases and the violin behind them up the front path.

'Motel or house entrance?' Abigail asked.

Madeleine shrugged, but continued towards the door to reception and Abigail followed. The little bell above the entrance to the motel jingled as Madeleine pushed it open but there was such a din from inside that it was barely audible.

Abigail breathed in the familiar smell that hung perpetually in the motel air; old carpet, beer and overcooked steak. The aroma should have made her turn up her nose, but instead she smiled. It smelt like home and after everything she'd been through lately, she couldn't think of any place she'd rather be.

'You know, we could check ourselves into a room, grab a good night's sleep and then surprise everyone in the morning,' Madeleine said, looking to Abigail with a cheeky glint in her eyes.

'Hmm ... tempting.' Although the motel beds weren't the comfiest on the planet, Abigail reckoned she'd zonk out the moment her head hit the pillow. Yet she kind of wanted to announce themselves. While she deliberated, the decision was made for them.

Lucinda rushed into reception, grabbed the camera off the desk and was almost gone again when she halted and turned slowly to look at Abigail and Madeleine still standing just inside the door. Her face was flushed as if she'd been in a hot kitchen or run off her feet. When she saw them her mouth fell open and she almost dropped the camera. 'What … I … What are you two doing here?'

'Surprise!' Madeleine held her hands up in the air as if she'd just popped out of a birthday cake.

Abigail laughed and rushed forward to grab her stunned sister in an embrace. 'It's so good to see you.'

Lucinda recovered enough to wrap her arms around Abigail. 'You too, but … I can't believe it. What are you both doing here? It's not because of me is it? I know my life is a debacle but you haven't come all the way across the world to make me feel better?'

'As a matter of fact we have,' Madeleine said, a deadpan expression on her face. 'We've come to tell you all about our disastrous lives, to show you that you are not alone.'

'Huh?' Lucinda pulled back and glanced from Madeleine to Abigail and back again. '*Your* disastrous lives? I'm lost.'

Charlie stormed into reception before either of them had the chance to answer. 'Lucinda, what's taking you so long? Have you got the camera?' She halted and glanced at the three sisters huddled together like they were visitors from outer space. 'What's going on?'

'That,' Madeleine said, 'is going to take quite a while to explain and I'm thinking we'll need wine. Seems like you guys are a little busy for that right now. What's going on in there?'

'It's Rosie Jean's fiftieth birthday,' Lucinda replied. 'Her kids have organised a surprise dinner for her and she has a big family. They've come from all over the country. We're run off our feet.

I came in here to get the good camera so I could take a photo for the local paper.'

'And I came looking for her,' Charlie added.

'What are you girls doing? Everyone is posed and ready,' came their father's voice just before he appeared in the doorway. He froze and blinked twice, shaking his head as if he couldn't believe his eyes. 'Madeleine? Abigail?'

'Yes, it's really us, Dad.' Abigail sprang away from her sisters and went over to hug her father, pleased to see him looking less tired and a whole lot healthier than he had been at Christmas. She held onto him tightly, taking comfort in his embrace.

'This is such a surprise. I don't know what to say,' he said, patting her on the back before extracting himself to briefly hug Madeleine. She'd never been as touchy-feely as the others but Abigail heard her oldest sister utter a contented sigh as Dad's arms closed around her. She was trying to be strong, trying to put on a brave face, but Abigail knew Madeleine was hurting just as bad as she was.

'A good surprise, I hope,' Madeleine joked, extracting herself.

'Sure.' Dad shrugged and then grinned. 'Free labour is always welcome. If you two stick around, maybe I can retire sooner than I thought.'

'Don't go getting any ideas, Daddy dearest.' Madeleine winked at him.

'Who's getting ideas?' Mrs Sampson asked, bustling into reception. 'Oh, my, girls, so my ears weren't playing tricks on me. I thought I heard your voices.' She rushed over and gave them each a quick hug and kiss on the cheek. 'This is a lovely surprise.'

'It is,' Lucinda agreed, 'but as great as it is to see you both, we need to get back to our guests.'

'It's fine.' Madeleine yawned and grabbed hold of her suitcase handle again. 'We'll check ourselves into a room and catch up tomorrow.'

'Oh.' Lucinda paused on her way back out and looked to Charlie and then Dad. 'We're actually all booked out. No vacancies till tomorrow afternoon.'

Madeleine raised an eyebrow.

'Really?' Abigail couldn't recall the last time they'd been fully booked. 'That's great news. In that case we can sleep on the couches.'

'Don't be silly.' Lucinda shook her head. 'You've both had a long journey. One of you can have my bed and I'm sure Charlie won't mind giving up hers for the night.'

'Not at all. I could always go stay in the spare room at Mitch's.'

'And I can sleep in the caravan,' Dad piped up, his grin ridiculously huge. 'I've been wanting to give it a dry run and that way one of you can have my bed.'

'Where is this caravan we've heard so much about?' Madeleine asked.

Dad blushed and looked to Mrs Sampson. 'It's at Sal's place.'

Abigail tried to stifle her grin. She'd never heard him call Mrs Sampson by her first name before. Any uncertainly she'd harboured about their relationship vanished in the face of Dad's happiness. If Mrs Sampson had made him smile again, then who were any of his daughters to stand in the way?

'Looks like we're sorted then.' Lucinda held up the camera, reminding the others why she'd come into reception in the first place. 'Everyone will be wondering what's happened to us.'

'Ooh, yes.' Mrs Sampson wiped her hands on her apron. 'And I'd better help Rob plate up the cake.'

'Do you need any extra hands?' Abigail asked as the others made their retreat.

'We'll be fine,' 'You girls get some rest,' 'See you in the morning,' came the various replies, and then Madeleine and Abigail were once again alone in the reception area.

'Did you see Dad blush when he talked about the caravan and Mrs Sampson?' Abigail asked, wriggling her eyebrows. 'It was so sweet.'

Madeleine rolled her eyes. 'I never knew you were such a romantic.' She started towards the house door.

'Neither did I.' Abigail sighed as she gathered her things and followed Madeleine. It was all Nigel's fault. Until she'd met him, she hadn't known what she was missing out on in the world of love and romance. But now that she did, she wondered if her heart would ever feel right again.

This thought led her into the house where it was obvious Lucinda had been hard at work. The place was immaculate in a way it had never been when Mum was alive. Not that Mum had been a bad housekeeper but she'd always put her efforts into the motel, which left little time to be a domestic goddess.

'Fancy a drink?' Madeleine asked, dumping her suitcase, handbag and overnight travel bag on the lounge room floor. 'I'm physically exhausted but my mind is wide awake.'

'Sounds good.' A nightcap with her sister was a better idea than heading to bed where she'd no doubt toss and turn for hours with thoughts of Nigel and her mega stuff-up. 'I'll just go dump my things and get changed into something more comfortable.'

The two of them went off to the bedrooms, returning a few minutes later wearing warm pyjamas and fluffy slippers. They grabbed glasses and a bottle of wine and then trekked into the lounge room.

Chapter Forty-three

After bidding their patrons and staff goodnight, Lucinda, Dad and Charlie tiptoed inside so as not to disturb their surprise overseas houseguests.

'I wonder how long they're staying?' Dad whispered.

'I guess we'll find out tomorrow,' Lucinda said.

Dad and Charlie planned to collect their toothbrushes and a change of clothes and then head off to Mrs Sampson's and Mitch's to spend the night, but they were all surprised to find Madeleine and Abigail still awake.

After a long day and the prospect of another sleepless night, Lucinda welcomed the sight of the wine bottle. 'Can I join you?'

'Sure, grab a glass.' Abigail gestured towards the kitchen.

Madeleine lifted her glass as if in toast. 'The more the merrier. Dad? Charlie?'

'Well … I shouldn't stay up too late, but maybe just one quick drink,' Dad said. 'It's not very often I have all my girls under one roof now, is it?'

Charlie sighed. 'I'm shattered, but I'll have a quick one too. I don't want to miss out on the gossip. What brings you two home in the middle of the year?'

As Lucinda went to get the glasses and another bottle of their favourite McLaren Vale chardonnay, she heard Madeleine say, 'Does there have to be a reason besides wanting to see our beloved family?'

'Yes,' Lucinda called over her shoulder and everyone laughed. That simple sound made her heart feel lighter than it had in days. She returned and began to pour glasses for herself, Dad and Charlie who'd already taken up residence in the two armchairs. Lucinda handed out the drinks and then perched on the edge of Dad's chair, looking in anticipation to Madeleine and Abigail who were sitting, legs curled up behind them on the couch. 'Well?'

Madeleine took a long sip of her wine and shrugged. 'I've been getting itchy feet for a while. Coming home at Christmas made me a little homesick, believe it or not. I missed you guys and I started to think about maybe looking for a position in Australia. It's been on my mind a bit, but when Abigail called and told me her news, I made up my mind.'

Lucinda got the feeling this wasn't the whole story—Madeleine wasn't the type to suffer homesickness—but she looked to Abigail. 'News?'

Abigail bit her lip, glanced down at her wine glass and then back up again. She looked as if she were close to tears. 'I got sacked from the orchestra.'

'What?' Lucinda, Dad and Charlie asked in unison. 'When?'

Abigail didn't give a definite time or very many details but, like Madeleine, she said she thought it a sign that it was time for her to return Down Under. 'I'm thinking of trying my hand at teaching music,' she confessed. And then she looked to their father. 'Are you terribly disappointed in me, Dad?'

'Baby girl. Of course not.' He crossed the shag rug, then bent down and pulled Abigail up into a hug. 'I'm proud of all you girls, and your mum was too.'

At his words, Abigail lost her battle with tears and Lucinda felt her own throat and eyes burning with emotion. So much had changed in the last year; it was as if the moment Mum died, the rest of their lives had started to unravel as well.

'So, do you mean studying teaching at university?' Charlie asked when Abigail had stopped sniffling.

'Yep. Well, possibly.' She shrugged. 'I might just see if there's anyone interested in lessons in Meadow Brook first and save a little money. I'll do my bit round here too.'

'Have you had much interest in the motel, Dad?' Madeleine asked.

He shook his head. 'I knew it wouldn't happen overnight, but I hoped we'd have had a few nibbles by now. Ah well, you can't rush these things—and having Charlie and Lucinda here to help has eased my load.' He put his hand over his mouth but failed to hide a yawn. 'I'm sorry my princesses, I'm going to have to head to bed but I'm so happy to have you all back home for a bit.'

'Thanks, Dad.' Abigail kissed him on the cheek and then flopped back down onto the couch. 'Sweet dreams.'

'You too.' He moved around the room, kissing each of his daughters goodnight before heading to his bedroom to collect the few things he needed for his first night in the caravan.

When he was gone, Madeleine looked to Charlie and Lucinda. 'Is this thing with Mrs Sampson serious then?'

They both shrugged.

'We don't know,' Lucinda conceded.

'He hasn't actually admitted there is anything going on,' Charlie mused. 'I think he's embarrassed.'

'And maybe worried about what we'll all think,' Lucinda added. 'But they sure do spend a lot of time together.'

'What *do* we think?' Madeleine asked.

'I admit I was a little upset by the prospect at first,' Lucinda said, twirling her wine glass between her fingers. 'But I don't want Dad to be alone for the rest of his life, and how long do we expect him to mourn? He'll always love Mum, but that shouldn't mean he has to be miserable forever.'

Her other sisters nodded.

'You know, I didn't know her name was Sal until tonight.' Abigail laughed and her wine splashed over onto her knuckles.

'Neither did I,' Madeleine admitted, plucking a tissue from the box on the coffee table and passing it to her sister.

'Do you think they'll be, like, sharing the caravan?' Abigail screwed up her nose.

Madeleine almost choked on her wine. 'Let's not even go there. I'm not ready to think about such things. I'm not sure I'll ever be ready.'

Lucinda laughed, leaned back in the seat she'd stolen when their dad left and took another sip. The conversation and wine flowed easily. Lucinda and Charlie filled the others in on the latest dramas in Meadow Brook and all the improvements they'd been doing at the motel.

'What about you, Luce?' Abigail asked. 'How are *you* doing?'

Lucinda immediately knew her sister was thinking of Joe. She swallowed. 'I'm taking it a day at a time.'

'Are you in contact with him?' This from Madeleine, who always got straight to the point.

'A little. I write to him every night and it's helping me sort out my feelings.'

'That's great.' Abigail smiled and then lifted her glass to her lips. 'Ahh,' she sighed. 'I had some fabulous French wines in London, but nothing beats the homegrown South Aussie plonk. Being able to drink is one very positive aspect of not being pregnant.'

'Pregnant?' Lucinda's grip on her glass tightened at Abigail's strange choice of words. 'Why would you be pregnant?'

Abigail's eyes widened. She'd obviously said something she hadn't intended.

Madeleine lifted one shoulder and looked at Lucinda. 'Apparently, you and Joe weren't the only ones trying to make a baby these last few months.'

Abigail went bright red and lifted her wine glass as if hoping to hide behind it. 'You promised you wouldn't say anything,' she hissed.

'Sorry.' And Madeleine sounded genuinely so. She reached out and took Abigail's hand in hers. 'I get loose lips when I have a few too many wines but, like I said, no one's going to love you any less.'

Lucinda didn't care about Madeleine's loose lips or Abigail's obvious mortification. Her heart was pounding at the possibility of her little sister getting pregnant before her. 'What's going on? Did you have a pregnancy scare?'

'If you don't want to tell us, you don't have to,' Charlie said at the same time.

Lucinda glared at Charlie but when Abigail's face crumbled and a tear snuck down her cheek again, her anxious curiosity made way for concern. When Madeleine put down her wine glass and pulled Abigail into a hug, Lucinda's heart clenched. Madeleine didn't hug lightly.

'What's going on?' she whispered, her mind running away with a hundred awful possibilities.

Abigail sniffed. 'I miss him so much.'

'Who?' Charlie asked.

'Nigel.' She sobbed again.

Lucinda frowned, recalling that Abigail had mentioned a boyfriend at Christmas. She hadn't spoken about him in emails or phone calls since and Lucinda hadn't given it much thought, assuming they must have broken up. 'I thought your boyfriend's name was Jack.'

'It's complicated,' Madeleine said, rubbing her palm up and down Abigail's back. 'Do you want me to tell them?'

'Yes, please,' Abigail managed.

Madeleine took a quick breath and then launched into the dramas that had unfolded in Abigail's life since she lost her job just before Christmas.

'I can't believe you didn't tell any of us when we were all home.' Lucinda couldn't keep the recrimination from her voice.

'I didn't want you to know how pathetic I was. To be honest, I wasn't really thinking at all. Without music, I was lost.'

'But then she met Nigel,' Madeleine said.

Abigail nodded, a soft but sad smile forming on her face. 'He was amazing, but he said he didn't want anything more than a fling, so I got it in my head that if I got pregnant I'd have reason to come home. I also wanted to disprove the curse. I didn't tell him but we started sleeping together and he thought I was on the pill, but … I wasn't.'

'Geez,' Charlie said. 'I wish you'd confided in us earlier.'

Lucinda bit her tongue on giving Abigail a lecture on her irresponsible behaviour. Who was she to talk? It wasn't as if she'd made such a great job of her life lately either.

Abigail looked as if she were losing the battle with her emotions yet again.

'She realised the error of her ways and forgot the whole idea,' Madeleine said. 'She fell in love with Nigel and has been giving music lessons in London but Nigel found out what she'd planned and he … he ended it.'

'I'm sorry.' Charlie handed Abigail the whole box of tissues. She yanked one out and blew her nose.

But Lucinda's brain was ticking. 'How long were you trying to get pregnant?'

'Three months.' Abigail admitted, wiping her eyes with another tissue.

'And are you sure you were trying at the right time?'

Abigail nodded. 'I read up on ovulation and timing and everything and even bought an ovulation kit from Boots.'

Lucinda's heart lurched at this new information. 'I *knew* it. Surely this proves there is some truth in the curse.'

'Lucinda,' Charlie warned, 'I thought you'd agreed to forget about that.'

Lucinda ignored her. 'Three of us have tried to conceive and failed. If that's not evidence enough, I don't know what is.'

'I agree,' Abigail said, her shoulders slumping and her tone defeatist.

'Hang on? What do you mean *three* of us?' Charlie asked. 'I haven't been trying to get pregnant.'

'I have,' Madeleine confessed and Lucinda couldn't help but smile at the look of shock on Charlie's face as their oldest sister explained what had happened between herself and Hugo. She continued to explain the fiasco that had gone down and had initiated her decision to return to Australia. Lucinda hadn't known about this latest development.

'I'm sorry things ended that way,' she said, trying and failing to recall a time when Madeleine had ever sounded so broken. And as she looked at her sisters, all so dejected, her belief in the power of the curse returned with a vengeance.

Three sisters, all of them actively trying to get pregnant to no avail.

It couldn't simply be coincidence.

Madeleine reached out and snatched a tissue. 'Turns out the curse grabbed hold of me as well. The logical part of me knows it's ridiculous, but I couldn't stop thinking about it. I didn't like the idea that if I wanted to have a baby, some ridiculous old curse might stand in my way. I'm a doctor for God's sake. So I decided to prove it wrong.' Madeleine laughed. 'I still don't believe in it, but if there is any truth in it, maybe it isn't just a fertility curse. Maybe it's a love curse as well.'

'What do you mean?' Lucinda asked.

'Well, look at you and Joe.' She paused, then gestured to Abigail. 'And the two of us made a right royal balls-up of our latest attempts at romance. And if we consider our family history, well, Aunt Mags, Victoria and Sarah were also ill-fated in that department. Maybe we are all destined to be old spinsters, living alone with a bunch of cats.'

A chill washed over Lucinda at this terrible possibility. But it made more sense than she cared to admit.

'I quite like cats,' ventured Abigail.

'That's not the point,' snapped Lucinda and Madeleine at the same time. Their gazes met and for the first time in her life, Lucinda knew she and Madeleine were on the same page, fear and fury bonding them.

'So what are we going to do about it?' she asked.

'You're the one who's researched curses,' Madeleine said, pointing her finger. 'What are our options?'

'There aren't many, which is why I've been so depressed about it. But the only one that makes any sense is confronting the person who cast the curse and asking them to reverse it. Of course, we can't do that because she's dead. Some people say psychics might be able to help, but I looked a few up on Google and they all charge a fortune. Besides, it's hard to tell which ones are legitimate—if any.'

'Do you know anyone?' Abigail looked to Charlie.

'No.' Charlie shook her head and if Lucinda wasn't mistaken she sounded a little annoyed. Her mouth opened as if she were about to say something else, but Abigail suddenly jumped up in excitement.

'We could have a séance,' she suggested, her whole face brightening at this idea.

Lucinda immediately imagined a bunch of adolescent girls scaring themselves silly with ouija boards, and was about to poohpooh the idea when Madeleine suggested something else.

'Or,' she said, gesturing for Abigail to calm down, 'we could go and speak to Wanda. Maybe her mother told her about the curse. It's a long shot … but if we talk her around, she might know how we can get it lifted. She might even be able to do it herself.'

'So you believe in the curse now?' Abigail asked.

Madeleine shrugged, taking another sip of her wine before she replied. 'I have no freaking idea, but I don't see any harm in investigating it further.'

'What if she just shuts the door in our faces?' Lucinda thought it a real possibility.

'Then we knock until she answers it. Us Patterson girls aren't quitters, are we?' Madeleine raised her glass as if for a toast. Maybe it was the wine spurring her on but she'd never been one to admit defeat. 'I for one am not going to let some dead old woman rule my life. Wanda, or … what did Aunt Mags say her real name was? Anyway she's the closest kin to Doris. She *must* know something. So, what do you say, sisters?'

Lucinda didn't need to think about her answer. She'd thought of little else for the past six months and the idea of doing something about the curse made her giddy. The truth was she'd contemplated visiting the old woman before but common sense had always talked her round. Right now, she felt as if common sense were hugely overrated.

She lifted her own glass and grinned. 'Count me in.'

'And me,' added Abigail. 'When will we go?'

'I'd say there's no time like the present,' Madeleine said, 'but it's midnight and we've all had too much to drink. What about first thing tomorrow morning?'

'I've got to do the breakfast service and then help Mrs Sampson with the rooms, but I can do after that,' Lucinda replied. 'That'll give you girls a chance to have a sleep in if you need it.'

'It's a deal.' Madeleine lifted her wine glass. She, Lucinda and Abigail clinked glasses and then each took a sip to seal it.

Chapter Forty-four

Despite the late night, Lucinda woke early, adrenalin rushing through her body when she remembered her sisters were home and the plans they'd made for today. After months of feeling helpless, it felt empowering to finally have a strategy. Who knew if confronting the old woman would achieve anything, but it was better than sitting on her hands, sulking about how unfair her life was. Maybe if they could really put the curse behind them, she'd be in a better place to move forward and fix things with Joe.

And having Madeleine onside made her feel justified in pursuing it because her oldest sister never did anything silly. Madeleine didn't abide fools and never wasted time on anything she didn't think worthwhile.

Lucinda all but jumped out of bed, hurried in the shower and then dressed quickly, eager to get the breakfast service over and done with. Charlie wasn't there yet when she went into the restaurant, so she turned on all the lights—this time of the year it was still pitch black outside at this hour of the morning—and went into the kitchen to get started. She switched on Rob's radio, half-heartedly listening to the ABC news while she worked, and by the time Charlie ambled in half an hour later, everything was almost ready to go.

'You don't look so great,' she said as her younger sister made a beeline for the tea. Charlie had gone to bed earlier than all of them last night and hadn't drank as much as the others, but this morning her face was a grey-green colour. By rights, Lucinda should have the killer hangover it looked like Charlie was suffering.

'I'm fine,' she said, but then caught sight of the bacon sizzling over the big hob stove and almost dry-retched. Lucinda raised an eyebrow. She knew Charlie didn't like cooking meat, but she always did it when necessary.

Charlie frowned and placed a hand on her stomach. 'Actually, I am feeling a little under the weather.'

Lucinda crossed to her sister and put a hand on her forehead. 'You're a little warm. Maybe you should go inside and lie down.'

'Are you sure you can manage without me?'

'Of course. You've been nose to the grindstone these last few months. Maybe you just need a day off.'

'Thanks.'

Charlie turned to go and Lucinda added, 'But remember, we're going to Wanda's this afternoon. Don't want to miss that.'

Madeleine woke up disorientated. It took her ten seconds to place herself. She was home ... back in Meadow Brook, back where it all began. Her head throbbed more than a little from last night's drinking with her sisters but she couldn't deny it had felt good to let loose. Travelling with Abigail and then last night with Lucinda and Charlie had reminded her that, if you let them, sisters could be the best kind of friends.

Maybe it was because they were all misery guts at the moment and could sympathise with each other's feelings of woe or maybe it was something else. Something more primal. She could only imagine how things might have turned out if she'd confided in Lucinda or Abigail or even Charlie about her desire to have a baby, instead of laying it on Hugo and Celia.

What had she been thinking? Could she really have coped with a baby on her own? And at the same time maintain such a demanding career? She thought back over the past year—the shock of losing her mother and then the weirdness of finding out about the Patterson curse. Would she have even contemplated getting pregnant if it wasn't for all that?

She couldn't deny the curse had made her start thinking about her ticking biological clock. She'd always hated the idea that she couldn't have something if that's what she wanted. Her mind went to the man she'd left in Baltimore. Had that been part of Hugo's attraction too?

At that thought, she shuddered as if a red-back spider had crawled into bed with her.

It was bizarre not to have to rush out of bed, not to have appointments to get to or babies to deliver. She'd never been good at taking holidays because being idle made her twitchy. She guessed it wouldn't be very long before she was chomping at the bit to get back into some kind of work.

And no, she didn't think pouring beer in the bar or changing dirty bed linen would suffice, but she could probably handle a few days while she worked out what to do next.

Never one to lounge around for hours after waking, she tossed off her blankets and climbed out of bed, glad that for today at least she had something to do. As much as she didn't want to believe in the curse, it was like a little ticking clock in the back of her head that wouldn't shut up and she hoped their visit to the old woman would give them all something to go forward with.

*

The house was silent when Charlie snuck back inside, and thankfully, when she shut the door to the motel behind her, the stench of bacon and sausages disappeared. She took a deep breath and headed for the kitchen, hoping a cup of herbal tea and some plain toast would settle her stomach. The last thing she needed was a bout of gastro because she had her first online exam in a couple of weeks and needed all her energies to study.

Only Mitch knew about the course and he'd been a great encouragement, but she'd never been good at tests and hadn't done anything like one since high school, so maybe it was simply the stress of the unknown combined with last night's wine that was making her queasy. She thought of Lucinda's excitement when she'd reminded her about going to see Wanda and shook her head in irritation. For years her sisters had teased her about her belief in supernatural, new age-type things and now they were all gung-ho over this so-called curse.

If only she hadn't been trying not to throw up, she'd have told Lucinda she wouldn't be going with them. The others might have nothing better to do than harass old ladies but Charlie had plenty. Possibly she believed in the curse but she was philosophical about such things and didn't want to get consumed with negativity like her sisters.

They'd been so caught up in their scheming last night that they either didn't care or hadn't noticed her reticence. Probably the first—her sisters had never rated her opinion highly as she didn't have a university degree to back it up.

But had they listened to themselves?

She'd almost told them about she and Mitch, simply to shut them up. Her confession would have put an end to their ridiculous notion that this was a love curse as well as a fertility one, but something had made her hold her tongue. She didn't want to sully their love with crazy curse talk, and the way Lucinda and Madeleine had been carrying on, they wouldn't have listened anyway.

She'd always thought her sisters were smarter than her, but right now they weren't acting it. They were almost like three vigilantes, planning to storm over and confront that poor old woman. She could only imagine what Dad would say if he found out. He hadn't wanted them to know about the curse and now she understood why. Mum had been right to want it to be forgotten.

Things were getting out of control.

Shaking her head, Charlie stuck two pieces of bread into the toaster, made tea and then lathered on butter and Vegemite when the toast popped. Feeling suddenly exhausted, she took her breakfast through to Lucinda's bedroom and closed the door behind her. Unsurprisingly Lucinda had made the bed with hospital-corner precision before she'd left that morning, and it looked comfy and welcoming. The only evidence that anyone even occupied the room was the tiny packet of tampons that sat on the bed, open as if Lucinda had grabbed one before heading out that morning.

Charlie put her tea down on the bedside table and then flicked the box off the bed onto the floor, a childish joy rushing through her at the thought of messing up Lucinda's immaculate space. She plonked herself down and had already taken her first bite of toast when a thought struck.

She stopped chewing.

When was the last time she'd had her period? She swallowed slowly, calculating back in her head. It had to be four or five weeks, maybe longer. Definitely before she and Mitch got together. She'd never bothered much with keeping track of her cycle but she'd have remembered if she'd had a period in the last few weeks as it might have messed with their love-making-at-every-opportunity routine.

She sat up straight, her stomach tightening as she discarded the toast and Vegemite.

I couldn't be. Could I?

They'd used condoms every time … every single time, except … that first time, when, half-in and half-out of his ute, they'd both been too desperate to wait any longer. Or to think about anything quite so mundane as contraception.

Her skin flushed instantly at the recollection, but she forced herself to think clearly. What if she *was* pregnant? How would she feel about that? How would Mitch feel? How would her sisters feel? Would they be happy it proved the curse nonsense, or jealous because she'd succeeded at something they'd so far all failed to do? Now that would be a turn-up for the books. She couldn't help feeling a little enchanted by the prospect.

Even as all these thoughts and questions whirled in her head, she found her fingers sneaking into her pocket to grab her mobile phone. She pressed dial on Mitch's number without thinking about what she was going to say. He'd always been the person she'd called first with good or bad news. He was the first person she'd phoned when she'd found out about Mum's death, and the only person she'd confided to about her ambitions to study.

He answered within a matter of seconds. 'Hey gorgeous. Your sisters still driving you wild?'

When she'd fallen into bed with him last night, she'd told him all about the evening's events and he'd done his best to cool her fury and restore her equilibrium.

'Not exactly.' She'd never been one for beating round the bush. 'I think I might be pregnant.'

'What?' There was nothing sinister in Mitch's tone, only surprise. And then, 'Are you okay? Do you need me to come over?'

'I'm not entirely sure,' she said and then explained how she'd come round to this suspicion.

'We need to do a test.'

She smiled—he was such a doer, always planning action and solutions—and she loved him for it. 'We'd have to drive all the way to Port Augusta to get one on a Sunday. Maybe we should wait until tomorrow. I'm pretty sure the general store stocks pregnancy tests.'

Wow. Were they really talking about this? She'd only just gotten used to the wonder of her and Mitch as a couple and now … this. It was almost too much to get her head around.

'Meet me at my place in half an hour,' he said. 'I've got an idea.'

He hung up before she had the chance to ask him what it was.

The half hour dragged and Charlie, wide awake now, arrived early at Mitch's place to find it deserted. He'd recently given her a key, so she let herself inside and sat down on his well-worn but comfortable couch. She picked up his remote and turned on the TV, but paid little attention to *Weekend Sunrise,* unable to think about anything but the possible new life inside her. About what it might mean to her, to them—to her sisters. Things were so fabulous between her and Mitch at the moment. Would a baby change all that?

Of course it would. She might not have had much to do with children but she knew from the way Kate and Lisa talked that a baby, although wonderful, altered the dynamics of a relationship. But hers and Mitch's relationship had only changed dynamics recently and she liked the new dynamics very much indeed. Her hand kept drifting to her tummy as if she might already be able to feel movement, but that was ridiculous and she told herself to be patient, to worry about the situation when (and if) she had something to worry about.

Finally, Mitch pulled up in the driveway and she dashed to the front door. He climbed out of his ute, beeped it locked and then strode around the front, moving towards her with cocky confidence and a smile on his face. He didn't seem cut up about the possibility of her being pregnant.

He jogged up the few steps onto the front verandah and she noticed the little box in his hand as he leaned forward and kissed her. Heat curled in her belly at the touch of his lips on hers but she pulled back, doing her darn best to ignore it. Now wasn't the time for her libido to dance and shout.

'Is that what I think it is?' She gestured to the box as he stepped inside and kicked the front door shut behind them.

'It's a pregnancy test,' he said, handing it to her.

'Where did you get it?'

Mitch shrugged out of his worn leather jacket and tossed it onto the floor near the door. 'I saw it a while back in Kate and Macca's bathroom cupboard, so I went over and stole it.' The grin on his face told her he felt pretty happy with himself for this.

'Is it still in date?' She turned the small cardboard box over, searching for a use-by date.

'Yep.' He pointed to the little black numerals on the bottom corner. 'Macca and Kate had a scare recently. You'd think after four kids, they'd know how babies are made and all but ...' He threw his hands up in the air good-naturedly, his easygoing way lessening the wild beating of her heart.

She pursed her lips and stared down, her hands shaking as she tried to garner the courage to take this next step.

Again, as if he could see inside her head, Mitch stepped close and took her free hand. 'Just do it, Charles. Whatever the result, it'll be a good one. I love you, you love me, so all is right with the world.'

She looked up into his beautiful, big brown eyes and drank in his heartfelt words, her own eyes watering at the emotion behind them. 'I love you too,' she said, blinking back tears. 'This could be nothing. I may have miscalculated my dates—you know math has never been my strong point. And if you listen to my sisters we're all cursed, so ...'

'I don't listen to your sisters. I listen to you.' He squeezed her hand and then brought it up to his lips and lightly kissed her knuckles. 'So let's stop speculating and do the damn test.'

She smiled and laughed nervously. 'Okay.'

Together they went into Mitch's tiny bathroom and read the instructions more carefully than either of them had ever read instructions before. Then Mitch stepped outside, giving Charlie privacy while she peed on the stick.

'Okay. I'm done,' she called as she placed it on the vanity.

He opened the door and then came up behind her, wrapping his arms around her and resting his head on her shoulder as they stared down at the test together, waiting for the result to appear.

Chapter Forty-five

Lucinda returned to the house to find Abigail and Madeleine nursing mugs of coffee at the kitchen table. They both looked tired and hung-over and for a moment she wondered if they'd changed their minds.

'Morning,' she said as she crossed the kitchen to make herself a cup of coffee. 'Did you both sleep well?'

Abigail groaned. 'Don't ask.' And then took another long sip.

'About the same,' Madeleine said, her tone dry. 'Will you be ready to set off on our mission soon?'

Lucinda guessed Madeleine's cryptic question was in case Dad happened to be lingering nearby, but she knew he was ensconced in book work in the office. 'You still want to?'

'Of course.' Madeleine stood and went to put her empty mug in the sink. 'It's not like I have other grand plans for the day.'

Lucinda let out a relieved giggle. 'I'll just go see if Charlie's up to it.'

'Where is she?' Abigail frowned.

'She wasn't very well this morning, so I sent her back to bed.'

Abigail's shoulders slumped. 'We can't go without her. This is a job for all the Patterson girls.'

Nodding, Lucinda headed down the hallway and knocked once before pushing open her bedroom door. Aside from the fact that her packet of tampons was now on the floor, its contents spilling out of the open lid, it didn't look like Charlie had even been here.

'That's odd,' she said to herself as she returned to the kitchen. 'She's not there,' she told the others.

Madeleine shrugged one shoulder. 'Maybe she felt better and went to continue her decorating or whatever it is she's been doing lately. We haven't seen her all morning.'

Feeling a little irritated—she'd had to work hard on her own in the kitchen with the motel being fully booked—Lucinda dug her mobile phone out of her pocket and dialled Charlie's number. It rang out.

'You know, she didn't seem all that keen last night,' she said, putting her phone down on the table and glancing between her sisters. 'Maybe she doesn't want to come with us.'

They were discussing whether or not they should go ahead without her when the door opened and Charlie appeared, followed by Mitch. She looked anything but unwell. In fact, her whole face was glowing. So that explained it. While Lucinda had been slaving away over a hot stove, washing dishes and then scrubbing toilets, Charlie had been getting up to who knows what with Mitch.

'I thought you were sick,' she snapped, unable to keep her annoyance to herself.

Mitch put a hand on Charlie's shoulder and glared at Lucinda in a way that made her straighten up and blink.

Before Lucinda could respond, Charlie said, 'You haven't been to see Wanda yet, have you?'

'No,' Lucinda said. 'We were waiting for you.'

'Oh, thank God.' Charlie breathed out deeply and pushed Mitch further into the house. 'Where's Dad?'

'In the office.'

'Good. There's something I need to tell you all, but he needs to hear it too. Be right back.' Charlie rushed off through the house and disappeared into the motel.

'What's going on?' Abigail asked, looking to Mitch.

He simply shoved his hands in his jeans' pockets and grinned, his smile stretching almost from ear to ear. No one said anything for the minute it took for Charlie to return with Dad.

'Come into the lounge room and sit,' she instructed everyone, an uncharacteristically bossy and confident edge to her voice.

Curious, Lucinda did as she was told and so did the others. Once again Abigail and Madeleine commandeered the couch and Dad sat in his favourite armchair. Mitch and Charlie didn't seem inclined to sit down, so Lucinda sat next to Dad in the second chair and looked to Charlie expectedly.

'I'm pregnant,' she announced, her eyes sparkling and her smile almost as crazy-wide as Mitch's.

The words sank into Lucinda's head but she found it hard to digest them.

'Who's the father?' Even as Abigail asked this question, Lucinda knew it was a stupid one. The answer was obvious.

'Mitch.' Charlie looked at him, her face radiating warmth and love.

He grinned back, his eyes saying what Lucinda had always known. Those two were meant for each other. They were like two peas in a pod and she was happy they'd finally got it together, but … a baby! Her chest muscles tightened, making it difficult to breathe.

'How long have you two been together?' Madeleine asked.

'Since …' Charlie's voice trailed off.

'Forever,' Mitch finished, taking hold of her hand.

Charlie laughed and a tear trickled down her cheek. 'But it took us about twenty years to get our act together.'

'Better late than never,' Mitch added.

Everyone remained frozen in their seats, staring at Mitch and Charlie as if they couldn't believe the news. And then something inside Lucinda snapped. She leapt from her chair and rushed across to her sister and her old friend.

'That's wonderful,' she said, drawing them both into a hug as tears of relief flowed down her cheeks. 'I'm so happy for you.'

She kissed them both and then pulled back, grinning.

'Are you sure you're okay about this?' Charlie asked.

'Okay?' Lucinda swallowed. 'I'm over the moon.' And she meant it. This sense of pure joy surprised her. She felt as if a weight had been lifted off her shoulders. She always thought she'd be plagued with jealousy if any of her sisters managed to get pregnant so easily when she hadn't been able to, but the relief was stronger than any other emotion. She couldn't say anything in front of their father because he didn't know how much they knew about the curse, but this proved Mum right.

It was a load of codswallop. And she'd been an idiot to let it consume her so.

'I'm so pleased,' Charlie said, her eyes locking with Lucinda's.

Lucinda felt herself being gently eased aside as Dad stepped in beside her and pulled Charlie into his arms. 'I'm gobsmacked,' he admitted. 'And maybe happier than I've ever been in my life. I'm going to be a granddad.' He half laughed, half cried as he hugged his daughter, and Lucinda wondered if he too were thinking about the curse.

'Thanks, Dad.'

He let go of Charlie and shook Mitch's hand. 'You've always been part of the family, but this makes it official. Welcome, son.'

Mitch grinned as Dad clapped him on the back. 'Thanks. I was scared you'd get out the shotgun and shoot me or something.'

Dad laughed more naturally than he had in a long time. 'I'm thinking about breaking out the good champagne instead. What do you say? When are you going to tell Rick?'

The answers to these questions were lost in more congratulations. Abigail and Madeleine took turns hugging and kissing Charlie and Mitch. Lucinda stepped back and watched the happy scene, wishing Joe was here to share it. She imagined him here now, drawing her into his warm embrace and comforting her over the fact that Charlie would have what she herself so desperately wanted.

But as she watched Charlie and Mitch, it wasn't the thought of their baby that she envied. It was the warmth and love that shone between the two of them.

Lucinda had that with Joe. Or at least she used to, before she'd let her desperate desire for a baby and then this damn curse nonsense come between them. Her heart ached thinking about how her obsession must have made Joe feel. He'd done his best to be there for her, to try and cheer her up whenever she felt low, but what had she done to comfort him?

Absolutely nothing. Instead she'd made him the enemy.

Shame and sadness washed over her. She'd been gone less than a month but it seemed like forever and she hoped to God it wasn't too long. The emails had helped her feel somewhat connected to him, but they weren't enough. She needed to hear his voice. She needed to tell him how much he meant to her, that he was her world and she was the biggest idiot in it.

Please God, give me another chance.

'Here you are, Lucinda.' Dad held out a crystal flute of champagne and she took it, summoning a smile. It wasn't often he brought out Mum's best glasses.

'Thanks, Dad.' She lifted her glass as he made a toast to the lovebirds.

'Where are you going to live now?' Abigail asked, before taking a sip of her bubbly.

Mitch and Charlie looked at each other and shrugged. 'We haven't thought that far,' Charlie admitted. 'This is all very new.'

'And wonderful,' Abigail said.

'Yes,' agreed the sisters, quickly exchanging knowing glances. A baby was fantastic news, but what it meant—that the curse was broken—was also wonderful.

The five of them sat sipping champagne and Charlie drank orange juice, while she and Mitch fielded more questions about how long this had been going on, how they'd gotten together and whether they had any names for the baby yet.

'Give them time to digest the idea they're going to be parents first,' Madeleine said, shaking her head at Abigail's enthusiasm.

'Speaking of parents.' Mitch put his glass down on the coffee table. 'We should go and tell Dad. Don't want him hearing the news from anybody else.'

'Good idea,' Dad said, standing. 'And do you mind if I tell Mrs Sampson?'

'Not at all,' Mitch and Charlie said at once.

'And Dad?' Madeleine said, raising her eyebrows at him. 'Don't you think it's time you started calling her Sally? Now you're joint owners of a caravan and … everything.'

Lucinda suspected it was the 'everything' that made him blush.

Charlie and Mitch headed off to the care facility at Port Augusta and Dad went to find Mrs Sampson, leaving Lucinda, Madeleine and Abigail alone to discuss what had just happened. The first thing they mentioned was the curse.

'Well, that proves that wrong.' Madeleine slumped back against the couch, suddenly looking weary. 'Thank God we didn't go and confront that poor old lady. I can't believe I even harboured the possibility of it being real.'

Abigail laughed, reached across the table and emptied the last of the sparkling wine into her glass.

Madeleine shot her and Lucinda a glare. 'I blame you two for leading me astray.'

'Hey!' Lucinda objected. 'It was your idea to go see her.'

'Didn't you suspect anything was going on with Charlie and Mitch?' Abigail asked.

'No.' Lucinda shook her head. 'They've always spent a lot of time together, so I never thought anything of it.' Besides, she silently added, she'd been too full of her own woes to pay much attention to the goings on around her.

They were all quiet for a moment, as if digesting the news.

Madeleine finally broke the silence. 'Luce, are you okay about all this? We know how much you want a baby.'

'You guys did too.'

Madeleine shrugged. 'Yes, but my marriage hasn't broken up because of it.'

'And me wanting a baby was insanity.' Abigail half-laughed. 'I can barely cook toast without burning it. How would I ever have looked after another human?'

Lucinda forced a smile and held her head high. 'I'm okay about the baby, really. And ...' She couldn't wait another moment. She put her glass on the coffee table and stood. 'I'm sorry, there's something I need to do. I'll see you guys, later, okay?'

'Do you think she's just pretending to be fine?' Abigail asked Madeleine when they heard the door to Lucinda's bedroom close.

'I'm not sure. It's a lot to take in for all of us, but I do think it's possible to be happy for someone else while still being sad for yourself.'

'Is that how you feel?'

'I'm not sad,' Madeleine said, 'more like annoyed with myself for wasting my energies on a man who was never going to love me back. If I decide I still want to have a baby on my own, there are plenty of other options. But this time, I'll be more careful about who I choose as a donor.'

'I can't understand why Hugo would choose Celia over you. From what you've told me, she sounds like a mental case.'

'Thanks. But she's not that bad. And you might be a little biased where I'm concerned.'

'I don't think so.' Abigail shook her head and Madeleine felt so much love and affection for her little sister. If anything good had come of this whole debacle, it was that it had brought her and her sisters together again.

She and Lucinda had been talking and emailing more since Lucinda had confessed her fertility issues, and she and Abigail had bonded over tiny bottles of wine and broken hearts during their long flight home. They would recover from all of this, because they had each other and Charlie and Mitch's baby to look forward to. She had faith that Lucinda and Joe would work things out. Abigail was young and full of life, and love would find her again. And although Madeleine felt a lot older and a whole heap more cynical, she guessed things would turn out okay for her in the end as well.

The only thing that couldn't be fixed was the fact Mum would never meet Charlie's baby, or any other grandkids that might follow. That thought brought an ache to her heart far greater than the realisation that Hugo would never love her back had done. Maybe it was jet lag, maybe it was the surprising turn of events and emotion of the day—maybe she was just turning into a sook—but her eyes prickled with near-tears.

And then the buzzer sounded in the kitchen, indicating that someone was waiting at reception. Blinking, Madeleine pasted a smile on her face and heaved herself off the couch. 'I'll go,' she said, glad of the distraction.

She pushed open the door into the motel and found a tall, blond man standing there. He was incredibly good looking, built like an ironman and tanned, even though it was the middle of winter. Maybe he was a gift from God, a sign that there really were more fish in the sea. Pity this one looked about ten years too young for her.

'Hi there.' She leant over the computer and clicked on the bookings program. 'Do you have a reservation?'

'Uh, no.' He wiped his hand across his brow and she noticed there were beads of perspiration there. 'I'm looking for Abigail Patterson. Is she here?'

Madeleine raised one eyebrow and took a closer look at him. Was this? Could he be? 'Are you … Nigel?'

He blinked. 'Yes. And you are?'

She offered her hand across the counter. 'Madeleine. Madeleine Patterson. Abigail's older sister.'

'Oh, right, hi. Pleased to meet you. I can see the resemblance. She's told me lots about you. I thought you lived in the States?'

Madeleine chuckled. 'Not anymore. And don't believe a word she's said about me. I'm sure it's all lies.'

He smiled—it was a sexy smile and Madeleine could see why Abigail was so taken with him.

'You're a long way from home.'

'No, my family only lives in Adelaide.'

'I meant from London.' The poor man was shaking and she guessed she should put him out of his misery.

'So you want to see my sister?'

He nodded.

'You're not going to break her heart all over again are you? Because you should know, I may look sweet and harmless but if you mess with Abigail's emotions, the only way you'll be leaving Meadow Brook again is in a box.'

Nigel's eyes widened.

'Are we on the same page?'

'Yes, ma'am. I have a little sister I feel exactly the same way about.' He put a hand on his heart. 'I promise, if I wanted to hurt Abigail, I wouldn't be here.'

Satisfied, Madeleine nodded. 'In that case, come with me.' She beckoned him round the desk and he followed her through the door into the house.

Chapter Forty-six

'Hey.'

Lucinda said a silent prayer of thanks when Joe answered the phone, but then found herself tongue-tied. She had so much to say but didn't know where to start and the sound of his deep, sexy and ever-so-familiar voice had distracted her. 'Charlie's pregnant,' she blurted.

A moment's silence, the time necessary to register the news, and then, 'Shit, Luce ... Are you okay?'

Tears sprouted in her eyes at the warmth, concern and sympathy in his voice. It meant something that this was his first question, rather than the obvious, *Who's the father?*

'I am actually.' She found her words. 'And Joe, I'm not ringing to whine about the unfairness or to solicit sympathy, I'm ringing because I can't go another day without hearing your voice.'

He sighed. 'It's good to hear you too, but—'

'Please Joe, let me speak. I need to get this off my chest.'

'Okay. Sorry.'

As she settled back against the pillows on her bed, she took a deep breath, hoping she could get this right. 'Mitch is the father of Charlie's baby. Unbeknownst to us all they've become more than friends. Their relationship is still new and the baby was a surprise, but when they told us all, I couldn't get past how right it felt. Those two have always been meant for each other, it simply took a while for them to work it out. And I realised something else: you and I are exactly the same.'

She paused a moment, her throat choking up with emotion.

'We're meant to be together. I'm empty inside right now and it's not because of the baby thing. It's because my life has no meaning without you in it.'

'Lucinda,' he broke in, 'you say that now, but you can't help yourself. I'm a mess without you and I miss you like crazy, but I can't go through that stress again. I can't watch you selfdestruct and not be able to do a thing about it. It hurts too damn much that I'm not enough.'

'You are enough!' She knew that now, but why couldn't she find the right words to make him believe? '*Please*, Joe, I want to make this work. I love you and I want you and our marriage back again. I want it more than I want a baby. I know it won't be easy but I want to change. Please, give me the chance to try.'

He was quiet again and her heart beat wildly as she waited for him to say something.

She couldn't stand it. 'What do *you* want, Joe? Do you still love me?' As much as it would hurt, if he told her no she would some-how walk away.

'Dammit, Lucinda, what kind of question is that?' He exhaled. 'Will you agree to marriage counselling?'

A spark of hope lit inside her. He may not have confessed undying love and devotion, but marriage counselling? From a bloke who generally thought stuff like that was for sissies? That was a very good sign. 'Yes. I'll do anything.'

'Okay, then.'

'Okay?'

'Come home,' he said softly. 'The bed doesn't smell right without you anyway.'

She couldn't speak past the lump of emotion in her throat. Tears streamed silently down her cheeks.

Eventually, Joe broke the silence. 'So, Charlie and Mitch, hey? We picked that years ago.'

'Yes, we did.'

He chuckled. 'I guess this disproves that whole curse thing too.'

'Yes, it does.' Her cheeks felt hot. 'I can't believe I ever believed such nonsense.'

'To be fair,' Joe said, 'our situation even made me wonder.'

They both laughed.

And then somehow they talked—about Charlie and Mitch, Madeleine, Abigail, Dad and Mrs Sampson, about Rosa and the rest of Joe's massive family, about how Lucinda had cut her finger in the kitchen that morning and about the crap show Joe had watched on television last night because he'd lost the remote and couldn't be bothered to get up and change the channel manually. They talked for an hour and they could have spoken for longer, but Joe said he had to go because he was late for Sunday lunch at his parents' place.

'What did you tell them about us?' Lucinda asked.

'I said Brian needed you at the motel and you'd gone home for a few weeks to help.'

She did a little fist pump. This proved he never wanted her to stay away or he would have told them the truth. 'Say Hi to everyone for me,' she said.

'I will. And Luce, go book your plane ticket.'

What now? Abigail sighed and stretched out on the couch, her legs taking up the space that Madeleine had just vacated. She stared at the empty bottle of sparkling wine—although she'd had one more glass than everyone else, she could go another. Besides, it was Sunday afternoon and it wasn't like she had anything better to do now the visit to Wanda was off the agenda. She'd decided that morning that tomorrow was T-Day—*time* to stop wallowing and do something with her life. That something would involve printing up a flyer about being available to give music lessons and taking those flyers to the few shops around town. She might even splurge for an ad in the *Meadow Brook Messenger,* the local rag run by volunteers, which usually had more adverts than actual news.

But all those things were for tomorrow, so she might as well indulge herself today.

Maybe when Madeleine returned, she'd suggest they crack open another bottle. After all, they were going to be aunties. The sisterly thing to do would be to celebrate. Although Lucinda might not feel up to it. The ache in Abigail's already tender heart grew even stronger whenever she thought about Lucinda and Joe. Most of the time she forgot about it because the idea of them *not* being together was ludicrous, but when she remembered she felt utterly helpless and miserable. Should she get up off her lazy bum and go check on her, or did Lucinda need some time alone?

Lamenting this dilemma, she barely registered the door from the motel opening and she startled when Madeleine appeared again. 'You have a visitor,' she announced.

Abigail glanced behind Madeleine to where a tall figure stood, slightly shadowed by the corridor wall.

No! She had to be hallucinating.

Her heart slammed into her chest cavity. Maybe she'd drunk more champagne than she thought. She leapt off the couch at the same moment Madeleine stepped out of the way and Nigel— looking more gorgeous than she remembered—came properly into view.

'Hi there.' Their eyes locked and she didn't know if her legs could handle the shock. They felt boneless; her whole body felt like that.

'It is you.' Those three words were barely more than a whisper. She couldn't take her eyes off him. Her fingers twitched, desperate to go over and touch him, to make sure he was real, but she was frozen to the spot.

'Yep,' was all he said as he walked towards her. Her heart pounded so loud and fast she felt like it would leap out of her body at any second.

He stopped about a ruler's length away and simply stared at her. The only thought in her head was that if she'd known he was going to turn up like this, she'd have made more of an effort when she got dressed that morning. Instead, she was standing there in front of the love of her life, her hair barely brushed, no makeup, her eyes red and puffy from nightly crying, wearing yoga pants and an old sweatshirt a few sizes too big.

Dammit, he probably wasn't gazing at her with adoration and affection. More likely he wondered why he'd come all this way for such a scruff. Why *had* he come all this way?

'What are you doing here?' she finally managed.

The lips she'd kissed so many times curled up at the edges. 'Apparently Livia is refusing to practise with the new violin teacher, so Daniel told me to get you back or find a new job.'

Her mouth fell open in shock, her stomach clenched in disappointment. 'He didn't!'

'He did but I think it was an empty threat. He simply couldn't stand to put up with my misery for another day.' Nigel came one step closer, reached out and placed his hands on her arms. 'I missed you, Abigail.'

'Oh?' she squeaked as the breath hitched in her throat.

'Yes.' His hands slid down her arms, claiming her hands in his. Delicious shivers scuttled down her spine. 'This last week felt like years without your cheery voice at the end of the phone or your smile or violin playing at the end of each day.'

Tears leaked from the corner of her eyes at his confession.

Nigel stooped his head and kissed one as it fell. 'What do you say?' he asked. 'Will you forgive me for overreacting? I want you to come back to London and make me the happiest man alive.'

That sounded almost too good to be true, but … '*Me* forgive *you*?' Had he forgotten what she'd done?

As if reading her mind, he said, 'I'm still upset about what happened, but I know you are as well and I want to put all that behind us. I've been a mess since we split. I can't think straight at work because all I'm thinking about is you and your damn violin. You don't know how many times I've listened to that CD you sent me.'

She'd been biting her lip since he started talking but she finally allowed herself a smile.

But he frowned slightly. 'Unless—' his Adam's apple moved slowly up and down as he swallowed '—you haven't missed me?'

'*What*?' Panic struck. She shook her head. 'I've never missed anyone or anything so much in my life. I just can't believe you're willing to take me back. This is—'

'Crazy. You make me crazy, Abigail, and I don't want anything to come between us ever again.' And then he dipped his head and kissed her. Her eyes closed and ripples of pleasure flowed through her. He tasted of coffee, with the tiniest hint of salt from her tear-drop. Nothing had ever tasted this good. His hands cradled her face as he deepened the kiss. She wrapped her arms around him and held him close. *This* was real.

She felt like a junkie, finally getting a fix after too long without, yet as much as her body begged her to take this further, she remembered they were standing in the lounge room with her big sister only a few feet away. Summoning every bit of willpower she possessed, Abigail pulled back but kept one arm wrapped around Nigel, unwilling to let him go.

She turned to introduce him to Madeleine, but Madeleine wasn't there.

'I guess she decided to give us some privacy,' Nigel said, stroking her hair back from her face and kissing her cheek.

Abigail grinned up at him. 'Unfortunately there's not that much of that around here at the moment. The motel is fully booked and the rooms in the house belong to Dad, Charlie and Lucinda.'

'Bugger. I suppose it'd be stupid to ask if there's another hotel or something in town?'

She snorted.

'Never mind.' He chuckled as he drew her into his arms again. 'Luckily, we've got the rest of our lives for violin playing.'

Chapter Forty-seven

Charlie couldn't wipe the smile off her face as she settled into the passenger seat of Mitch's ute. He looked over and grinned at her, his face brimming with all the emotions that were zapping through her body. Surprise. Excitement. Happiness. Contentment. There weren't enough words in the thesaurus to describe how she felt.

Sure, getting pregnant hadn't been on their agenda—not quite so soon anyway—but now that she knew she was carrying his baby, she couldn't think of anything she wanted more. It felt unbelievably right.

'We'll go see Dad and then while we're in Port Augusta we should pop in and tell your Aunt Mags in person too.' Mitch put his hand on her thigh and squeezed lightly. 'Don't want her hearing the news second-hand or she'll never forgive us.'

'Good idea.' She put her hand on top of his, wondering if she'd ever get sick of his touch. 'Mags always gave me the impression she didn't want to believe in the curse but that she couldn't help it.'

Mitch chuckled. 'That damn curse. Who'd have thought we'd be the ones to prove it wrong without even trying to?'

'I know.' Charlie sighed. 'And I know it's wrong, but I can't help feeling a little smug about that. I feel bad for Lucinda and hope she means it when she says she's okay, but I've always been the not-quite sister. Not quite as smart, not quite as talented, not quite as beautiful as them and—'

'Not in my eyes you weren't,' he interrupted, his tone fierce.

She licked her lips and smiled despite the lump that appeared in her throat. 'Thank you, but it was hard growing up alongside Madeleine and Abigail, who got top marks at everything they tried. Lucinda wasn't far behind and she was so much more organised than I could ever hope to be. I can't help feeling like the black sheep sometimes.'

'Don't you know how amazing you are? You're the sexiest woman alive. You're funny and courageous and giving, and when you decide to do something, you put your whole heart and soul into it. You might not have a certificate with letters behind your name, but neither do I, and you still love me, right?'

She nodded. 'More than you'll ever know.'

'Well then, it's time to forget this nonsense about your sisters being better than you. You're not the black sheep of the family, you're the shining star. Don't get me wrong, I think your sisters are great, but none of them have anything on you.'

'If you weren't driving right now, I'd climb onto your lap and show you exactly how much you mean to me.'

Mitch made a choking noise and swerved the ute a little. 'Don't tempt me. I could pull over anytime. You just say the word.'

She laughed. 'And get us arrested for indecent behaviour? We're going to be parents, Mitchell. We need to grow up. Be responsible.'

'I have to grow up?' He groaned.

Still laughing, she said, 'Oh my God, can you believe this? We're having a baby. We're going to be parents.' They hadn't had much time to digest the news after finding out because Charlie had wanted to go and catch her sisters before they stormed Wacky Wanda's. She suddenly realised she hadn't asked them about that. Oh well, whatever had happened, it was good to be able to put an end to the curse business once and for all.

Mitch chuckled. 'Looks that way. What are we going to call it?'

'Oh. I don't know.' Choosing a name was such a massive responsibility. She wanted something unique, something that meant something. 'Have you got any thoughts?'

'Yeah, I was thinking we should choose something traditional, in honour of your mum. She seemed to like all the old names. You know—Madeleine, Lucinda, Charlotte, Abigail. Or, if it's a girl, maybe we could call it Annette.'

Charlie couldn't speak. And dammit, she was crying again. Maybe it was pregnancy hormones making things worse but the thought of Mum never seeing their baby cast a shadow over her joy.

'Aw, I'm sorry.' Mitch did pull over to the side of the road now and he reached out and enveloped her in his lovely strong arms. 'I didn't mean to make you cry. I just thought—'

'It's a lovely idea,' Charlie managed through sobs. 'The best. I just wish she was still here to hear our news, to meet our baby, to be a grandma. She'd have made such a wonderful grandma.'

'I know she would have. And we'll tell the kid lots about her, make sure she's not forgotten.'

'Thank you.' Charlie sniffed, wiped her eyes and then kissed him firmly on the lips. 'Now, let's go tell your dad.'

'You sure you're okay?'

She nodded. 'Better than okay.'

Mitch pulled out onto the road again and Charlie said, 'What about if we have a boy?'

They put in the rest of the journey discussing other names, arguing and laughing over the outrageous suggestions they came up with. They weren't any closer to a decision by the time they arrived at the care facility where Rick McDonald lived but they'd ruled out a fair few.

'Thank God we have nine months to choose,' Charlie said as they walked up the path hand in hand.

'Yes,' Mitch agreed. 'Do you want to find out the sex?'

'Geez … I don't know. Let's talk about that on the way back home.'

Rick was sitting in his recliner by the window in his bedroom, looking out onto the nursing home's pretty courtyard garden and drinking tea from a plastic sipper cup when they arrived.

'Hey Dad,' Mitch said, striding across the room towards him.

Charlie followed and Rick looked a little confused as he glanced between them. 'This is a nice surprise. To what do I owe the visit?'

Mitch sat on his dad's bed and patted the space on the mattress beside him, indicating Charlie should do the same.

'How are you feeling today?' Mitch asked.

Rick shrugged as he put his plastic cup down on the small table beside him. His hands shook slightly as he did so and a pained expression crossed Mitch's face. Charlie could tell he wanted to help but also didn't want to make his dad feel any more useless than he already did. Her heart ached for both of them.

'All the better for seeing you two.' He glanced to Charlie. 'How's things at the motel?'

'They're good, thanks,' she said, wanting this small talk to be over.

'They're better than good,' Mitch said with a chuckle. Then he took hold of her hand.

A flicker of something like disapproval flashed across Rick's face and Charlie's stomach clenched in confused anxiety.

Mitch continued, oblivious. 'And that's because we have some news.' He met Charlie's eyes and grinned, before looking back to his dad. 'Charlie and I are going to have a baby.'

Rick's mouth dropped open, but no words came out. You could have heard a pin drop.

Charlie's gut churned. Mitch might think her the sexiest woman alive but maybe Rick thought he could do better. This wasn't the reaction they'd been hoping for.

'Dad?' Mitch asked, his tone apprehensive. 'Are you going to say something? We hoped you'd be over the moon about being a granddad.'

'I ... I ... I ...' Rick appeared to have developed a stutter and Charlie didn't think it had anything to do with his illness. 'I thought you were just good friends?'

'Charlie's my *best* friend, Dad.' Mitch squeezed her hand. 'And we've finally realised what that means. I've never been happier in my life.'

But Rick didn't look happy. He looked like he was about to be sick. Charlie wondered if she should call a nurse.

'Dad? What's going on?' Mitch let go of her hand, got off the bed and dropped to his knees beside Rick. 'Are you okay?'

Rick slowly shook his head and the solemn expression on his face set Charlie's heart racing. What the heck was going on? He didn't dislike her that much did he?

'I'm sorry.' He looked to Mitch, his eyes brimming with tears. It was disconcerting to see Mitch's father cry; Charlie could only remember her own Dad crying at Mum's funeral.

'What is it?' Mitch put his hand on Rick's shoulder. '*Dad?*'

'I'm sorry.' Rick closed his eyes a moment and then opened them again, looking sadly at Charlie and then back to Mitch. 'We should have said something years ago but then Charlie moved to Melbourne and we didn't think it was going to be a problem.'

'Think *what* was going to be a problem?' There was an edge to Mitch's voice Charlie had never heard before.

'It's not something I'm proud of,' Rick began, and then the alarm bells started ringing in Charlie's head.

'Annette was Theresa's best mate, but there was always something between us.'

Mitch frowned. He asked what Charlie also wanted to know. 'Between who?'

Rick looked up at her. 'Between Annette and me. We went out a couple of times before Brian whisked her off her feet and I guess I never really stopped loving her. Theresa always suspected it, and although I tried to put aside my feelings and be a good husband, I never quite managed. I tried to stay away but there was one night— Brian was out of town and I went for a drink at the motel. Annette was feeling flat, she confessed that since she'd had the two girls she sometimes wondered if Brian was still attracted to her. Somehow I got set to show her how damn attractive she was. Things got out of hand and—' he put his head in his hands '—we slept together.'

No! The air whooshed from Charlie's lungs. He had to be making it up.

'It's not true. You're lying. Mum would never have cheated on Dad,' Charlie all but spat at Rick. Her body shook. It was ridiculous. It didn't compute. They'd had the perfect marriage.

Mitch swore but somehow he sounded far away. 'What are you saying, Dad? When was this?'

'It was twenty-nine years ago,' Rick confessed. 'Therese was pregnant with you, Mitch, and threatening to leave me—take Macca and never let me see either of you. You know what she was like. Both Annette and I were feeling low and we … It was a mistake. It doesn't mean she didn't love Brian. Lord knows she did.'

Charlie squeezed her lips together. She'd heard enough. There was no excuse for infidelity.

'I don't need to hear excuses,' Mitch growled. 'Are you telling us … Charlie might be yours?'

Tingles prickled her skin at Mitch's choked words and they weren't the good kind.

Rick nodded. 'I promise, it only happened once. We both regretted it immediately. It was a mistake. We didn't want to hurt Brian or Theresa, but yes, we always knew there was a possibility, a very tiny one, that I was Charlie's biological father.'

Charlie snapped. 'You never thought to find out?'

Mitch glared at her. 'Charlie, calm down.' And then he turned back to Rick. 'Seriously, Dad, you never checked?'

'Don't tell me to calm down!' Charlie leapt off the bed and started pacing the room, her hands tearing through her hair. This was … this was … this was *wrong*, on so many levels.

'We decided not to,' she heard Rick say. 'If it was the case—if Charlie was my daughter—it would have destroyed your father, and Therese. And neither of us wanted to do that. We were just good friends who overstepped the boundaries. Just once.'

Mitch didn't say anything but the colour had bled from his face.

'Maybe we were wrong, but I convinced myself that the chances of you being my daughter were very slim. I still think they are but—'

'*Maybe?* What is *wrong* with people?' Charlie turned on Rick, cutting off whatever he'd been about to say, but then a thought struck and she froze. 'Hang on. What about blood types? Mum was O and Dad is A. I know because at one stage in high school Madeleine was obsessed with genetics and made all of us learn the basics. Anyway, I'm an A, so—'

'I'm an A too, Charlie,' Rick said gravely. 'You could be mine or Brian's.'

As his devastating words sunk in, Charlie stared at Rick, scrutinising him for clues. Any part of him that might resemble her. But while she couldn't see herself in his eyes or anything like that, a sinking feeling settled in her gut. This made terrifying, heartbreaking sense.

Was this why she'd always felt like the odd one out amongst her sisters? Why they all had light coloured hair like their parents and she was a brunette? Like Rick McDonald. Was this why she and Mitch got along so well? Until recently, she'd always joked that he was like a brother to her … Maybe that wasn't so funny. Rick warning her off at the St Patrick's Day party suddenly made sickening sense.

Feeling as if she might vomit up the contents of her breakfast, she placed her hand on her stomach but it offered none of the comfort it had only an hour ago.

Angry tears welled in her eyes.

And if she wasn't really a Patterson, maybe the damn curse did exist. So much for her being the family saviour. It looked like she might be the one to tear it apart. What would this do to her dad? Or rather to Brian—who knew if he was anything more to her than the fool who'd brought up another man's child? She squeezed her eyes shut, her heart feeling ripped in two at the thought of how he would feel when he found out about this.

Even if he wasn't her biological father, she loved him and couldn't stand to be the one to break his heart.

'Charlie.' She felt Mitch's hand on her arm, but she flung it off, not willing to allow herself to seek comfort from him.

'What?' She glared at him, knowing this wasn't his fault but unable to help herself.

'We should take some time to calm down and then work out if we want to do anything about this.'

'*If?!* Are you suggesting we just continue on as we were? Pretending life is fine and dandy and I might not be having a baby with—'

'No.' He shook his head, angrily ran a hand through his thick mop of scruffy dark hair. 'Fuck, I didn't mean that. I just meant we can't think straight right now, we need time.'

'Mitchell, I'm not going to be able to think straight until we know the truth. And we don't have much time. If this baby is …' She gestured to her still-flat stomach. 'If we are, you know, I can't have it.'

Mitch's face fell and his shoulders slumped. He looked utterly broken, as if someone had just thrown a bomb into his world. Half of her wanted to take him in her arms and kiss him, to tell him everything was going to be fine, but she couldn't … because maybe it wasn't going to be.

'Is everything okay in here?'

Charlie and Mitch spun to face the door to see one of the nurses standing in the doorway. She wore a crease-free white uniform and her hair was tied back in a high, neat ponytail. She raised an immaculately preened eyebrow as if annoyed they were disturbing her perfect world.

'Fine,' Mitch barked. 'We'll be going soon.'

'Good. I don't want Mr McDonald getting overtired.' She smiled, but it felt like a warning as she turned on her heels and marched back out.

No one said anything until the sounds of her shoes click-clacking along the corridor faded. Then, Rick spoke again. 'I'm sorry. I can't change the past. God knows I would if I could. But what's done is done. The question is, what are we going to do about it?'

'Paternity testing?' Mitch said, gazing out the window rather than at either of them.

'It was only a relatively new thing when Annette was pregnant with you,' Rick volunteered. 'I suggested it but the accuracy was only eighty percent or something and she said it was better if we didn't know. Better if we forgot about it.'

Charlie shook her head, quietly seething. Mum was lucky that bee had stung her because if she'd been alive when Charlie found this out, she'd have wished she wasn't.

'But,' continued Rick, 'I'm sure the tests are more accurate now.'

'I'll ask Madeleine about it,' Charlie said, finally starting to think straight. 'She'll know what to do, where to go.'

'You're not going to tell your father, are you?' Rick sounded worried. 'Annette wouldn't want that.'

'Not yet, but that doesn't mean I won't. He deserves to know what you did.' *What Mum did*, she silently added.

But no. She'd do her best to keep a cheerful face around Dad, to pretend she was overjoyed about the baby, and would worry about what to tell him when they had facts. She could barely bring herself to look at Mitch now, never mind her possible biological father, so she said, 'I'll be in touch,' and stalked out of the room.

Mitch caught up with her seconds later. He didn't take her hand as he had on the way in, and neither of them were smiling anymore. In the course of a few hours, they'd experienced the biggest high of their lives and then the greatest low. The visit to Aunt Mags was obviously off the agenda, just as—*Fuck*—the curse was back on.

They climbed into the ute in silence and neither of them said anything until they were heading back along the Eyre Highway.

'It might be okay,' Mitch said, slowly rapping his fingers on the steering wheel. 'He said it only happened once. The odds are Brian is your father.'

His optimism had always attracted her but right now it only grated on her nerves. Couldn't he see that she was more like him than any of her so-called sisters?

'We don't know that,' she snapped. 'I can't believe your dad came round to the motel when my dad wasn't around. I bet he planned to seduce her. It makes me sick.'

'Hey.' Mitch took his eyes off the road a second to glare at her. His nostrils flared. 'It takes two to tango. And besides, Annette's the one who wanted the secret kept all these years.'

'Don't yell at me. This isn't my fault.'

'It's not mine either!'

Charlie jumped at the fury in Mitch's voice. They rarely disagreed and barely argued about anything. Although she'd occasionally heard him raise his voice to someone on the footy field or in the pub, she struggled to remember a time he'd ever spoken to her like that. Then again, she'd never shouted at him either.

Silence reigned for a few long moments and then Mitch sighed. 'I'm sorry. I know this is an awful thing we have to face, but it's not going to do any good yelling at each other.'

'I know,' she whispered, shivering.

But she just felt so utterly helpless and alone. And sad. Whatever the truth, the knowledge that her mother had betrayed her dad made her feel very, very sad.

Chapter Forty-eight

And I thought scenes like that only happened in the movies.

Madeleine smiled at the romantic reunion happening before her eyes. Nigel seemed like a good guy and he had to really love Abigail to have travelled around the world to tell her. Feeling bittersweet—happy for Abigail and Charlie, but wondering if she'd ever get her own happy ending—she quietly retreated from the lounge room and headed down the hallway to check on Lucinda. Although Luce had put on a brave face and declared herself fine with Charlie's unexpected pregnancy, she had to be finding this difficult. Hell, Madeleine had only been trying to get pregnant for a few months and it felt like a slap in the face that Charlie had achieved it accidentally.

She knocked lightly on Lucinda's bedroom door. There was no answer. Worried, she twisted the handle and pushed it open to find Lucinda sitting on her bed, talking on her mobile phone. Tears were streaming down her cheeks. Lucinda was so caught up in whatever the person on the other end of the phone was saying that she didn't appear to notice her at all. Madeleine didn't know whether to let her sister know she was there or to sneak away unseen. Guessing she was talking to Joe, she chose the latter option. Whatever they were saying, the fact that they were talking at all was a good thing.

It was just after midday but jet lag had messed with her body clock so she wasn't yet hungry. Feeling at a loose end and not wanting to disturb the reunited lovebirds, who now looked to be checking out each other's tonsils on the couch, Madeleine donned her sneakers and then snuck past to go outside. It was a beautiful late autumn day—neither hot nor cold—perfect running weather. She ran through the main street of town, deserted because it was a Sunday and nothing opened in Meadow Brook on Sundays, and then headed out towards the bush.

Without thinking she found herself jogging past Wacky Wanda's house. She slowed, chuckling at the recollection of what had happened six months ago with Abigail. Although they now knew the curse was ridiculous, Madeleine had to admit that Wanda's witch-like appearance and her overgrown garden dotted with scruffy cats certainly fit with what Mags had told them about the curse. Their imaginations had run away with them and stories they remembered from the schoolyard had compounded their fears.

Shaking her head, she was about to continue on when she heard a screen door open and shut. She looked past the cats and the garden onto the derelict porch to see the old woman standing there surveying her kingdom. Something tugged inside her and she paused.

If Mags were right and Wanda's mother was of James Patterson's generation, then she must be in her nineties. When most women of her age were being taken care of by families or nursing homes, she was alone and fending for herself. Saddened by this thought, Madeleine lifted her hand and waved at the woman on the porch. For a few long moments Wanda simply stood there, staring, but then she lifted her arm and waved back.

That was all the encouragement Madeleine needed to take the few steps to the gate. She stopped there, not wanting to scare the elderly woman, unsure what she intended to do but wanting to make some kind of contact.

'Hi,' she called, pushing her sunglasses up onto her head. 'Lovely day, isn't it?'

Wanda slowly descended the steps, stooping to pick up a cat before continuing down the cracked garden path. Madeleine fought the urge to rush in and assist her because she guessed she was used to being independent.

She stopped a few feet before the gate and looked at Madeleine with an expression half confused, half intrigued. 'I don't get many visitors out this way,' she said eventually.

'I don't know why.' Madeleine smiled. 'It's beautiful out here away from the highway. Have you lived here long?'

Wanda cocked her head to one side and gave her a knowing look. 'I recognise you. You're a Meadow Brook girl from way back. I think you know I've been here forever.'

Was she referring to the crazy stories about her? Did Wanda know what people said? Up close she wasn't half as scary-looking as Madeleine remembered. She wanted to ask her if she knew about the curse, but decided against it. Out here, with the sun shining down, it all seemed so tenuous.

It was codswallop like Mum had said—and what good would raising the question do anyway?

So she smiled instead. 'You amaze me, living out here by yourself. You're a real pioneer, an inspiration.'

Wanda snorted but her eyes sparkled. 'And who are you, my dear?'

'My name is Madeleine. Madeleine Patterson.' She finally held out her hand, wondering if Wanda would accept the gesture or even if she would recognise the Patterson name. She wanted to talk more, to offer support if the old woman needed it.

Wanda put down the cat and tottered forward, finally stretching out her own hand and placing it inside Madeleine's. It was cold and her skin felt papery thin. 'I'm Lorraine. And it's lovely to meet you.'

Later, when Madeleine returned to the house, she found Nigel and Abigail in the kitchen making a late lunch of toasted sandwiches. She almost told them about her meeting with Lorraine, but decided to wait until she had all her sisters together.

'Want some?' Abigail asked.

Madeleine nodded as she grabbed a glass and filled it at the tap. 'That'd be great. I'll have a quick shower and see if Lucinda and Dad want to join us.'

'Dad's having a lie-down before he has to help Rob this evening,' Abigail said, slicing cheese for the toasties. 'I think today's been a wee bit exciting for him.'

Nigel grinned. 'Abigail told me about your sister's news. That's awesome.'

'Sure is.' Madeleine smiled, still struggling to come to terms with the whole Mitch-and-Charlie thing, never mind that her flighty, sometimes ditzy sister was going to be a mum. 'So you met Dad then?' she asked, lifting the glass to her lips.

Nigel nodded. 'Yep. I told him I loved his daughter and asked if he'd give me his blessing to marry her.'

'You *what*?' Madeleine almost choked on her water.

Abigail laughed and turned to smile at Nigel with gooey eyes. 'Surprised me too. Want to be my maid of honour?'

Recovering, Madeleine said, 'Isn't that a bit fast?'

Nigel and Abigail gazed into each other's eyes and then he said, 'When you know, you know.'

'I guess.' Madeleine felt a little nauseated by all this romance, so guzzled the rest of her water and then headed for the bathroom. She stood under the hot water and closed her eyes, letting it soothe her over-exerted muscles. It looked like Abigail might not be staying in Meadow Brook that long after all. Although happy for her little sister, she'd had fun hanging out with her these last few days and was disappointed their time together might be over so quickly.

Remembering she had another sister who might need her, Madeleine turned off the water and climbed out of the cubicle. She dried and dressed quickly and then went to try Lucinda again. This time, she got an answer when she knocked.

'Come in.'

Madeleine pushed the door open. 'Are you okay?'

Lucinda nodded from where she was folding laundry into piles on her bed. 'I know no one probably believes me but I'm genuinely happy for Charlie and Mitch. They are both wonderful people and they deserve love and … Wow, the baby is just such a special surprise. At least now we know the curse is crap.'

Madeleine laughed. 'As if there was ever any doubt. Have you met Nigel yet?'

Lucinda looked up and frowned. 'Abigail's Nigel?'

'One and the same. He arrived from London a couple of hours ago to declare his undying love and affection and to beg Abigail to marry him.'

Lucinda's mouth dropped open, then, 'No! Are you serious?'

'I don't think there was much begging involved, but yes.' She nodded. 'He's here in all his tall, blond glory and I'm going to be *maid-of-freaking-honour*.'

Lucinda started laughing. 'Must be the day for surprises.'

'Yep, looks like everyone gets a happy ending except us.' Madeleine shifted a pile of neatly folded underwear and plonked herself on the bed.

'Actually …' Lucinda looked down, her expression sheepish. 'I've decided to go home. Joe has asked me to go to marriage counselling and we're going to do our best to work things out.'

'Oh …' For a split second Madeleine's heart cramped in disappointment—she'd been looking for someone to share her woe—but then she got over herself. 'That's wonderful. I'm so happy for you.'

'Thanks.' Lucinda sniffed and smiled. 'I'm not kidding myself that this is the end of our troubles or that the road ahead is going to be easy, but being apart has made us both realise how much we want to be together. I've booked a flight back to Perth for tomorrow evening. And I can't wait to see him.'

'So—' Madeleine gestured to the piles on the bed as she registered the suitcase open and off to one side on the floor '—you're packing?'

'Yep. I know you and Abigail have only just gotten home and everything, but I have to put my marriage first. You don't mind, do you?'

'No, of course not. I'll even drive you to Adelaide for your flight if you want. But first, do you want to come get some lunch? Abigail and Nigel are making toasties and I can't handle them making eyes at each other across the table on my own.'

'Now you mention it,' Lucinda said, 'I'm starving. And I do want to meet Nigel if we're going to be related.'

Madeleine heaved herself up off the bed. 'Come on then.'

The two of them went to the lounge room where Abigail and Nigel had laid out a massive plate of toasted sandwiches on the coffee table. This time Abigail and Nigel took the couch and Lucinda and Madeleine sat in the armchairs, shooting sisterly questions at the newly engaged couple between mouthfuls. Dad woke from his nap, came in for a while and did his best with his own questions, but it turned out they all adored Nigel almost as much as Abigail.

When Dad went into the motel to do some work, the others half-heartedly watched a movie. It was a very chilled, pleasant afternoon.

'I wonder when Mitch and Charlie will be back?' Abigail asked as the credits rolled up the TV screen.

'Maybe we should have a celebratory dinner in the restaurant tonight?' Lucinda suggested.

'Good idea,' Madeleine said. 'That way Dad can be with us while he's seeing to the patrons and we can help in the bar. We should ask Mrs Sampson to join us.'

'Yes, I'll go give her a call.' As Lucinda rose from the armchair, the front door opened and Charlie appeared by herself. 'Where's Mitch?' Lucinda asked, the concern in her voice indicating she'd noticed Charlie's pale, shaky demeanour.

This Charlie was like a different person from the one who'd left the house a few hours earlier and Madeleine immediately switched into medical mode. 'What's wrong? Have you got cramps, bleeding or something?'

Charlie shook her head as she closed the door and stepped further inside. She lifted her arms and wrapped them around herself as if she were freezing. 'Where's Dad?'

'In the motel,' Abigail answered.

'Good, because he doesn't need to hear this.'

'What?' Madeleine, Lucinda and Abigail asked in unison.

'I ... I ...' She glanced at each of them and then her gaze fell on Nigel. She frowned. 'Who are *you*?'

He got up off the couch where he'd been sitting nuzzling Abigail and offered Charlie his hand. 'I'm Nigel. Abigail's fiancé.'

'Oh right,' Charlie nodded and shook it, accepting his explanation without question, which Madeleine thought a testament to the fact something was very, very wrong. 'I need to speak to Madeleine,' she continued as Nigel sat back down, 'but you may as well all hear this. It sort of affects you all.'

'What is it?' Lucinda asked as Madeleine leaned forward in her chair.

Charlie sighed, her whole body rising and then sagging again. She looked close to tears and she wasn't the type to cry over nothing. 'I've just found out that Mum and Mitch's dad had a … a brief—' she lowered her voice '—*liaison* around the time she fell pregnant with me.'

She paused as Madeleine and the others gasped, but didn't wait for the first blow to settle before she hit them with the second. 'It's possible that Rick is my real father. Which means—'

'What the fuck?' Madeleine launched into a stand, shaking her head as if she thought this was one very sick joke. Lucinda and Abigail looked numb.

'My feelings exactly,' Charlie said, dropping her arms and placing one hand against her stomach as she felt the nausea rising again. She wasn't sure whether it was morning sickness, terror or a menacing cocktail of both. 'Which is why I need your help. How do Mr McDonald and I go about getting a paternity test done?'

'You're going to find out?' Abigail asked, her tone disbelieving. 'But … what if you are Rick's daughter? What is that news going to do to Dad?'

Charlie felt annoyance and frustration building alongside the nausea. As if this was her fault! 'I can't think about that right now. What about our—' she squeezed her eyes shut, not wanting to cry '—the baby?'

She couldn't allow herself to think about it as hers and Mitch's because if they were … Well, she couldn't have it, could she?

'I don't believe it,' Lucinda whispered. 'I *can't* believe it. Mum would never have cheated on Dad.'

'That's what I thought, but Rick swore it. And why would he lie about something like this?' Charlie didn't want to go over it all but her sisters needed to know. 'Apparently it happened only once. They both agreed it was an accident and it never happened again.'

'An *accident*?' Lucinda scoffed. 'An accident is running into someone else's car or spilling a drink on the table. It's not falling into bed with someone else's wife. And Mum? Christ, what was she thinking?'

'I might go make some tea,' said the guy on the couch next to Abigail as he pushed into a stand. *Had he said he was her fiancé?* Charlie shook her head, not ready to deal with that mystery right now.

She sat down next to Abigail on the space he'd vacated. Madeleine came over and squeezed in next to her and Lucinda sat on the edge of the coffee table in front of them. They reached out for each other's hands and Charlie couldn't help the tears that came. She loved and admired them all so much, had always looked up to them, even Abigail who was younger. She hated the thought that she might not be one of them as much as she hated the terrible possibility that she might be related to Mitch.

After a long silence, she whispered, 'I'm sorry.'

Madeleine squeezed her hand. 'What are you sorry for? This isn't your fault.'

'It'll be alright,' Lucinda promised. 'We're here for you whatever happens.'

'But I might only be your half-sister.'

'Even if we do have different fathers, and let's not get carried away before we know the facts,' Abigail said, sounding a lot calmer than she had a few moments ago, 'we're still sisters. Nothing is going to take that away.'

'Damn straight,' Madeleine said at the same time as Lucinda said, 'Exactly.'

'But don't you see?' Charlie pursed her lips together and then sucked in a breath. 'If Rick is my biological father, then I'm not a Patterson. Which means … maybe the curse is real.'

They were all quiet for a moment and then Lucinda said fiercely, 'We don't care about the damn curse right now. We care about you.' And then she slipped her hands from the sister chain, knelt on the floor in front of Charlie and pulled her into a hug. 'You're all that matters.'

Coming from Lucinda, that meant a lot.

'Thank you.' Charlie sniffed. When Lucinda finally let her go, she turned her head to look at Madeleine. She needed to focus. 'What are the logistics of getting paternity testing done? Is it hard?'

Madeleine shook her head. 'Not these days. There's a simple test. I'll make some calls first thing tomorrow morning and find out if it can be done at the pathology unit in Port Augusta. There are tests we can get via mail order but it'll be quicker and more reliable if you and Rick can go in person.'

'Okay, thanks.' Charlie felt grateful she had Madeleine to do the groundwork because she could barely think straight herself. 'Is it very invasive?' She'd always been a wimp where needles were concerned.

'No. It's very simple and pain free. They'll collect some cells from on the inside of your cheek, and Rick's, using what's called a buccal or cheek swab. It's a little wooden or plastic stick that has cotton on a synthetic tip. The person performing the test will collect as many cells as possible and these cells will be sent to the lab for testing.'

'And that's … accurate?'

'Yes. As accurate as taking a blood sample because the DNA is the same.'

'Okay.' Charlie couldn't believe this nightmare was her life. 'And how long will it be before we have the result?'

Madeleine shrugged. 'I'm not sure. It depends on the pathology unit. Anywhere up to ten days at a guess, but I'll see if I have any contacts there who may be able to put a rush on it.'

'Thanks.' Although right now ten days sounded like a lifetime. 'How am I supposed to face Mitch? Or Dad?'

Her other sisters exchanged glum looks.

'Where's Mitch now?' Abigail asked.

'I told him to go home and said I'd call him when I'd worked out what to do. I can't face him at the moment.' Looking at him hurt too damn much.

'Fair enough.' Lucinda reached behind her for the box of tissues on the coffee table. She offered the box and Charlie snatched up a couple.

What was she supposed to do now? What she wanted was to get very, very drunk, but she wouldn't add *that* to this baby's problems. She started by blowing her nose and wiping her eyes.

'About Dad,' Lucinda said. 'Why don't we try and get him away for the next week or so? We'll suggest that since we're all home at the moment, he and Mrs Sampson should take the chance to try out the caravan and—'

'But,' Madeleine interjected. 'Aren't you—'

'More than happy to take on Dad and Mrs Sampson's work,' Lucinda butted in. 'I'm sure you and Abigail will help.'

'Of course,' Abigail said. 'No way I'm going back to London until all this is sorted.'

'That's settled then.' Lucinda stood. 'I'll go tell Dad.'

'You don't think he'll be suspicious?' Charlie asked. 'And ... don't you think he has a right to know? About Mum?'

Lucinda took a deep breath. 'Look. Let's deal with this ourselves first and when we've got a handle on it, then work out what and if to tell Dad. What if it turns out to be nothing? Besides, he's so desperate to play with his caravan, he'll jump at the chance to get away. Remember, this will be his first holiday in Lord knows how long.'

Charlie was more than happy with his suggestion. She had enough crap to deal with herself without worrying about how all this might affect their father.

'Well, if you're sure.' Madeleine gave Lucinda an odd look.

'Good.' Lucinda smiled, started out the room and then looked back to Charlie. 'We were going to suggest dinner together in the motel tonight. Would you be up for that or would you prefer I made us something here?'

Charlie didn't know whether she'd be able to stomach food, but if they were in the restaurant she'd have to keep a happy face for appearances sake. And being with her family would be better than hiding away in her room. 'I'm up for it.'

As Lucinda headed off through the kitchen and into the motel, Charlie turned to Abigail, needing distraction. 'So? Nigel? What's the deal?'

'Oh.' Abigail's lips twisted into a grin and then she glanced towards the kitchen. 'Honey, it's safe, you can come out now. Come meet Charlie.'

Nigel returned carrying a tray with a teapot, five mugs and a packet of Tim Tams.

Charlie raised her eyebrows at Abigail, trying to focus on her sister's news rather than the continuous churning of her stomach. She moved over on the couch so Nigel could sit down next to Abigail. 'Hello there,' she said, offering him her hand, forgetting that she'd already shaken his earlier. 'Sorry about before. I hope our family dramas haven't scared you off.'

'Not at all. I come from a big family so I'm used to drama.' Nigel's hand was warm and solid but felt nothing like Mitch's. She inwardly cursed, not wanting to think about him right now.

'Did you say fiancé before?' she asked.

'Yes.' Nigel and Abigail nodded, already speaking as one.

'Nigel flew all across the world to tell her that he loves her, and to ask for Dad's blessing to marry her,' Madeleine said, sounding amused.

'Well, at least someone's love life is going smoothly,' Charlie said dryly, before she could think better of it.

'I'm sorry, Charlie.' Abigail reached across Nigel to pat her sister's knee. 'This royally sucks.'

'It does, but I'm honestly happy for you both. Congratulations.' She meant it, but all of a sudden she felt the need to be alone. 'Think I might just go have a shower before dinner. I'll see you love birds later.'

'Bye,' they said, again in unison.

Charlie stood and Madeleine followed her out of the room.

'You sure you don't need company?' she asked once they were in the hallway that led to the bedrooms.

Charlie shook her head. 'I'll be okay. See you at dinner.'

After saying goodbye to Charlie, Madeleine put her sneakers back on and walked the short distance to Mitch's house. Charlie had confided in them but Mitch was a bloke and she guessed his coping mechanisms might be different. Still, he was a friend and she wanted to check on him.

His ute was out the front and lights were on inside the house. She knocked on the door but the sound could barely be heard over the music blaring from inside. Thankfully no one bothered to lock their doors in Meadow Brook, so she wiped her feet on the scruffy doormat and let herself inside.

She found Mitch sitting on his couch nursing a beer. Three empty bottles were already lined up on the floor at his feet. He was staring straight ahead at the TV but it wasn't on and although she cleared her throat, he didn't notice her. Madeleine stepped into the room and yanked the stereo's plug out of the wall. The room went silent and Mitch finally turned to look at her.

'Hey.' He lifted his beer in a slight wave and then took a sip.

'Got any more of those?' she asked, nodding to the bottle.

He shrugged. 'In the fridge. Help yourself.'

Madeleine wasn't much of a beer fan but if she drank one, it'd be one less for him to drown his sorrows in. She grabbed a bottle and then sat herself on the couch beside him. She'd never been very good at knowing what to say to comfort people in times of need, so she took a sip and waited for him to talk.

'How's Charlie?' he asked.

'A mess,' she said honestly.

'Fuck.' Mitch slammed his bottle down on the table and ran a hand through his hair. 'I feel so bloody helpless. I want to help her through this but she said she can't see me right now. I don't know what to do. I just want to fix it.'

'I know. And first thing tomorrow we'll organise a paternity test. I'm fairly certain we'll be able to get it done in Port Augusta. Will you be able to break your dad out of the nursing home for the testing?'

Mitch nodded. 'Yeah, you just tell me where I need to take him.'

They were both quiet again and Madeleine took another sip of beer, ignoring the bitter taste on her tongue. How anyone could love this stuff, she had no idea.

'I don't know what I'm going to do if …' Mitch faltered and then sucked in a deep breath. 'I don't know how I can go back to just being friends. She's the love of my life. How can I just switch that off?'

Her heart aching for him, Madeleine reached out and squeezed Mitch's hand. 'Let's try not to worry about that yet. One step at a time, hey? We just have to get through the next few days.'

'We'll know in a few days?'

'It might take a little longer, but we'll know soon.'

He cleared his throat. 'How exactly do they test? It's not gonna hurt Dad or Charlie, is it?'

'No.' Madeleine shook her head and explained the procedure to him as she had to her sisters.

'That sounds all right.' Mitch started to get up and clear the empty bottles. 'Can I get you something to eat?'

'No, thanks. We're having dinner in the motel. Keeping up appearances for Dad.' She put her half-full bottle down on the coffee table and stood. 'Will you be okay?'

He nodded. 'I'm not going to drink myself silly if that's what you're asking.'

'Good.' She started towards the door and he followed to see her out.

As Mitch held open the front door for her, she said, 'Charlie or I will call you tomorrow as soon as we've made an appointment. Will you be around?'

'I'll make sure of it.'

Somehow Charlie got through dinner, managing not to throw up when Mrs Sampson threw her arms around her and squealed her congratulations. Instead she smiled sweetly and asked if she'd keep the news quiet for now as it was still early days.

Of course Dad wanted to know where Mitch was but Charlie told him he had a migraine and reminded them they had an engagement to celebrate as well. Her sisters kept the conversation going, suggesting ideas for Nigel and Abigail's wedding and asking Dad and Mrs Sampson where they planned to travel over the next couple of weeks.

'Are you sure you girls can do without us?' Dad asked.

Charlie looked at her sisters, panicking at the idea of him sticking around, but they all jumped in to assure him they'd be fine.

'You may as well make the most of us while we're all here,' Abigail said. 'I'll be heading back to London soon.'

'Well, in that case ...' Dad lifted his beer and took a sip, his grin stretching ridiculously across his face.

Charlie picked at her dinner as she tried to participate in conversation but was unable to eat a mouthful of her favourite dessert. 'Do you mind if I call it a night?' she asked, pretending to stifle a yawn.

Mrs Sampson chuckled. 'You go and get some rest. There's nothing like that fatigue in early pregnancy. You can't fight it.'

'Thanks.' Charlie smiled weakly around the table as she pushed back her chair.

She went into the house alone, more exhausted than she could recall ever feeling in her life. Whether that was early pregnancy or the emotional upheaval of the day, she couldn't say. She brushed her teeth, changed into her pyjamas and then snuck under the bed covers but sleep didn't come easily. She tossed and turned for hours, unable to think about anything but Mitch. How was he coping? Was he also having difficulty getting sleep?

She longed to call him, to hear his soothing and familiar voice, but that might only make everything worse. She couldn't allow herself to need him. Not now. Not until. Just in case. So instead, she rolled over onto her side, curled up in the foetal position and cried.

Chapter Forty-nine

While Madeleine was on the phone to the pathology unit in Port Augusta on Monday morning, Dad and Mrs Sampson were packing up the caravan, oblivious to the drama going on around them. They headed off towards the Nullarbor—destination Esperance in Western Australia—just after midday, waved off by all the sisters and Nigel. The girls kept their fake smiles plastered to their faces until the caravan was well and truly out of sight and then they turned to Madeleine.

'Well?' Charlie asked.

'You and Rick have an appointment this afternoon. We'll have to leave in an hour or so. Do you want to tell Mitch yourself or would you like me to call him?'

Charlie's stomach twisted, both at the thought of what lay ahead and also at the prospect of phoning Mitch. What had seemed so normal only a day ago now felt awkward and wrong. 'Can you?'

Madeleine nodded. 'Of course.'

'Do you want us to come with you?' Lucinda asked.

Charlie shook her head. 'You and Abigail better stay here and man reception. It's not like we're going to have a result today anyway.'

465

*

'Hi.' Charlie barely croaked the greeting as Mitch jumped into the back of the Meadow Brook Motel van. Madeleine was at the wheel and Charlie sat in the passenger seat, feeling queasy already —despite never having experienced travel sickness before.

'Hi ladies. Thanks for picking me up.' Mitch clicked his seat-belt into place and Charlie noted his voice sounded slightly different to normal. As if he were trying too hard to *be* normal.

'You're welcome.' Madeleine smiled over her shoulder and then turned back to face the road as she pulled away from the kerb outside Mitch's fibro house. 'Did you manage to get in contact with your dad?'

'Yep. The nurses will have him ready when we arrive.'

'Great.'

When Mitch didn't say anything else, Madeleine leant forward and switched on the radio. The monotone voice of some ABC journalist crackled out of the ancient speakers and Charlie had never felt more thankful for talkback radio in her life. The old van couldn't tune into the more popular FM stations, but right now she didn't care. She was simply thankful for something to fill the silence.

It felt like the longest journey ever, but then they were finally in front of the nursing home. Madeleine pulled into a short-stay parking bay and Mitch leapt out to fetch his dad.

Madeleine glanced across at Charlie. 'You hanging in there?'

'I can't believe this is happening,' she replied, sagging into the seat. 'Mitch feels like a stranger, when only yesterday we ...' She couldn't finish her sentence. Her throat felt like it had clogged up with cement.

Madeleine tapped her fingers on the steering wheel. 'I wish I could say something to make you feel better.'

Charlie sniffed. 'I don't think there's anything anyone could say right now. If you believed in God I'd ask you to pray that all this was a nightmare.'

'Is that what you're doing?'

She nodded. 'I'm praying to God, begging Mother Nature. I think I'd even sell my soul to the devil if he could make this right. Whatever it takes.'

'Right.' Madeleine stared out the window. A few more minutes passed in silence and then she said, 'They're coming.'

When Charlie turned her head towards the building, she saw Mitch wheeling his father down the ramp towards the van. Rick looked like he'd deteriorated—physically—since they'd visited him yesterday. His confession seemed like a lifetime ago and now she found herself torn between anger and pity.

While Charlie struggled with her emotions, Madeleine got out to help Mitch with Rick and the wheelchair.

'Hello Madeleine, love, long time no see.'

Charlie bristled at the familiarity in Rick's voice and the sympathy she'd almost felt towards him evaporated. How dare he speak to Madeleine as if he were an old friend of the family. Friends didn't do what he'd done.

She didn't know how she'd cope if he was her father. Would everyone suddenly expect her to transfer her affections from Brian onto Rick? Hell would freeze over before that happened. Brian would always be her dad, the man who'd loved her her whole life and would do anything for her. Rick would simply be the cheating scumbag who'd shattered her world.

She folded her arms across her chest as she listened to Madeleine and Mitch struggle Rick into the seat. Mitch finally climbed into the van and as he pulled the sliding door shut, Rick said, 'Hello Charlie? How are you?'

She almost snorted at the question, but chose to ignore it. Telling him how she felt would involve a number of colourful words and she didn't want to upset Mitch. This was hell for him as well and feeling like he was torn between her and his dad wouldn't help.

Madeleine turned the key in the ignition and again the dry voice of the ABC radio presenter wafted into the van. He'd moved on to discussing incontinence in Australia's ageing population, but luckily the distance from nursing home to hospital was short and they arrived at the pathology unit, an old single-storey brick building in the grounds of Port Augusta hospital, before they had to hear the listeners phoning in with their stories.

As Madeleine parked, Charlie's heart began to pound. Although she knew this was a simple, pain-free procedure and that they wouldn't have the results for at least a week, it felt akin to looking over the cliff top of a massive canyon and preparing to throw herself off. If it weren't for the new life inside her, would Rick have ever come clean?

If it weren't for her pregnancy—or Mitch—would she even want to know?

To think that a few cells on the inside of her cheek could dictate the rest of her life.

'You coming?' Madeleine opened the passenger door and Charlie realised they'd already got Rick out and into the wheelchair.

No, she wanted to say. Why couldn't someone just pinch her and wake her up? 'Okay.' She nodded, picking up her patchwork handbag from the floor of the van.

Charlie took Madeleine's lead and followed her into the building and over to the reception desk, aware of Mitch and Rick close behind.

'How can I help you?' asked a grey-haired woman with a stern face and glasses.

'Appointment for Charlotte Patterson and Richard McDonald,' Madeleine said, slightly leaning over the counter.

The woman scanned her computer, then picked up two clipboards. 'Which of you are Charlotte and Richard?'

Charlie raised her hand at the same time as Rick said, 'I'm Richard.'

The woman thrust a clipboard at each of them. 'Fill in these forms and take a seat. Your names will be called soon.'

'Thank you,' Charlie managed.

The four of them walked over to a row of plastic chairs. Mitch positioned the wheelchair on the edge and sat down next to it. Charlie sat beside him, the little hairs on her arms standing up at being so close. She swallowed and tried to focus on the page.

'Do you want me to fill it in?' Madeleine asked a few moments later.

Charlie glanced sideways and saw Mitch busy filling in the answers for his dad, his tongue poking slightly out of his mouth in concentration. Damn, he was cute.

'Yes, please.' She nodded and handed her sister the clipboard. Madeleine didn't have to ask Charlie about most of the answers, so Charlie sat there, her hands pressed tightly down on her knees to try and stop them jittering.

When Madeleine had finished, Mitch took both clipboards across to the desk.

'Will we go in together?' Charlie asked her sister.

Madeleine shook her head. 'I doubt it. They'll call you both separately.'

As Mitch returned to their seats, a tall thin woman in a white uniform appeared at the edge of the waiting room. 'Richard McDonald,' she called, scanning the faces on the plastic chairs.

'Come on, Dad.' Mitch grabbed hold of the wheelchair and started after the woman.

Charlie's throat felt dry.

'Do you want me to come in when it's your turn?' Madeleine asked.

'No, thanks.' She lifted her hand to touch her neck. 'But do you reckon you can find a vending machine or something for when we're finished? I'm parched.'

'Sure. There'll be something in the hospital. I'll be back soon.' Madeleine stood quickly.

Charlie watched her go and took a deep breath as she disappeared through the door. She stretched across and picked a tattered copy of *New Idea* from the table in the middle of the waiting room.

Flicking aimlessly, she'd barely glanced at a few pages when Mitch and Rick reappeared.

'All done,' Mitch said, repositioning his dad's wheelchair and then sitting back down beside Charlie. He hit her with a warm, comforting smile that almost unravelled her. She wanted to hold his hand, wanted him to come into the treatment with her as support. How could he possibly be her brother? Could life really be that screwed up?

'Charlotte Patterson.'

Not used to her full name, Charlie blinked as the woman in white called her up.

'Where's Madeleine?' Mitch asked.

'Gone to get me a drink,' she replied, not daring to look at him as she stood.

'Do you want me to come with you?'

'No,' she said, unable to resist turning to look at him. She smiled. 'I'll be fine.'

And then she walked off to start the ball rolling on what could be the worst news of her life.

*

Madeleine stared at the ancient coffee machine in the waiting area of the main hospital and then decided to get a selection of cool drinks from the vending machine next to it instead. Bad coffee simply wouldn't cut it. The drive to Port Augusta had been painful. The tension between her sister and her old friend was excruciating. They'd been so loved up yesterday morning, but now they could barely bring themselves to look into each other's eyes.

She'd wanted to say something to break the heartbreaking silence but small talk had never been her forte. That's why she'd chosen not to become a GP; she couldn't stand the thought of nattering to all those pensioners day in day out, simply because they had no one at home to talk to. She sighed as she dug around in her purse, slotted coins into the machine and pressed the different buttons, stooping each time a drink fell into the bottom. Unsure what either Mitch or Charlie would feel like, she bought a Diet Coke for herself and a selection of other soft drinks, juices and water.

And then there was Rick. Maybe she shouldn't but she felt for him also. He'd been carrying around this guilty secret for years, no doubt dreading but also half hoping that it might come out. If Charlie *was* his daughter then it had been wrong of their mother to cover it up. No matter how painful it might have been, she should have known the truth would come out eventually.

Her head aching, she gathered up the drinks in her arms and started back towards the exit. She'd barely walked two steps when someone called her name.

'Madeleine?' Assuming there must be another person with the same name somewhere nearby, she turned anyway and saw a giant of a man striding towards her wearing blue scrubs. As he approached she saw he was all hard muscle and tanned skin, and his face gave new meaning to the word chiselled.

'Dylan?' Her mind jolted in recognition.

'Long time no see,' said the man whom she'd spent almost a decade studying with at university. A man who looked better in scrubs than any other man she'd known. Even Hugo. He smiled as he nodded towards the drinks in her arms. 'I'd shake your hand, but I'm scared you'd drop your bundle.'

She half-laughed, half-snorted and one can slipped from her grasp. Dylan caught it and held it up like he'd caught her out in a game of baseball.

'Thanks,' she said as he balanced it back on the top of the drink pile. A zillion questions were running through her mind about why he was here in Port Augusta—obviously working, though he'd never given her the impression he'd choose to work in the country—but he got in first.

'How are you doing? Last I heard you were living in the States.'

She smiled. 'Your contacts are only slightly out of date. I've been back all of three days. Still slightly jet lagged.'

'But you're home for good? In South Australia? Didn't your folks live not far from here? Have you got a job lined up?'

'I thought you were a doctor, not a journalist.'

'Sorry.' He grinned sheepishly. 'Just curious.'

She licked her lips. 'Home in Australia for good. Not sure about where exactly. I haven't started looking for work.'

'You're having a … holiday?' He looked horrified at the idea, which made her laugh.

'I'm not exactly sure,' she admitted. 'It's a long story. So, you work here?'

'Yup.' He nodded. 'Been here six months. Loving every minute of it.'

'And … is Alice working in town too?' Madeleine had heard on the grapevine years ago that he'd married his high school sweetheart. She wasn't a doctor but they'd been together a long time and she'd come to a lot of social events with him when they were at university.

Madeleine had had a mega crush on Dylan—as had every other girl in their year—but he'd never so much as flirted with any of them.

He grimaced and shook his head. 'Alice and I parted ways just over a year ago. The divorce is almost through. I needed to get away from Melbourne and our life there.'

'Oh, I'm sorry.' And while she meant it, she couldn't help the little leap in her heart at the thought that he was now single.

He shrugged. 'These things happen. People grow apart. Women fall into other men's beds.' He chuckled as if this didn't hurt and Madeleine wondered if Alice had a few screws loose. Why stray when you had someone like Dylan to come home to? But then, her own mother had strayed, hadn't she?

'I'm sorry,' she said again, hating how inadequate it sounded.

'I'm over it, really. I'm just glad we didn't have kids yet. What about you? Married? Mortgaged? Children?'

'No to all of the above.' A sad sigh slipped from her lips before she could catch it.

'Are you going to tell me who all those drinks are for then?' he asked, nodding towards her collection. 'Looks like you're about to have a party.'

'I wish. I'm here with my sister. She's getting tests done in pathology and said she was thirsty.'

He frowned. 'I hope nothing serious.'

Madeleine shook her head. 'Not health-wise. Look, it was so good seeing you, but I'd better be getting back to her.'

'Sure. Of course.' He nodded and then shoved his hands in his pockets.

'Well, I might see you round,' she said, not making a move to leave.

'If you're not busy some night and feel like catching up for a drink, you want to give me a call?' he asked, not quite meeting her gaze.

She moistened her bottom lip, delighted by this prospect. 'You'd have to give me your number.'

There it was; his irresistible grin. 'You got your phone on you?'

'In my pocket.' She nodded towards her thigh, trying to work out how to wrangle it out without dropping all the drinks.

'Allow me.' And then, he slipped his fingers into the top pocket of her skinny jeans and pulled out her iPhone. Her legs quivered at the interaction and she prayed he didn't notice her increased breathing rate. She watched as he slid his finger across the screen to unlock it and then started punching his details into her contacts list.

When he'd finished, he slipped the phone right back into place, his fingers again brushing her thigh and making everything inside her feel like liquid.

'Call me,' he said.

'I will,' she promised, hoping her voice didn't sound as husky as it felt.

'And I hope your sister's okay.'

'Thanks.' She finally turned to walk away, a wide smile on her face and a spring in her step as she headed outside and back to the pathology unit.

Charlie, Mitch and Rick were outside waiting for her. One look at the dejected, resigned look on their faces had her tamping down her smile and feeling guilty that she'd been enjoying seeing an old friend while her sister had been having the scariest test of her life.

'All done?' she asked as she approached them.

'Yep.' Three glum faces nodded back at her.

Not long after the wannabe grey nomads left on their trip and Charlie, Madeleine and Mitch set off for Port Augusta, another surprise visitor turned up at the motel. Lucinda had sent Abigail and Nigel off for a tour of town and cake at Rosie Jean's and was settling into some work at the reception desk to try and distract her thoughts from Charlie and Mitch when the door opened and the bell above it tingled.

She glanced up, ready to paste on a smile for a guest and her mouth fell open.

'Hi Luce.' Joe stepped inside, the door clanged shut behind him and he dropped his backpack to the floor.

'Joe?' Tingles flushed through her body as she gaped at her husband.

He grinned. 'Last time I checked. How are you?'

She forced herself to breathe. The answer to that question was complicated, as was knowing what to do now the man she'd been separated from stood before her looking like he'd just stepped off an Italian football team's charity calendar. Part of her wanted to rush around the desk and throw herself at him, to kiss him like they hadn't kissed since they were first dating. But she wasn't sure how he'd react. Maybe she needed to tread carefully.

Was there a protocol in situations such as this?

'I'm—' she paused a moment '—very happy to see you.'

'I'm glad. When you called last night and told me about Charlie and said you couldn't come home yet, I knew what I had to do. I'm supposed to head back to work tomorrow, but I told my boss I needed to take some urgent family leave. I had to see you. I flew out on the red-eye and hired a car when I landed. Drove straight here.'

'The car hire places at Adelaide Airport must be making a killing from our family.'

He laughed and then she couldn't hold back any longer. Despite shaky legs, she pushed herself off the swivel chair and walked around the desk right into his arms. They didn't kiss but his hands closed around her back and they stood there together, just holding each other. Lucinda inhaled deeply, loving the familiar scent of her husband. Meadow Brook might be the Pattersons' home, but Joe was hers.

'Are you checking to see if my clothes are clean?' he asked with a chuckle.

'No.' She shook her head. 'I'm checking to see if you're real. I missed you, Joe.'

'You too, babe. When you told me everything that was going on here, I had to come to make sure you were okay. Are you sure you're okay?' He looked down into her eyes, his expression serious.

She knew he was referring to the baby and she nodded. 'I'm just worried about Charlie and Mitch. And I can't believe Mum cheated on Dad. That's just—'

'People make mistakes, Luce. Everyone. They do things they're not proud of.'

She swallowed. 'Are you talking about us?'

He nodded. 'Yes, but the important thing is to make it right in the end. Now, are you going to make me a cup of coffee or what?'

Chapter Fifty

The next few days were agonising, and by the end of the week Charlie felt like she was losing the plot. The routine of the motel kept everyone going and they put a good face on for the guests, but whenever she and her sisters were alone the conversation went straight back to 'the McDonald issue'—as she'd come to call it in her head.

Have you talked to Mitch today? Do you really think Mum had an affair? How could she have done that to Dad? What else might she have kept from us?

And then there was the big one: *Should we tell him?*

Charlie understood their need to talk, to analyse, but she couldn't cope with their emotions on top of her own. As if the question inside her own head wasn't enough to deal with right now.

Am I a Patterson or—heaven forbid—a McDonald?

This one thought kept going through her mind like a broken record. She would just about convince herself that she was who she'd always known herself to be—a Patterson—and then one of her sisters would say or do something that was so far from anything she'd ever say or do herself that she decided she must be a McDonald.

The uncertainly was driving her insane, as was her enforced separation from Mitch. He called her every night to check how she was coping but their conversations were brief and strained. It was breaking her heart but she couldn't allow herself to feel connected to him. In the same way she couldn't allow herself to think about the baby—it would hurt too much if she had to say goodbye. Occasionally she'd slip into a daydream, imagining the first time she felt it kick or what it might be like to hold it in her arms, but whenever she caught herself doing this she found something else to occupy her time.

Many hands were supposed to make light work but there were almost too many hands at the motel with all the sisters and Joe and Nigel chipping in. When they weren't working, they were taking turns sticking close to her and mollycoddling. Charlie understood her sisters were worried, but she was beginning to feel as if she were a patient on suicide watch and they were all on roster to look out for her.

Even Nigel had been schooled in the ways of Charlie-sitting, but unlike the others she found his company soothing. He was the only one who didn't ask her prying questions—perhaps because he didn't know her well enough—and she could see why Abigail was smitten.

Still, sometimes Charlie wished she could run away in a caravan like Dad and Mrs Sampson.

'I'm going into Port Augusta to visit Aunt Mags,' she announced one morning when she could no longer cope with sitting around and waiting. She needed a break but she also wondered if maybe their aunt would have a better idea of how they should all handle this situation. Although Mags was Dad's older sister, she could be trusted to keep this secret if that's what they decided to do.

'Oh, I'll come too.' Madeleine jumped at the opportunity for a few hours away from Meadow Brook and Charlie reluctantly accepted her company. At least she'd only have one sister—or half-sister; who knew?—in tow.

After finishing their motel duties—Charlie still in the kitchen and Madeleine once again battling with the room cleaning—they drove to the 'entertainment centre'.

Charlie didn't feel like talking and for part of the way Madeleine remained quiet too. She'd taken the wheel and looked to be intently staring at the road ahead even though she'd driven this trip a hundred times before. Then, out of the blue, she said, 'I talked to Lorraine a couple of days ago.'

'Who?' Charlie racked her brain for a face to put to the name but came up blank.

'You know … Wacky Wanda. Turns out her real name is Lorraine.'

Charlie sat up straighter and twisted to look properly at Madeleine. 'Really? What was she like? Why haven't you said anything?'

Madeleine half-chuckled. 'It kind of slipped my mind after you came back from visiting Mitch's dad, but I met her that morning when I went for my run.'

'What did you say to her? Did she mention the curse?' Now who was asking endless questions?

'It was strange. Actually, no … You'd just told us about Mitch and the baby, and I was feeling ashamed of the way we'd latched onto the old tales about her. So I said hello and she surprised me by saying hello right back. We had quite a little chat. She's a very strong, independent old woman. Not scary at all. Someone to be admired, not feared.'

'I never bought into those stupid stories,' Charlie said, but a cold flooded her body. Wanda—*Lorraine*—might be a harmless old dear, but that didn't mean her mother hadn't been a bitter harridan seeking to avenge her sister's suicide. 'Did you ask her about the curse?'

Madeleine shook her head. 'I thought about it. But I felt sorry for her and I didn't want to make a connection and then ruin it. I still feel stupid even thinking that it might be real. I'm a doctor for fuck's sake, but—'

'It might be,' Charlie interrupted. 'If I'm not a Patterson then this pregnancy doesn't disprove anything.'

'Let's worry about that later.' Madeleine reached over and patted Charlie's knee. 'Are you going to tell Aunt Mags about … You know?'

'I want to,' Charlie confessed. 'You don't mind, do you?'

'No. I think it's a good idea. I'd love to know if she ever suspected Mum's affair and ask if she thinks we should tell Dad.'

Charlie didn't say anything on that matter. The sisters were divided on this.

Madeleine believed that the truth always came out in the end—she'd used the Charlie–Mitch–Rick situation as an example—and that it would be better if Dad found out from them now. 'Think about how he'll feel if he finds out down the track and knows we all kept it from him?'

For once Lucinda agreed with her, but Charlie and Abigail were of the opposite opinion.

Charlie couldn't help thinking about the baby. What if—*please God*—she and Mitch could keep it? She didn't want her child's two grandfathers to have disharmony between them. And quite frankly, she couldn't see how tainting his memory of Mum would help Dad in any way; it was in the past, and Mum was unable to explain or defend herself—or to apologise.

When the girls arrived at the retirement village, they found Mags lording over a game of Uno in the communal hall. Her friends voiced their objections but she happily left the game to go and visit with her nieces.

'To what do I owe this pleasure, my darlings?' she asked as she linked arms with them and led them outside into the garden. 'I thought you'd be run off your feet with my brother and Sal off gallivanting around the outback.'

Despite her mood, Charlie couldn't help but smile. Aunt Mags had that effect. Dad had phoned her about his impromptu road trip but of course she didn't know the real reason the girls had suggested it.

But then the sisters exchanged a look and Mags's expression darkened. 'Oh no!' She slapped a hand against her chest. 'Is it Brian? Has something happened to him on the road?'

'No, no, nothing like that.' Madeleine reached out a hand to steady their aunt as she rushed to reassure her. 'Shall we go to your place so we can talk?'

'You're scaring me, girls, and you know I don't scare easily,' Mags said as they walked the short distance to her villa. She unlocked the door and they followed her inside. 'Can I get you a cup of coffee, or will we need something stronger?'

'Coffee will be fine,' Madeleine said as Aunt Mags shuffled over to the kettle.

'I'll just have some water, please.' Charlie absentmindedly placed a hand against her stomach in the way pregnant women often did. Realising what she'd done, she quickly wrenched her hand away, but not before Aunt Mags noticed.

'Charlie!' she exclaimed, the kettle hanging in midair. 'Are you having a baby?'

Trying to swallow the lump in her throat, Charlie nodded.

'Mitch's!' Aunt Mags dumped the kettle back on the bench, clapped her hands together in glee and rushed over to hug her.

Not one to normally succumb to hysterics, Charlie burst into tears. What should have been a time of utter joy was anything but.

Her aunt pulled back and frowned. 'Surely the pregnancy hormones haven't got hold of you already?'

No one answered the question. Instead Charlie felt Madeleine ushering her over to the couch and then gently pushing her down to sit.

'What the devil is going on?' Aunt Mags asked, abandoning all efforts to make drinks as she sat herself down next to Charlie. Madeleine sat guard on the other side. 'Don't tell me that boy doesn't want it? Or is it you having butterflies? Because let me tell you, girl; Mitch McDonald is a good man and you'd be stupid to let him slip through your fingers. Anyone can see you two are made for each other.'

This only made her sob more.

'Please, Aunt Mags,' Madeleine pleaded, squeezing Charlie's hand. 'Let us explain. We came to visit because Charlie needed to clear her head and we hoped you'd have some wisdom to offer.'

Aunt Mags snorted, but sounded secretly pleased. 'Just because I'm as old as God, doesn't mean I'm wise.'

'We'll give you a try,' Madeleine replied dryly.

Finally Mags went quiet and Charlie looked to her sister, telling her she had permission to spill all. As she listened to Madeleine speak, she couldn't believe this was really happening to her. To them. Madeleine explained how Mitch and Charlie had surprised them all with the baby announcement and that they'd only been getting used to the idea themselves when Rick had dropped his bombshell.

Even though she'd known what was coming, Charlie appeared more shocked by Madeleine's announcement than Aunt Mags, who merely pursed her lips and said. 'That Rick McDonald always was a strapping young bloke.'

Charlie nearly choked, and Madeleine looked aghast. 'You're not surprised?' she exclaimed. 'About Mum and Rick?'

Mags shook her head. 'Of course I'm surprised, but if it's true, at least your mother had the good sense to choose someone like him.'

'Aunty Mags!' Charlie couldn't believe her ears. It almost sounded like Mags condoned such behaviour.

'I'm sorry, my darlings.' Mags patted Charlie's knee. 'I can imagine this has come as quite a shock.'

'You reckon?' Charlie asked, her tone sarcastic.

'They wouldn't be the first people to make a mistake and they won't be the last,' Mags said matter-of-factly.

'That's what Abigail keeps saying.' Madeleine stood and started pacing. 'But it doesn't make anything right. We don't know what to tell Dad and we're all going out of our heads waiting for the paternity results.'

'Paternity results?'

'Yes.' Madeleine nodded. 'Charlie and Rick McDonald were tested a few days ago. To find out if—'

'Ah of course … Now I'm catching up. *Sheesh.*' She gave Charlie a look of sympathy. 'Of course an affair with anyone else wouldn't have been quite so worrying.'

This was only slightly soothing to hear. It would still have made them think differently about Mum, but that on its own would have been easier to work through. Charlie's voice shook as she asked, 'Do you think I might not be a Patterson?'

Aunt Mags took her time replying. 'No matter what your genes are, you'll always be a Patterson to me. You're a Patterson in your heart and that's what counts.'

Charlie tried to smile. The sentiment was sweet, but … 'It might matter for me and Mitch.' A lump sprung up in her throat at the thought she'd been trying but failing to ignore since Rick's revelation.

'Ah, Charlie.' Mags sighed. For the first time in Charlie's life she thought her wise old aunt might not have all the answers.

Instead she pulled Charlie into her arms and held her tightly while she cried. It was the first time Charlie had sobbed in front of anyone since her happy tears with Mitch over the pregnancy test. It felt cathartic to let it all out.

The three of them sat there a while—the only sounds in the room that of tissues being ripped from their box to mop up tears.

Eventually, Madeleine broke the silence. 'Do you think we should tell Dad?'

Charlie knew the question was directed to their aunt and was grateful for the change of focus in conversation.

Mags pondered the question for a while, and finally looked up. 'That's between the four of you, but I want you all to think long and hard about why you'd want to tell him, and what you would hope to achieve. I wouldn't rush into anything just yet because you're all still in shock. Remember, once things like this are out in the open, they can never be buried ever again.'

Charlie bit back a sigh. It was a response but it wasn't the black-and-white answer she'd been hoping for. Still, maybe there was wisdom in waiting … at least until they knew exactly what they were dealing with.

'Thanks, Aunty Mags.'

Three days later, Charlie looked up at the ceiling after reading the page in front of her for about the tenth time in as many minutes. It was no use. Try as she might to focus on anything besides her real-life soap-opera drama, she couldn't. Today was day eight since testing and the results were due any day now.

'What are you doing?' Abigail asked, coming in from the motel and heading straight for the fridge.

'Studying,' she replied without thought.

'Huh?' Abigail grabbed a bottle of orange juice and crossed the kitchen to peer over Charlie's shoulder at the article about holistic principles. 'What's all that about?'

Too tired to keep secrets, Charlie sighed and handed over the article. 'I'm doing an online course in naturopathy.'

'Wow.' Abigail's face lit up. 'That's awesome.'

'Is it?' Charlie shrugged. Once upon a time her little sister's approval would have made her day, but right now she struggled to recall why she'd ever felt that way. 'I've got my first ever exams next week and this may as well be in Dutch for all I can understand.'

'I'll help.' Abigail handed back the paper and then pulled out a seat and sat down. 'You're probably just finding it hard to concentrate with—'

'It's all right,' Charlie interrupted before she could finish. 'You're absolutely right.' She glanced at the time on the kitchen wall clock. 'Thanks for your offer, but I might go check the post.'

Not mentioning that she'd already been in to the post office four times that day, she pushed back her chair. The wooden legs scraped against the floor as the door from the motel opened again. Madeleine marched through, Joe, Lucinda and Nigel following closely behind. Charlie noted the anxious expressions on their faces and guessed that the yellow envelope in Madeleine's hand was the news they'd all been waiting for.

'It's here,' Madeleine announced, crossing the kitchen to Charlie. She handled the envelope delicately, as if its contents were explosive. 'Do you want me to open it? Or do you want to do it alone?'

Charlie reached out to take it, her hands shaking and stomach churning. 'I'll do it, but you may as well all stay.' Whatever the result, she'd have to tell them eventually.

She sucked in a breath as she turned the envelope over and stared at the sender's address. *SA Pathology*. This was it. She heard the distant tingle of someone entering reception but they could wait. *This* was more important than anything.

'Should we call Mitch?' Abigail asked as Charlie slid her finger beneath the seal. 'Maybe he should be here when you open it?'

Before Charlie had a chance to reply or even think this suggestion through, someone cleared his throat. They all turned to find Mitch standing in the open doorway. Ripped, faded denim clung to his legs and her heart turned over in her chest at the sight of him.

'Open it,' he said, his dark eyes serious. 'Dad just called. He got the letter a few minutes ago.'

'So … you know?' she whispered.

He nodded, his eyes watery with tears she couldn't decipher. 'Go on.'

All eyes glued on her, Charlie tried to steady her hand enough to open the envelope. She tore out the piece of paper, dropped her gaze to the middle of the page, bypassing the letterhead, date and preamble and zooming in on the information that would make or break her life.

Oh. My. God.

She lost her grip on the letter and it fluttered to the floor. Shivers racked her body, tears swelled in her eyes. She glanced up and looked straight at Mitch.

'I'm a Patterson,' she said, biting her lower lip as the tears barrelled down her cheeks. Tears of relief and sorrow and pure joy.

'I know.' He stepped towards her and pulled her into his arms. It felt so unbelievably good, so right, that she barely heard the voices of her family around her.

'Thank God.'

'Thank fuck.'

'I knew you were.'

'This calls for champagne,' Joe said.

Charlie laughed. 'Yes.' She pulled back slightly from Mitch's embrace. 'But I'll have to have soda water. No booze for me for the next eight months.'

'No.' Mitch kissed her forehead as he pressed his hand against her stomach. The smile on his face said it all.

'I'll go get a bottle from the motel. We've got lots to celebrate,' Madeleine said, turning and heading through the adjoining door.

'Yes.' Charlie could barely manage to speak as she made a mental catalogue of *all* the things. Her and Mitch's baby, Joe and Lucinda back together, Abigail's engagement, even Dad and Mrs Sampson. The fact they'd found out about Mum's mistake—even all these years later—somehow made accepting Dad's new relationship easier. He deserved happiness as much as the rest of them.

And as for the curse? Well, perhaps it was time to leave that in the past.

By the time Madeleine returned with a bottle of Moët and a can of soda water, Lucinda had lined up Annette's best champagne flutes on the kitchen table. Madeleine handed Joe the bottle and he popped the cork in the flamboyant way that only an Italian could. He might have been third generation Aussie, but Italy was in his blood. He filled the glasses with the skill of someone who'd spent the last eight nights behind the bar of the Meadow Brook Motel.

Everyone grabbed a glass and, as they lifted their drinks, Madeleine made a toast. 'To Charlie Patterson and Mitch McDonald. And to their baby, for finally laying the Patterson curse to rest.'

There was still a lot to discuss, but all that could wait. Right now, all Charlie wanted to do was enjoy.

Epilogue—Six months later

'I can't believe this will be our last Christmas in Meadow Brook,' Lucinda exclaimed as she lifted one of their ghastly decorations onto the tree. None of them had been able to bring themselves to throw them out.

'I know.' Abigail sniffed, sounding as near to waterworks as Lucinda felt. Knowing this day had been coming for a while didn't make it any easier. Lucinda shot her an understanding smile.

'Actually—' Dad leaned over to switch on the fairy lights that adorned the tree, then straightened and grinned '—I have some news about that.'

It was Christmas Eve and all the family, including partners, were gathered in the motel bar where they'd decided to place the tree for their very last Christmas as owners. Charlie's redecoration had done its job and Lucinda liked to think her spring-cleaning had helped as well. The motel had been sold and the girls had been summoned home for one final Christmas. Dad hadn't told them anything about the new owners, but they hadn't asked many questions either.

The important thing was that he'd finally be able to retire.

Lucinda couldn't be happier for him and she knew her sisters felt the same, but while they were stoked for Dad and Mrs Sampson— who had their big trip around Australia planned down to days, hours and even places they would stop for lunch—saying goodbye to the motel was like closing the final pages of a much-loved book.

It had been in Mum's family for four generations, and although the place would live on in their hearts, although they'd always remember the crazy times they'd had there together, it was time to move on. The year and a bit since Mum's death had been an emotional rollercoaster—shock, grief, anger that she'd left them so young—and then dismay and hurt when they'd discovered she wasn't the perfect person they'd always believed. This had hit them hard and they'd all come to terms with it in different ways. Lucinda had taken comfort in the knowledge that Mum was human, just like she was. And just as Joe had forgiven her craziness, Lucinda had forgiven her mother's.

'Hurry up, Dad,' Abigail pleaded, snapping Lucinda back to the present.

She looked back to her father, who had a massive grin on his face as if he were enjoying the curiosity and impatience of his daughters.

Could he and Mrs Sampson be getting married? Nothing could shock Lucinda anymore and she stifled a giggle as she imagined herself and her sisters dressed in ghastly pink flower girls' dresses.

'Without further ado,' he said, with a game-show host wave of his arm, 'I'd like to introduce you to the new owners of the Meadow Brook Motel.'

Confused, Lucinda followed the gazes of her sisters to the door, expecting to see strangers standing there waiting to be introduced. But no one new had entered.

She frowned as Madeleine echoed her thoughts. 'What's going on?'

Before anyone could say anything else, Charlie and Mitch stepped into the middle of the group. Their faces said it all.

'You two?' Abigail clapped a hand over her mouth before doing a little jig on the spot.

Lucinda was speechless. Could it be true? Now that the possibility was out there, she couldn't think of anything more perfect.

Charlie, her hand linked with Mitch's, nodded, a slow smile stretching across her face. 'After all the work we put in, we couldn't bear to say goodbye. And this way, Mitch won't need to work away from home and will be here for the baby.' She paused while everyone took this in, then asked, 'Are we insane?'

'No.' They shook their heads in mutual agreement.

'I think it's wonderful,' Madeleine said.

Lucinda agreed. 'It seems right to keep the motel in the family.'

Aunt Mags, who'd been unusually quiet the last few minutes, suddenly spoke up from where she was reclining on one of the new leather couches in the bar, nursing a tumbler of Baileys on ice. 'Well, maybe a little bit.' Beaming, she gestured to Charlie's burgeoning bump. 'But as I was the one to put the idea into your head, I'll take some of the blame.'

Charlie laughed, let go of Mitch's hand and went over to hug Aunt Mags, which was quite a feat considering she was seven months pregnant and showing heavily. 'I love you, Aunty Mags.'

The tears Lucinda had been fighting broke free and she felt Joe's arm close around her as he pulled her into his side.

'Oh stop,' Mags said, clearly loving the attention. When Charlie pulled back, she put her hand on Charlie's bump. 'Are you sure you're not having twins?'

Lucinda laughed along with everyone else, her tears happy not sad.

'Not that we know of.' Mitch shrugged. 'But Lord knows, where Charlie's concerned there's one surprise after another.'

'Speaking of surprises.' Madeleine, perched on a bar stool at the edge of the gathering, cleared her throat and took the hand of the tall, dark man beside her. Dylan was his name, although Lucinda thought he looked more like a Patrick, and apparently Madeleine had been dating him for almost six months. Where she'd found the time while working for an aid organisation that ran mobile antenatal clinics in remote areas, Lucinda had no clue. It would be easier to understand if she'd taken up with the pilot that flew her round the country.

Him walking in the door with Madeleine only a few hours ago had been the first time Lucinda had any inkling of his existence and her family had seemed equally surprised. She guessed after the debacle with Hugo, Madeleine wanted to be sure before she introduced him to the clan.

'Dylan and I are ...' She glanced at him and her voice cracked. 'We're pregnant!'

Lucinda's heart shot into her throat as happy gasps and utterings of joy and congratulations erupted around her. Charlie, Abigail and Dad rushed forward for hugs, but she seemed to be frozen to the spot.

Joe, still clutching her to his side, leaned in and kissed her cheek. 'You okay, babe?'

The announcement had been a shock, but now that she'd had a few seconds to digest the information, she nodded. 'Our time will be soon. I just know it.'

After months of marriage counselling, she and Joe were closer and more connected than ever. He'd quit working away and found a job that paid almost as much in the company's Perth office. It didn't involve blowing things up on a daily basis but he told her constantly that the improvement in their marriage was worth the sacrifice. Lucinda had been relief teaching the last six months, which she enjoyed because she still got to do what she loved, the pay was fabulous and yet she didn't have so much stress.

And the best part? They'd finally decided they were strong enough as a couple to begin assisted insemination.

'Geez,' Abigail declared, glancing at Nigel as she moved away from Madeleine to give someone else a chance to congratulate them. 'Maybe we should bring forward the wedding or our maid-of-honour won't fit into her dress.'

He chuckled and Lucinda only just made out his whispered words, clearly meant only for Abigail. 'I'll marry you tonight if you want.'

Abigail pretended to pout. 'Um, it's Christmas? I think the church is booked.'

Lucinda grinned as she watched her youngest sister interact with her doting fiancé. The local gossips would be so busy drooling when she brought him to midnight mass that they wouldn't be able to speak.

Abigail and Nigel were spending Christmas at the motel and then heading to Adelaide to celebrate New Year with his family, before finally flying back to London where Nigel had recently scored another promotion and the two of them had put down a deposit on their own apartment. The way Abigail told it, it was tiny and a long way from Nigel's work and her music students, but it was theirs—and that made it perfect.

'I guess we'd better break out the champagne,' Dad announced. Tearing her gaze from Abigail and Nigel, Lucinda looked back to her father in time to see him wiping his eyes as he headed to the fridge.

'Great minds think alike.' Mrs Sampson, already there, grinned as she held up two bottles and gestured to the flutes she'd lined up along the bar.

'And that's why I love you,' Dad proclaimed, a grin stretching from ear to ear. Lucinda blushed a little as he closed the distance between himself and the old housekeeper, pulled her towards him and pressed a big kiss against her lips.

'Go Brian,' Mitch yelled as Joe wolf-whistled. Lucinda dug him in the ribs, but was secretly ecstatic.

She and her sisters exchanged happy glances and then everyone started to clap.

'About time you two came out of hiding,' Madeleine said. 'And I can't even have a proper drink to celebrate.'

Lucinda grinned at her. 'Don't worry, sis. I'll have your share.'

She stepped forward and plucked a crystal flute off the bar. Because although her life might not be unfolding exactly as she'd planned it, she felt blessed. She had Joe, she had her sisters, and soon there'd be a new generation of Pattersons.

If these weren't reasons to celebrate, she didn't know what was.

Acknowledgements

Thanks as usual to the wonderful crew at Harlequin Australia—Sue, Michelle, Cristina, Annabel, Adam, Lauren, Sam, Lilia, Adrian, Camille and Romina to name but a few. You people are awesome.

To my gifted editor, Lachlan Jobbins—thank you for all your hard work with this book. Your insight was spot-on and without you this wouldn't have become half the book it is. Thanks also for listening to me and often understanding what I meant better than I did myself. And to my agent, Helen Breitwieser—thanks for all you do. I'm glad you're in my corner.

Thank you to my writing friends—some of you have been with me on this journey from the start, others are more recent, but I wouldn't be without any of you. Beck Nicholas, Cathryn Hein, Janette Radevski, Amanda Knight, Lisa Ireland, Alissa Callen, Scarlet Wilson, Fiona Palmer and Fiona Lowe—your support, early reading, brainstorming, counselling and friendship mean the world to me.

A special mention to my old friend Penny who planted the seed for this story when she said I should write a book called *Paterson's Curse*. Feel free to give me title suggestions anytime.

In every book, there is research and I want to thank the people who shared their fertility stories with me for the Patterson sisters. Thanks to Shea, Amanda, Nardia, Joanne, Karen and Kaetrin for being so open.

And last but never least to my family—my husband Craig, my three heroes-in-training and my mum Barbara, who put up constantly with me drifting off into my own little world. I couldn't do any of this without your love, support, cooking, cleaning and babysitting.

Turn over for a sneak peek.

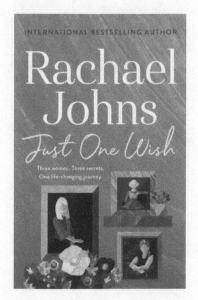

Just One Wish

by

Rachael Johns

Out now

Prologue

1964

'Alice Louise Abbott, you are the girl of my dreams, the love of my life, you light up my heart like the sun lights the sky. Please, will you do me the greatest honour of becoming my wife?'

Oh God. Alice's heart shook as she stared down into the dark eyes of the gorgeous Henry French. Any other girl would be jumping at the chance to marry him. Henry, who'd been courting her for almost twelve months, was without a doubt the best person on the planet. She loved everything about him—from his cheeky smile to his warm heart, not to mention the way he looked when he got all dolled up in his swish grey suit. Within moments of making Henry's acquaintance at the birthday party of her best friend's brother, Alice had fallen head over heels.

But Alice wasn't the marrying kind. The way she saw it, marriage benefited men way more than it did women and, for this reason, she didn't think she'd ever enter into such a contract. And she'd thought Henry knew this about her. She'd thought he understood and respected her stance.

So why the *hell* was he down on bended knee at the end of St Kilda Pier on this beautiful summer's night that had been perfect in practically every way? They'd had a delicious dinner at Leo's Spaghetti Bar and were enjoying a lovely stroll before heading back to his place for a 'nightcap'. Or so she'd thought.

She laughed as if she thought he were joking, when in her heart of hearts she knew he was not. 'Henry! Get up. You'll ruin your trousers and people are looking at us.'

Henry didn't make a move to stand. Instead, he reached into his jacket pocket and pulled out a small, black velvet box. 'I don't care who looks at us—I only care about you and me. I've been offered a big promotion at work and the new role is in Geelong.'

'Geelong?' she whispered, feeling as if she'd been punched in the gut.

Still smiling, he nodded. 'And I want you to come with me. I want you to come as my wife. So … will you marry me?'

He opened the box and a stunning square-cut diamond glistened up at her, almost winking in the moonlight. Alice couldn't deny its beauty, and for a moment she tried to imagine what being married to Henry French would be like, but all she felt was dread.

Maybe in a couple of years or if his proposal involved staying in Melbourne, she might have relented, but right now she needed to establish her career. And while she was happy for Henry's promotion, he didn't seem to have considered her work at all. Geelong might only be a few hours away but it felt like the ends of the earth. No way would she be able to commute there on a daily basis. She'd finally secured a role in the labs at the university, but she had ambitions far bigger than that.

A voice from deep inside told her that if she said 'no' she could kiss Henry French goodbye. That thought was almost too awful to bear, but even worse would be giving up her dreams for a man.

'You know I can't,' she whispered as Henry gazed up at her.

His face fell.

Had he really expected any different ending to this uninvited, unanticipated, *undesired* proposal?

Still, her heart squeezed and twisted at the tortured look on her beloved's face.

'I'm sorry, Henry.' Alice's own voice choked. 'You know I love you, I'll always love you, but I can't marry you. Congratulations on the promotion. I'll support you, and come visit as much as I can. I'd move in with you in a second if you were staying in Melbourne, but I can't move to Geelong. My work is here.'

But Henry didn't hear anything about her work. 'Move *in* with me?' he scoffed as he jumped to his feet, his cheeks turning crimson as he snapped the box shut and shoved it back in his pocket. 'Your head is stuck in the clouds if you think that would be possible. I don't know what fantasy world you're living in, but if I want to be a respectable businessman, I need a wife, not a floozy!'

'F-f-floozy?' Alice spluttered, unable to believe the words coming out of his mouth. How *dare* he!

'I'm sorry, Alice. I didn't mean …' His face a picture of distress, he reached out to grab her, but she stepped back.

The damage was done. She'd seen the real Henry—a Henry she'd dared to believe didn't exist. But he was just like every other man. Just like her father. The fact he genuinely thought she'd be overjoyed by such a romantic proposal only showed how little he really knew her. And she him. She held up her hand and shook her head, unable to speak. Tears threatened at the back of her throat.

'I didn't mean that. You're not a floozy,' he said, his tone desperate, pleading. 'But can't you see that you're being unfair? I love you and I want to be with you, but the bank doesn't take kindly to unmarried couples living together, and long-distance relationships never work.'

Alice raised her eyebrows, unable to believe her ears. She didn't give a damn about the opinion of a bunch of stuffy bankers.

'And what about children?' he went on. 'You can't believe it's okay to bring them into the world out of wedlock?'

To be honest, she hadn't given much thought to children—possibly she didn't want them, definitely she didn't want them in the near future. There were other things more pressing, more important for her to dedicate her time and energy to. As much as she loved Henry, accepting his proposal, becoming his wife, would mean turning her back on everything she believed important.

'I'm sorry, Henry,' she said, gulping back her tears, 'but I just can't.'

And that was the last time Alice Abbott saw Henry French for over fifty years.

1

Now

'Carly and I are thinking about getting back together.'

What? Christos could not be serious! I almost gagged on my prosecco as I yanked the sheets over my bare chest and searched his flushed face. Was this some kind of sick joke? After almost a year together, I was comfortable, confident, in our relationship. But my boyfriend didn't look like he was joking. Although his eyes refused to meet mine, the serious expression on his face turned my insides to ice.

But hang on, he'd only said 'think'.

'What do you mean you *think* you're getting back together? Are you? Or are you not?'

He slowly raised his head and when his gaze met mine his eyes were watery. *No.* Dread poured into my stomach and slithered up my chest like a snake working its way up my oesophagus.

'I'm so sorry, Ged. I love you, but first and foremost I'm a dad, and things haven't been that great for the kids lately. They're really struggling with our living situation and Carly and I have been wondering if the best thing for them is if we try to make a go of things again.'

Make a go of things? Again?

He made it sound so casual, so easy, but they were divorced, which I'd thought was final. I couldn't believe my ears. Surely in a second he'd pull me back into his arms and tell me he was pulling my leg.

But there was no laughter. Only a man who thirty seconds ago I thought I knew better than anyone else in the world. A man who, despite his complicated living situation, I believed only had eyes for me.

'Oh my God. You're serious?'

'Nothing's set in stone yet—we're just considering our options. But I didn't want to keep you in the dark. I'm sorry.'

'Sorry?' I'd left work early for *this*!

It was Christos's week with his kids, so we'd arranged a Thursday afternoon rendezvous at a fancy city hotel around the corner from our office and I'd been looking forward to it all day.

But suddenly I felt sick, dirty, like some kind of harlot.

'Does this mean we're breaking up?' I hated the way my voice cracked. 'You're choosing your kids and your ex-wife over me?'

'Ged, please. It's not like that.'

'But you are considering getting back together with Carly?'

He confirmed my worst fear with another slow nod.

'I can't believe you still came here, that you let us …' I couldn't bring myself to say the words as I tried to swallow away the pain that suddenly burned in my chest. 'Why couldn't you have told me in a text message like a normal bloody person? Or at least in a cafe where I could have thrown a hot drink over you?'

We both eyed the half-flute of prosecco still in my hand but no matter how mortifying the situation, no way was I wasting good alcohol on Christos. I poured it down my throat instead, threw back the sheet and leapt from the bed.

I snatched up my tangled black lace knickers and tailored navy pants and yanked them apart. I couldn't put them on fast enough. My top had landed on the plush velvet armchair and my heels were near the door but where the hell was my bra?

'Ged. Baby. *Please*. Don't be like this.'

Holding my silk blouse against my bare breasts, I glared at him. 'How the hell do you expect me to be?'

Oh Lord, my eyeballs prickled painfully but I refused to cry in front of Christos. To hell with the bra. It had been a gift from *him* anyway.

I tugged the blouse over my head, grabbed my handbag and raced out the door. Half-walking, half-running and occasionally hopping, my hands shook as I tried shoving my feet into my shoes without stopping. God, how far was the lift? The long corridor stretched out in front of me in a tear-blurred tunnel and I hauled in a noisy, snot-filled breath. A guy from housekeeping glanced up, presumably to smile, but took one look at me and retreated into the room he was attending to.

At the elevator, I stabbed my finger so hard at the down button that it hurt. I winced but the pain had nothing on the ache in my heart. How could Christos do this? He didn't love Carly—not in the way he loved me.

I glanced over my shoulder, half-expecting to see him running after me, ready to tell me he'd made a mistake. But all I saw was the cleaning man venturing back into the corridor.

Maybe I should go back and talk to him? Make him see sense.

My grandmother's voice rang out loud and clear in my head. *You do not need a man to give you value. Certainly not one who could treat you with such disrespect.*

And, no matter how much I loved Christos, what he'd just done hadn't made me feel respected in the slightest. I wasn't about to beg. I was furious at him for making me even consider it.

The lift pinged and the doors opened to reveal it was empty. I rushed inside and scrutinised my reflection in the mirrored walls. Mascara streaked down my bright red cheeks like some ghastly painting; my hair had taken the term 'bird's nest' to a whole other level and my nipples were clearly visible through my crumpled blouse. No chance I could slink back to the office looking like this.

I emerged into the hotel lobby, feeling as if everyone's eyes were on me, and rushed out onto Little Collins Street, where I dug my phone out of my handbag. I couldn't call Darren, my boss, because I wasn't sure I could talk without crying, and overwrought female wasn't the persona I wanted to give off in the office—especially not when I was vying for a promotion against two other capable colleagues.

I started tapping out a message instead: *Sorry. Something's come up. Family emergency. I need to take the rest of the day off. Will explain la*

In the nick of time I realised the error of my ways: *Won't be back in the office today as I just had a lead on a story*—but I was interrupted by the buzzing of my phone.

I grimaced as the word 'Mum' flashed up at me. I didn't feel like talking to anyone right now, least of all my mother, who would immediately pick something off in my voice and start an interrogation. I pressed the little icon that would autoreply that I was in a meeting (which she'd believe as she was always berating me for working too hard) and then finished texting my boss.

I'd barely pressed send when a message from Mum popped up—since when had she got so speedy at thumb typing? Only two years ago she didn't even have a mobile and now, not only did she have a smartphone, but also an Instagram account, Snapchat *and* a YouTube channel, but that's a whole other story. And possibly my fault, since I was the one who'd dragged her into the modern age and got her on Facebook so she could see all the photos my sister-in-law posted of her grandbabies.

Don't forget, you're picking Gralice up for her birthday dinner tonight. And wear something nice—I'm filming the whole thing. She ended with a little emoji of a movie camera.

My heart slammed to a halt. Could this day *get* any worse?

I adored Gralice—my Grandma Alice—and wanted to celebrate her eightieth birthday, just not tonight. Not when all my family would be there and I'd have to pretend everything was okay, or admit it wasn't and subject myself to their sympathy. I wanted to be strong, but one kind word and I was likely to fall apart. An image of me sobbing on the sofa between Granddad Philip and Granddad Craig landed in my head. That probably wasn't something Mum wanted on her YouTube channel.

And wear something nice?

The audacity! I'd once worked in fashion mags for goodness' sake.

I stared at the screen as I headed towards my tram stop, trying to work out how to respond to my mother, when suddenly I was falling. My hands shot out to break my fall and my phone catapulted out of my grip even before I worked out what had happened. Two seconds later I heard the crunch of whatever iPhones are made of against the bitumen as a car drove over it.

No. My whole life was in that device—my emails, my appointments, my banking, all my photos of Christos. My heart squeezed. And hang on, was that blood I could taste on my lip? Dirt in my mouth? Pain throbbing in my ankle?

Apparently, this day *could* get worse.

'Are you okay?' sounded an elderly male voice.

I raised my head enough to see not only was there indeed an elderly gentleman peering down at me, but a small crowd had gathered around us.

'Shall I call an ambulance?' someone asked.

'I've got a first aid kit in my bag,' announced another.

'No. No. I'm fine.' I felt as if I'd been hit by a freight train as I tried to heave myself to my feet, but I did not want attention drawn to me this close to the hotel or the office. A couple of people reached out to help and within seconds I was upright, however, it immediately became clear that standing on two feet was going to be a challenge. My ankle hurt so badly I had to lift it off the ground and hover on one leg.

'I think this is yours.' A twenty-something with a grotty cap on backwards and a skateboard under one arm held out the remnants of my phone. The sight brought tears to my eyes all over again.

'Thank you.' I took the pieces and shoved them into my bag.

'Looks like you've done a right number on your foot,' said the old man. 'Can we call someone to help you?'

My mind went to Christos and immediately rejected that thought. 'No, thank you. I was heading to the tram. I'll be fine once I get home.'

'Let me call you a cab.' The concerned gentleman was already leaning into the road, his hand outstretched.

Almost immediately a taxi slowed to a stop by the curb—at least one thing was working in my favour. The gentleman held the door open for me and I crawled into the back seat, eager to escape this mortification. My rescue crew on the pavement waved me off like I was on a royal tour and I forced myself to wave back when all I wanted to do was bury my head in my hands and bawl.

'Where you headed?' The driver had a strong British accent, Geordie I thought, although it had been over ten years since my gap year backpacking around the UK.

I told him my address in Carlton, was thankful when he didn't complain about the short trip, and even more so when he didn't try and engage me in conversation. Was there anything worse than beauticians and taxi drivers who wanted to know your whole damn life story?

As he parked on the street outside my apartment block, I dug my purse out of my bag.

'It's all paid for. Your granddad gave me a fifty when you got in. Said I could keep the change.'

Ah, so that accounted for why he hadn't grumbled about the distance. After Christos's behaviour I'd been beginning to lose hope in humankind but the stranger's actions helped remind me the world wasn't all bad. I would get over this—it would likely just take a little time and an ocean of alcohol.

I thanked the driver and limped into the building, grateful not only that my apartment was on the ground floor but also that I didn't run into any of my neighbours in the lobby. If I hadn't already looked a sight with my tear-stained make-up and messy hair, the grazes I could feel burning on my face had sealed the deal. Pity it wasn't Halloween—I wouldn't even have to hire a costume!

My five-year-old groodle greeted me as I pushed open the door. I sank to the floor and buried my face in her soft fur. 'Oh, Coco. You won't believe my day.'

If she had any idea what had happened, she'd be as distraught as I was. She adored Christos. Let's face it, everyone did. All my friends—especially the coupled ones—were hugely jealous of our relationship.

Dating a divorced father of three had never been a walk in the park, especially because he and his ex were involved in the new custody trend of nest parenting where their three kids stayed in their marital home and Christos and Carly took turns living there, one week on, one week off. They'd rented a two-bedroom apartment to use on their weeks 'off'—they had a bedroom each and strict rules about keeping the communal areas clean—but recently it had become more Carly's place as Christos had all but moved in with me on his non-kid weeks.

In theory having a week-on-week-off partner was pretty much the perfect arrangement. I had plenty of evenings where I didn't have to share Netflix with anyone and I always knew that sex and companionship were just around the corner. But oh, how I missed him on those long weeks between. A fresh wave of pain washed over me as I realised not only would there be no more lunchtime rendezvous, but that I wouldn't be coming home to Christos ever again.

I looked around my apartment; it suddenly felt cold and empty.

Coco whined, and for a moment I thought she was commiserating with me, until she put her paw against the door. I hauled myself to my feet, grabbed a tissue and my keys and took her out into the communal garden at the back of the building.

Each step felt like torture. I wondered if I'd broken my ankle. Perhaps I should get an X-ray, but the thought of going to the hospital or even to a doctor … it was too much right now.

After Coco had relieved herself we went back inside and I hobbled to the freezer. Wasn't ice supposed to fix everything?

I popped a couple of Panadol and then, with my foot dressed in the finest of frozen veggies and elevated on the sofa, I opened my laptop and logged into Messenger.

Happy birthday, Gralice. Hope you're having a great day. Really sorry but I can't drive you tonight. I tripped this afternoon and sprained my ankle. It's pretty bad. Also broke my phone—so if you need to contact me for the next couple of days it'll have to be via email or here. And I'm not feeling so great so think I'll have to give

*tonight a miss. I'll drop round tomorrow after work and give you
your present. xo*

I felt awful bailing on Gralice's big birthday bash, but she'd have
the rest of our family to celebrate and this felt more like Mum's
party than hers anyway.

I decided not to break the news to my mother for a few more
hours in order to delay the lecture that would inevitably come—
at least she couldn't call me—and, in an effort to try and distract
myself from the train wreck that was my heart, turned my attentions
to the next issue. Buying a new phone.

In this day and age, but in my line of business especially, a mobile
was something I couldn't live without.

I woke a few hours later to the buzzing of my intercom and Coco
barking up at it as if she'd never heard the sound before. I tried to
get up but groaned when pain shot through my ankle, bringing back
all the horrid events of the day.

Christos had ended our relationship.

Could it be him at the door?

My heart tingled. Maybe he'd called and, unable to get through,
had hurried over to beg me to take him back. *Well, stuff him!* It
would take a lot of grovelling to put the pieces of my heart back
together. Let him feel a little of the anguish I had.

It was only when the buzzing continued—no pauses at all, as if a
little child had their finger jammed on the button and was refusing
to let go—that I realised Christos still had a key and wasn't the
type to be kept waiting. If he wanted to talk he'd already be here,
standing in my small apartment, saying his piece. Disappointment

filled me as the pain in my ankle travelled through my body and settled back in my chest, making it difficult to breathe.

I couldn't remember ever experiencing such heartache over a guy before, but I'd honestly thought Christos was it, *the one* I'd spend the rest of my earthly days with. I'd dated heaps of men on and off throughout my twenties, but, far more focused on my career, I hadn't been serious about anyone.

Then I hit thirty, met Christos at work and 'serious' suddenly became my middle name. My feelings for him had blindsided me. I didn't care that I might never have sex with anyone else in my life, I only wanted him. He was the perfect guy for me—we were both in newspapers so understood the pressures that came with the job and, as he already had children, he didn't want things from me I didn't think I wanted to give.

We'd been together for almost a year now and had been planning an overseas holiday to spend Christmas and New Year in New York. I'd thought he might propose while we were there. Christos came from a family as Greek as his name and was very traditional about stuff like that. I didn't really see the point of marriage, but I must admit I'd already had the odd schoolgirl fantasy about becoming the next Mrs Panagopoulos. Not that I'd take his surname, I couldn't understand why any woman would, so there'd be no double-barrelled surnames either. Can you imagine Mrs Geraldine Johnston-Panagopoulos? *No, thank you.*

But, I loved him and was quite prepared to compromise if he thought the piece of paper important.

I hadn't actually given much thought to how such a marriage would co-exist with Christos's current arrangement with Carly, but I guess I never thought the nest-parenting thing would be permanent. Everything I'd read about it indicated it was a temporary situation while the kids got used to their parents being apart, and also while finances and permanent custody arrangements were finalised. That's certainly the way Christos sold it to me. His and Carly's divorce had just come through, so I'd assumed it wouldn't be long before he moved in permanently with me or we got our own house so his children could stay with us every second weekend. I might have already been perusing real-estate-dot-com in my spare time. Even with Christos's child support obligations, we might have been able to afford to buy something nice if we went a little further out of the city or if I got the promotion I was working my arse off towards.

But it looked like my fantasy was about as unlikely to come true as it was for me to find a baby unicorn at the local pet shop. At least I still had my job.

The buzzing continued to echo loudly through my apartment and I was this close to screaming and giving it a run for its money. Who on earth could it be? I still hadn't got around to messaging my mother and letting her know I wasn't coming, so it couldn't be her come to drag me to their place by my hair. *Could it?* I might be thirty years of age, but the way Mum sometimes acted you'd think the three and zero were the other way around.

Whoever it was, if they didn't stop pressing that buzzer soon, I was going to set my dog on them.

One look at Coco jumping up against the door like a crazed chipmunk and I realised the idea that she would ever hurt anyone was also a fantasy and I was going to have to give the intruder what for myself.

It hurt to stand and hurt even more to shuffle across the room to the intercom, which only exasperated my shitty mood.

'Who IS it?' I yelled into the speaker on the wall.

talk about it

Let's talk about books.

Join the conversation:

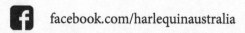 facebook.com/harlequinaustralia

 @harlequinaus

 @harlequinaus

harpercollins.com.au/hq

If you love reading and want to know about our
authors and titles, then let's talk about it.